*This little segment comes with special
appreciation for both Rik and Sebby Catter, who
kept me sane during all of the madness...*

The Final Lullaby - Volume 2. First printed September 2021.
Published by Feff Silvers T/A Feff.Works. Copyright 2021 Feff
Silvers. All rights reserved. All names, characters, and events,
are entirely fictional. Any resemblance to actual persons (living
or dead), or events, without satiric intent, is coincidental.
Printed in the United Kingdom.

ISBN: 978-1-9196289-2-9

Special Dedications
and
Thanks

Daniel Widding Salas
Richard Scholes
Charley Mather
Arron Sobers
Mick Bardason
Nic Royal
Daniel Jennings
June Samuels (Psychoticmime)
spanio
Ashleigh Crosby
Albert ARIBAUD
Fernando Zamora
Billy Monks
Doreen Tyler
Gary Sobers
Richard Sharp
bd648
Meg D
Natasha Liff
MeeMee
Moonbearonmeth
Jason Kimble
Jay Pink
Scantrontb
Jonathan Cole
Anton Ooms
Nick Shearon
Jennie Gyllblad

and the rest of the Kickstarter Backers for helping to make
this happen!

Chapter 5
Hunter Hunted

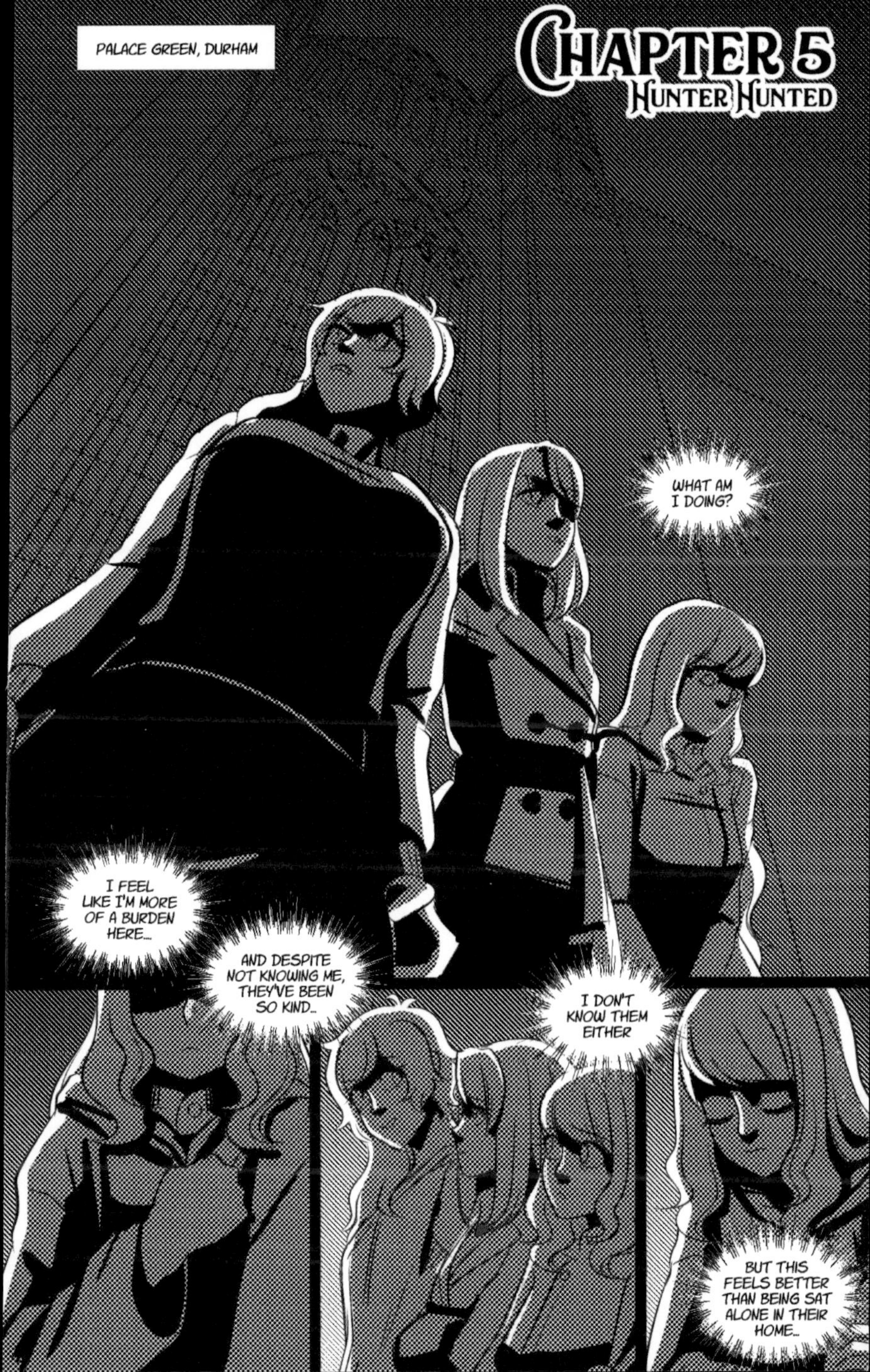

PALACE GREEN, DURHAM
WHAT AM I DOING?
I FEEL LIKE I'M MORE OF A BURDEN HERE...
AND DESPITE NOT KNOWING ME, THEY'VE BEEN SO KIND...
I DON'T KNOW THEM EITHER
BUT THIS FEELS BETTER THAN BEING SAT ALONE IN THEIR HOME...

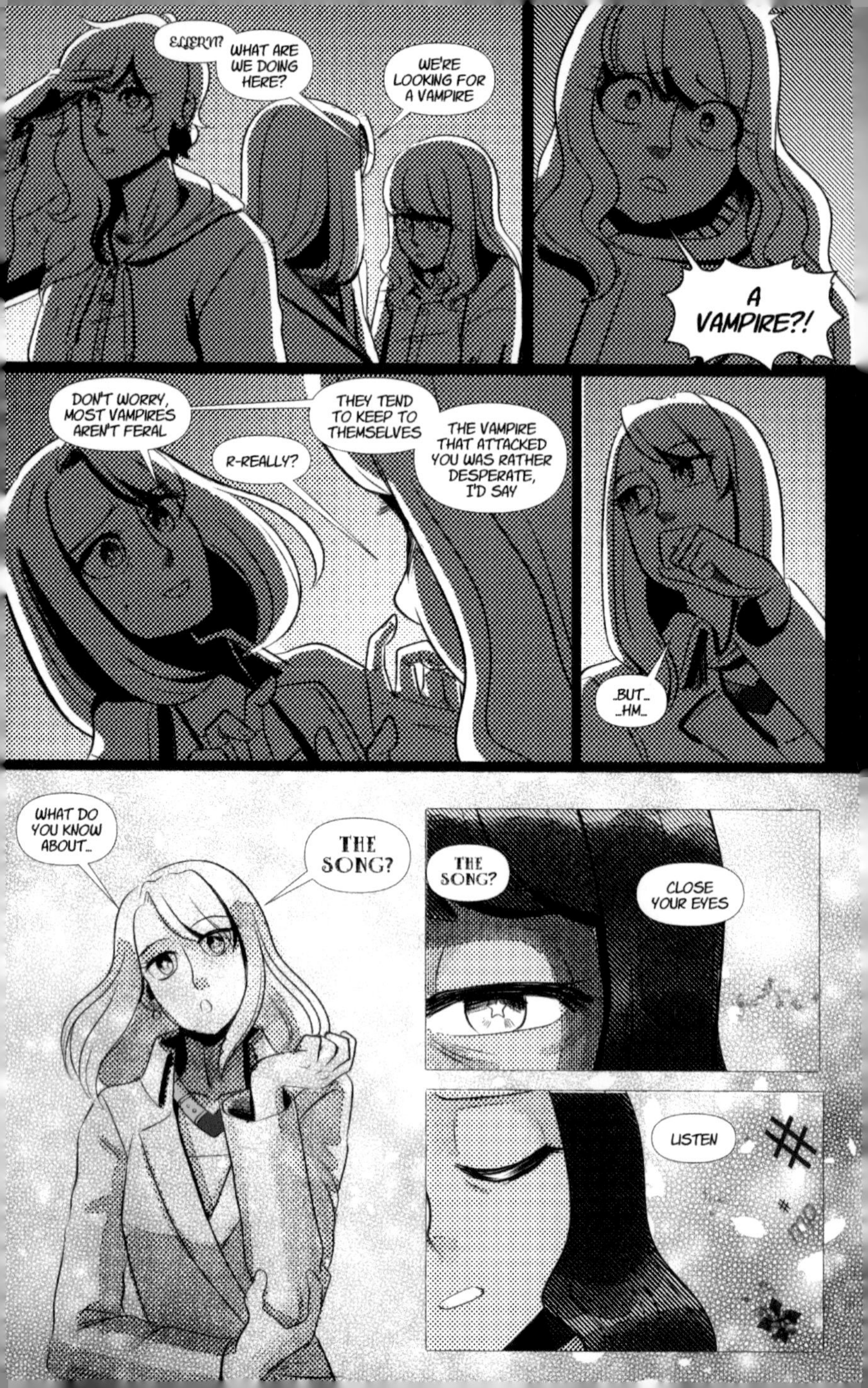
ELLERY?
WHAT ARE WE DOING HERE?
WE'RE LOOKING FOR A VAMPIRE
A VAMPIRE?!
DON'T WORRY, MOST VAMPIRES AREN'T FERAL
THEY TEND TO KEEP TO THEMSELVES
R-REALLY?
THE VAMPIRE THAT ATTACKED YOU WAS RATHER DESPERATE, I'D SAY
..BUT.. ..HM..
WHAT DO YOU KNOW ABOUT...
THE SONG?
THE SONG?
CLOSE YOUR EYES
LISTEN

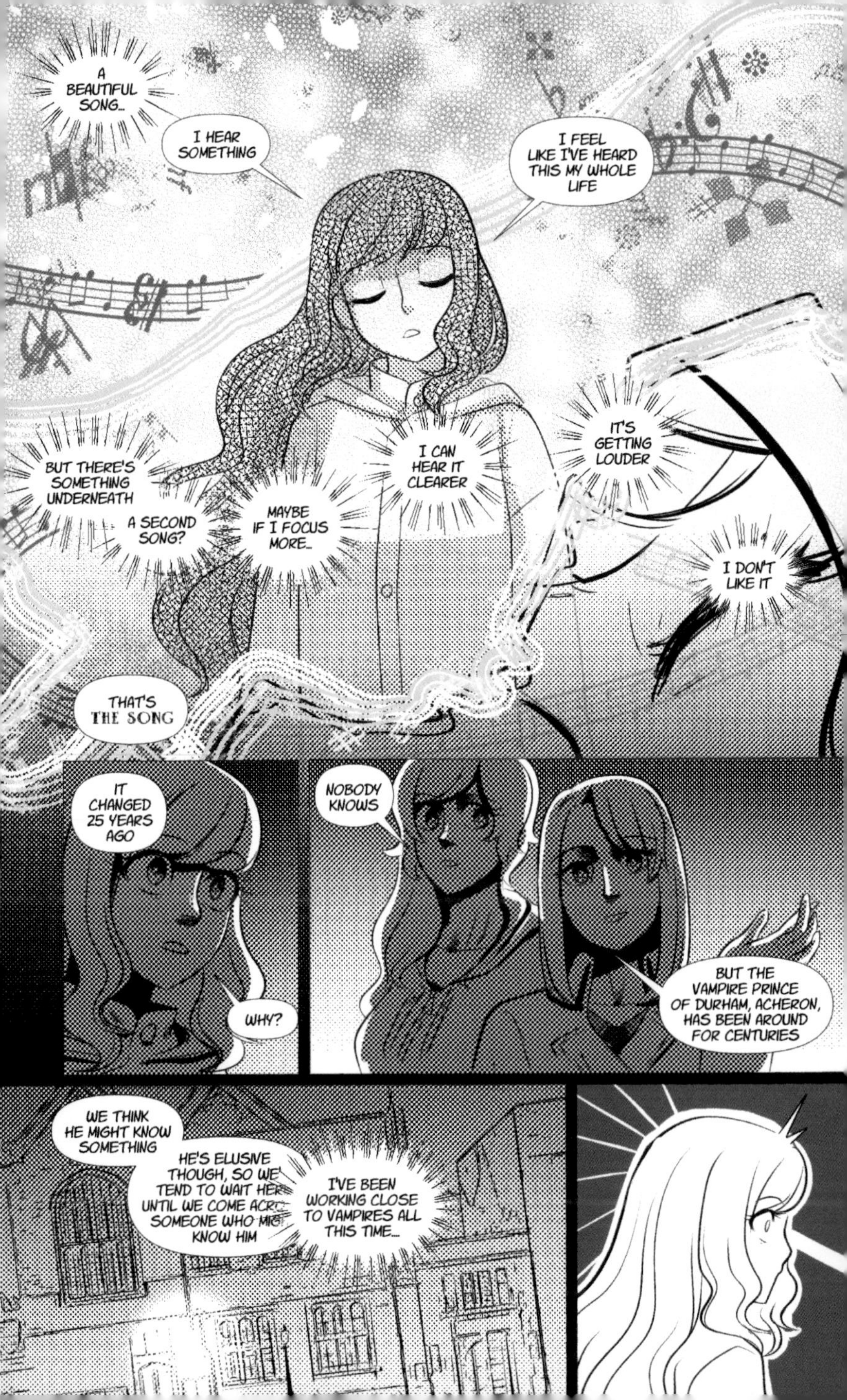
A BEAUTIFUL SONG..
I HEAR SOMETHING
I FEEL LIKE I'VE HEARD THIS MY WHOLE LIFE
BUT THERE'S SOMETHING UNDERNEATH
A SECOND SONG?
MAYBE IF I FOCUS MORE..
I CAN HEAR IT CLEARER
IT'S GETTING LOUDER
I DON'T LIKE IT
THAT'S THE SONG
IT CHANGED 25 YEARS AGO
WHY?
NOBODY KNOWS
BUT THE VAMPIRE PRINCE OF DURHAM, ACHERON, HAS BEEN AROUND FOR CENTURIES
WE THINK HE MIGHT KNOW SOMETHING
HE'S ELUSIVE THOUGH, SO WE TEND TO WAIT HE UNTIL WE COME AC SOMEONE WHO MI KNOW HIM
I'VE BEEN WORKING CLOSE TO VAMPIRES ALL THIS TIME...

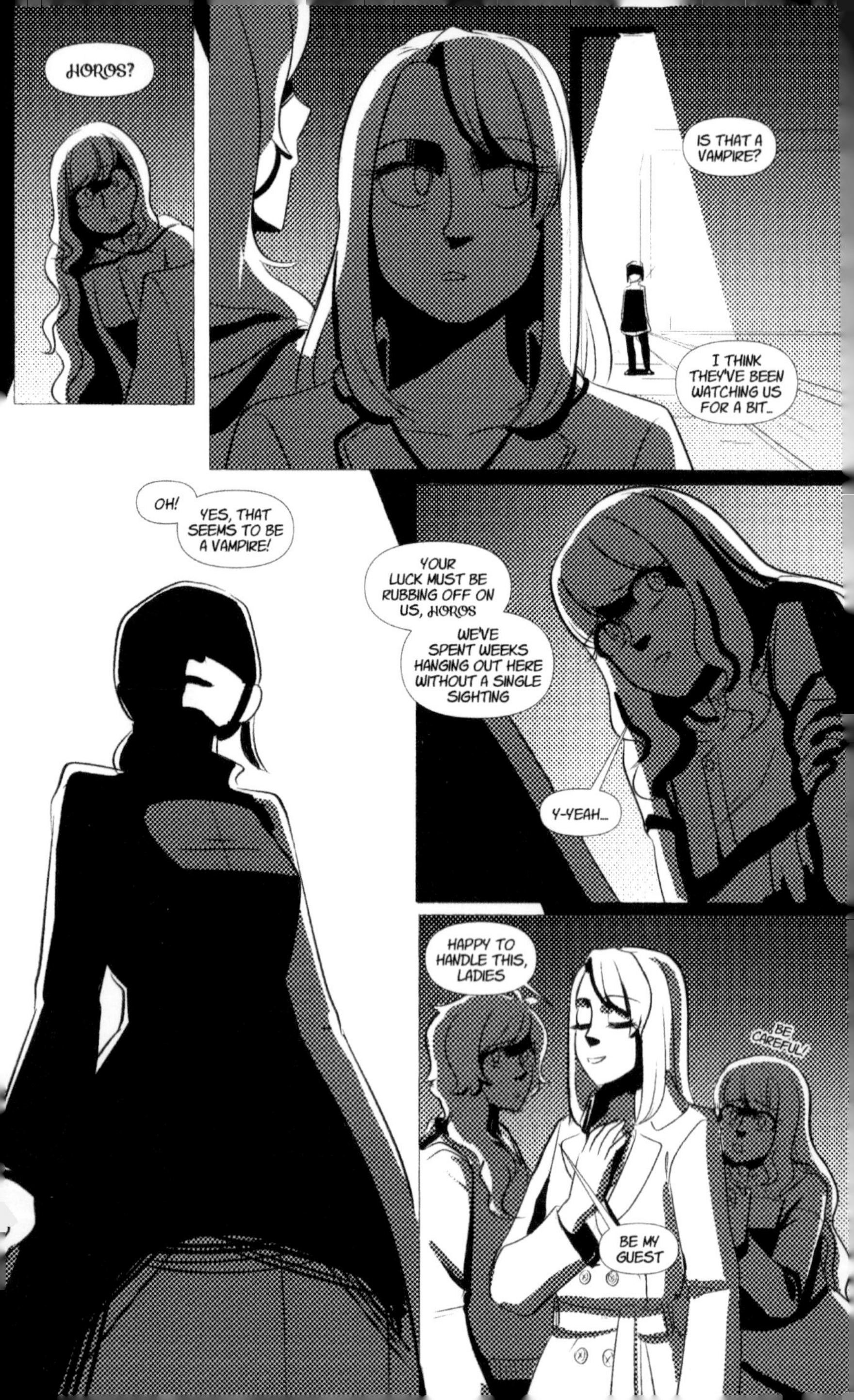
HOROS?
IS THAT A VAMPIRE?
I THINK THEY'VE BEEN WATCHING US FOR A BIT..
OH!
YES, THAT SEEMS TO BE A VAMPIRE!
YOUR LUCK MUST BE RUBBING OFF ON US, HOROS
WE'VE SPENT WEEKS HANGING OUT HERE WITHOUT A SINGLE SIGHTING
Y-YEAH..
HAPPY TO HANDLE THIS, LADIES
BE CAREFUL!
BE MY GUEST

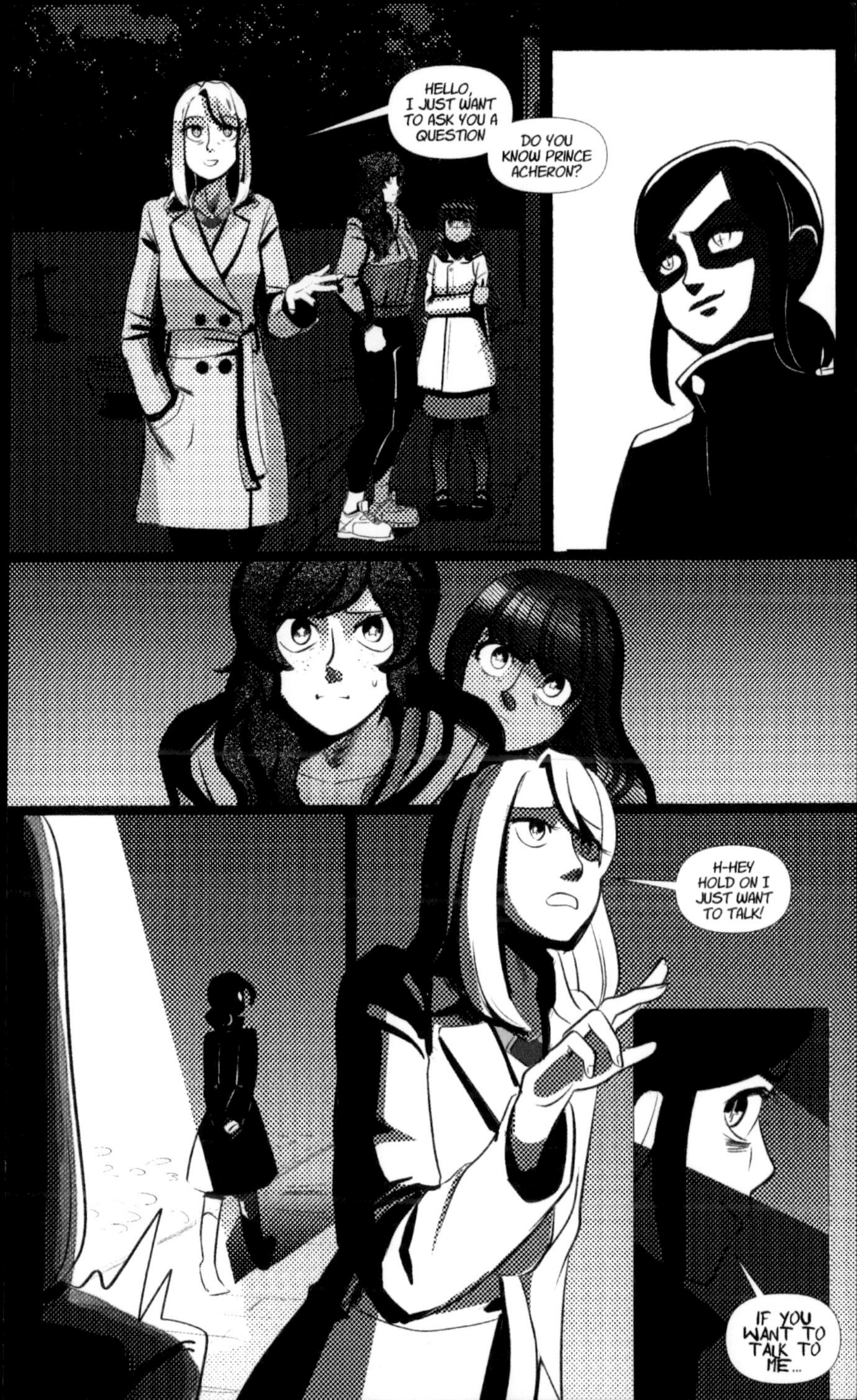
HELLO, I JUST WANT TO ASK YOU A QUESTION
DO YOU KNOW PRINCE ACHERON?
H-HEY HOLD ON I JUST WANT TO TALK!
IF YOU WANT TO TALK TO ME...

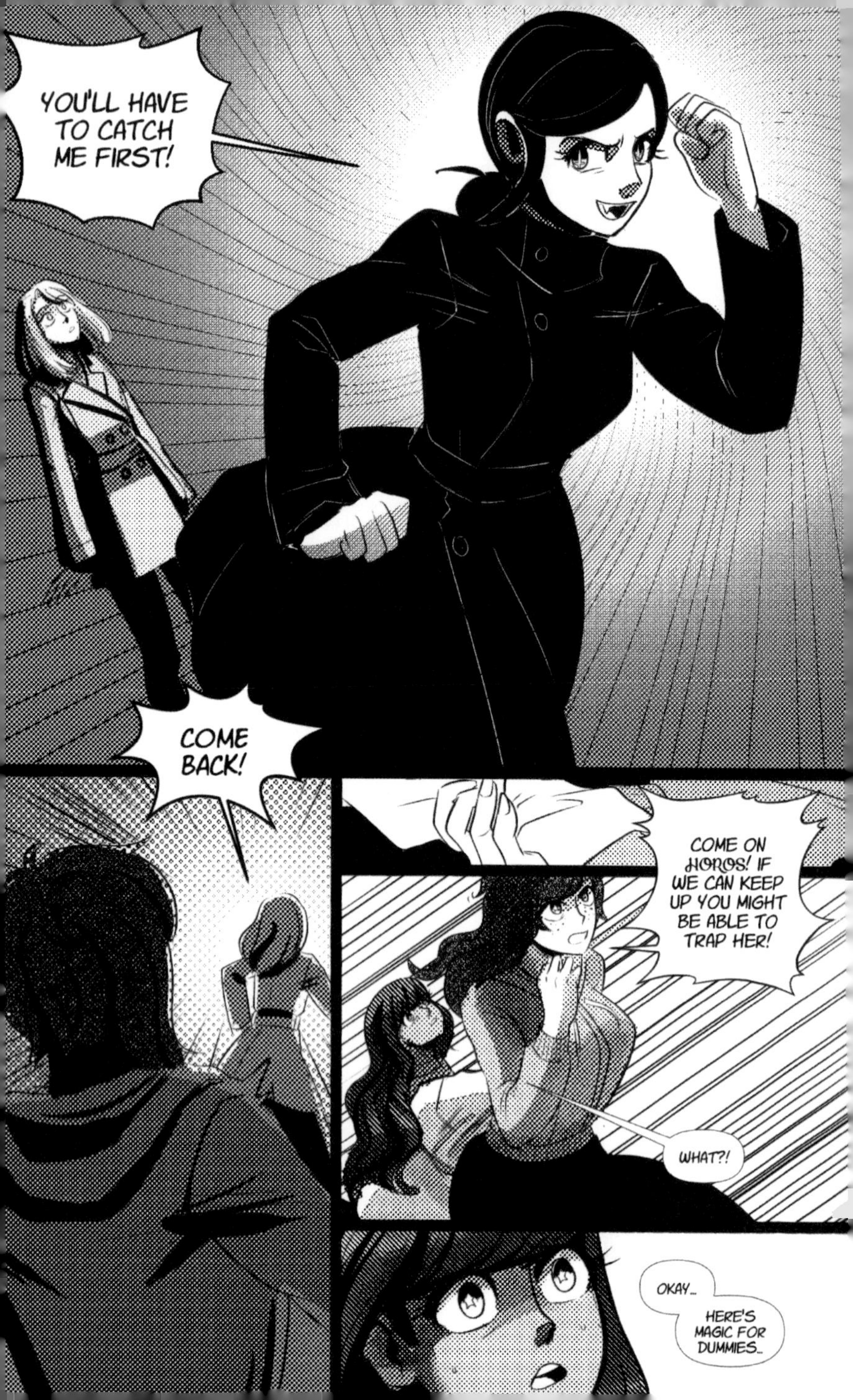
YOU'LL HAVE TO CATCH ME FIRST!
COME BACK!
COME ON HOROS! IF WE CAN KEEP UP YOU MIGHT BE ABLE TO TRAP HER!
WHAT?!
OKAY...
HERE'S MAGIC FOR DUMMIES...

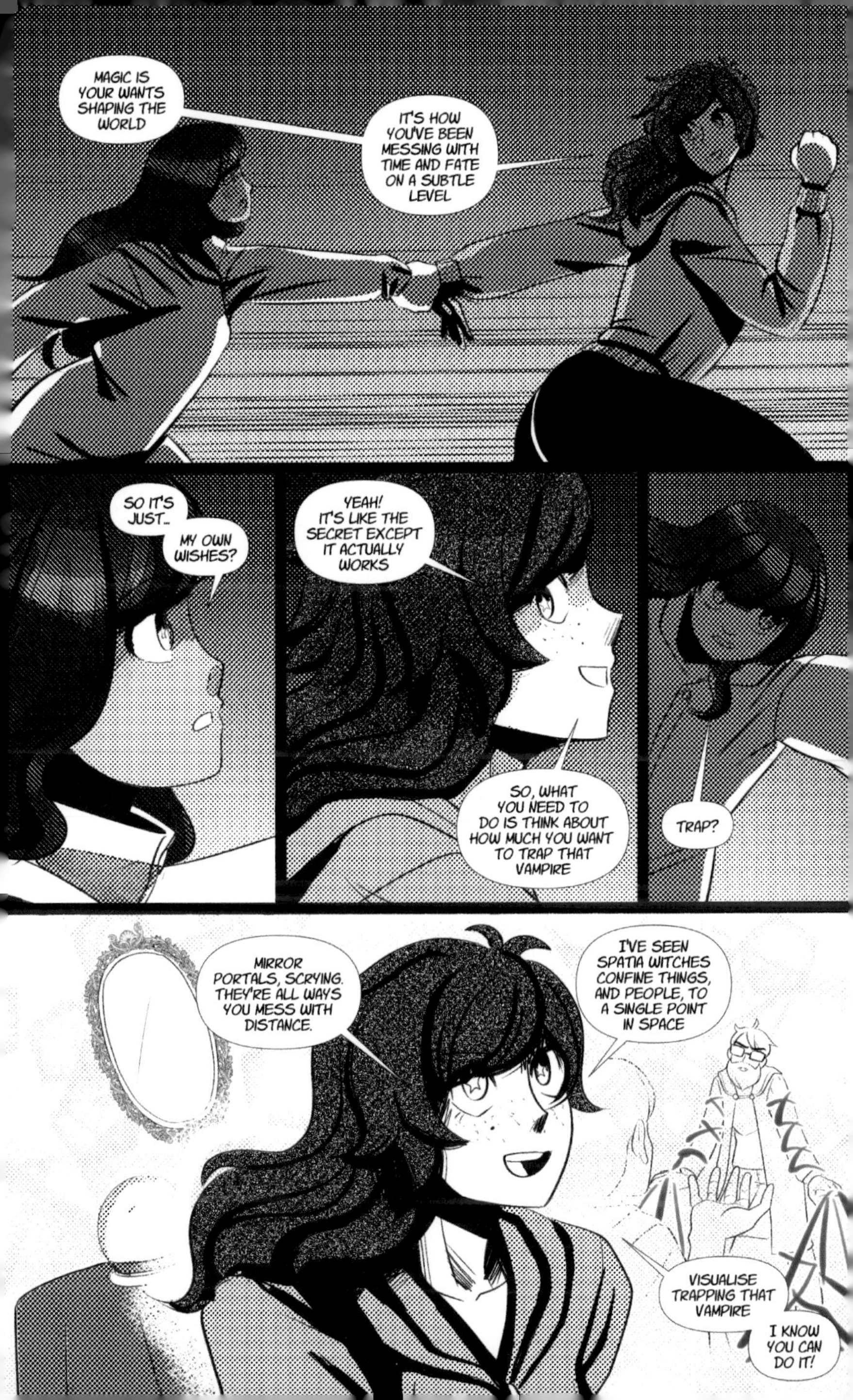
MAGIC IS YOUR WANTS SHAPING THE WORLD
IT'S HOW YOU'VE BEEN MESSING WITH TIME AND FATE ON A SUBTLE LEVEL
SO IT'S JUST...
MY OWN WISHES?
YEAH! IT'S LIKE THE SECRET EXCEPT IT ACTUALLY WORKS
SO, WHAT YOU NEED TO DO IS THINK ABOUT HOW MUCH YOU WANT TO TRAP THAT VAMPIRE
TRAP?
MIRROR PORTALS, SCRYING. THEY'RE ALL WAYS YOU MESS WITH DISTANCE.
I'VE SEEN SPATIA WITCHES CONFINE THINGS, AND PEOPLE, TO A SINGLE POINT IN SPACE
VISUALISE TRAPPING THAT VAMPIRE
I KNOW YOU CAN DO IT!

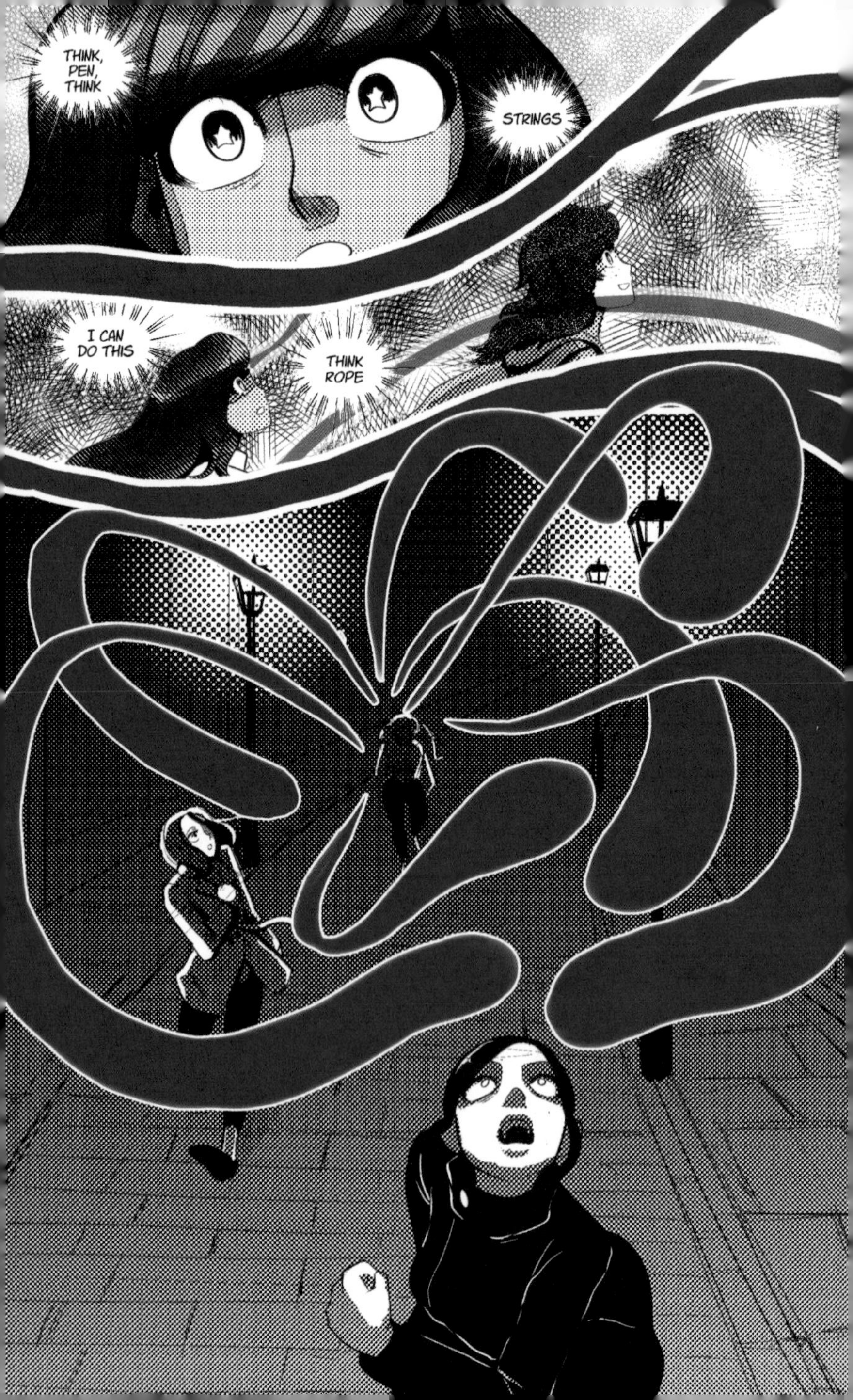
THINK, PEN, THINK
STRINGS
I CAN DO THIS
THINK ROPE

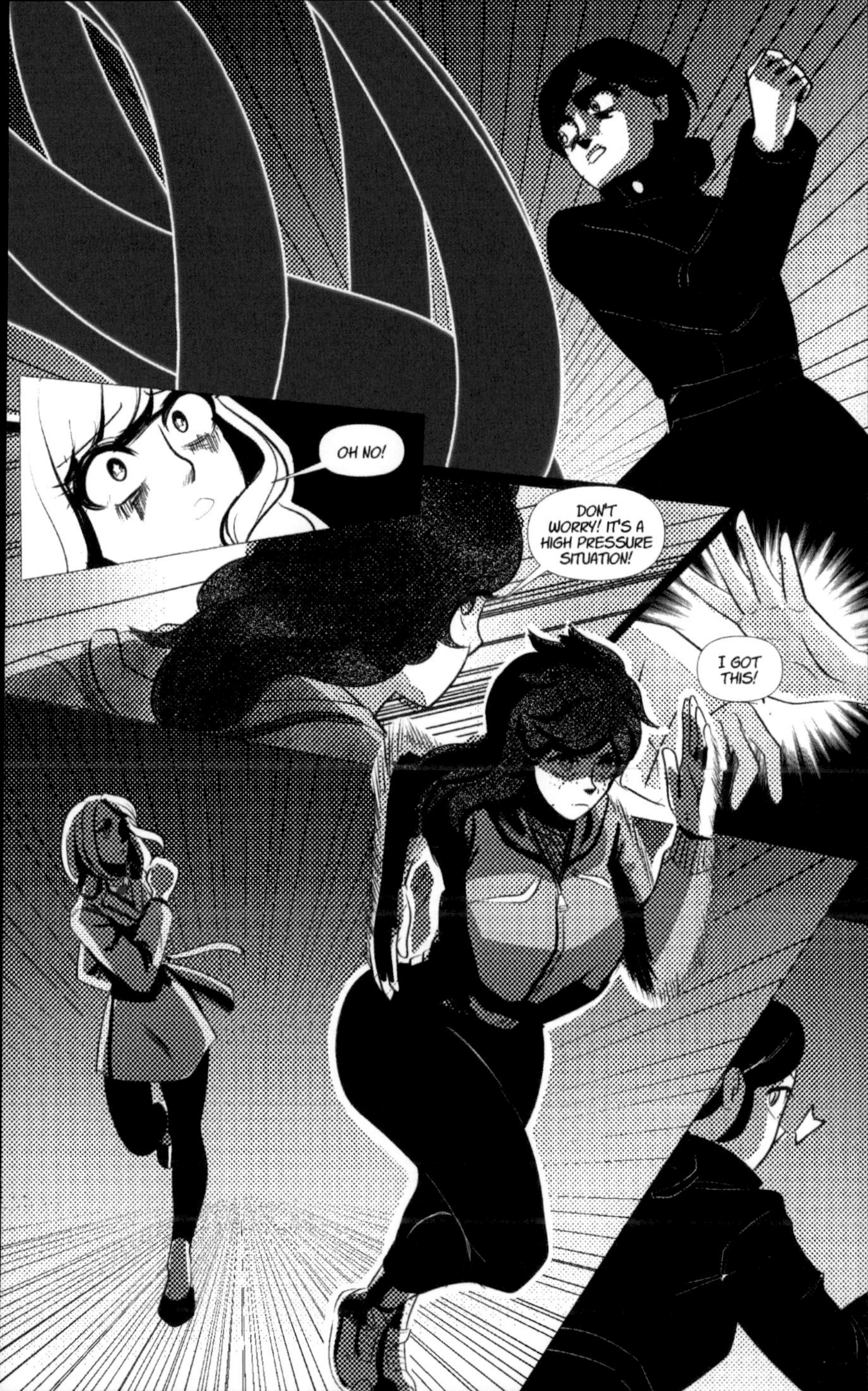
OH NO!
DON'T WORRY! IT'S A HIGH PRESSURE SITUATION!
I GOT THIS!

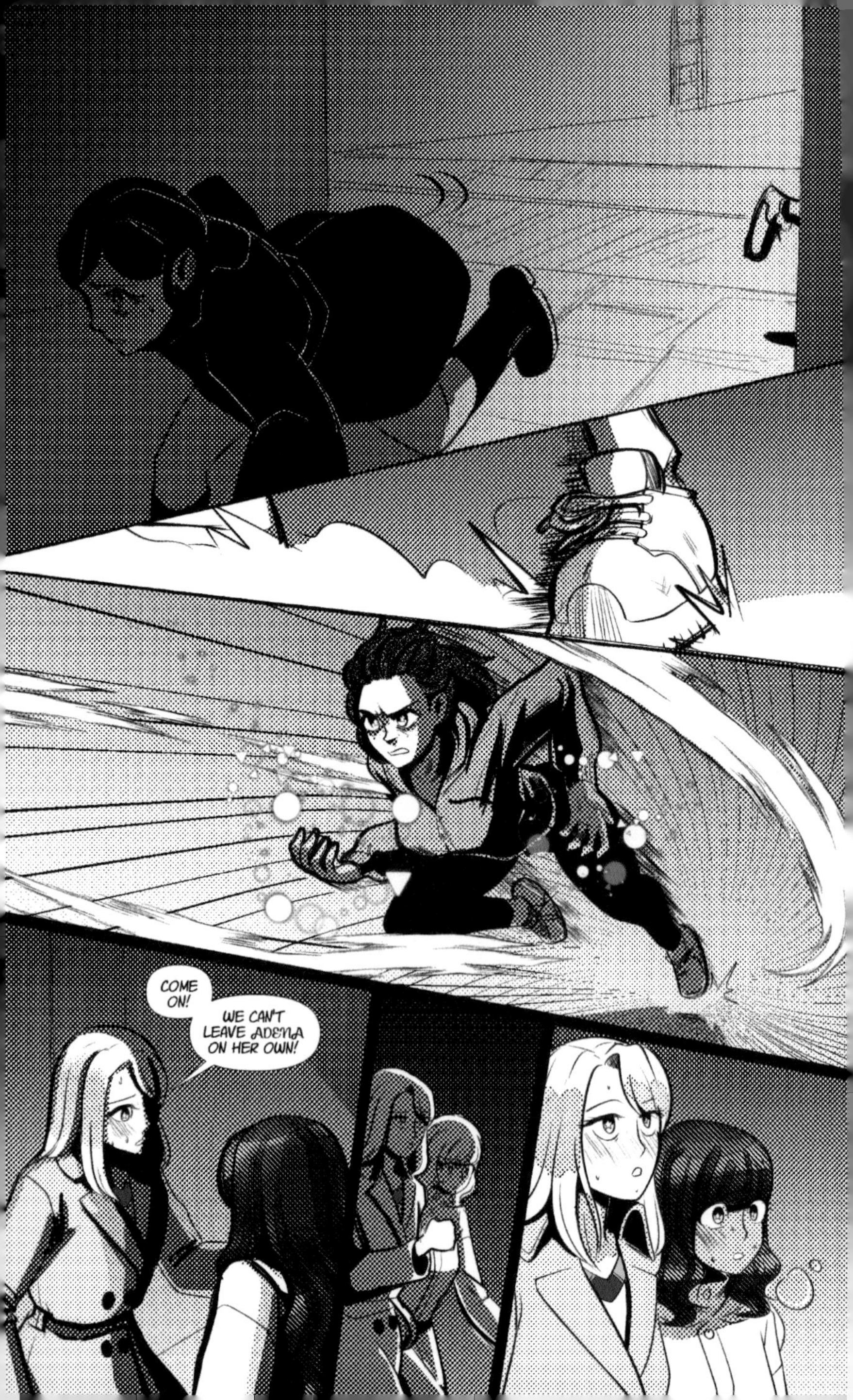
COME ON!
WE CAN'T LEAVE ADENA ON HER OWN!

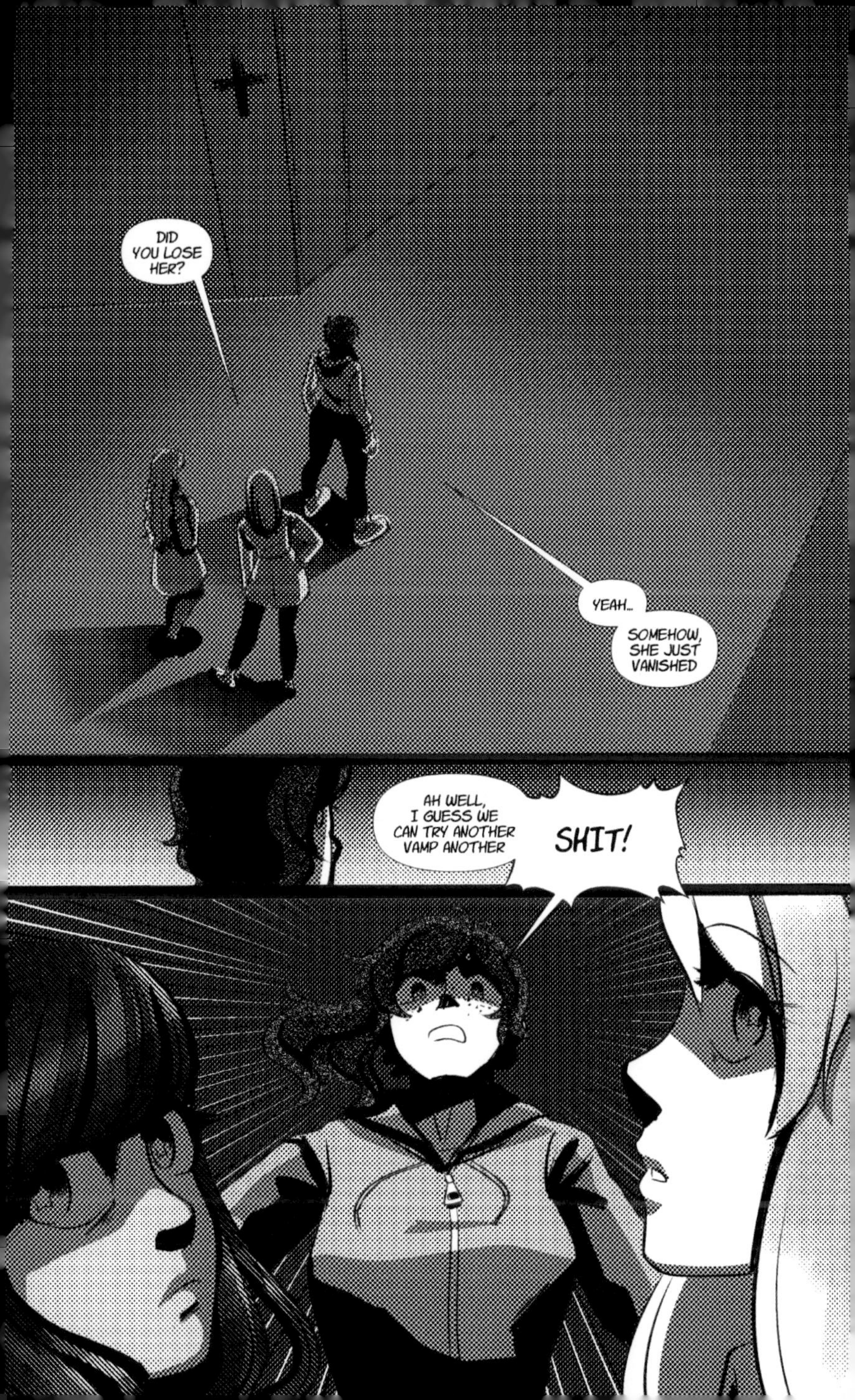
DID YOU LOSE HER?
YEAH...
SOMEHOW, SHE JUST VANISHED
AH WELL, I GUESS WE CAN TRY ANOTHER VAMP ANOTHER
SHIT!

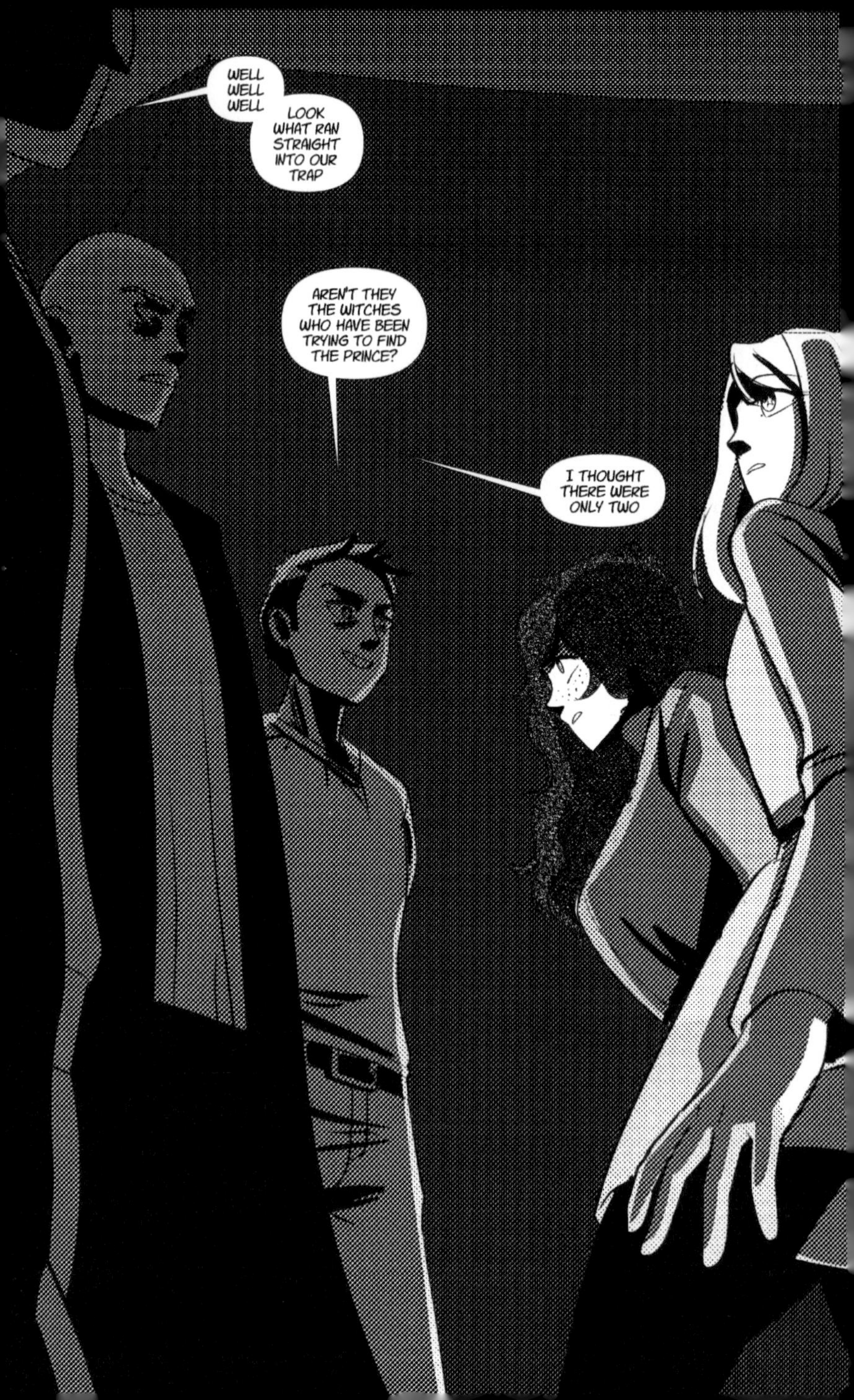
WELL WELL WELL
LOOK WHAT RAN STRAIGHT INTO OUR TRAP
AREN'T THEY THE WITCHES WHO HAVE BEEN TRYING TO FIND THE PRINCE?
I THOUGHT THERE WERE ONLY TWO

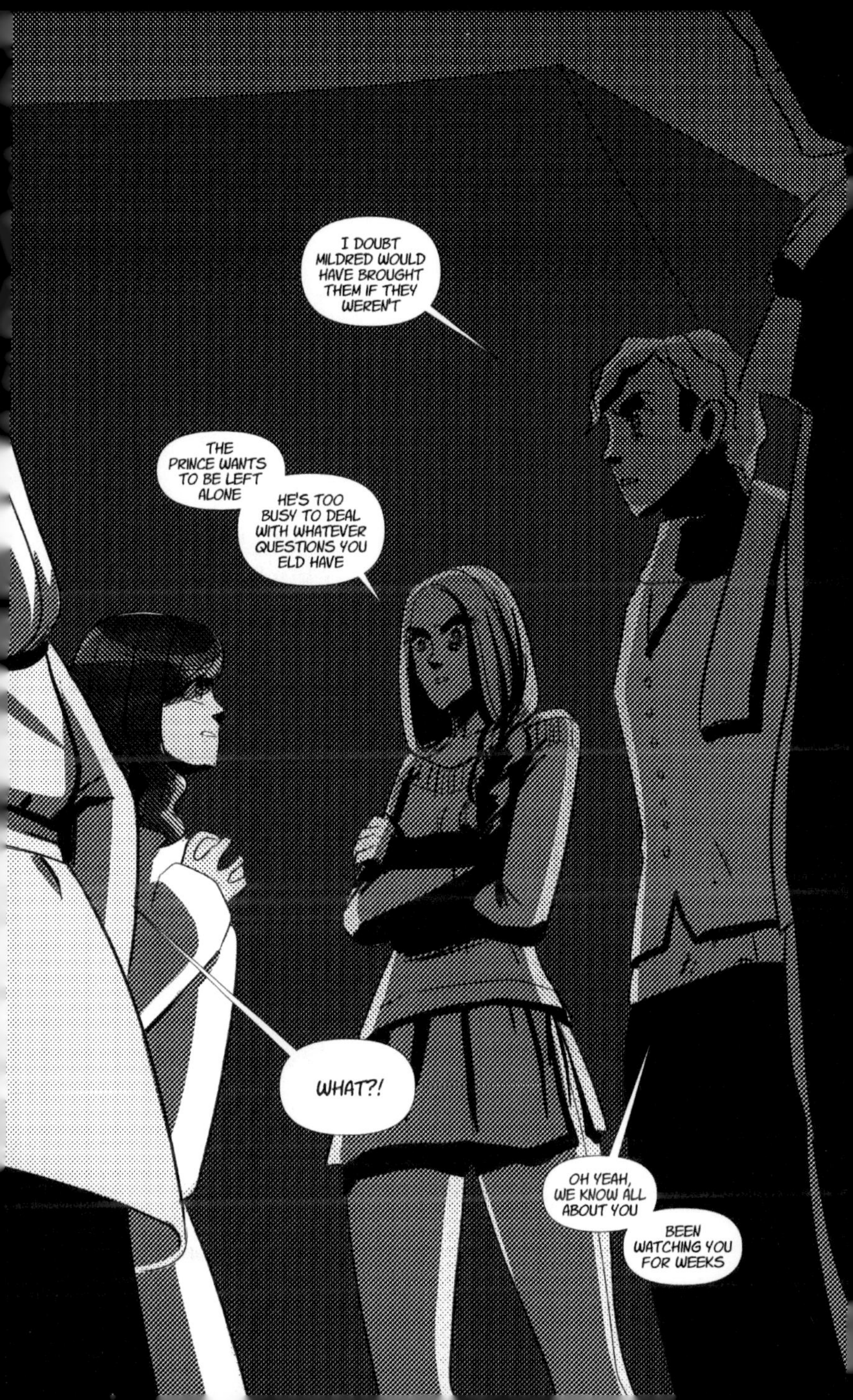
I DOUBT MILDRED WOULD HAVE BROUGHT THEM IF THEY WEREN'T
THE PRINCE WANTS TO BE LEFT ALONE
HE'S TOO BUSY TO DEAL WITH WHATEVER QUESTIONS YOU ELD HAVE
WHAT?!
OH YEAH, WE KNOW ALL ABOUT YOU
BEEN WATCHING YOU FOR WEEKS

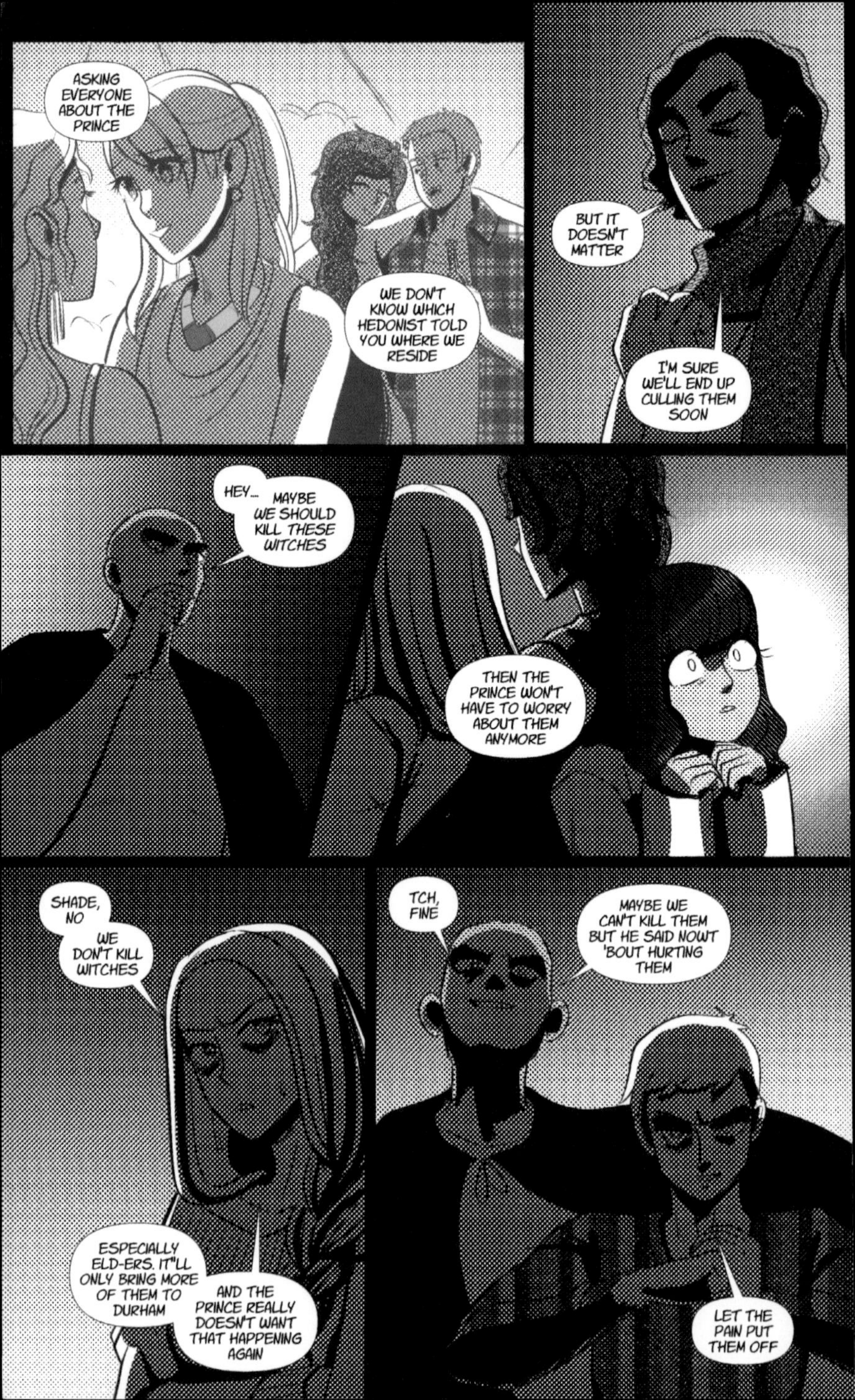
ASKING EVERYONE ABOUT THE PRINCE
WE DON'T KNOW WHICH HEDONIST TOLD YOU WHERE WE RESIDE
BUT IT DOESN'T MATTER
I'M SURE WE'LL END UP CULLING THEM SOON
HEY...
MAYBE WE SHOULD KILL THESE WITCHES
THEN THE PRINCE WON'T HAVE TO WORRY ABOUT THEM ANYMORE
SHADE, NO
WE DON'T KILL WITCHES
ESPECIALLY ELD-ERS. IT"LL ONLY BRING MORE OF THEM TO DURHAM
AND THE PRINCE REALLY DOESN'T WANT THAT HAPPENING AGAIN
TCH, FINE
MAYBE WE CAN'T KILL THEM BUT HE SAID NOWT 'BOUT HURTING THEM
LET THE PAIN PUT THEM OFF

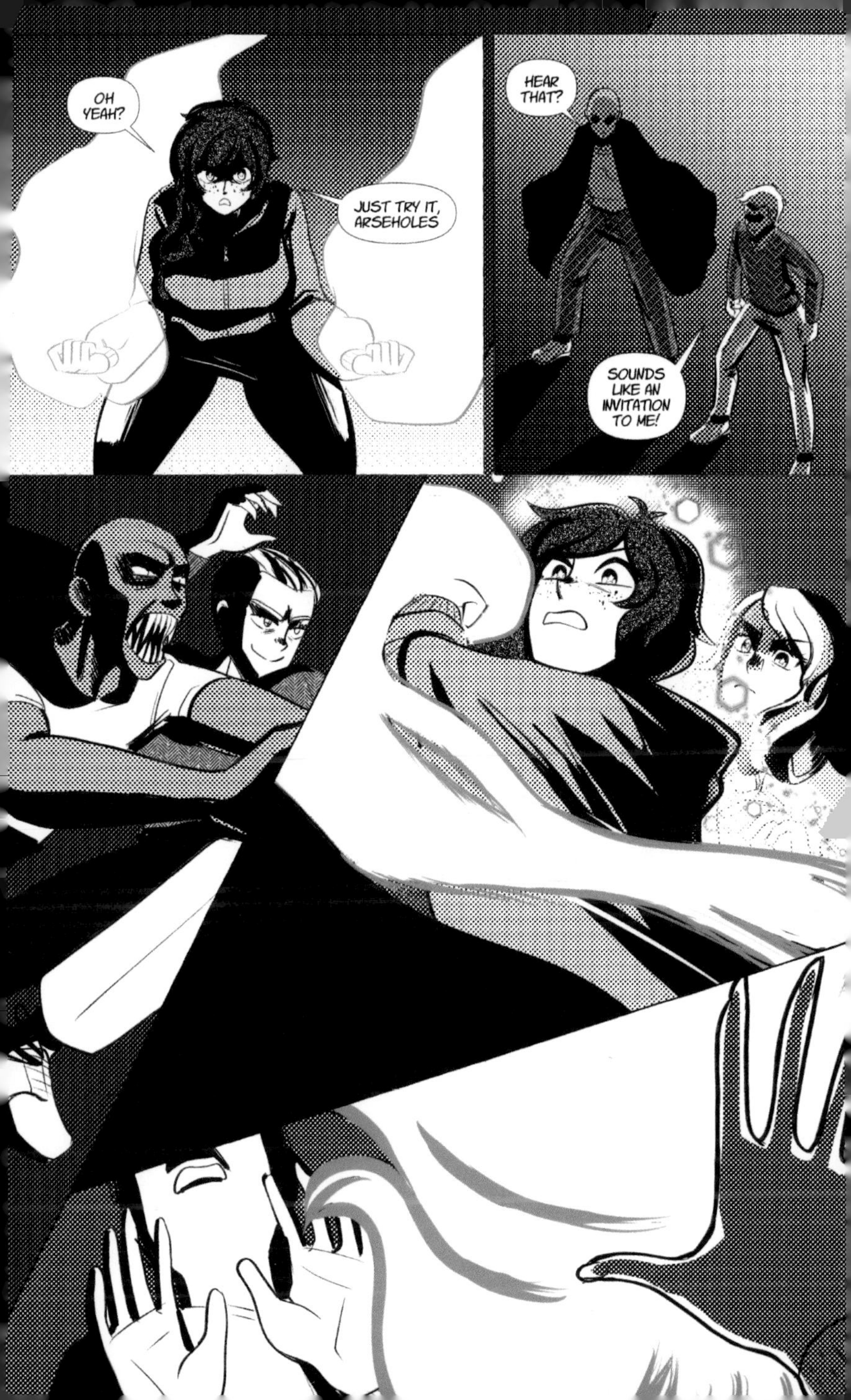
OH YEAH?
JUST TRY IT, ARSEHOLES
HEAR THAT?
SOUNDS LIKE AN INVITATION TO ME!

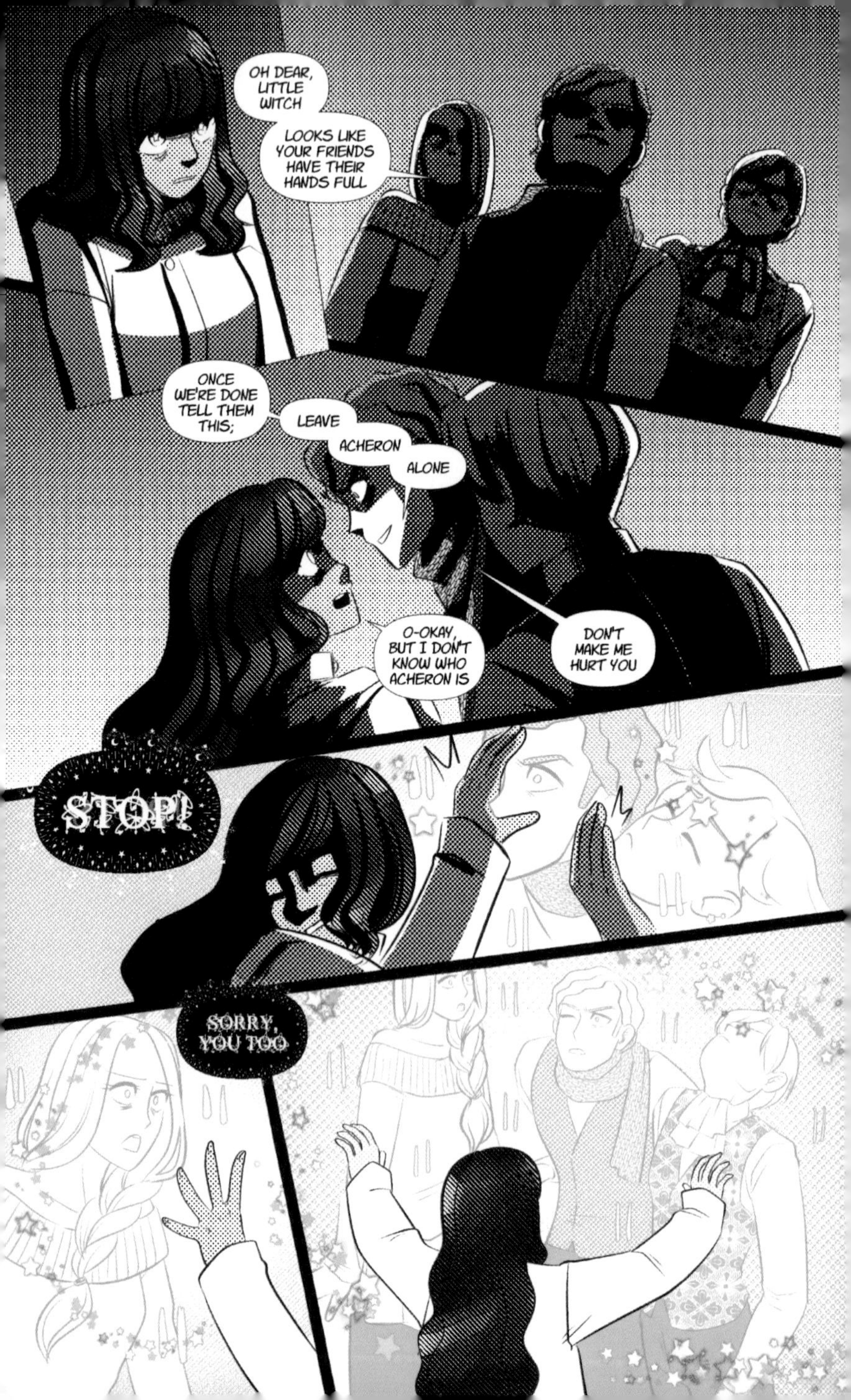
OH DEAR, LITTLE WITCH
LOOKS LIKE YOUR FRIENDS HAVE THEIR HANDS FULL
ONCE WE'RE DONE TELL THEM THIS;
LEAVE
ACHERON
ALONE
O-OKAY, BUT I DON'T KNOW WHO ACHERON IS
DON'T MAKE ME HURT YOU
STOP!
SORRY, YOU TOO

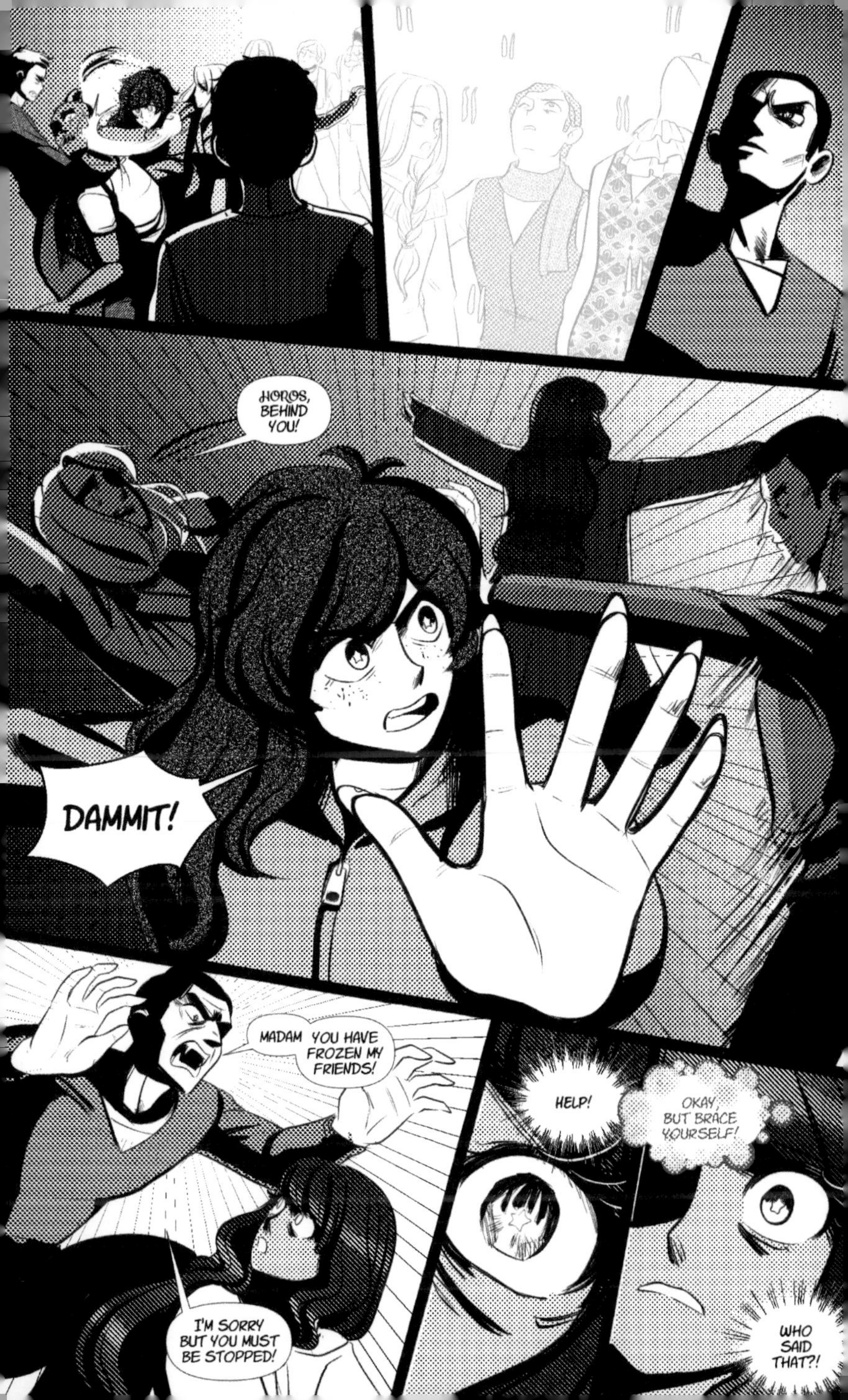
HOROS, BEHIND YOU!
DAMMIT!
MADAM YOU HAVE FROZEN MY FRIENDS!
I'M SORRY BUT YOU MUST BE STOPPED!
HELP!
OKAY, BUT BRACE YOURSELF!
WHO SAID THAT?!

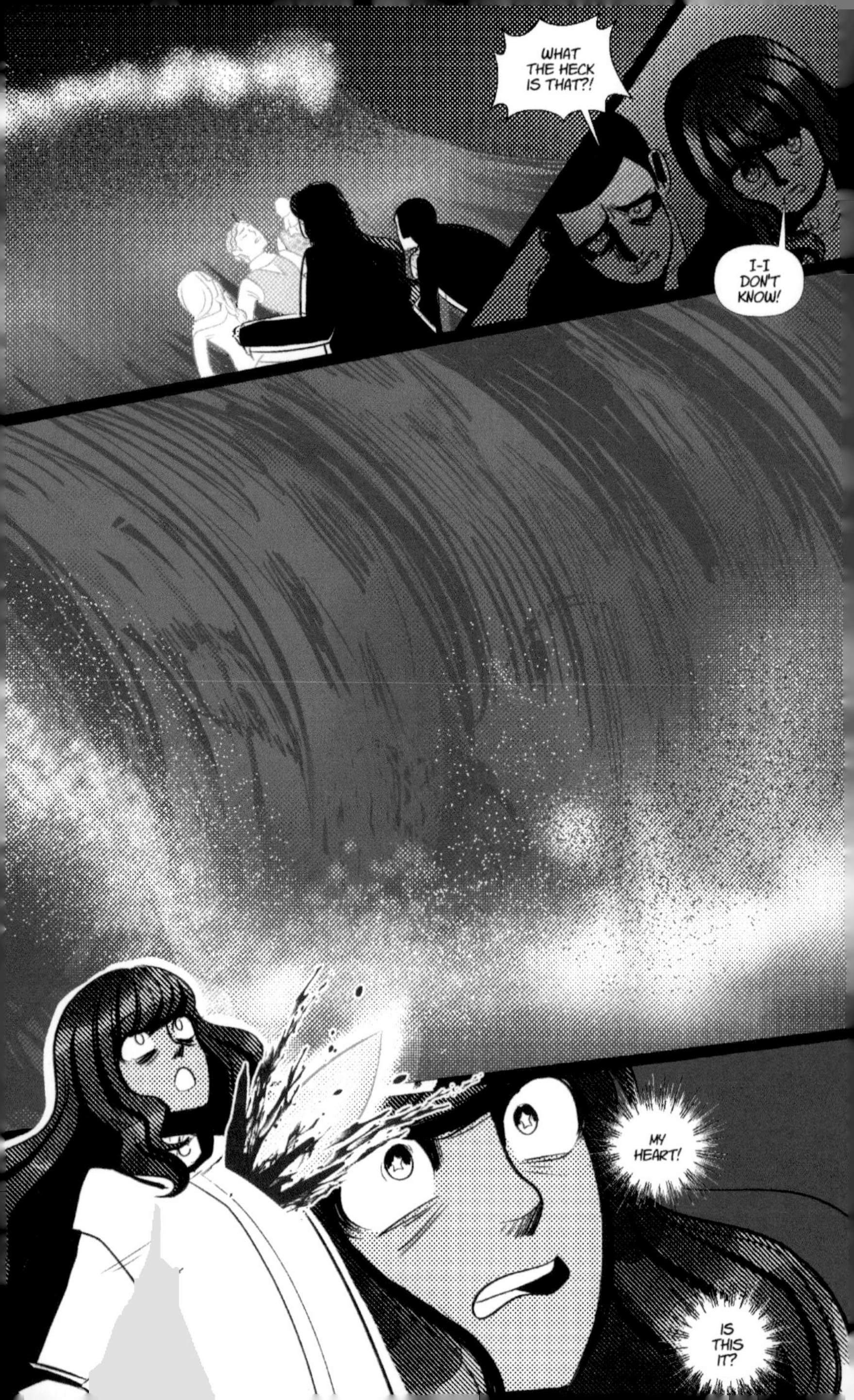
WHAT THE HECK IS THAT?!
I-I DON'T KNOW!
MY HEART!
IS THIS IT?

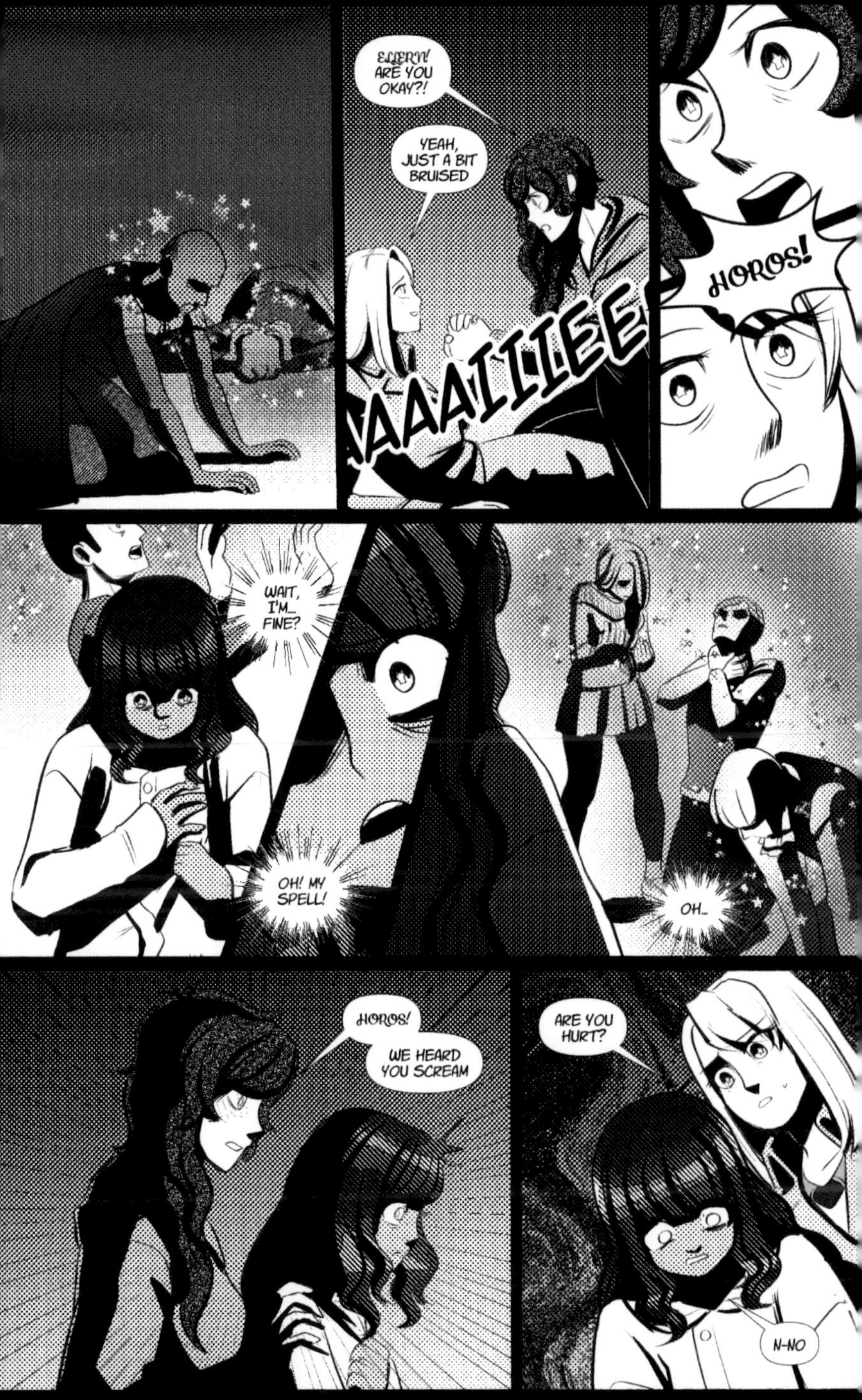

ELLERY! ARE YOU OKAY?!
YEAH, JUST A BIT BRUISED
AAAAIIIEEE
HOROS!
WAIT, I'M... FINE?
OH! MY SPELL!
OH...
HOROS!
WE HEARD YOU SCREAM
ARE YOU HURT?
N-NO

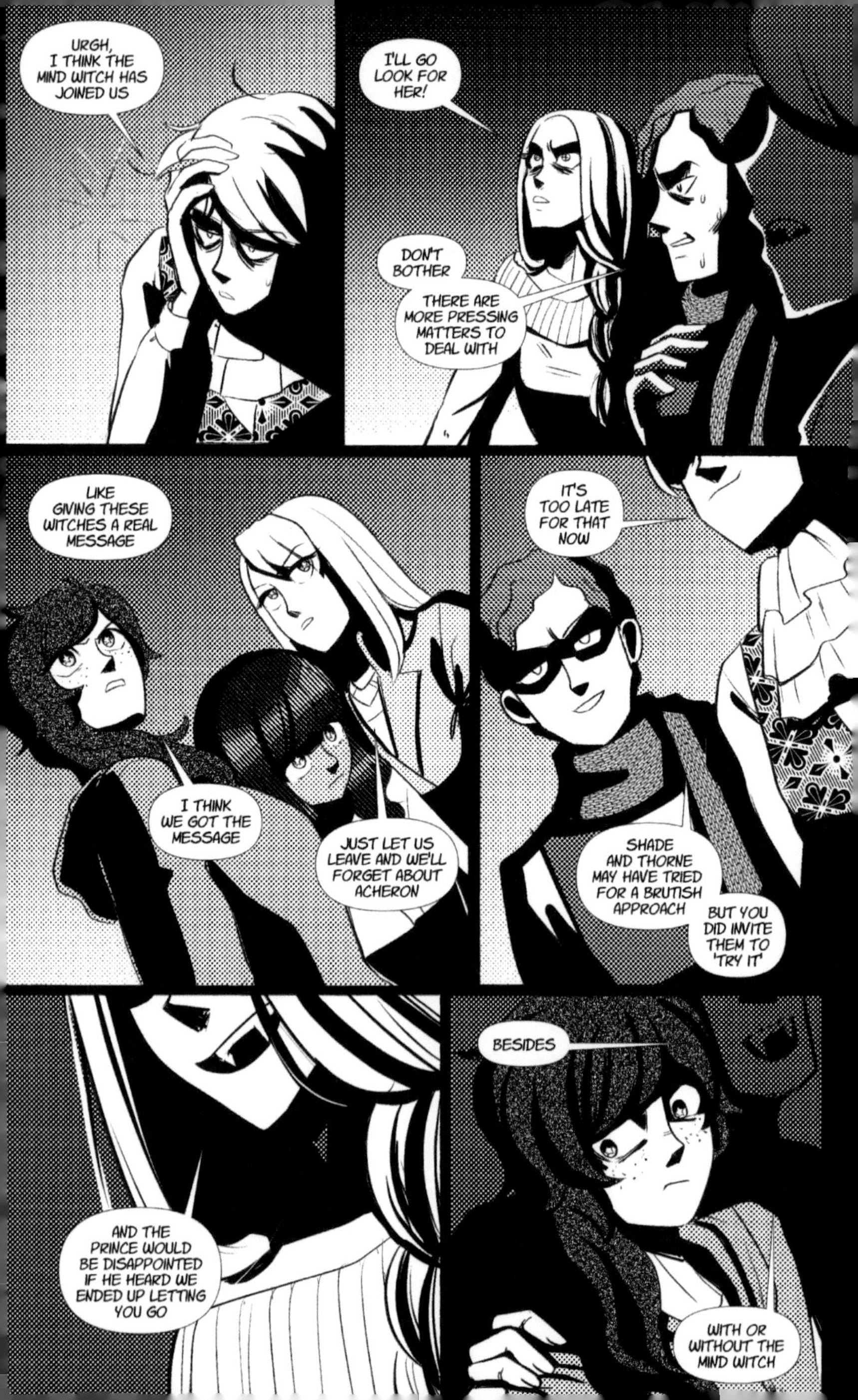
URGH, I THINK THE MIND WITCH HAS JOINED US
I'LL GO LOOK FOR HER!
DON'T BOTHER
THERE ARE MORE PRESSING MATTERS TO DEAL WITH
LIKE GIVING THESE WITCHES A REAL MESSAGE
I THINK WE GOT THE MESSAGE
JUST LET US LEAVE AND WE'LL FORGET ABOUT ACHERON
IT'S TOO LATE FOR THAT NOW
SHADE AND THORNE MAY HAVE TRIED FOR A BRUTISH APPROACH
BUT YOU DID INVITE THEM TO 'TRY IT'
AND THE PRINCE WOULD BE DISAPPOINTED IF HE HEARD WE ENDED UP LETTING YOU GO
BESIDES
WITH OR WITHOUT THE MIND WITCH

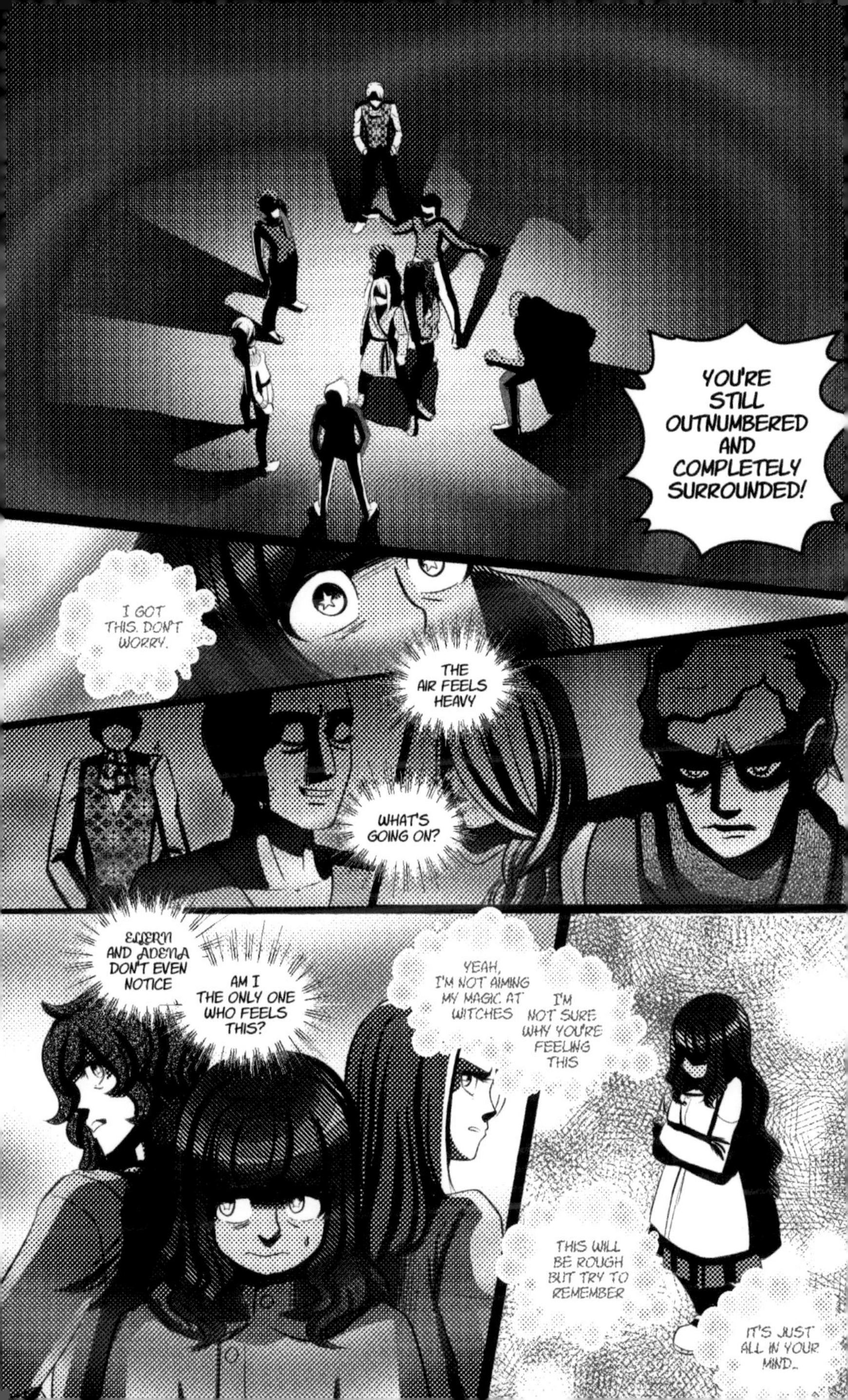
YOU'RE STILL OUTNUMBERED AND COMPLETELY SURROUNDED!
I GOT THIS. DON'T WORRY.
THE AIR FEELS HEAVY
WHAT'S GOING ON?
ELLERN AND ADENA DON'T EVEN NOTICE
AM I THE ONLY ONE WHO FEELS THIS?
YEAH, I'M NOT AIMING MY MAGIC AT WITCHES
I'M NOT SURE WHY YOU'RE FEELING THIS
THIS WILL BE ROUGH BUT TRY TO REMEMBER
IT'S JUST ALL IN YOUR MIND..

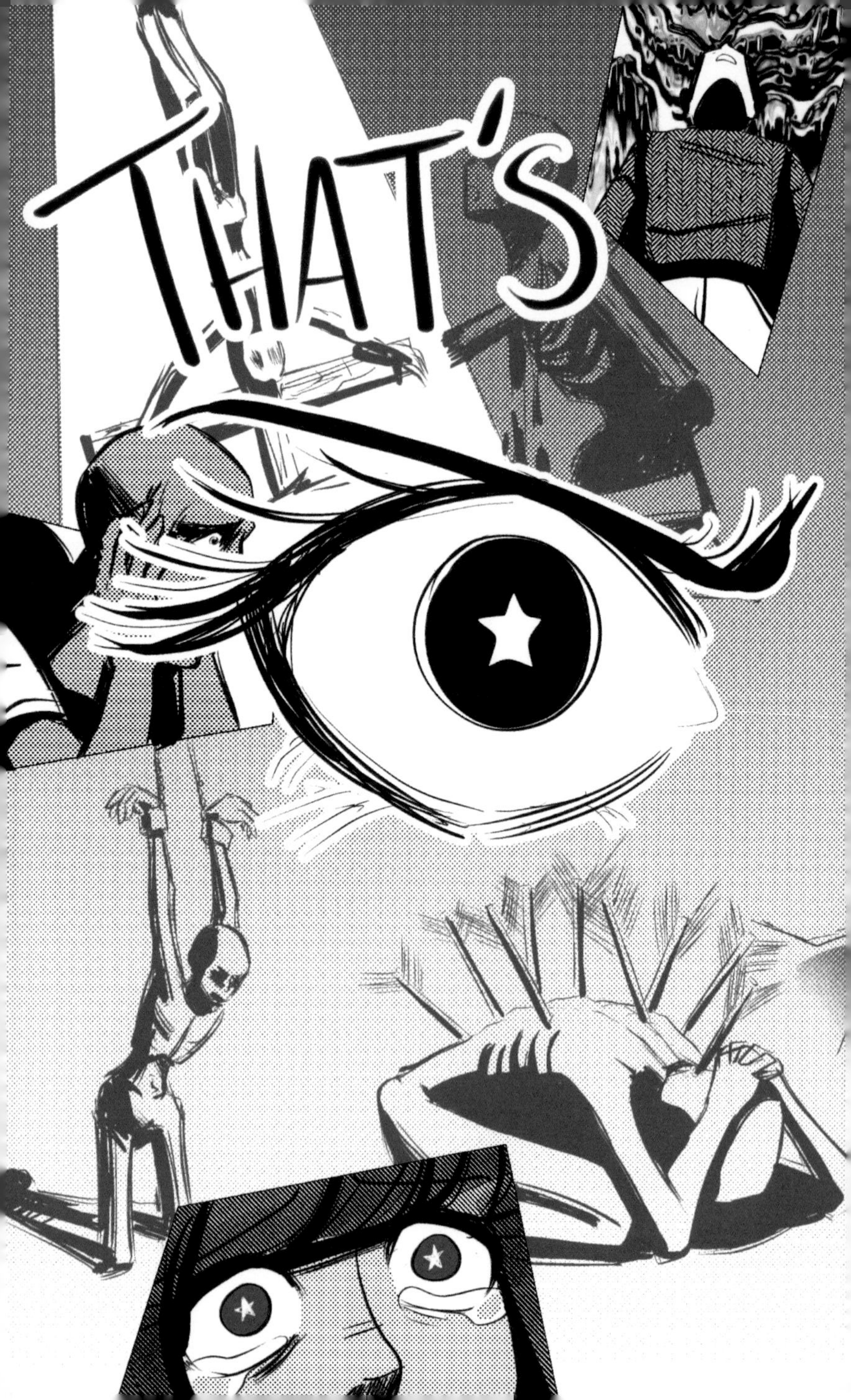
THAT'S

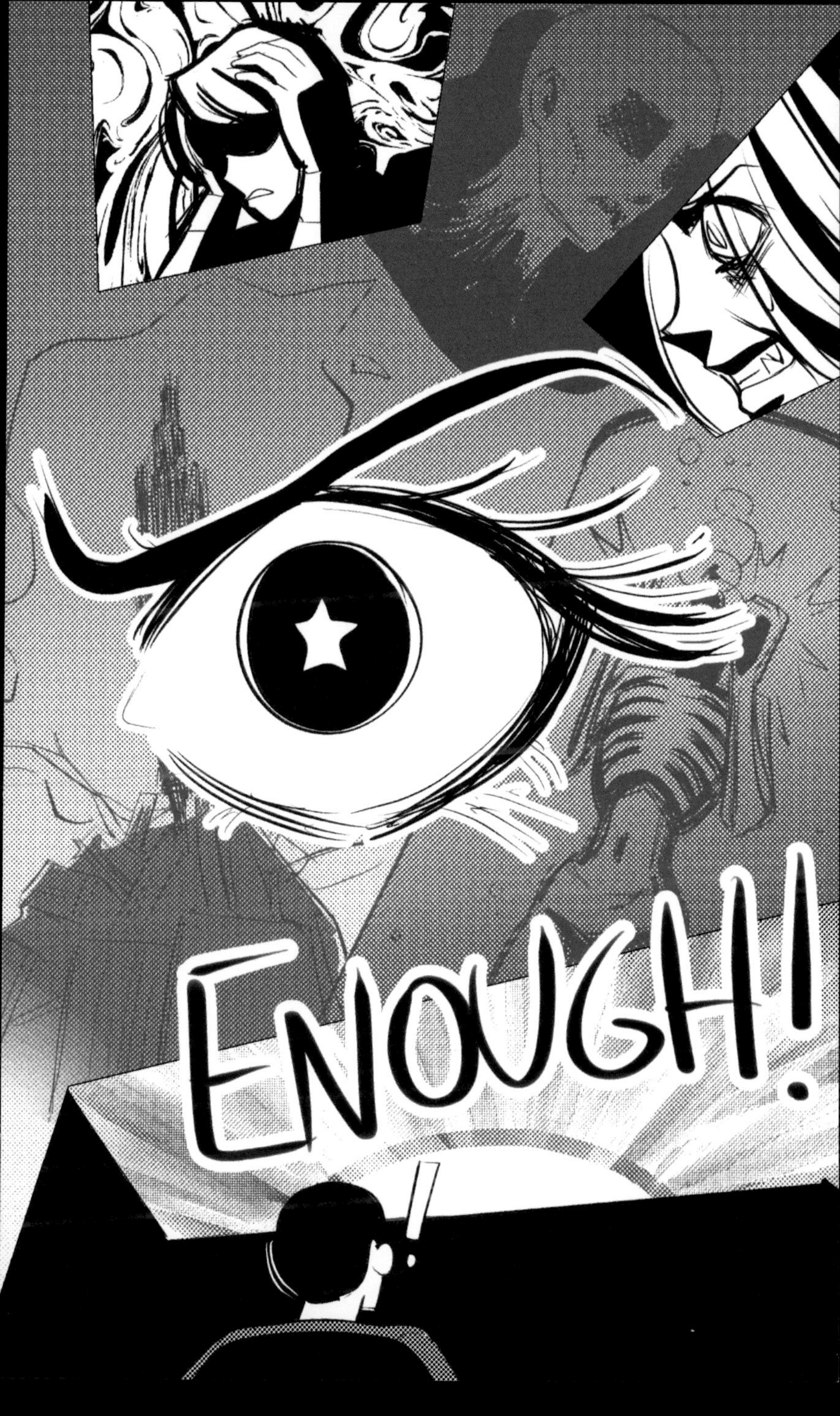
ENOUGH!
!

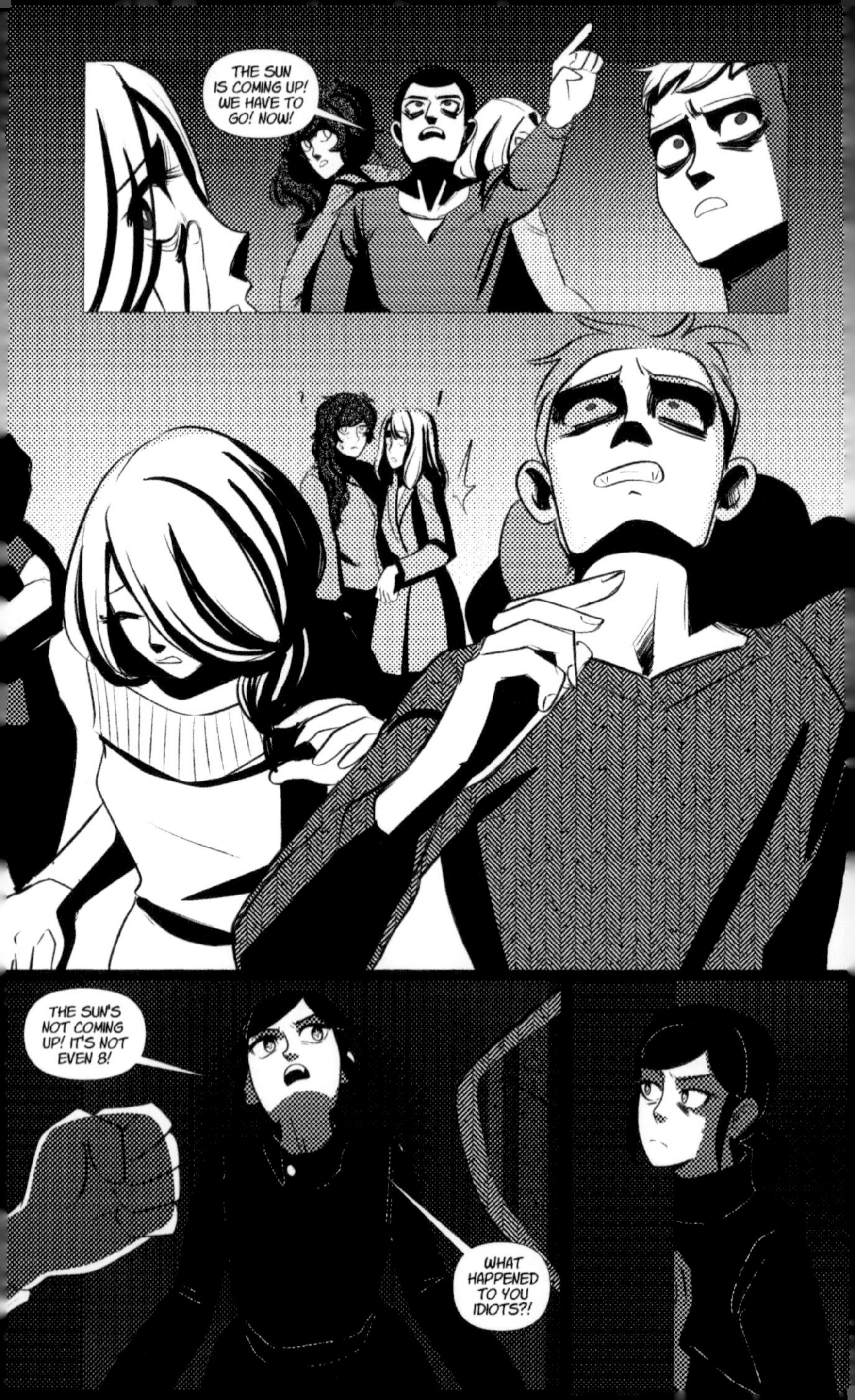
THE SUN IS COMING UP! WE HAVE TO GO! NOW!
THE SUN'S NOT COMING UP! IT'S NOT EVEN 8!
WHAT HAPPENED TO YOU IDIOTS?!

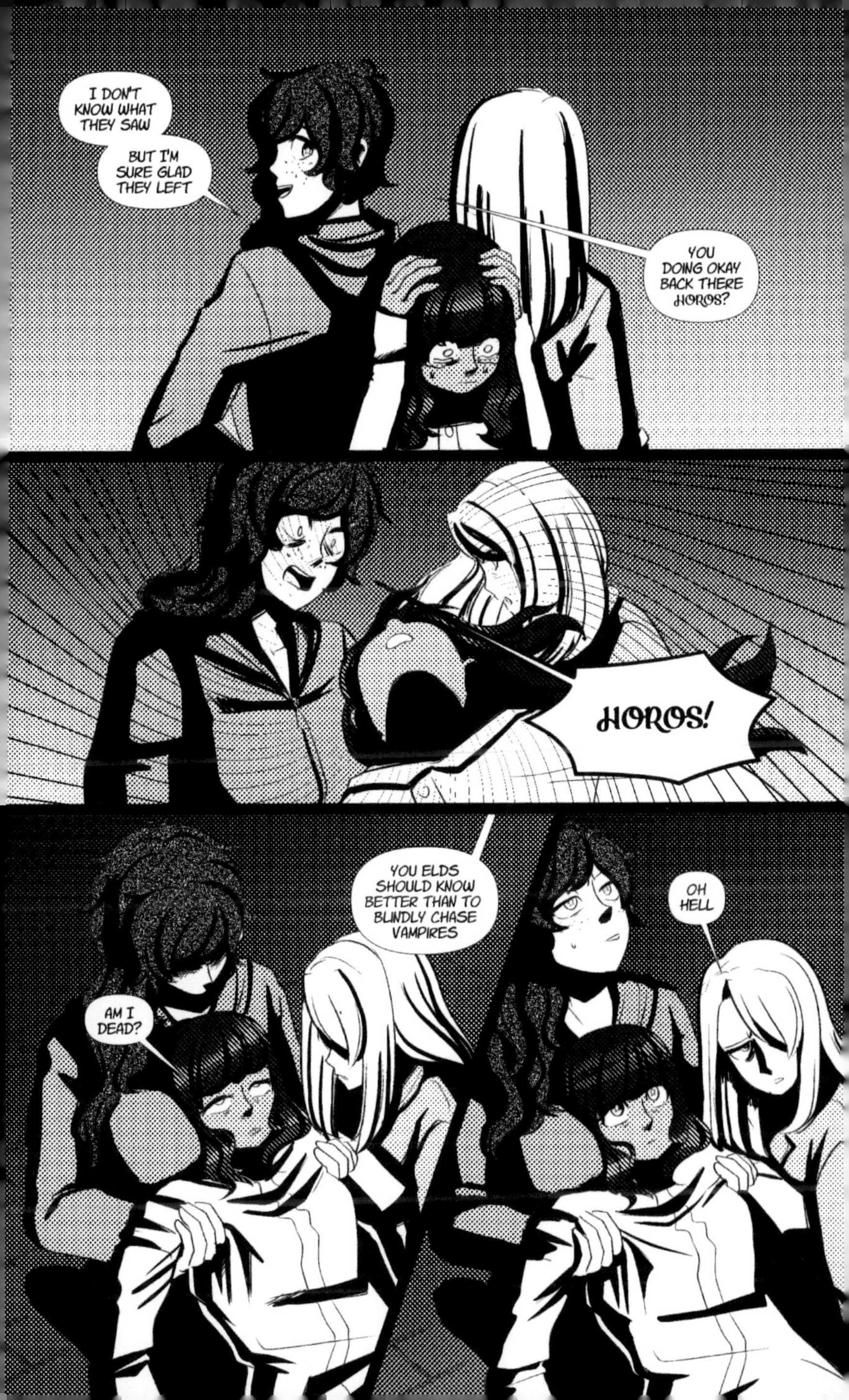
I DON'T KNOW WHAT THEY SAW
BUT I'M SURE GLAD THEY LEFT
YOU DOING OKAY BACK THERE HOROS?
HOROS!
AM I DEAD?
YOU ELDS SHOULD KNOW BETTER THAN TO BLINDLY CHASE VAMPIRES
OH HELL

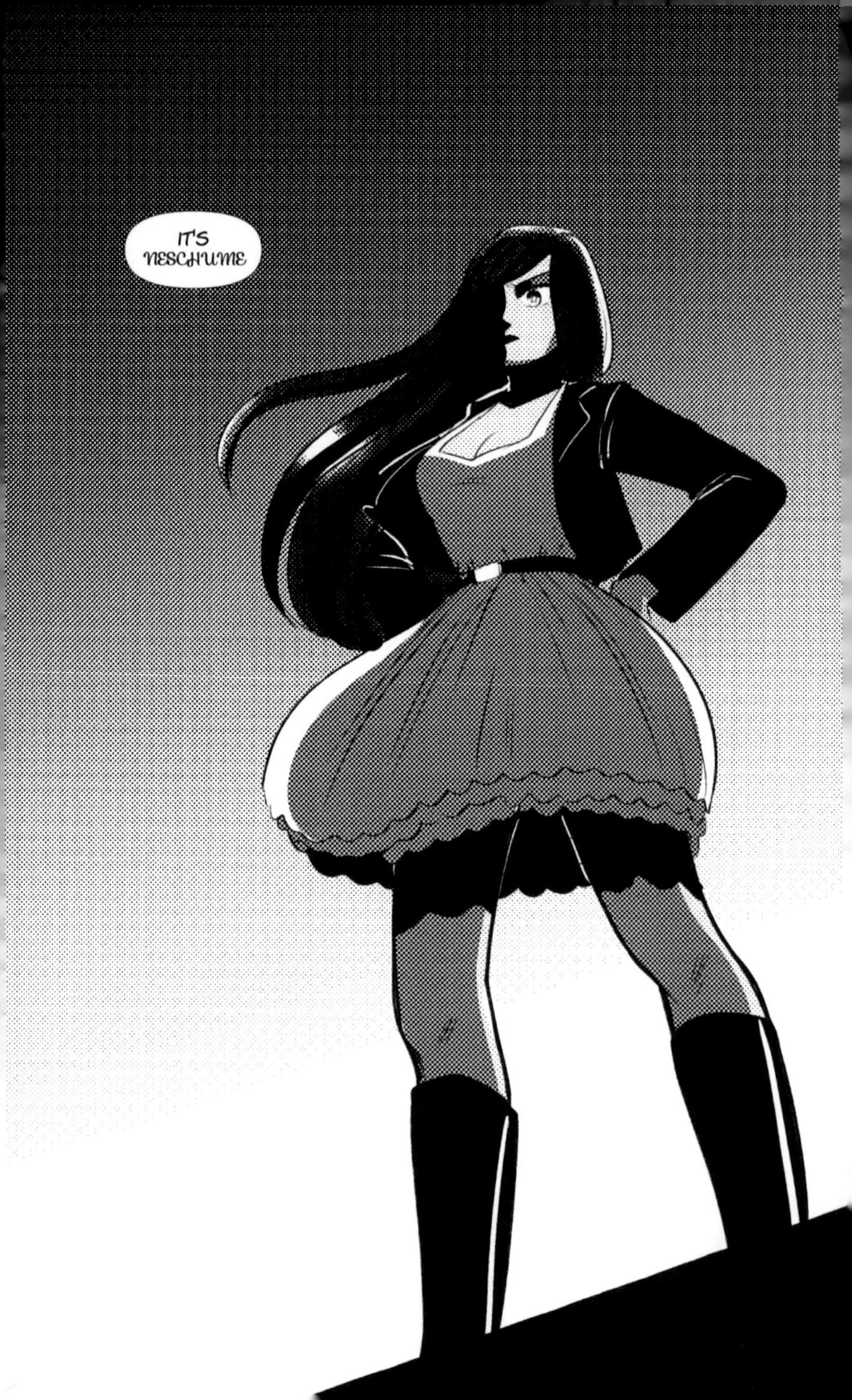
IT'S NESCHUME

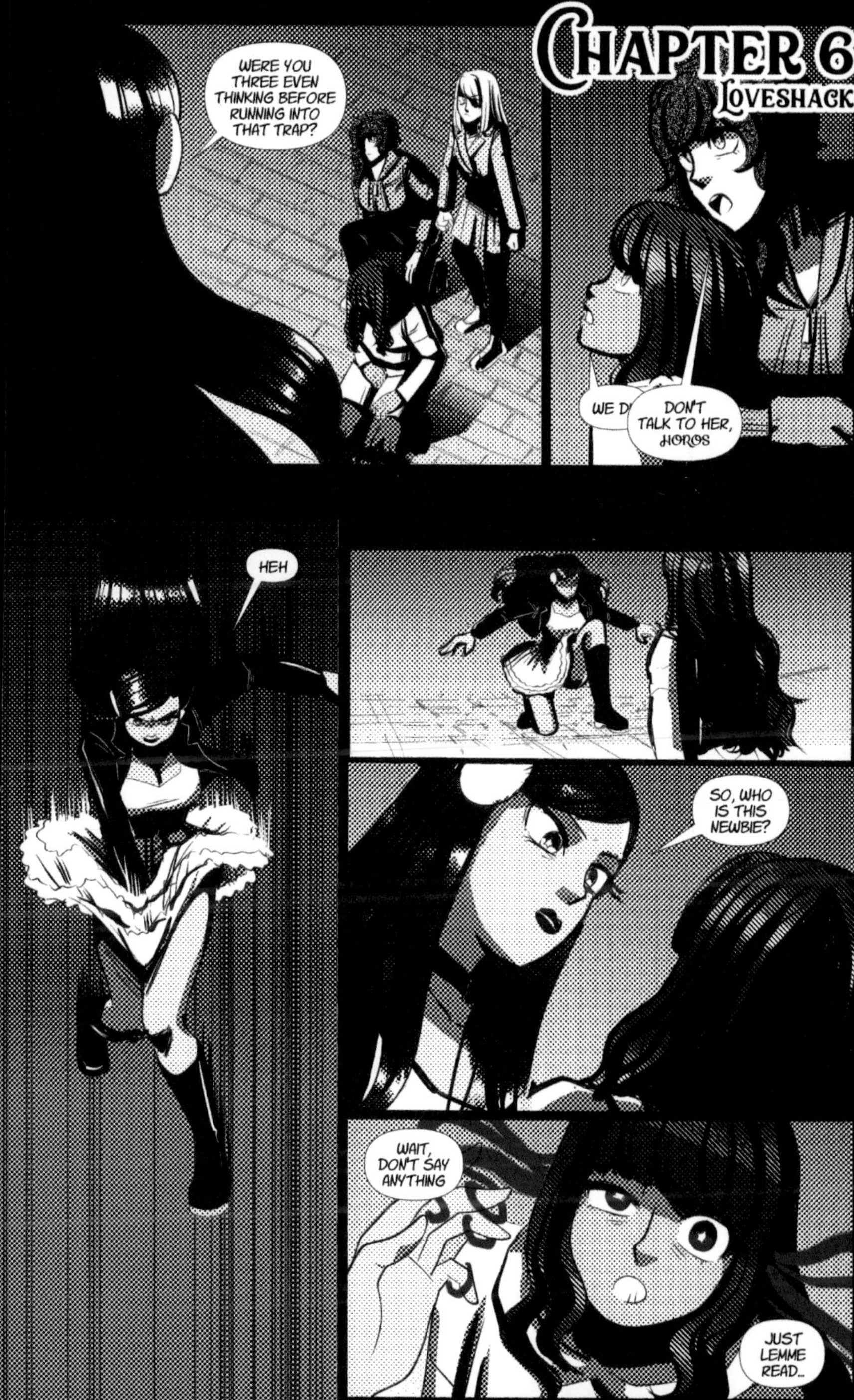
WERE YOU THREE EVEN THINKING BEFORE RUNNING INTO THAT TRAP?
CHAPTER 6
LOVESHACK
WE D
DON'T TALK TO HER, HOROS
HEH
SO, WHO IS THIS NEWBIE?
WAIT, DON'T SAY ANYTHING
JUST LEMME READ...

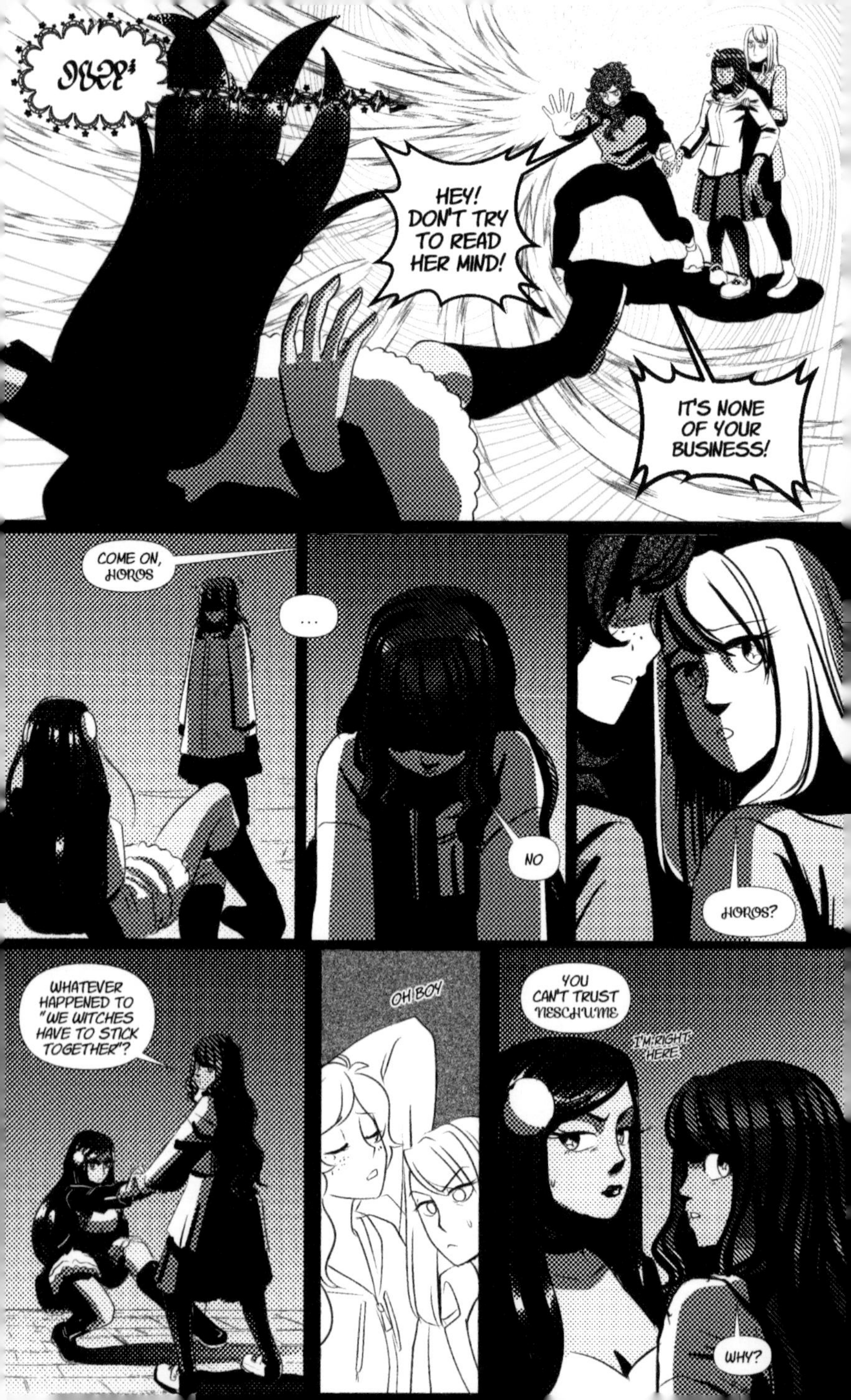
HEY! DON'T TRY TO READ HER MIND!
IT'S NONE OF YOUR BUSINESS!
COME ON, HOROS
...
NO
HOROS?
WHATEVER HAPPENED TO "WE WITCHES HAVE TO STICK TOGETHER"?
OH BOY
YOU CAN'T TRUST NESCHUME
I'M RIGHT HERE
WHY?

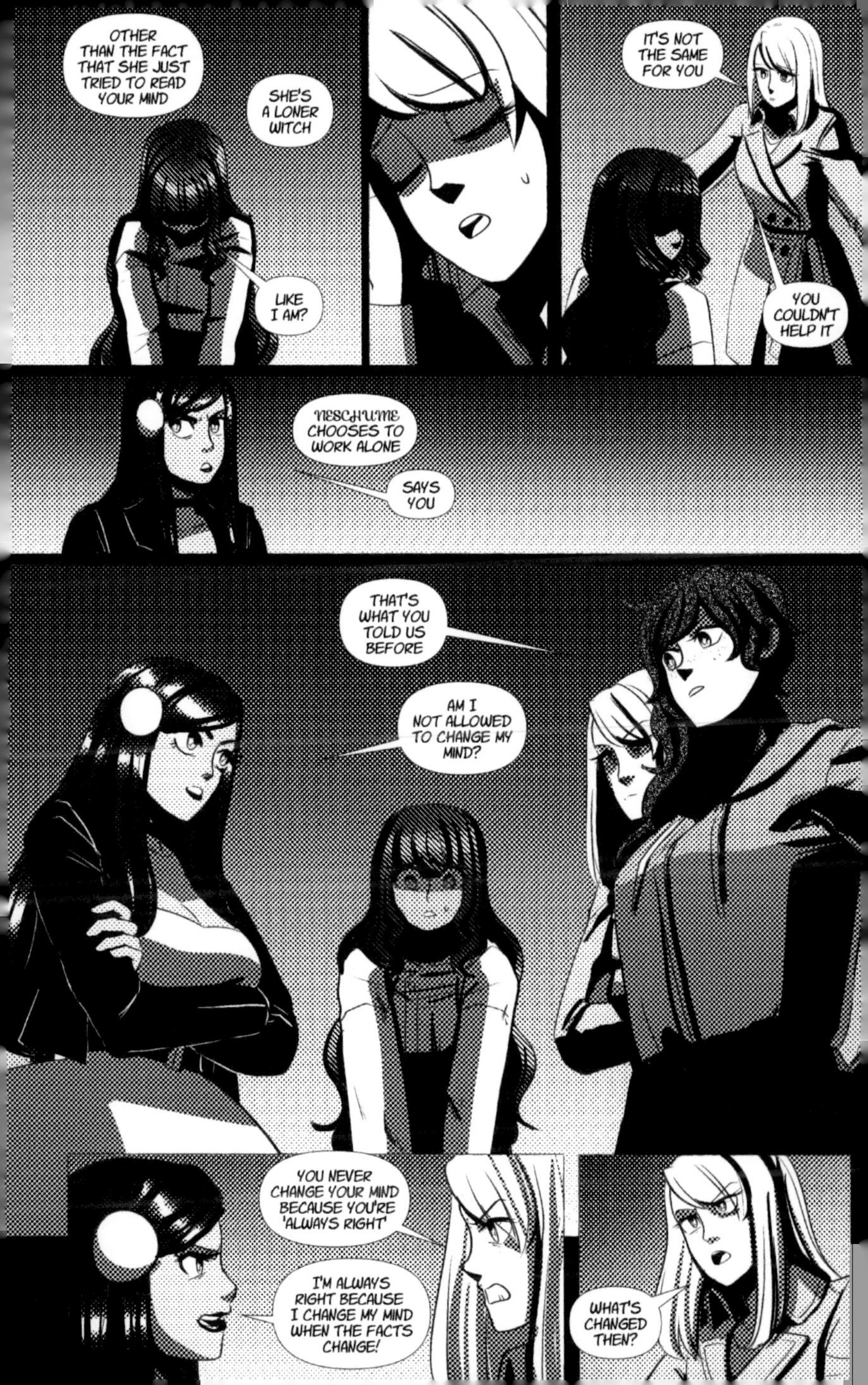
OTHER THAN THE FACT THAT SHE JUST TRIED TO READ YOUR MIND
SHE'S A LONER WITCH
LIKE I AM?
IT'S NOT THE SAME FOR YOU
YOU COULDN'T HELP IT
NESCHUME CHOOSES TO WORK ALONE
SAYS YOU
THAT'S WHAT YOU TOLD US BEFORE
AM I NOT ALLOWED TO CHANGE MY MIND?
YOU NEVER CHANGE YOUR MIND BECAUSE YOU'RE 'ALWAYS RIGHT'
I'M ALWAYS RIGHT BECAUSE I CHANGE MY MIND WHEN THE FACTS CHANGE!
WHAT'S CHANGED THEN?

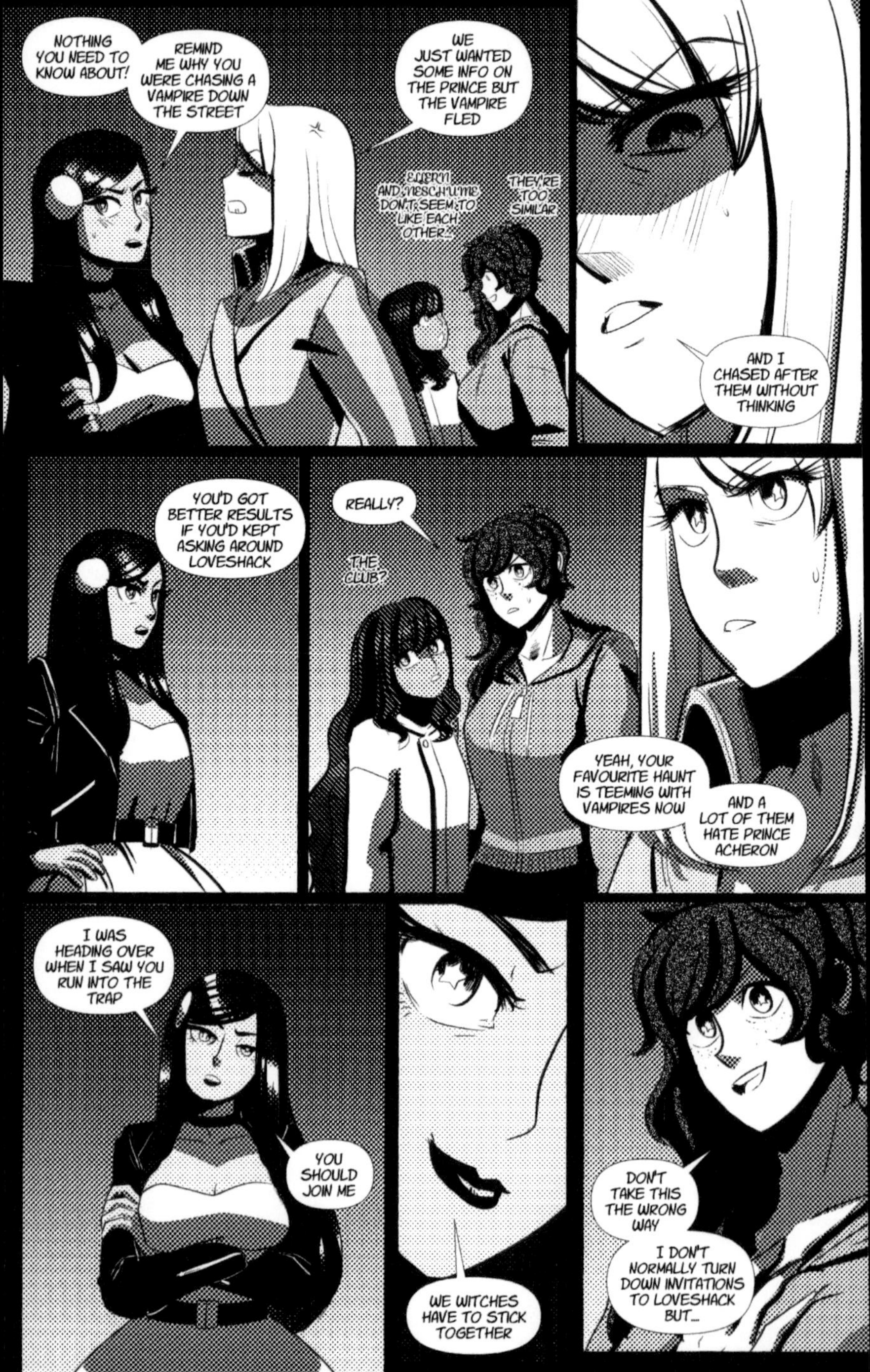
NOTHING YOU NEED TO KNOW ABOUT!
REMIND ME WHY YOU WERE CHASING A VAMPIRE DOWN THE STREET
WE JUST WANTED SOME INFO ON THE PRINCE BUT THE VAMPIRE FLED
ELLERN AND NESCHUME DON'T SEEM TO LIKE EACH OTHER...
THEY'RE TOO SIMILAR
AND I CHASED AFTER THEM WITHOUT THINKING
YOU'D GOT BETTER RESULTS IF YOU'D KEPT ASKING AROUND LOVESHACK
REALLY?
THE CLUB?
YEAH, YOUR FAVOURITE HAUNT IS TEEMING WITH VAMPIRES NOW
AND A LOT OF THEM HATE PRINCE ACHERON
I WAS HEADING OVER WHEN I SAW YOU RUN INTO THE TRAP
YOU SHOULD JOIN ME
WE WITCHES HAVE TO STICK TOGETHER
DON'T TAKE THIS THE WRONG WAY
I DON'T NORMALLY TURN DOWN INVITATIONS TO LOVESHACK BUT...

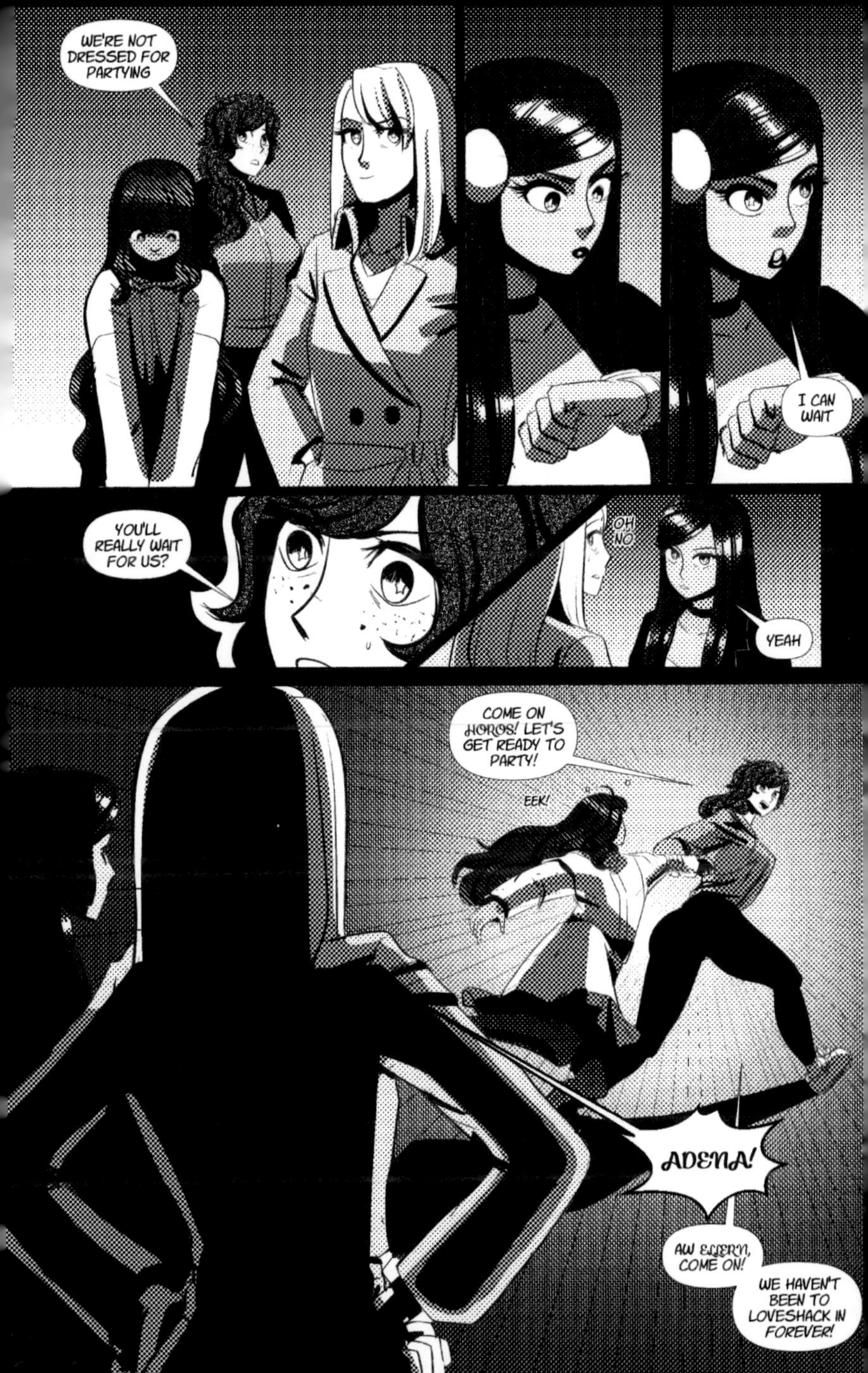
WE'RE NOT DRESSED FOR PARTYING
I CAN WAIT
YOU'LL REALLY WAIT FOR US?
OH NO
YEAH
COME ON HOROS! LET'S GET READY TO PARTY!
EEK!
ADENA!
AW ELLERN, COME ON!
WE HAVEN'T BEEN TO LOVESHACK IN FOREVER!

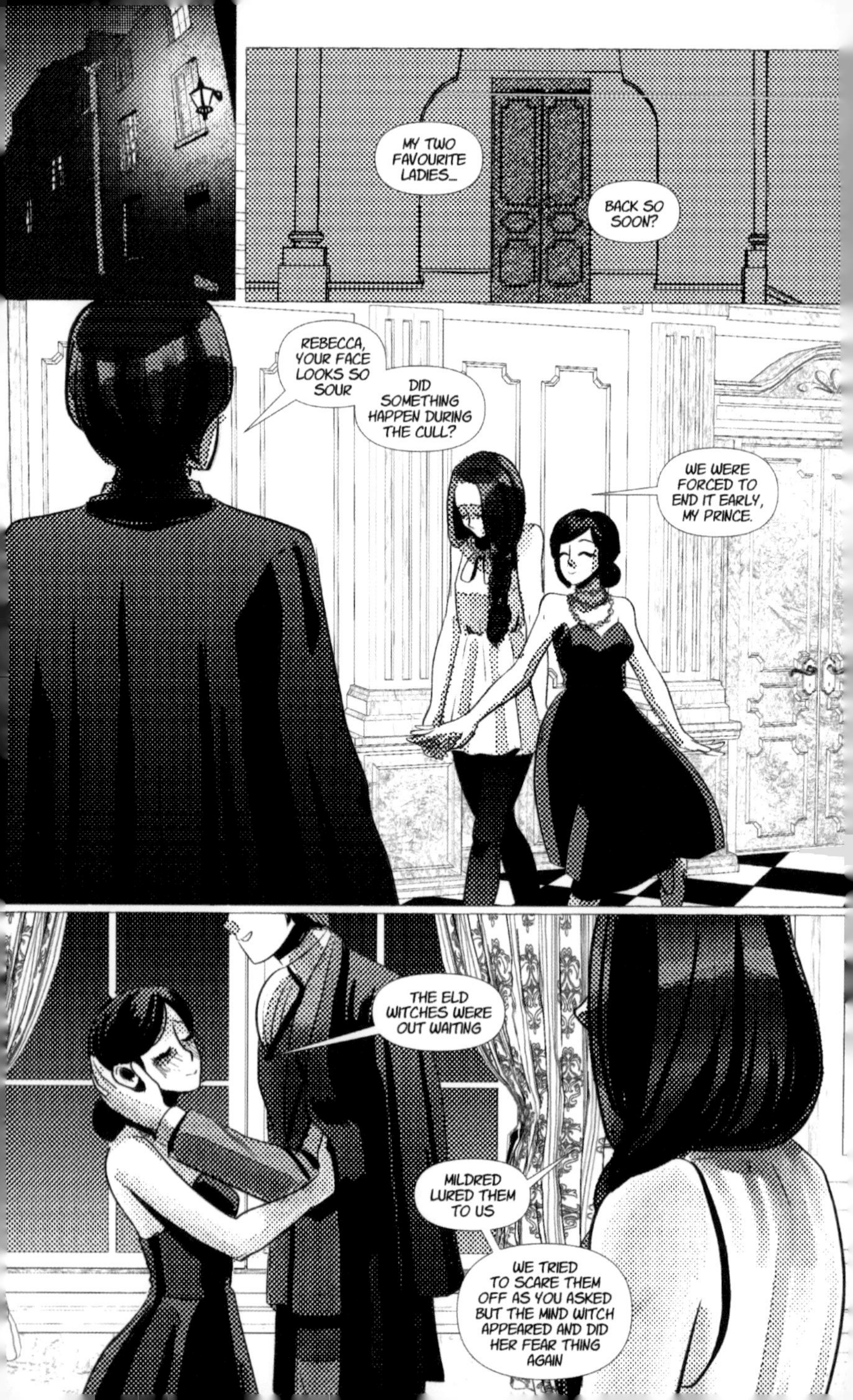
MY TWO FAVOURITE LADIES...
BACK SO SOON?
REBECCA, YOUR FACE LOOKS SO SOUR
DID SOMETHING HAPPEN DURING THE CULL?
WE WERE FORCED TO END IT EARLY, MY PRINCE.
THE ELD WITCHES WERE OUT WAITING
MILDRED LURED THEM TO US
WE TRIED TO SCARE THEM OFF AS YOU ASKED BUT THE MIND WITCH APPEARED AND DID HER FEAR THING AGAIN

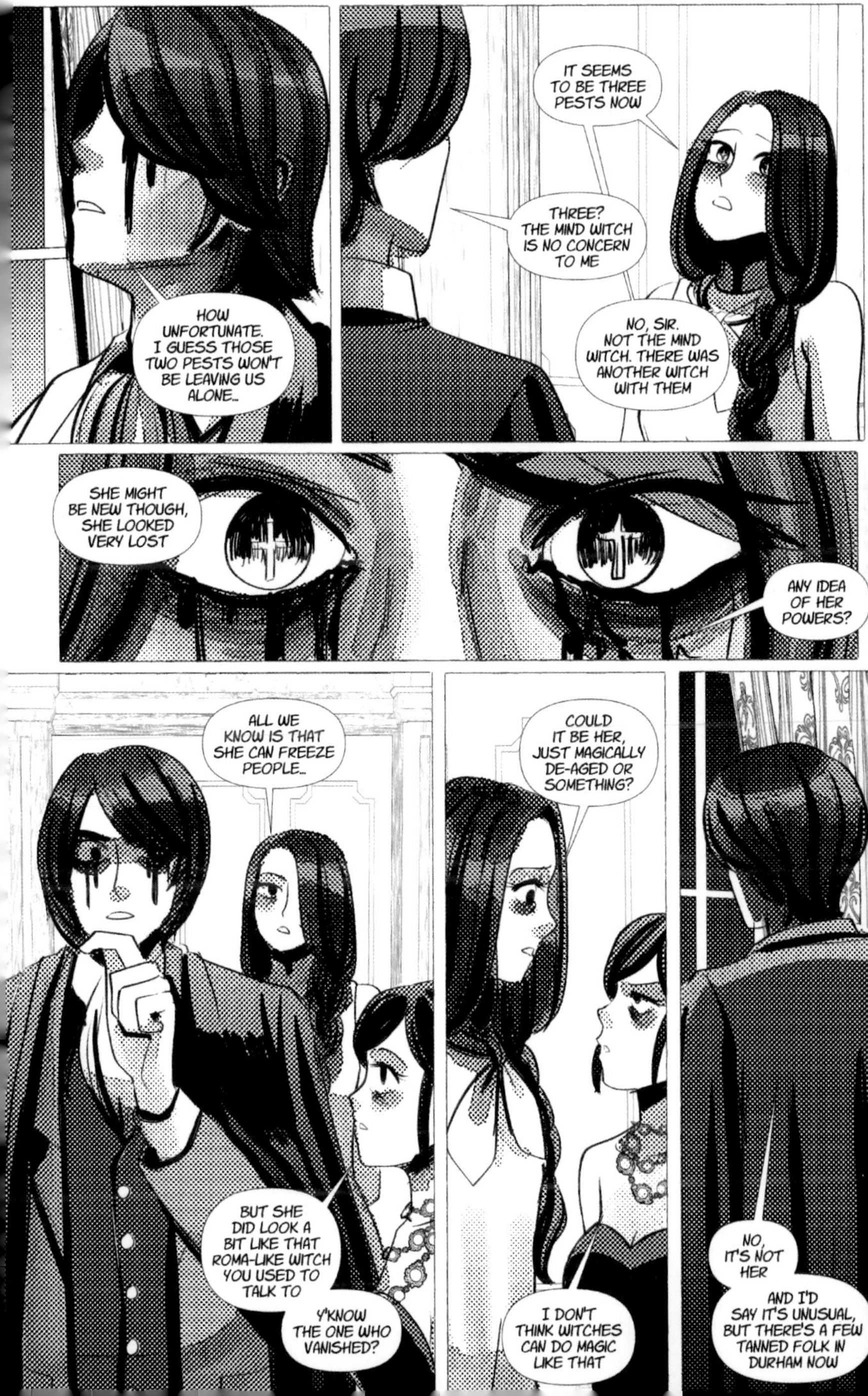
HOW UNFORTUNATE. I GUESS THOSE TWO PESTS WON'T BE LEAVING US ALONE..
IT SEEMS TO BE THREE PESTS NOW
THREE? THE MIND WITCH IS NO CONCERN TO ME
NO, SIR. NOT THE MIND WITCH. THERE WAS ANOTHER WITCH WITH THEM
SHE MIGHT BE NEW THOUGH, SHE LOOKED VERY LOST
ANY IDEA OF HER POWERS?
ALL WE KNOW IS THAT SHE CAN FREEZE PEOPLE..
BUT SHE DID LOOK A BIT LIKE THAT ROMA-LIKE WITCH YOU USED TO TALK TO
Y'KNOW THE ONE WHO VANISHED?
COULD IT BE HER, JUST MAGICALLY DE-AGED OR SOMETHING?
I DON'T THINK WITCHES CAN DO MAGIC LIKE THAT
NO, IT'S NOT HER
AND I'D SAY IT'S UNUSUAL, BUT THERE'S A FEW TANNED FOLK IN DURHAM NOW

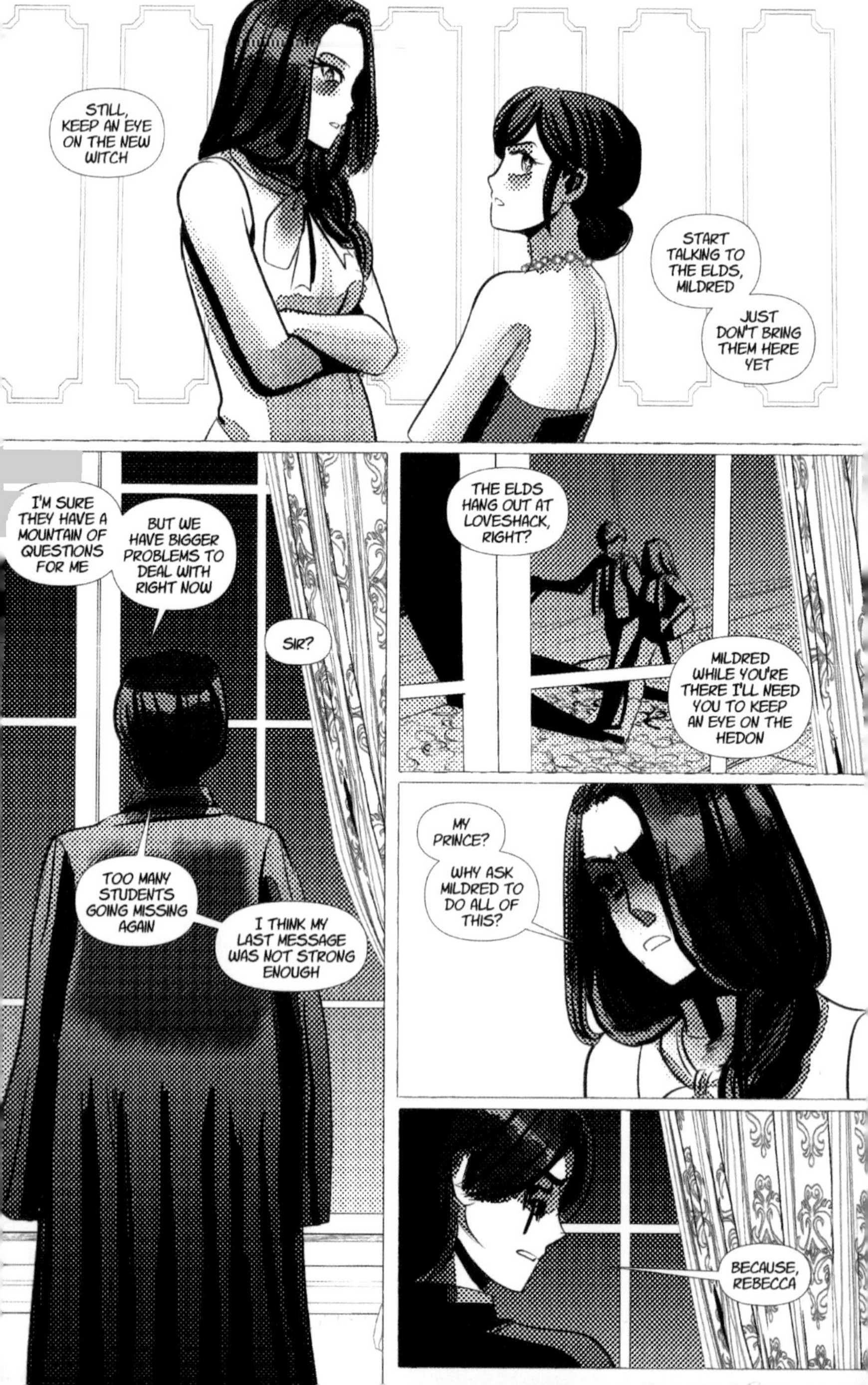
STILL, KEEP AN EYE ON THE NEW WITCH
START TALKING TO THE ELDS, MILDRED
JUST DON'T BRING THEM HERE YET
I'M SURE THEY HAVE A MOUNTAIN OF QUESTIONS FOR ME
BUT WE HAVE BIGGER PROBLEMS TO DEAL WITH RIGHT NOW
SIR?
TOO MANY STUDENTS GOING MISSING AGAIN
I THINK MY LAST MESSAGE WAS NOT STRONG ENOUGH
THE ELDS HANG OUT AT LOVESHACK, RIGHT?
MILDRED WHILE YOU'RE THERE I'LL NEED YOU TO KEEP AN EYE ON THE HEDON
MY PRINCE?
WHY ASK MILDRED TO DO ALL OF THIS?
BECAUSE, REBECCA

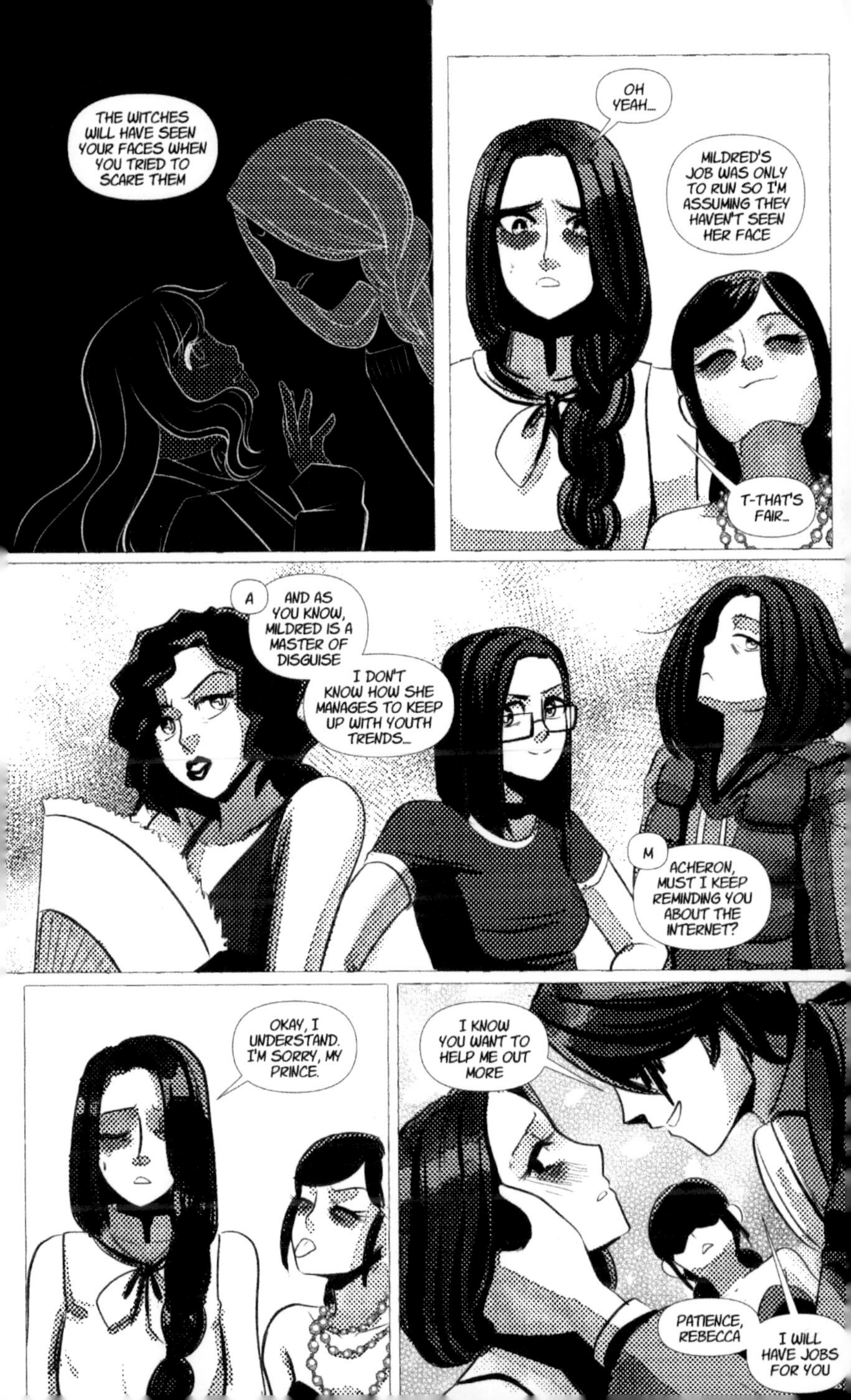
THE WITCHES WILL HAVE SEEN YOUR FACES WHEN YOU TRIED TO SCARE THEM
OH YEAH...
MILDRED'S JOB WAS ONLY TO RUN SO I'M ASSUMING THEY HAVEN'T SEEN HER FACE
T-THAT'S FAIR...
A
AND AS YOU KNOW, MILDRED IS A MASTER OF DISGUISE
I DON'T KNOW HOW SHE MANAGES TO KEEP UP WITH YOUTH TRENDS...
M
ACHERON, MUST I KEEP REMINDING YOU ABOUT THE INTERNET?
OKAY, I UNDERSTAND. I'M SORRY, MY PRINCE.
I KNOW YOU WANT TO HELP ME OUT MORE
PATIENCE, REBECCA
I WILL HAVE JOBS FOR YOU

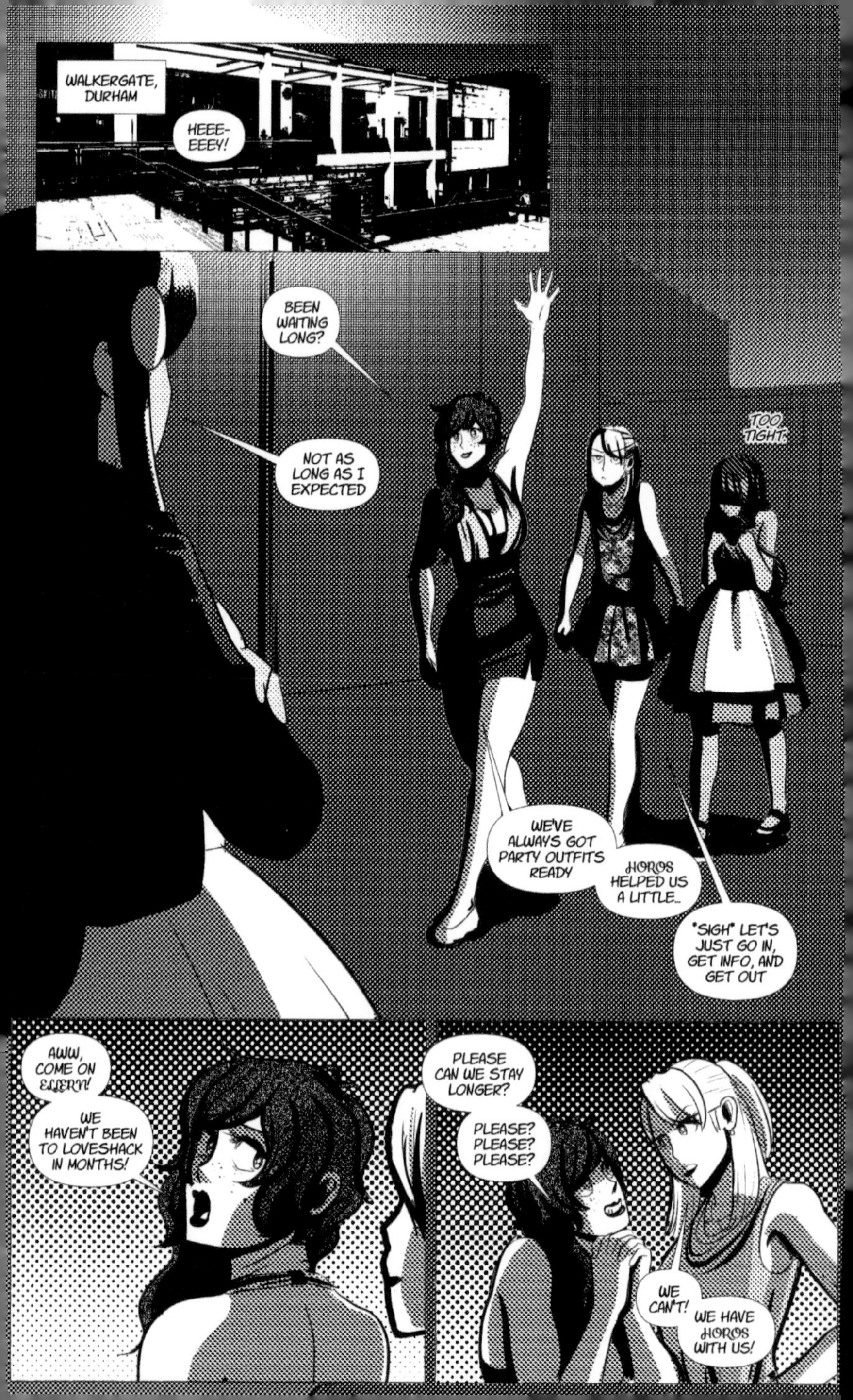

WALKERGATE, DURHAM
HEEE-EEEY!
BEEN WAITING LONG?
NOT AS LONG AS I EXPECTED
TOO TIGHT.
WE'VE ALWAYS GOT PARTY OUTFITS READY
HOROS HELPED US A LITTLE..
SIGH LET'S JUST GO IN, GET INFO, AND GET OUT
AWW, COME ON ELLERN!
WE HAVEN'T BEEN TO LOVESHACK IN MONTHS!
PLEASE CAN WE STAY LONGER?
PLEASE? PLEASE? PLEASE?
WE CAN'T!
WE HAVE HOROS WITH US!

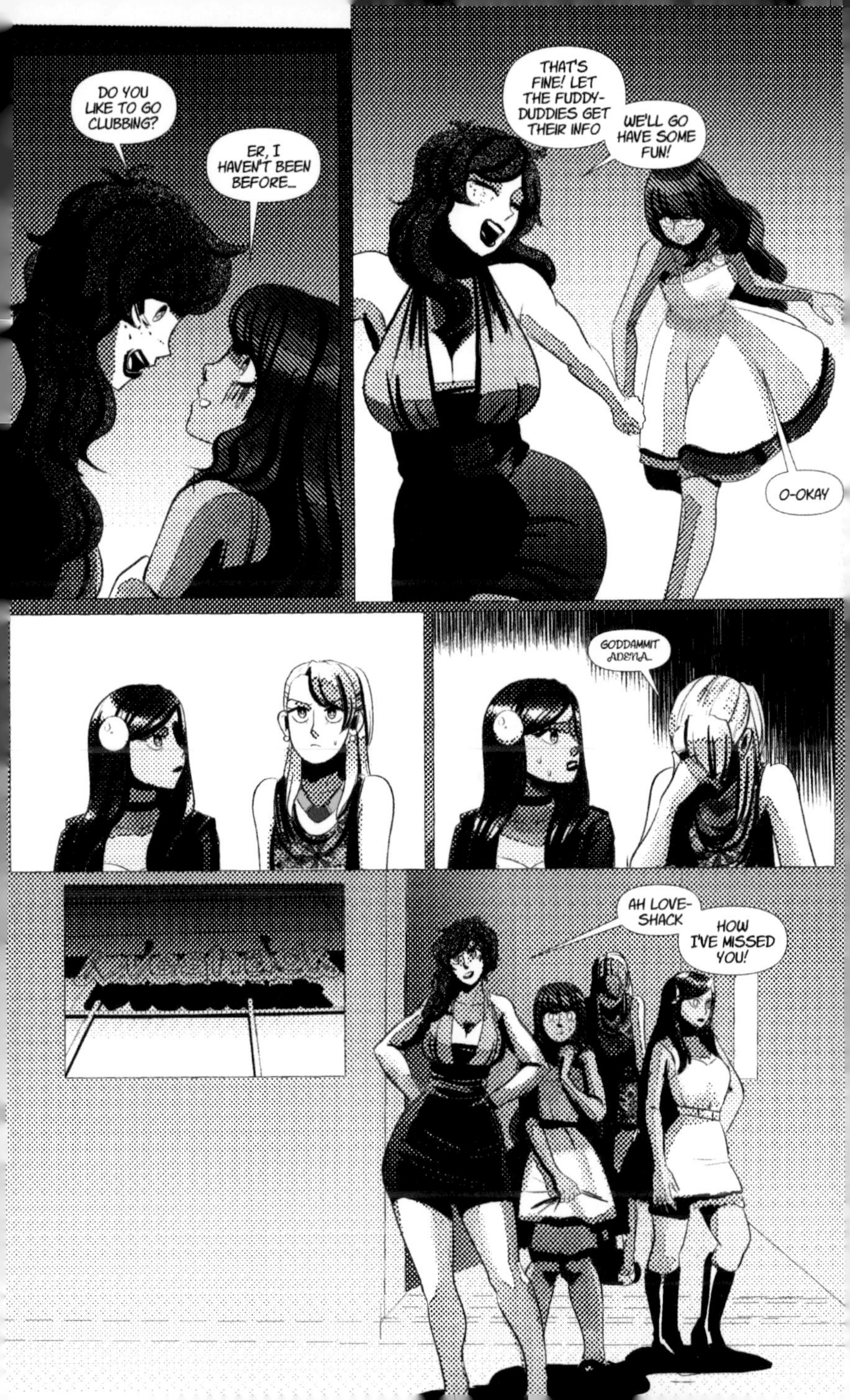

DO YOU LIKE TO GO CLUBBING?
ER, I HAVEN'T BEEN BEFORE...
THAT'S FINE! LET THE FUDDY-DUDDIES GET THEIR INFO
WE'LL GO HAVE SOME FUN!
O-OKAY
GODDAMMIT ADENA...
AH LOVE-SHACK
HOW I'VE MISSED YOU!

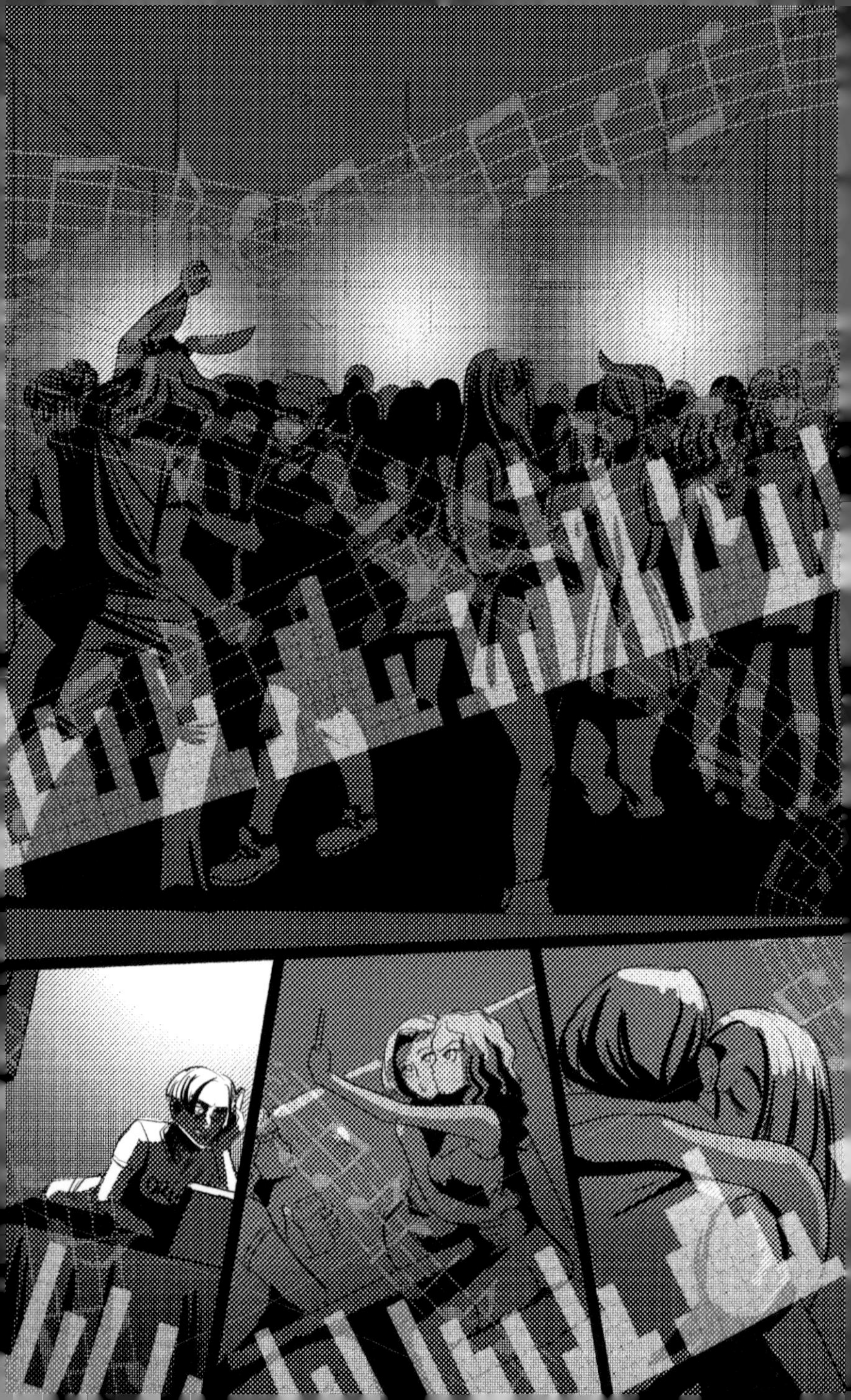

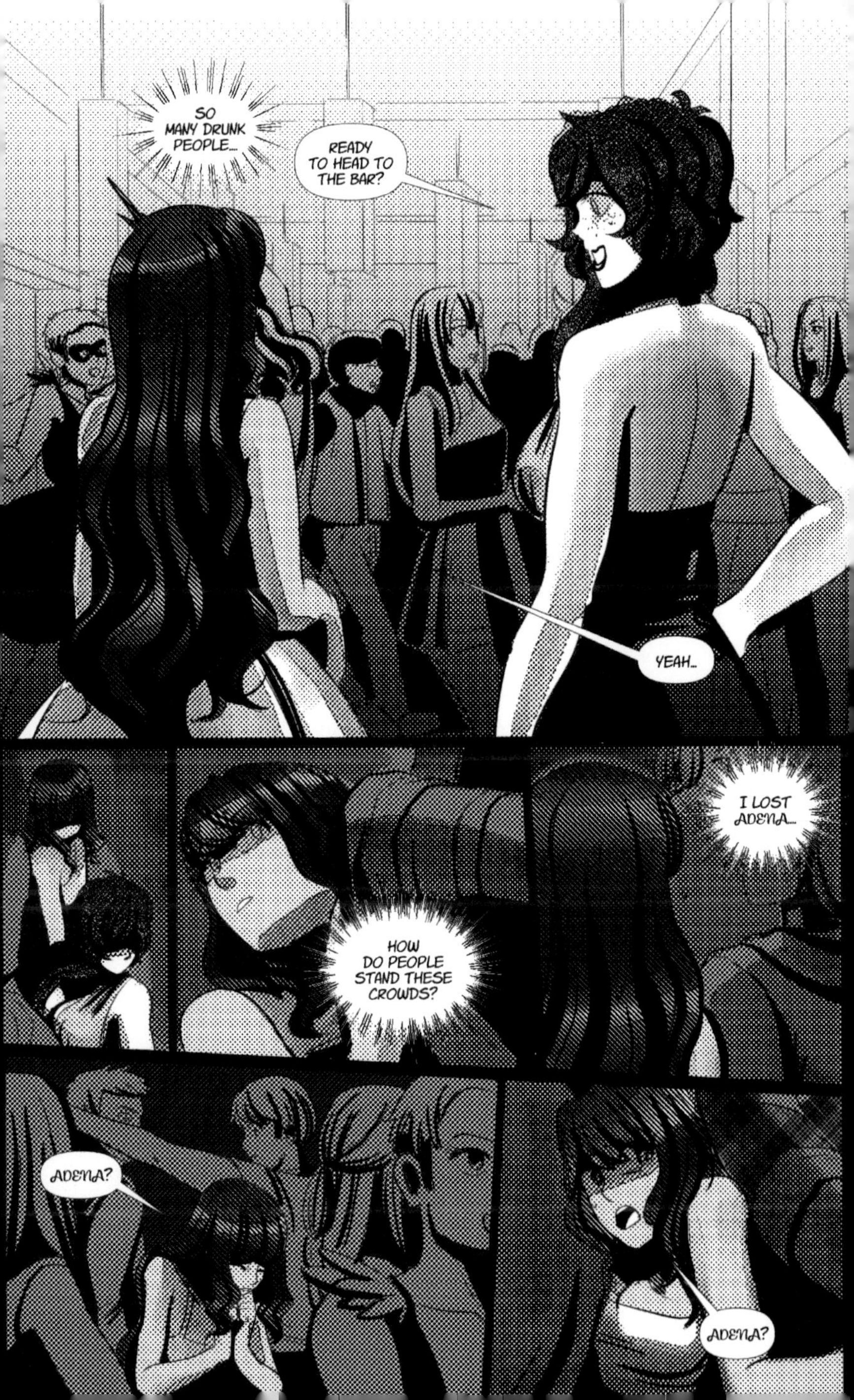
SO MANY DRUNK PEOPLE...
READY TO HEAD TO THE BAR?
YEAH...
HOW DO PEOPLE STAND THESE CROWDS?
I LOST ADENA...
ADENA?
ADENA?

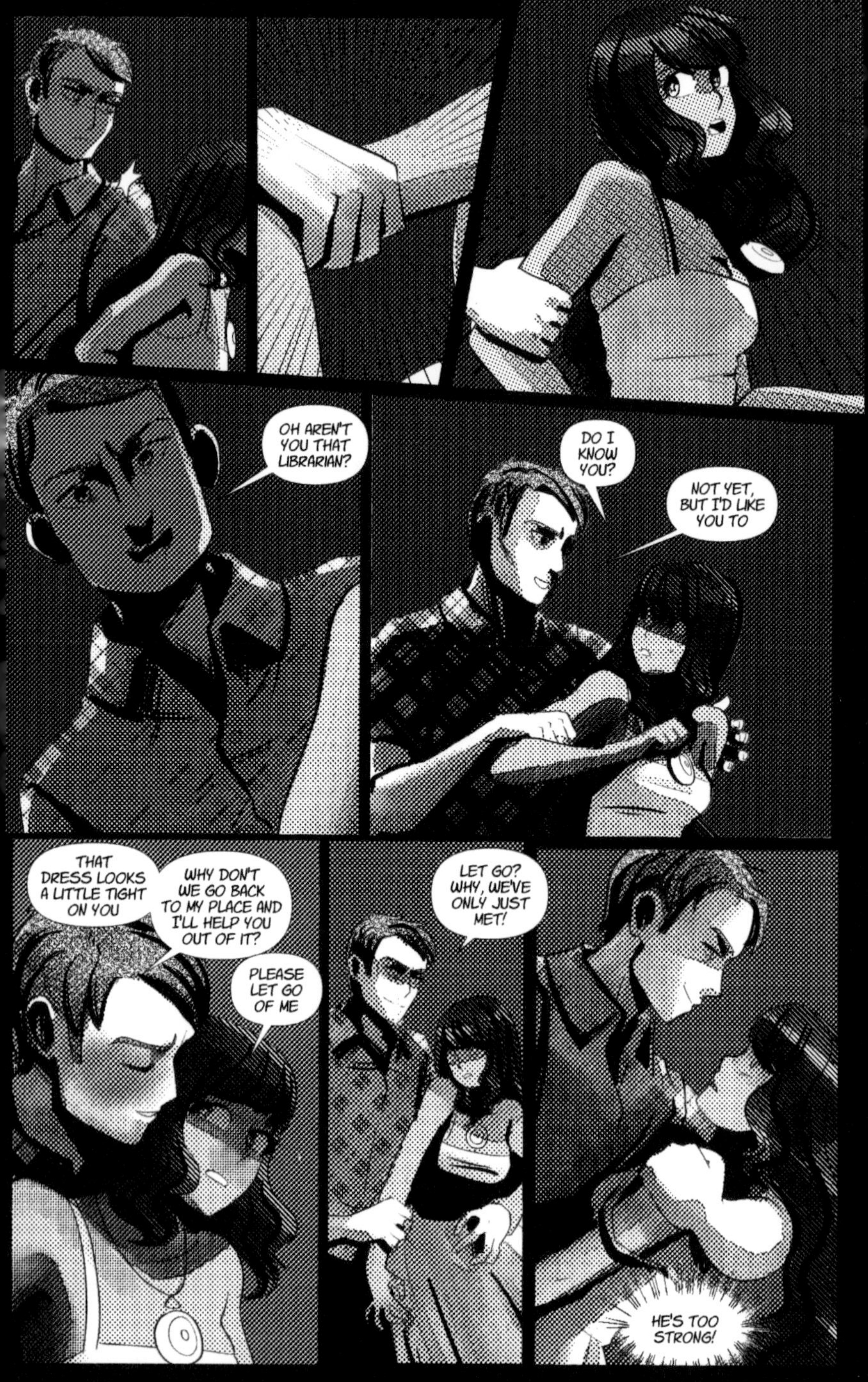
OH AREN'T YOU THAT LIBRARIAN?
DO I KNOW YOU?
NOT YET, BUT I'D LIKE YOU TO
THAT DRESS LOOKS A LITTLE TIGHT ON YOU
WHY DON'T WE GO BACK TO MY PLACE AND I'LL HELP YOU OUT OF IT?
PLEASE LET GO OF ME
LET GO? WHY, WE'VE ONLY JUST MET!
HE'S TOO STRONG!

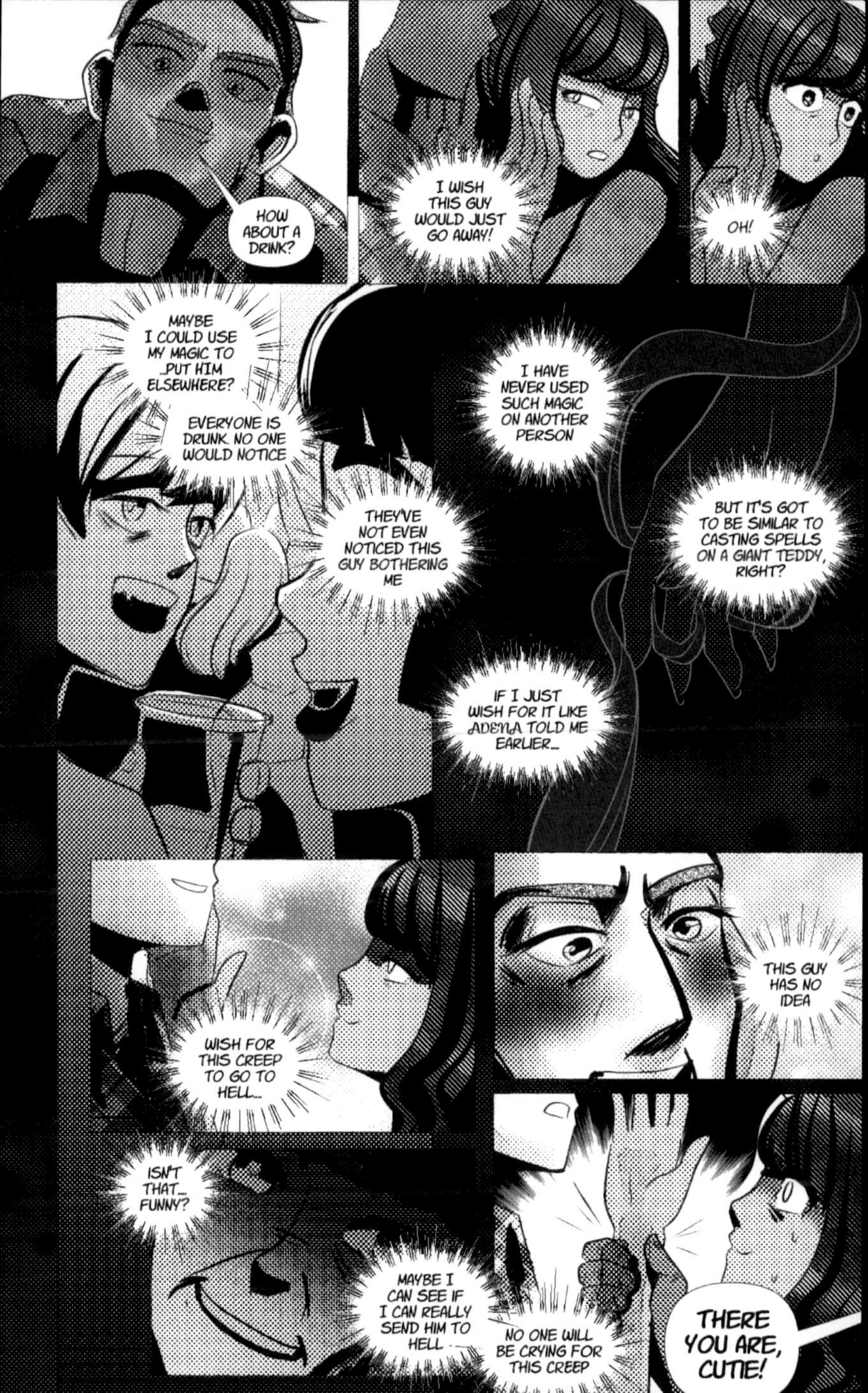
HOW ABOUT A DRINK?
I WISH THIS GUY WOULD JUST GO AWAY!
OH!
MAYBE I COULD USE MY MAGIC TO ..PUT HIM ELSEWHERE?
EVERYONE IS DRUNK. NO ONE WOULD NOTICE
THEY'VE NOT EVEN NOTICED THIS GUY BOTHERING ME
I HAVE NEVER USED SUCH MAGIC ON ANOTHER PERSON
BUT IT'S GOT TO BE SIMILAR TO CASTING SPELLS ON A GIANT TEDDY, RIGHT?
IF I JUST WISH FOR IT LIKE ADENA TOLD ME EARLIER...
WISH FOR THIS CREEP TO GO TO HELL...
THIS GUY HAS NO IDEA
ISN'T THAT... FUNNY?
MAYBE I CAN SEE IF I CAN REALLY SEND HIM TO HELL
NO ONE WILL BE CRYING FOR THIS CREEP
THERE YOU ARE, CUTIE!

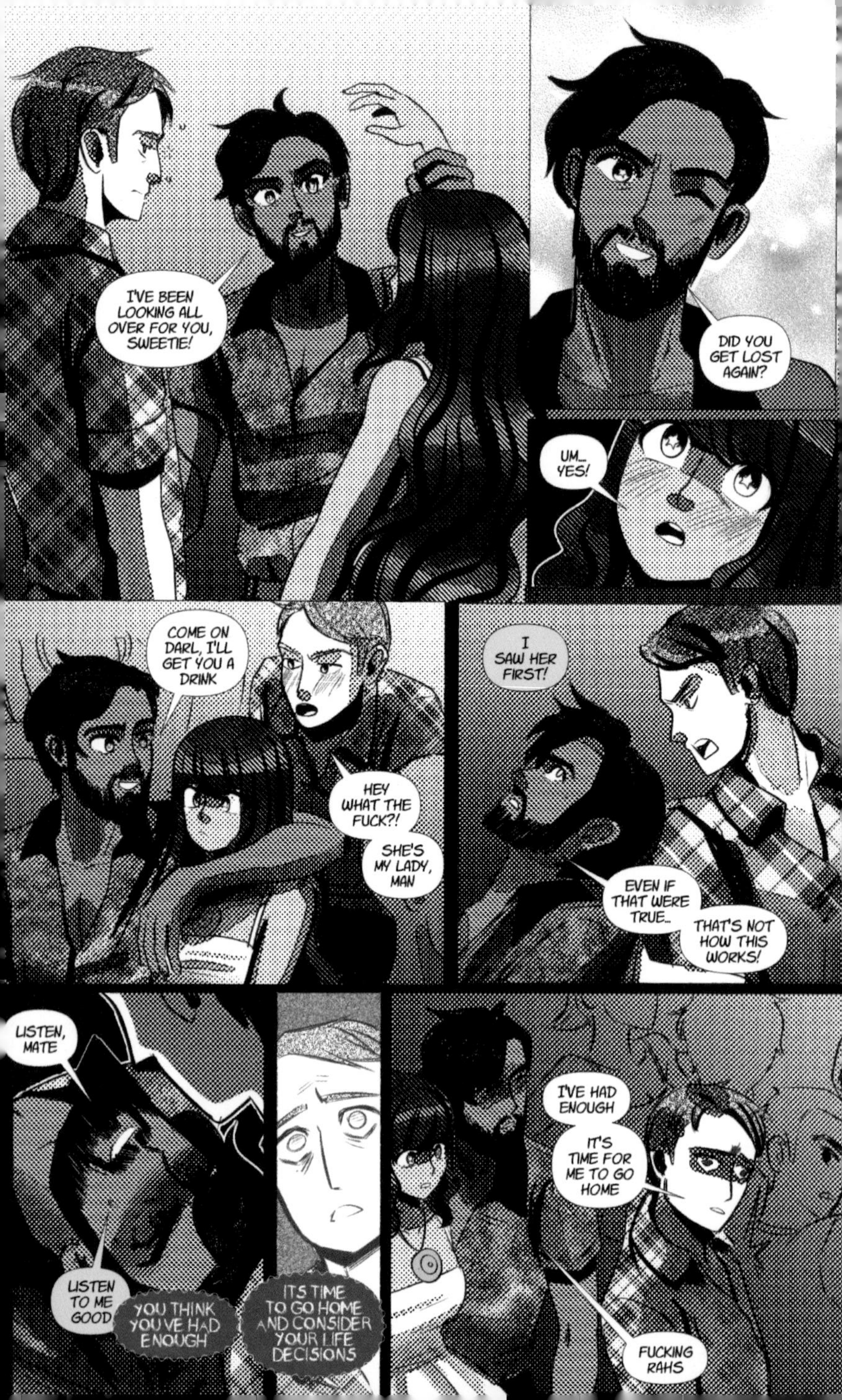
I'VE BEEN LOOKING ALL OVER FOR YOU, SWEETIE!
DID YOU GET LOST AGAIN?
UM... YES!
COME ON DARL, I'LL GET YOU A DRINK
HEY WHAT THE FUCK?!
SHE'S MY LADY, MAN
I SAW HER FIRST!
EVEN IF THAT WERE TRUE..
THAT'S NOT HOW THIS WORKS!
LISTEN, MATE
LISTEN TO ME GOOD
YOU THINK YOU'VE HAD ENOUGH
ITS TIME TO GO HOME AND CONSIDER YOUR LIFE DECISIONS
I'VE HAD ENOUGH
IT'S TIME FOR ME TO GO HOME
FUCKING RAHS

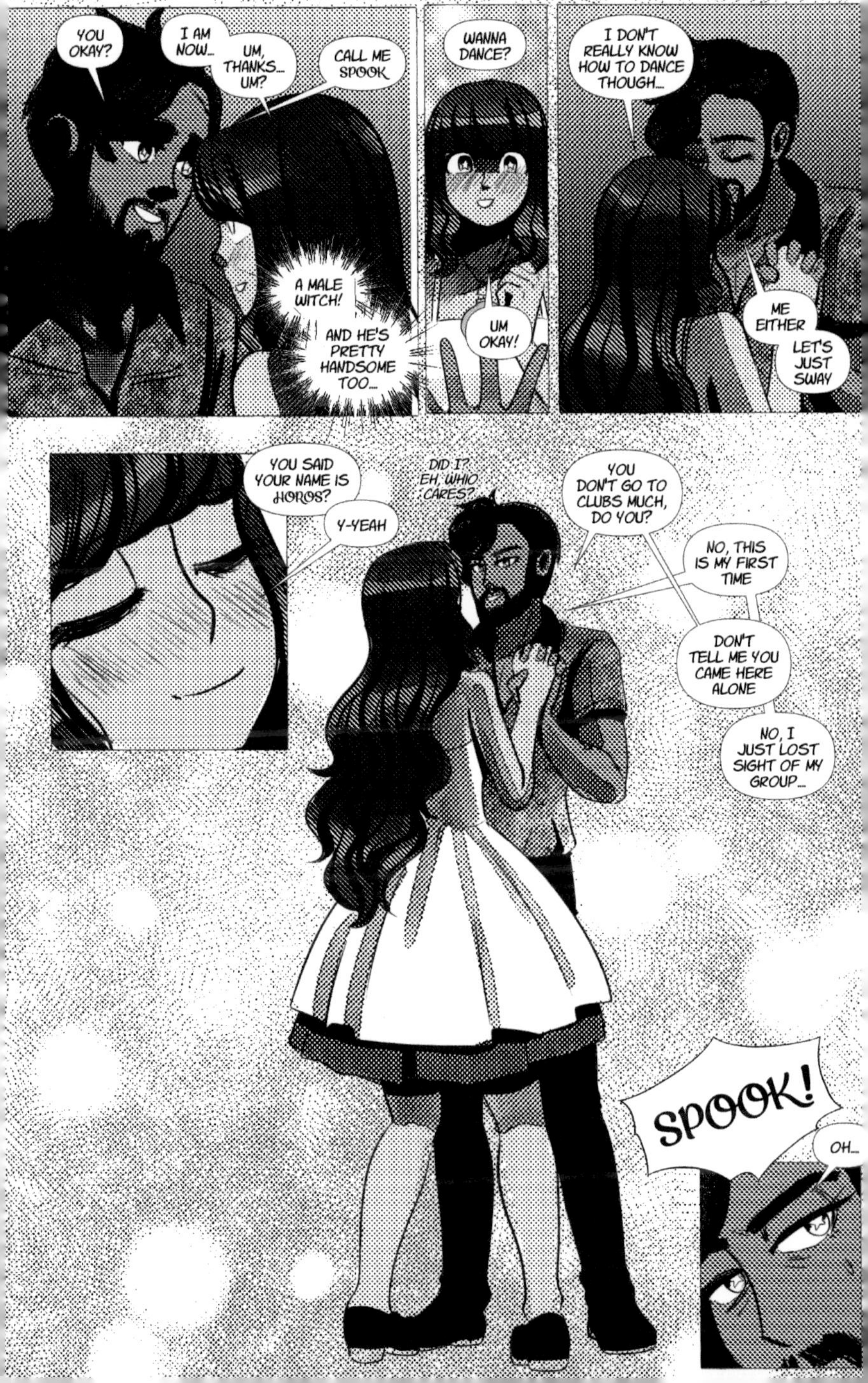
YOU OKAY?
I AM NOW...
UM, THANKS... UM?
CALL ME SPOOK
A MALE WITCH!
AND HE'S PRETTY HANDSOME TOO...
WANNA DANCE?
UM OKAY!
I DON'T REALLY KNOW HOW TO DANCE THOUGH...
ME EITHER
LET'S JUST SWAY
YOU SAID YOUR NAME IS HOROS?
Y-YEAH
DID I? EH, WHO CARES?
YOU DON'T GO TO CLUBS MUCH, DO YOU?
NO, THIS IS MY FIRST TIME
DON'T TELL ME YOU CAME HERE ALONE
NO, I JUST LOST SIGHT OF MY GROUP...
SPOOK!
OH...

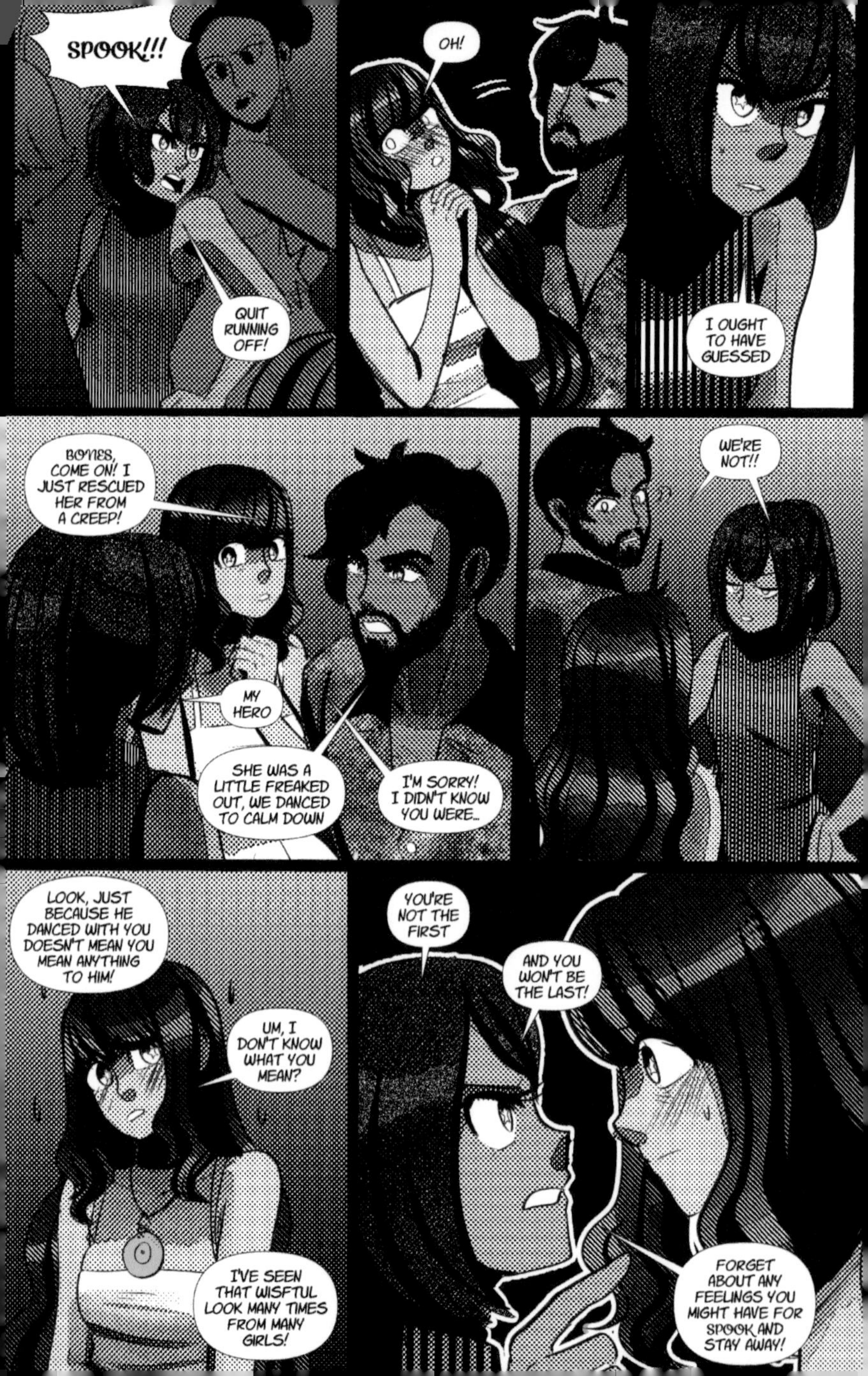
SPOOK!!!
QUIT RUNNING OFF!
OH!
I OUGHT TO HAVE GUESSED
BONES, COME ON! I JUST RESCUED HER FROM A CREEP!
MY HERO
SHE WAS A LITTLE FREAKED OUT, WE DANCED TO CALM DOWN
I'M SORRY! I DIDN'T KNOW YOU WERE...
WE'RE NOT!!
LOOK, JUST BECAUSE HE DANCED WITH YOU DOESN'T MEAN YOU MEAN ANYTHING TO HIM!
UM, I DON'T KNOW WHAT YOU MEAN?
I'VE SEEN THAT WISFTUL LOOK MANY TIMES FROM MANY GIRLS!
YOU'RE NOT THE FIRST
AND YOU WON'T BE THE LAST!
FORGET ABOUT ANY FEELINGS YOU MIGHT HAVE FOR SPOOK AND STAY AWAY!

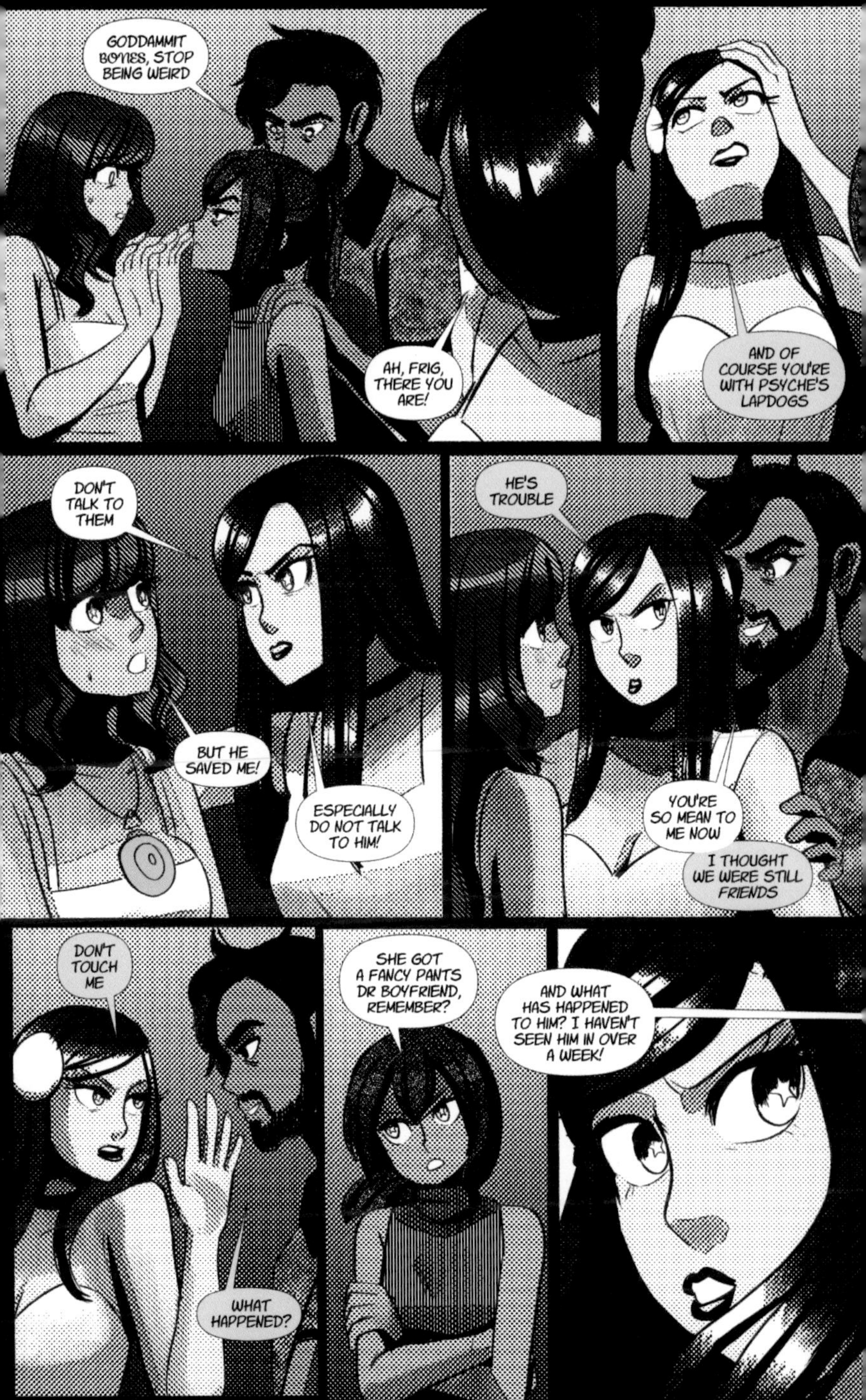
GODDAMMIT BONES, STOP BEING WEIRD
AH, FRIG, THERE YOU ARE!
AND OF COURSE YOU'RE WITH PSYCHE'S LAPDOGS
DON'T TALK TO THEM
BUT HE SAVED ME!
ESPECIALLY DO NOT TALK TO HIM!
HE'S TROUBLE
YOU'RE SO MEAN TO ME NOW
I THOUGHT WE WERE STILL FRIENDS
DON'T TOUCH ME
WHAT HAPPENED?
SHE GOT A FANCY PANTS DR BOYFRIEND, REMEMBER?
AND WHAT HAS HAPPENED TO HIM? I HAVEN'T SEEN HIM IN OVER A WEEK!

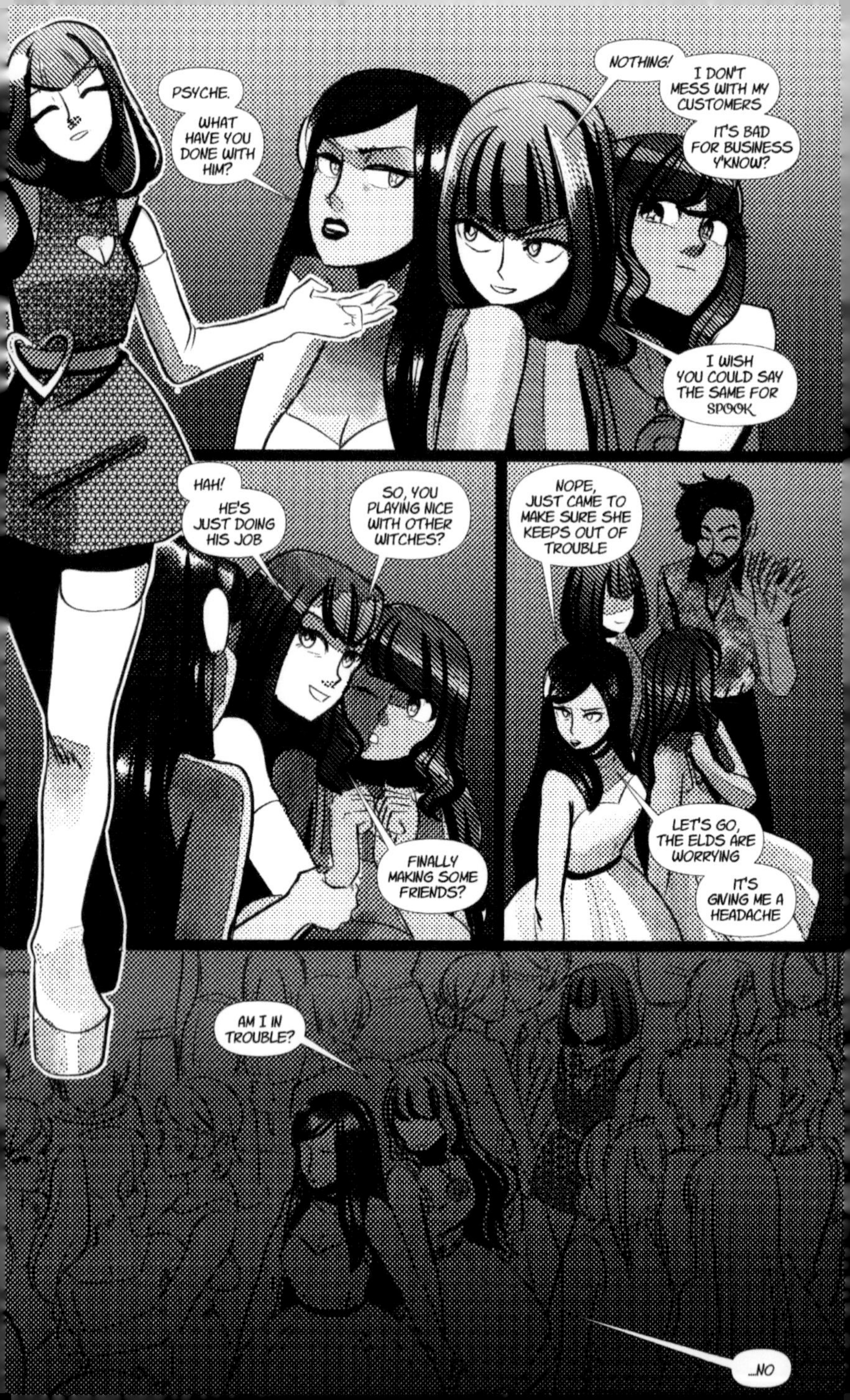
PSYCHE.
WHAT HAVE YOU DONE WITH HIM?
NOTHING!
I DON'T MESS WITH MY CUSTOMERS
IT'S BAD FOR BUSINESS Y'KNOW?
I WISH YOU COULD SAY THE SAME FOR SPOOK
HAH!
HE'S JUST DOING HIS JOB
SO, YOU PLAYING NICE WITH OTHER WITCHES?
FINALLY MAKING SOME FRIENDS?
NOPE, JUST CAME TO MAKE SURE SHE KEEPS OUT OF TROUBLE
LET'S GO, THE ELDS ARE WORRYING
IT'S GIVING ME A HEADACHE
AM I IN TROUBLE?
...NO

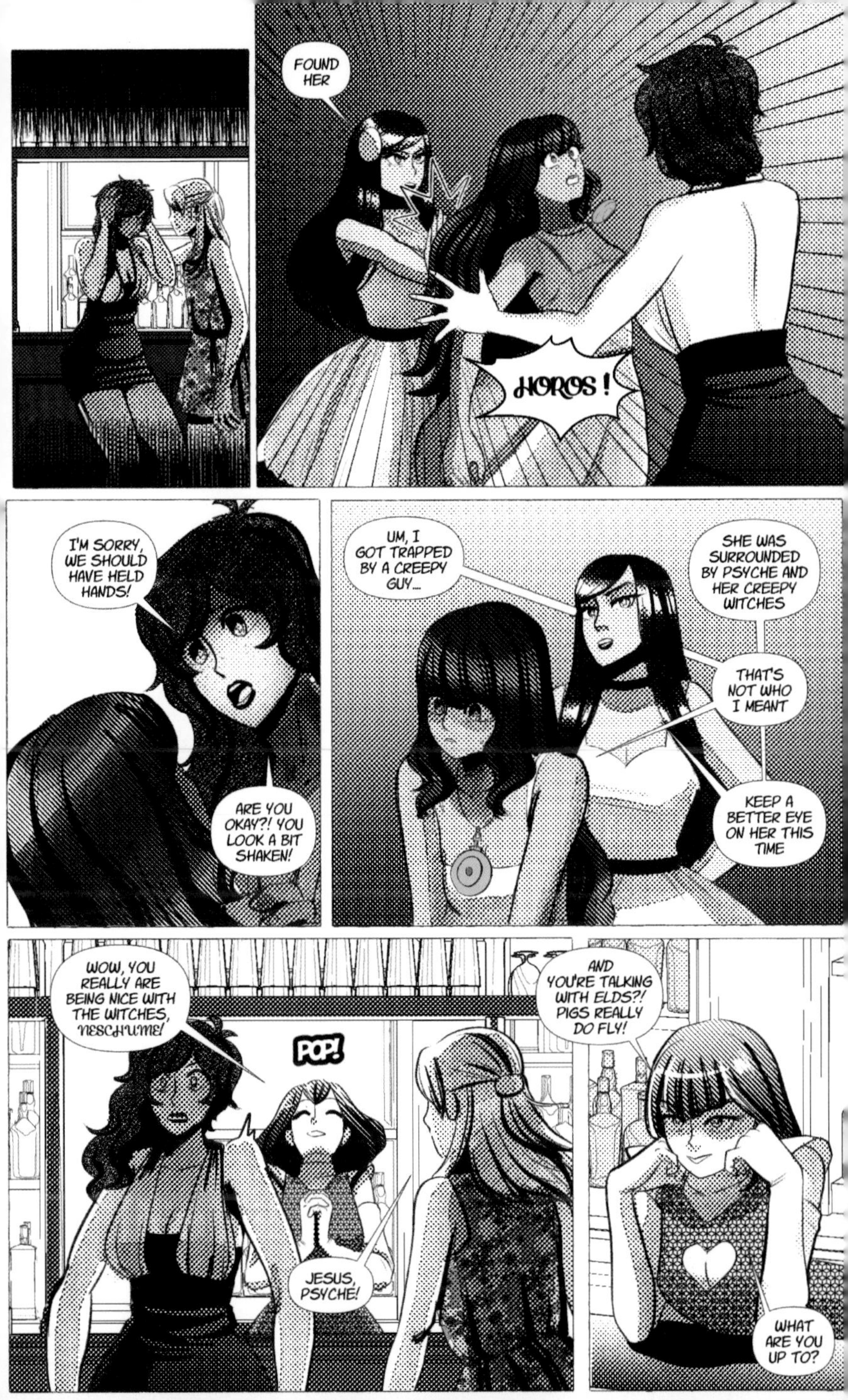
FOUND HER
HOROS!
I'M SORRY, WE SHOULD HAVE HELD HANDS!
ARE YOU OKAY?! YOU LOOK A BIT SHAKEN!
UM, I GOT TRAPPED BY A CREEPY GUY...
SHE WAS SURROUNDED BY PSYCHE AND HER CREEPY WITCHES
THAT'S NOT WHO I MEANT
KEEP A BETTER EYE ON HER THIS TIME
WOW, YOU REALLY ARE BEING NICE WITH THE WITCHES, NESCHUME!
POP!
JESUS, PSYCHE!
AND YOU'RE TALKING WITH ELDS?! PIGS REALLY DO FLY!
WHAT ARE YOU UP TO?

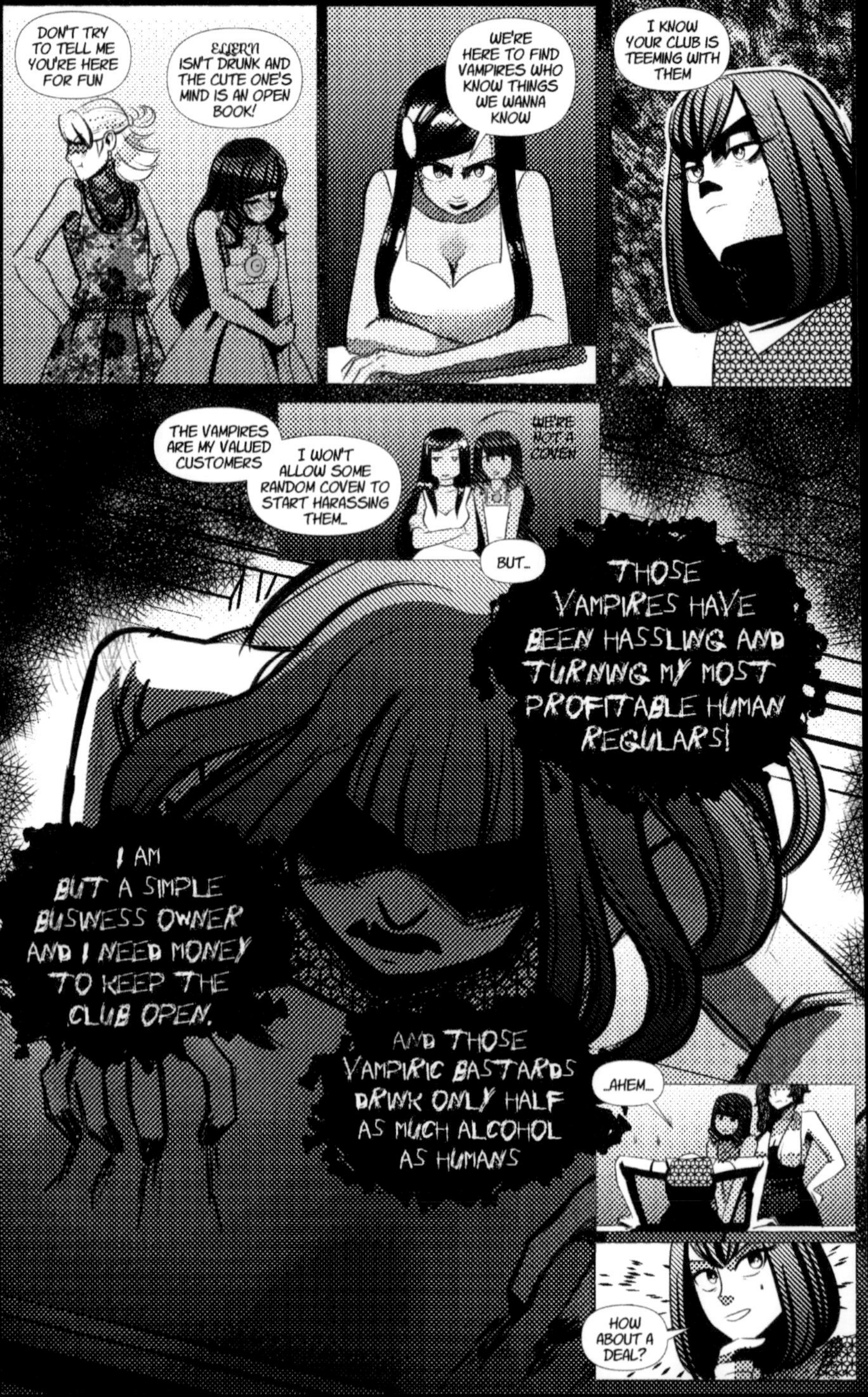
DON'T TRY TO TELL ME YOU'RE HERE FOR FUN
ELLERYN ISN'T DRUNK AND THE CUTE ONE'S MIND IS AN OPEN BOOK!
WE'RE HERE TO FIND VAMPIRES WHO KNOW THINGS WE WANNA KNOW
I KNOW YOUR CLUB IS TEEMING WITH THEM
THE VAMPIRES ARE MY VALUED CUSTOMERS
I WON'T ALLOW SOME RANDOM COVEN TO START HARASSING THEM...
WE'RE NOT A COVEN
BUT...
THOSE VAMPIRES HAVE BEEN HASSLING AND TURNING MY MOST PROFITABLE HUMAN REGULARS!
I AM BUT A SIMPLE BUSINESS OWNER AND I NEED MONEY TO KEEP THE CLUB OPEN.
AND THOSE VAMPIRIC BASTARDS DRINK ONLY HALF AS MUCH ALCOHOL AS HUMANS
...AHEM...
HOW ABOUT A DEAL?

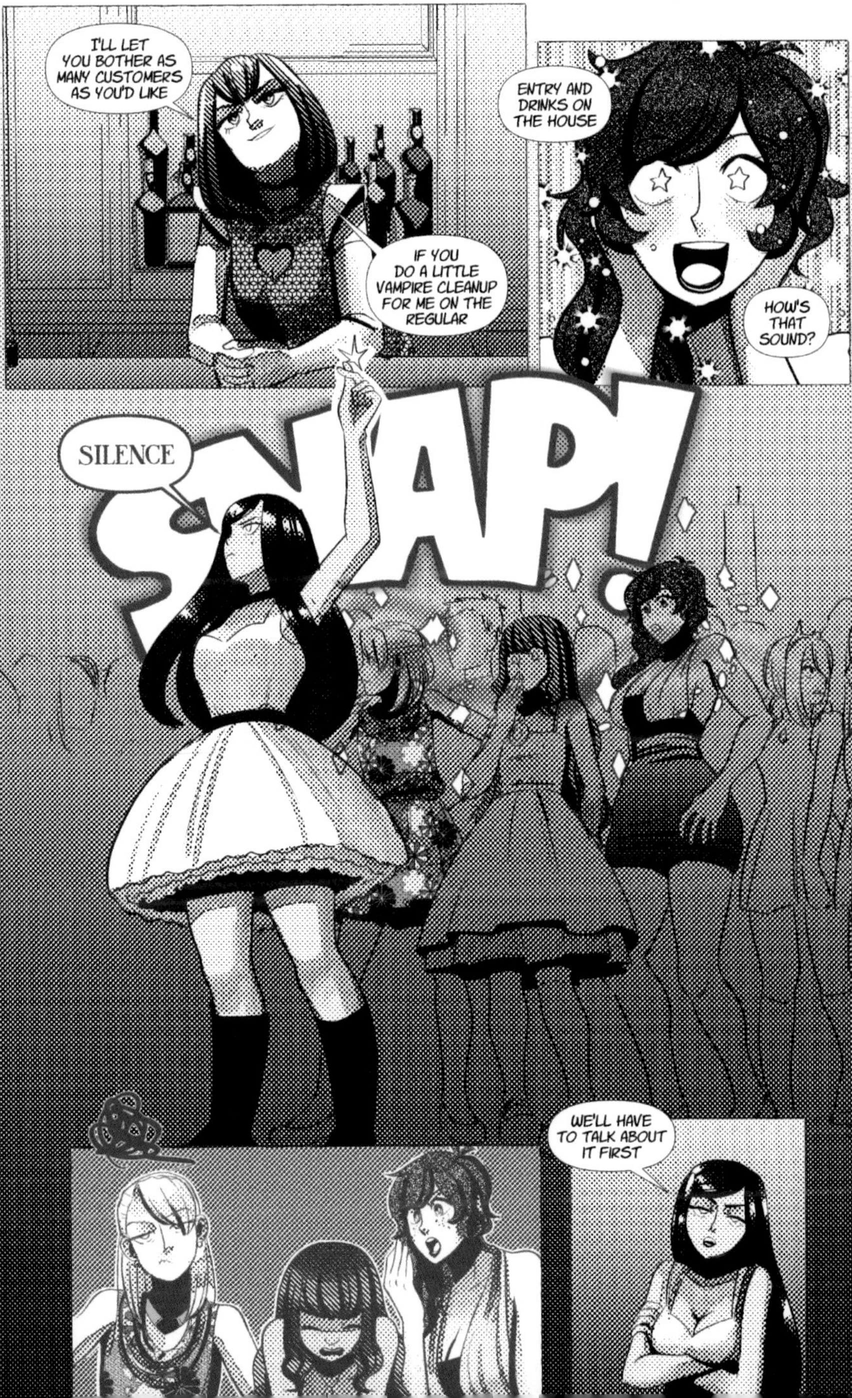
I'LL LET YOU BOTHER AS MANY CUSTOMERS AS YOU'D LIKE
IF YOU DO A LITTLE VAMPIRE CLEANUP FOR ME ON THE REGULAR
ENTRY AND DRINKS ON THE HOUSE
HOW'S THAT SOUND?
SILENCE
SNAP!
WE'LL HAVE TO TALK ABOUT IT FIRST

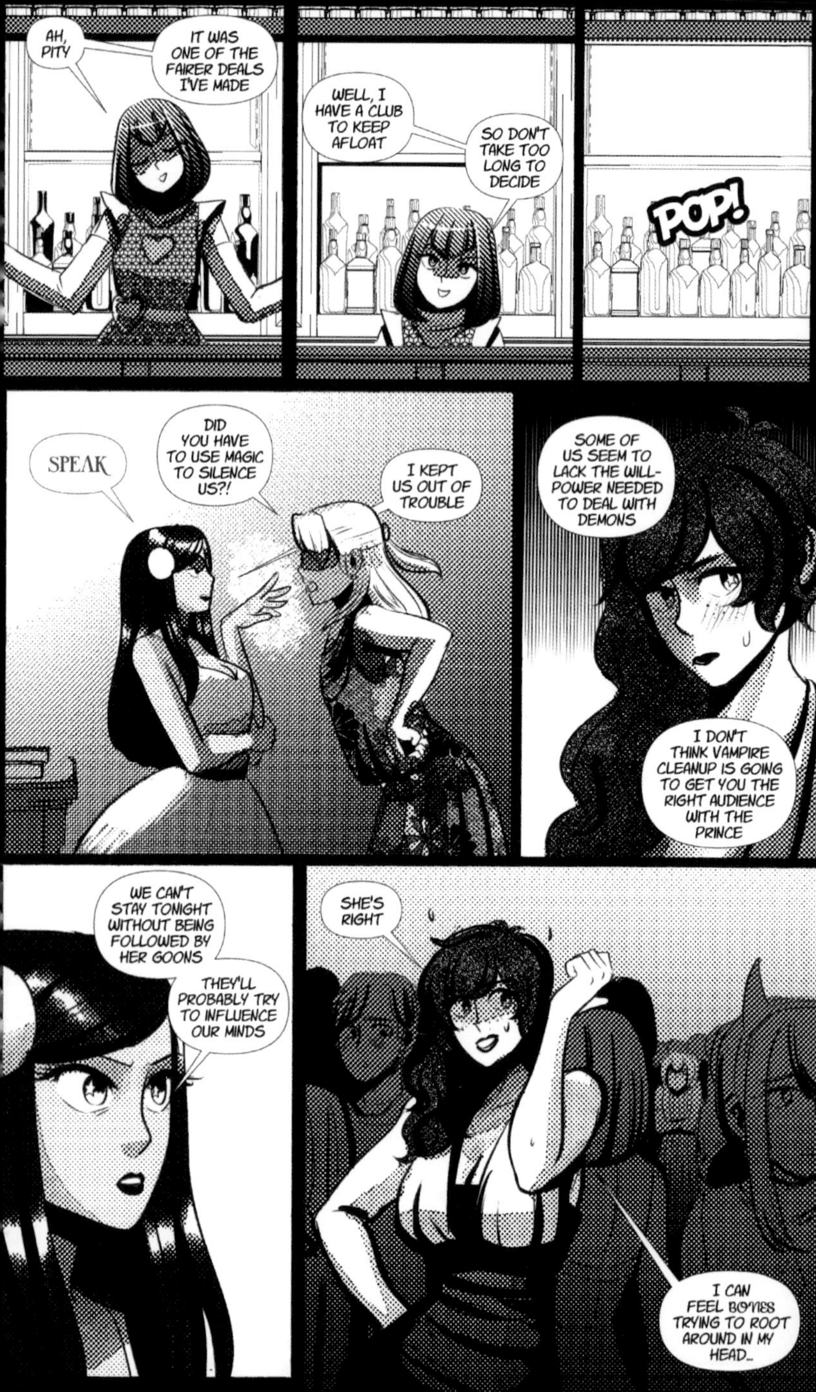
AH, PITY
IT WAS ONE OF THE FAIRER DEALS I'VE MADE
WELL, I HAVE A CLUB TO KEEP AFLOAT
SO DON'T TAKE TOO LONG TO DECIDE
POP!
SPEAK
DID YOU HAVE TO USE MAGIC TO SILENCE US?!
I KEPT US OUT OF TROUBLE
SOME OF US SEEM TO LACK THE WILL-POWER NEEDED TO DEAL WITH DEMONS
I DON'T THINK VAMPIRE CLEANUP IS GOING TO GET YOU THE RIGHT AUDIENCE WITH THE PRINCE
WE CAN'T STAY TONIGHT WITHOUT BEING FOLLOWED BY HER GOONS
THEY'LL PROBABLY TRY TO INFLUENCE OUR MINDS
SHE'S RIGHT
I CAN FEEL BONES TRYING TO ROOT AROUND IN MY HEAD...

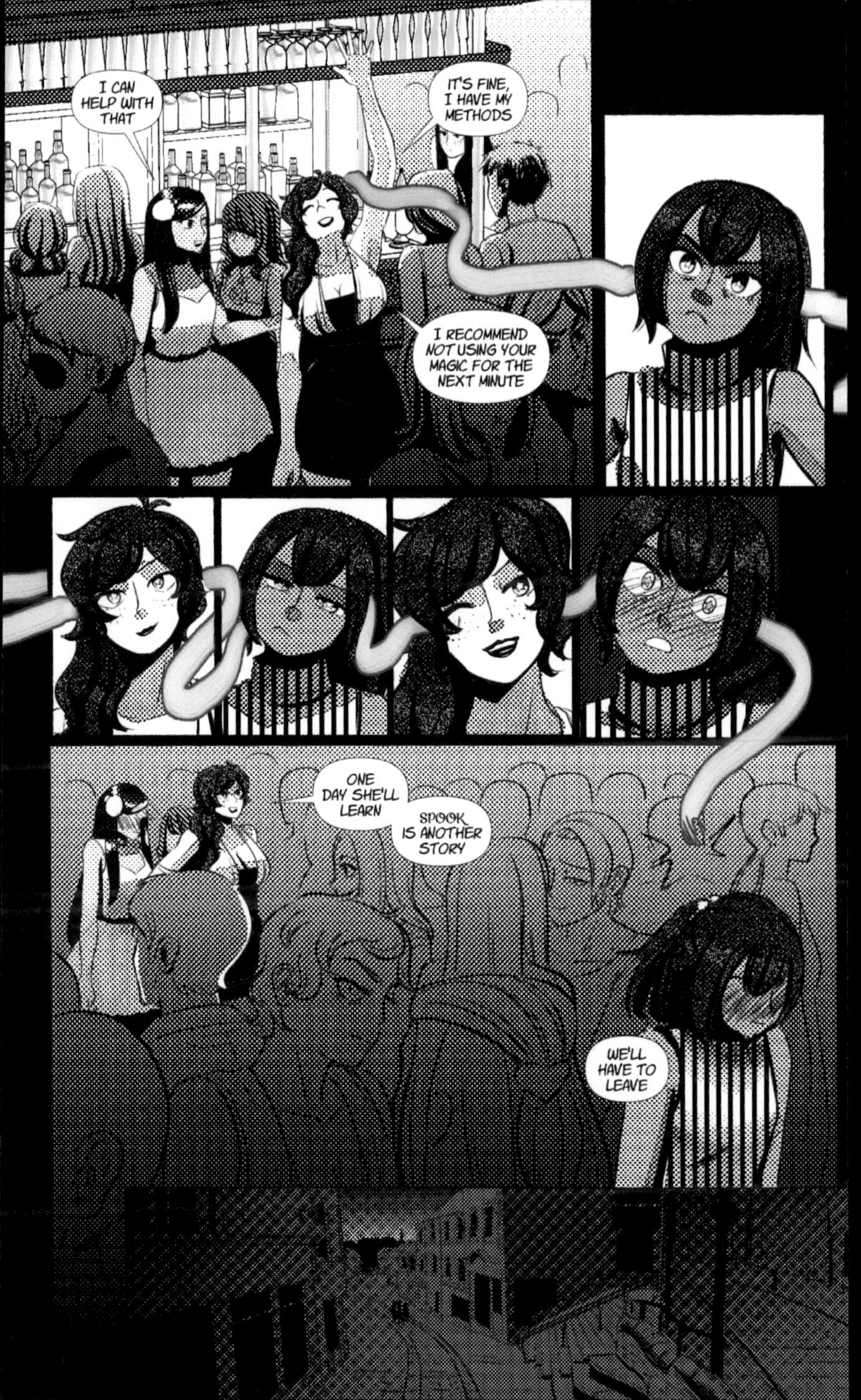
I CAN HELP WITH THAT
IT'S FINE, I HAVE MY METHODS
I RECOMMEND NOT USING YOUR MAGIC FOR THE NEXT MINUTE
ONE DAY SHE'LL LEARN
SPOOK IS ANOTHER STORY
WE'LL HAVE TO LEAVE

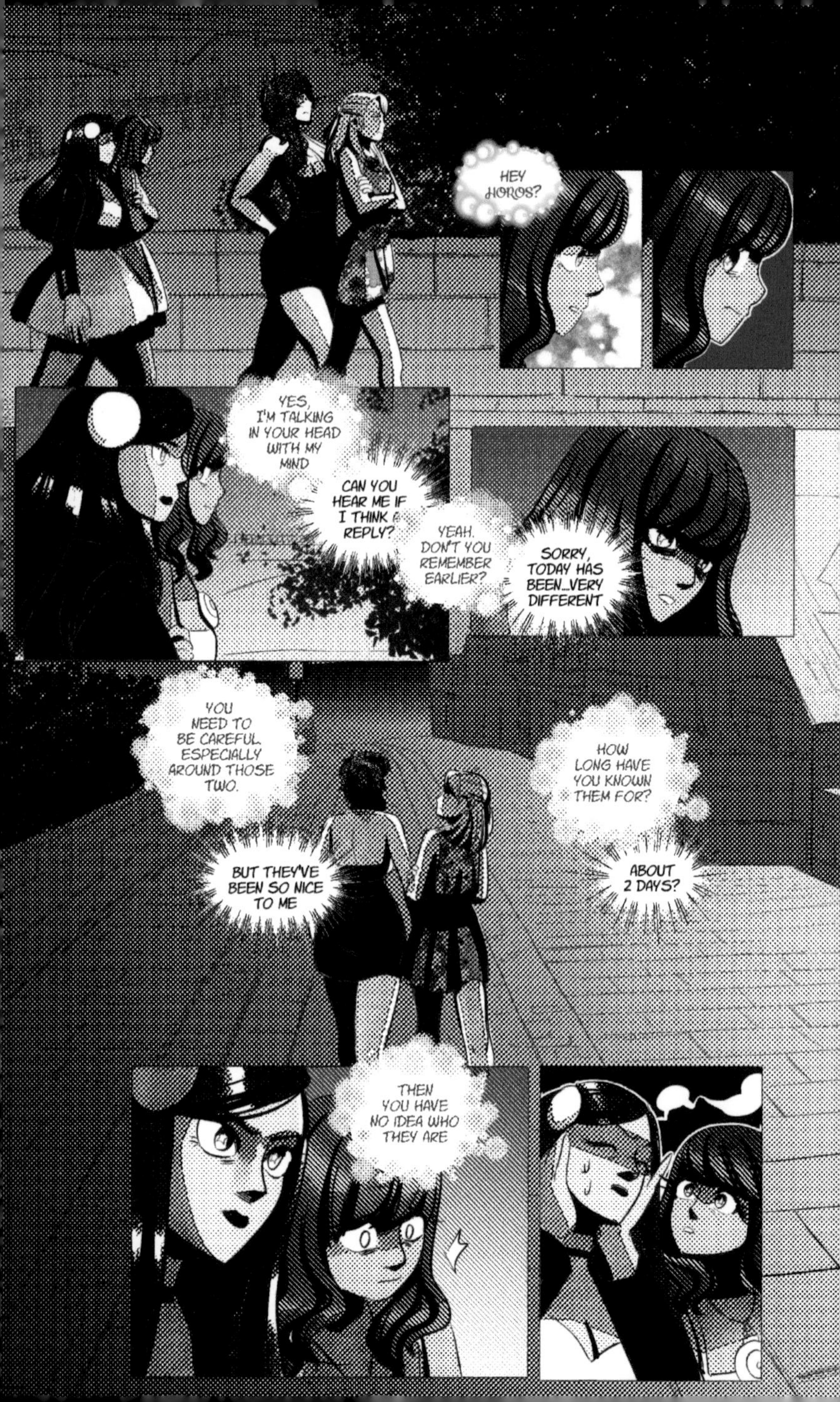
HEY HOROS?
YES, I'M TALKING IN YOUR HEAD WITH MY MIND
CAN YOU HEAR ME IF I THINK A REPLY?
YEAH. DON'T YOU REMEMBER EARLIER?
SORRY, TODAY HAS BEEN...VERY DIFFERENT
YOU NEED TO BE CAREFUL. ESPECIALLY AROUND THOSE TWO.
HOW LONG HAVE YOU KNOWN THEM FOR?
BUT THEY'VE BEEN SO NICE TO ME
ABOUT 2 DAYS?
THEN YOU HAVE NO IDEA WHO THEY ARE

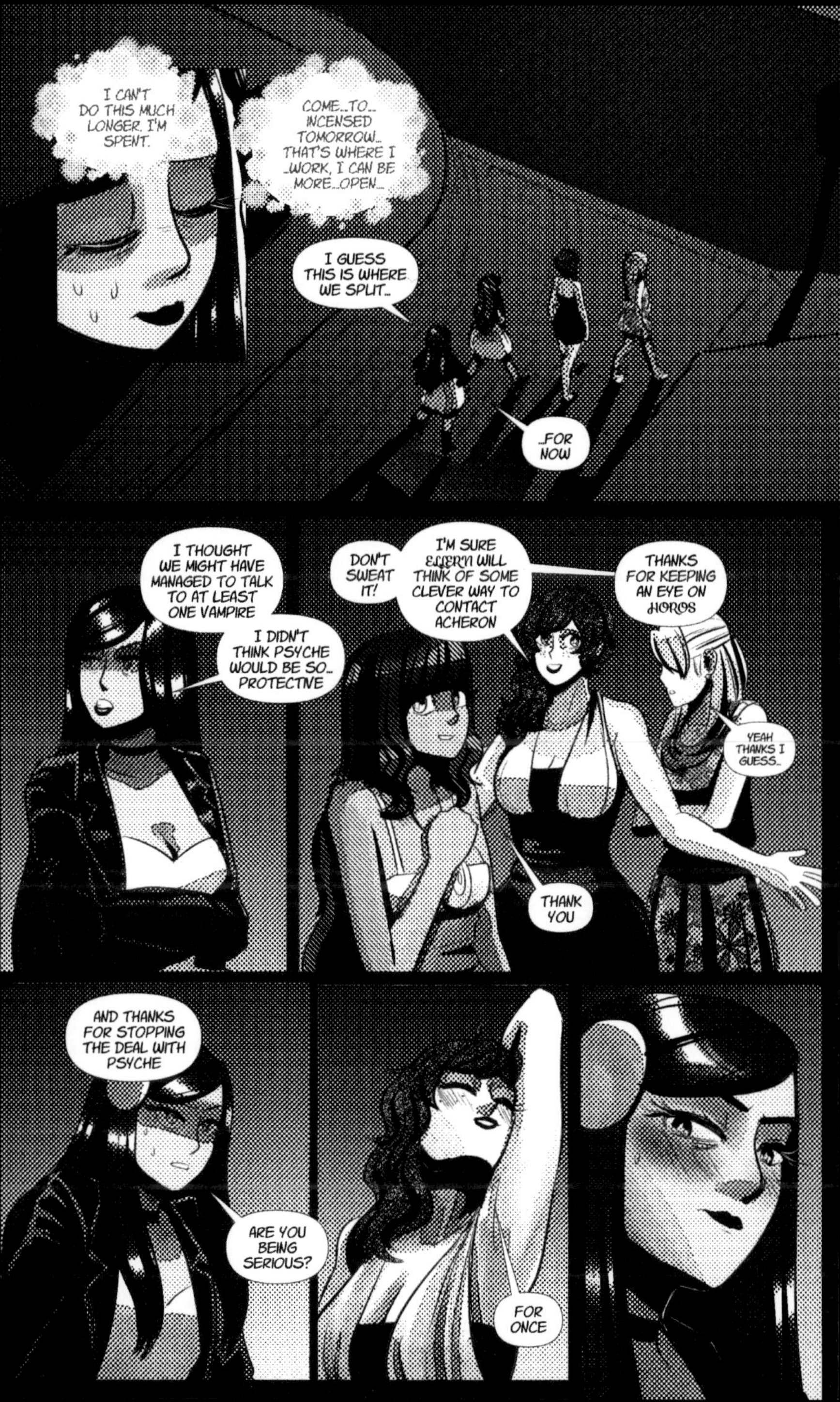
I CAN'T DO THIS MUCH LONGER. I'M SPENT.
COME...TO... INCENSED TOMORROW... THAT'S WHERE I ...WORK, I CAN BE MORE...OPEN...
I GUESS THIS IS WHERE WE SPLIT...
...FOR NOW
I THOUGHT WE MIGHT HAVE MANAGED TO TALK TO AT LEAST ONE VAMPIRE
I DIDN'T THINK PSYCHE WOULD BE SO... PROTECTIVE
DON'T SWEAT IT!
I'M SURE ELLERN WILL THINK OF SOME CLEVER WAY TO CONTACT ACHERON
THANKS FOR KEEPING AN EYE ON HOROS
YEAH THANKS I GUESS...
THANK YOU
AND THANKS FOR STOPPING THE DEAL WITH PSYCHE
ARE YOU BEING SERIOUS?
FOR ONCE

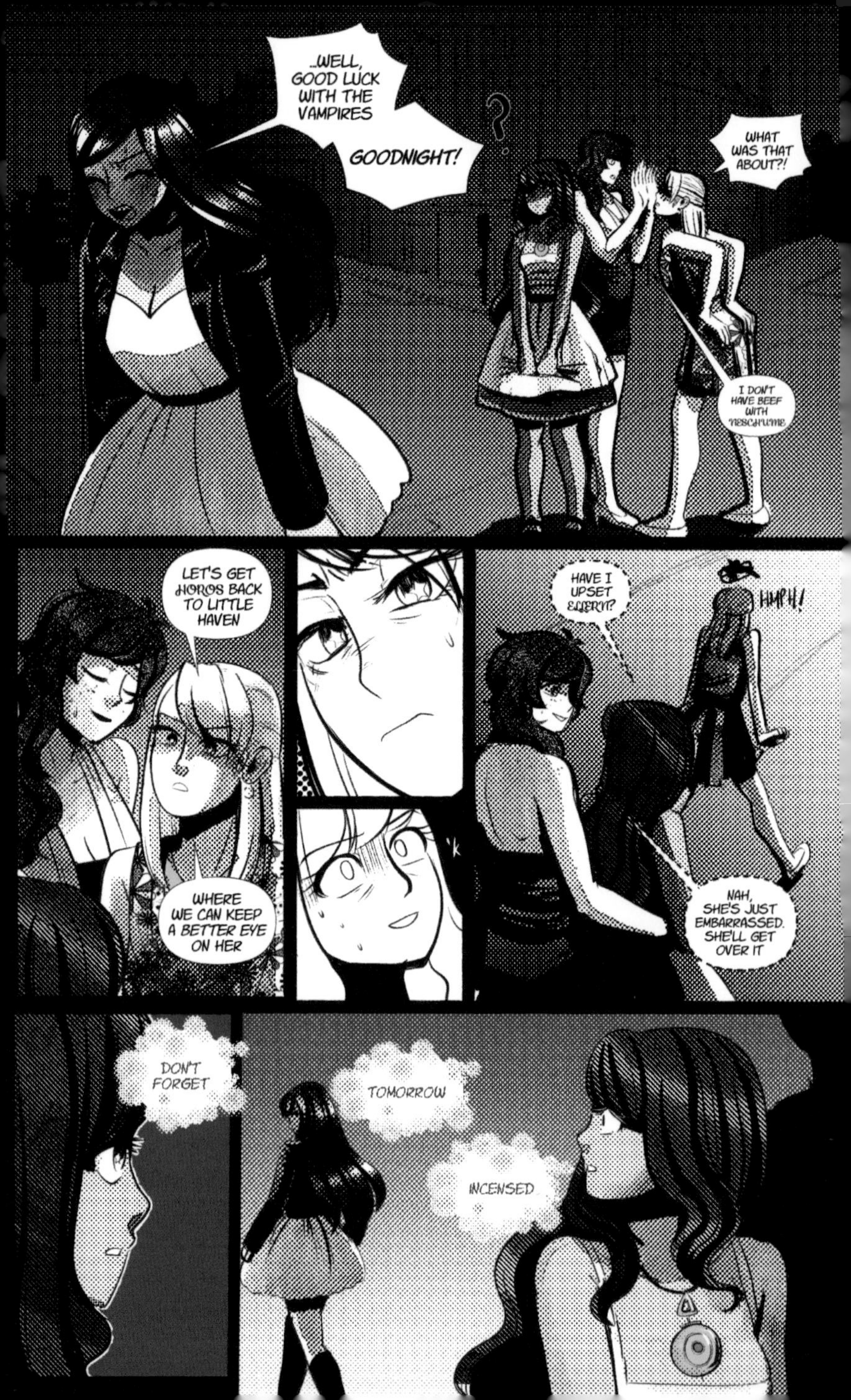

...WELL, GOOD LUCK WITH THE VAMPIRES
GOODNIGHT!
?
WHAT WAS THAT ABOUT?!
I DON'T HAVE BEEF WITH NESCHUME
LET'S GET HOROS BACK TO LITTLE HAVEN
WHERE WE CAN KEEP A BETTER EYE ON HER
HAVE I UPSET ELERYN?
HMPH!
NAH, SHE'S JUST EMBARRASSED. SHE'LL GET OVER IT
DON'T FORGET
TOMORROW
INCENSED

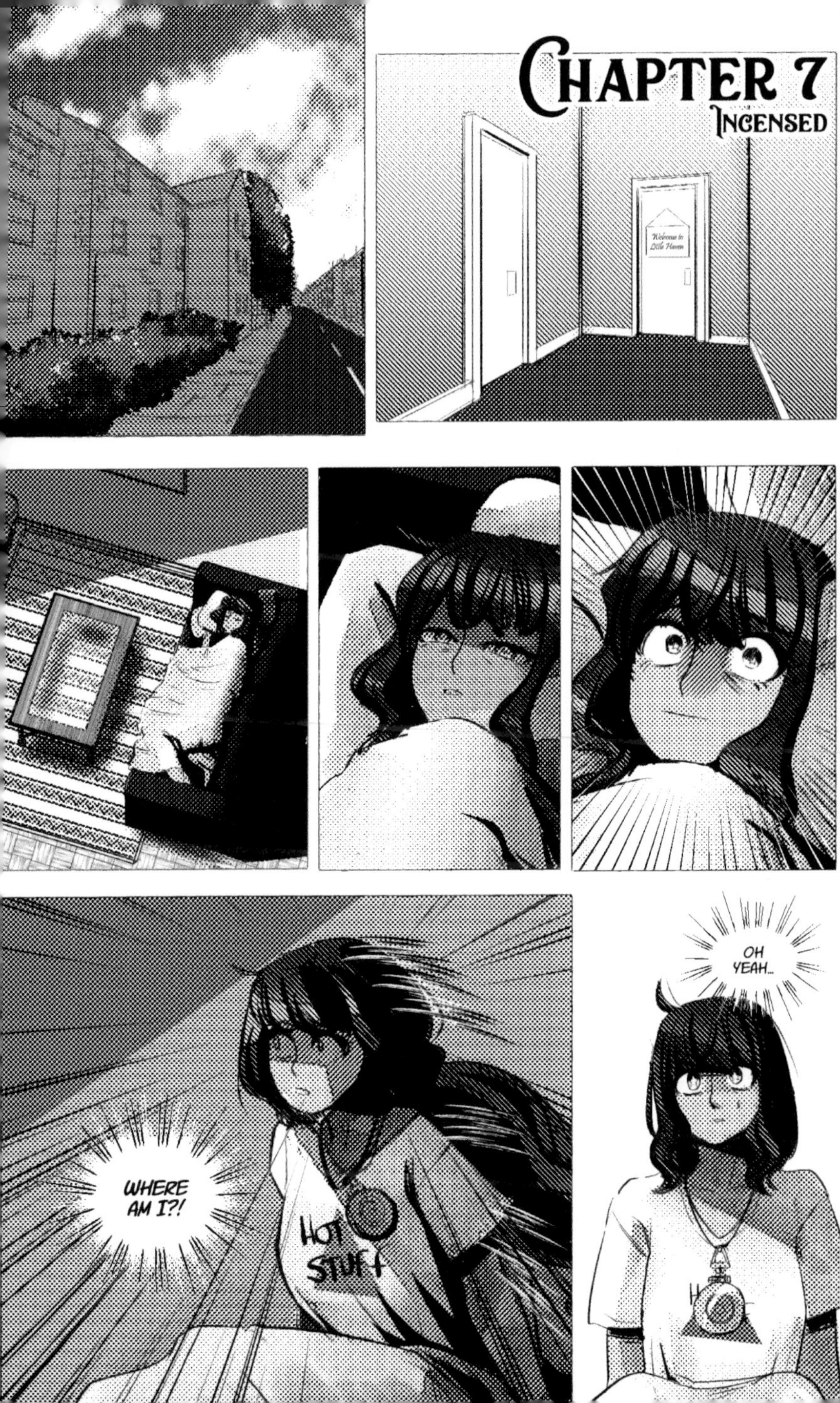
CHAPTER 7
INCENSED
Welcome to Little Haven
WHERE AM I?!
HOT STUFF
OH YEAH...

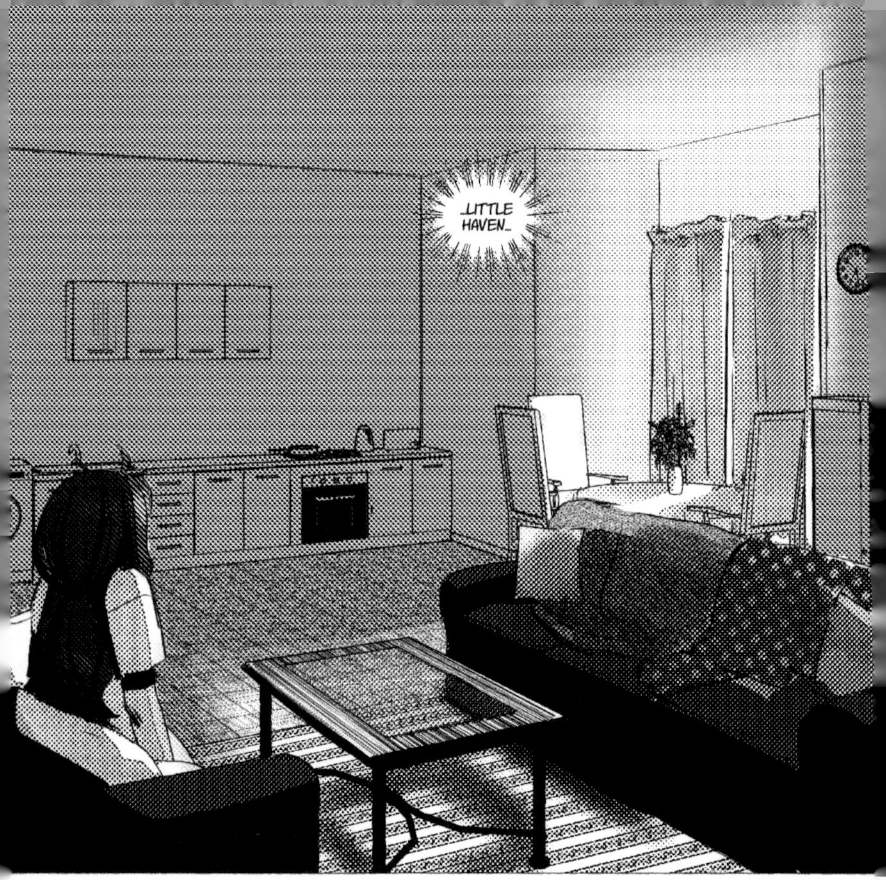
...LITTLE HAVEN...

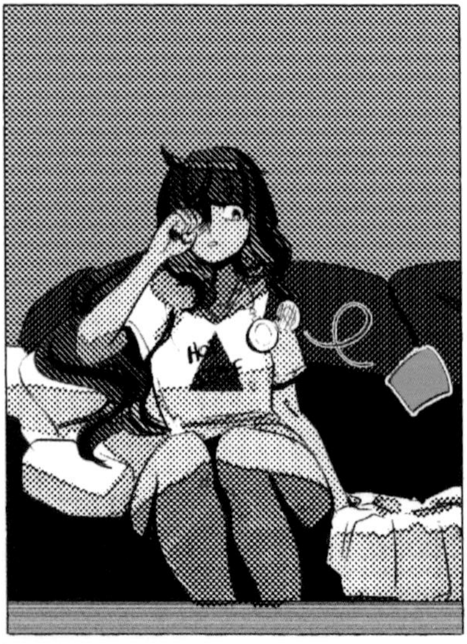

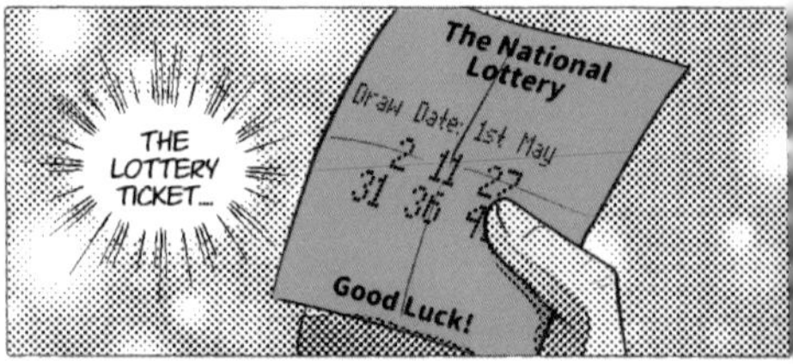
THE LOTTERY TICKET...
The National Lottery
Draw Date: 1st May
Good Luck!

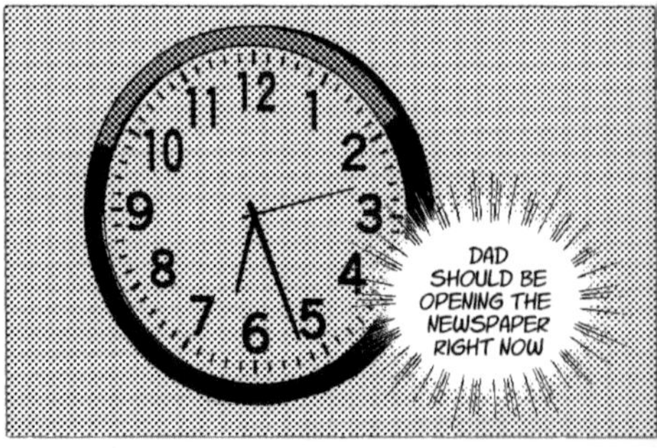
DAD SHOULD BE OPENING THE NEWSPAPER RIGHT NOW

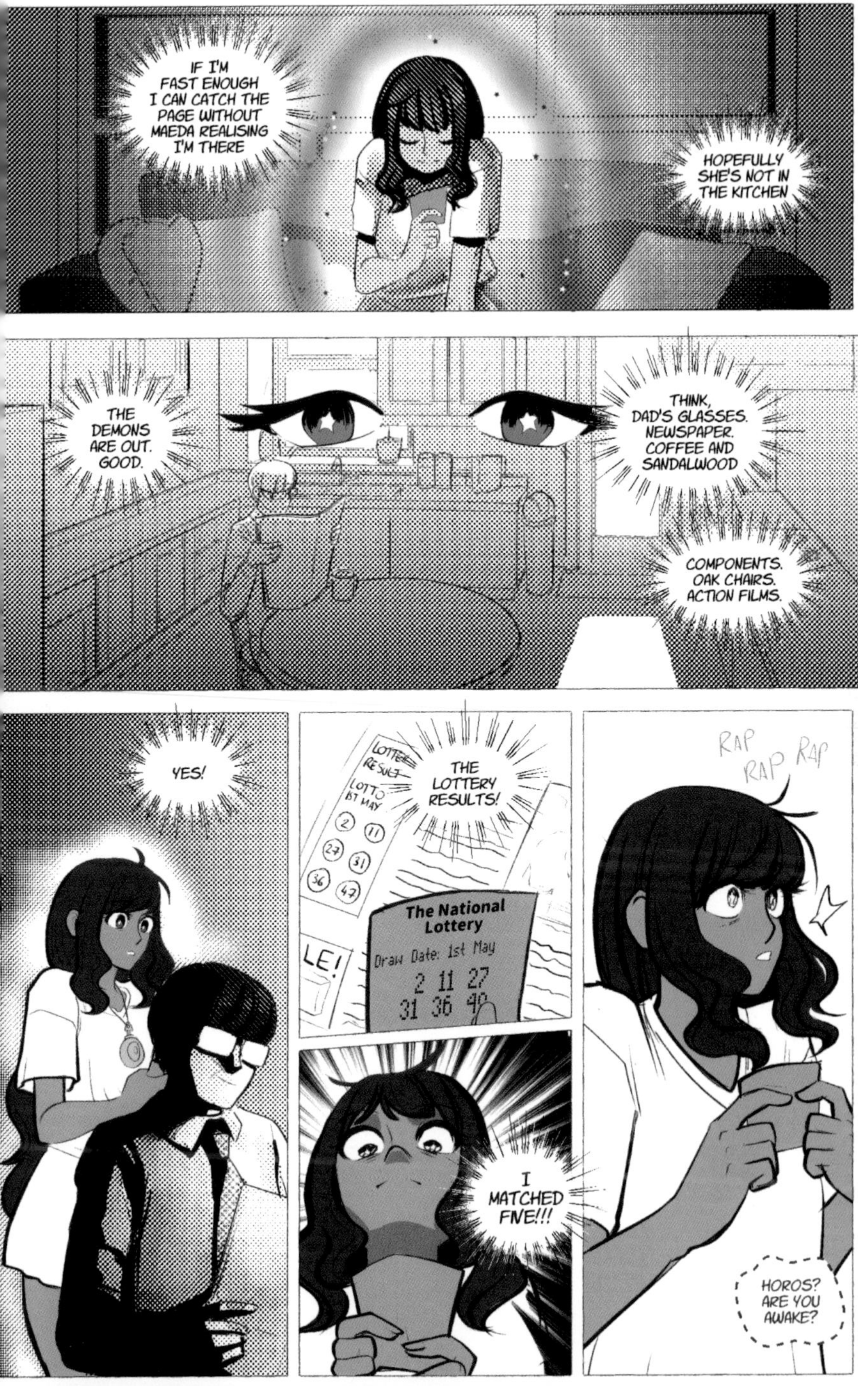
IF I'M FAST ENOUGH I CAN CATCH THE PAGE WITHOUT MAEDA REALISING I'M THERE
HOPEFULLY SHE'S NOT IN THE KITCHEN
THE DEMONS ARE OUT. GOOD.
THINK, DAD'S GLASSES. NEWSPAPER. COFFEE AND SANDALWOOD
COMPONENTS. OAK CHAIRS. ACTION FILMS.
YES!
THE LOTTERY RESULTS!
LOTTO 1ST MAY
2 11 27 31 36 47
The National Lottery
Draw Date: 1st May
2 11 27
31 36
LE!
I MATCHED FIVE!!!
RAP RAP RAP
HOROS? ARE YOU AWAKE?

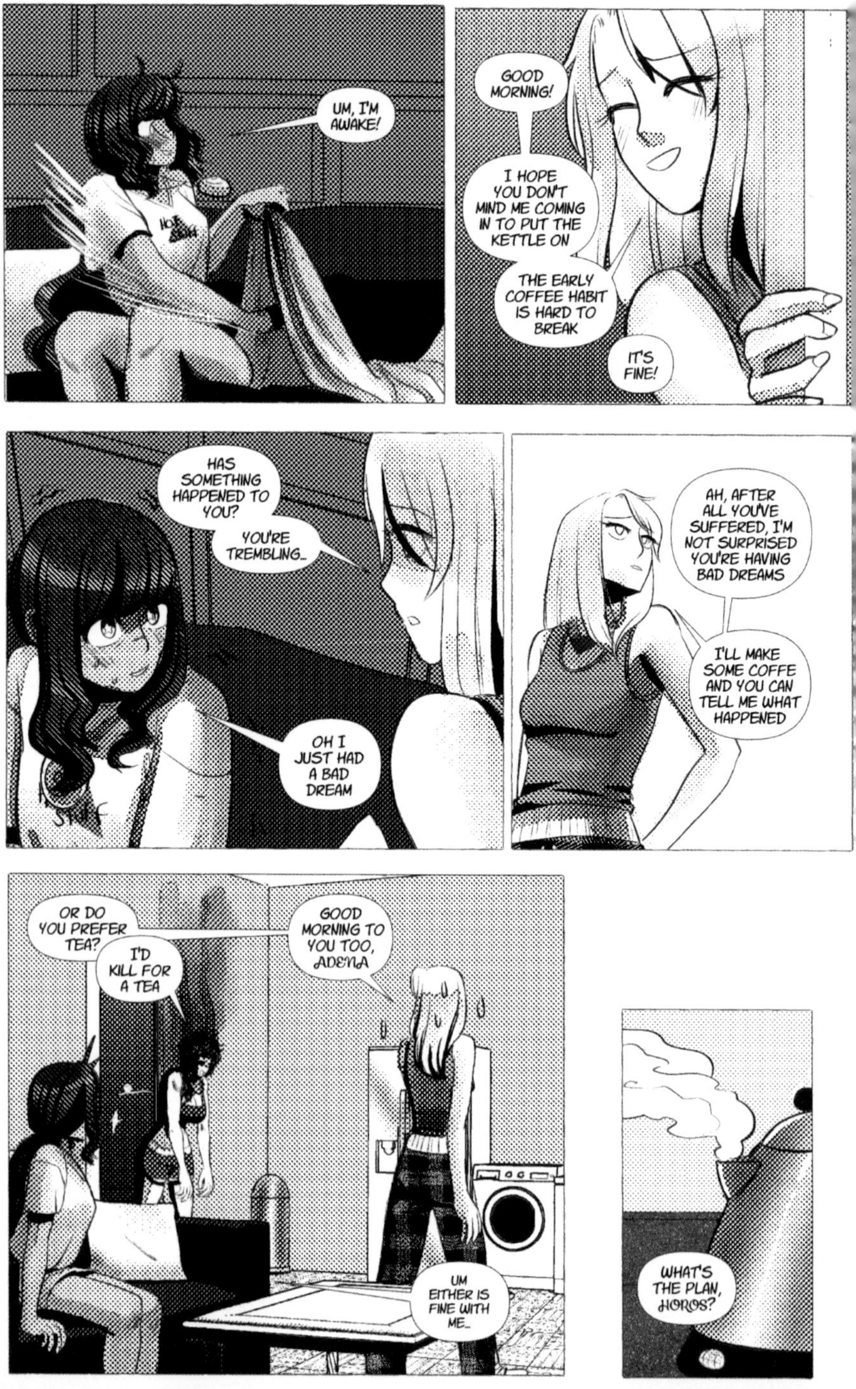
UM, I'M AWAKE!
GOOD MORNING!
I HOPE YOU DON'T MIND ME COMING IN TO PUT THE KETTLE ON
THE EARLY COFFEE HABIT IS HARD TO BREAK
IT'S FINE!
HAS SOMETHING HAPPENED TO YOU?
YOU'RE TREMBLING...
OH I JUST HAD A BAD DREAM
AH, AFTER ALL YOU'VE SUFFERED, I'M NOT SURPRISED YOU'RE HAVING BAD DREAMS
I'LL MAKE SOME COFFE AND YOU CAN TELL ME WHAT HAPPENED
OR DO YOU PREFER TEA?
I'D KILL FOR A TEA
GOOD MORNING TO YOU TOO, ADENA
UM EITHER IS FINE WITH ME...
WHAT'S THE PLAN, HOROS?

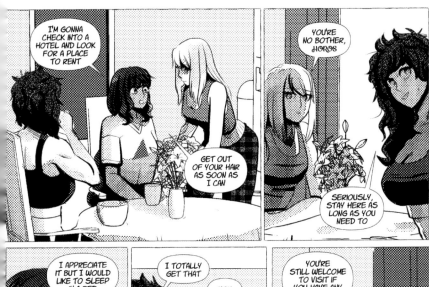

I'M GONNA CHECK INTO A HOTEL AND LOOK FOR A PLACE TO RENT

GET OUT OF YOUR HAIR AS SOON AS I CAN

YOU'RE NO BOTHER, HOROS

SERIOUSLY, STAY HERE AS LONG AS YOU NEED TO

I APPRECIATE IT BUT I WOULD LIKE TO SLEEP IN A BED

I TOTALLY GET THAT

YOU WOULD

YOU'RE STILL WELCOME TO VISIT IF YOU HAVE ANY QUESTIONS

ABOUT THAT...

UM, WOULD IT BE OKAY IF I CAME AROUND FOR, ER, WITCH LESSONS?

MAYBE ONE OR TWO NIGHTS A WEEK?

IF THAT'S OK?

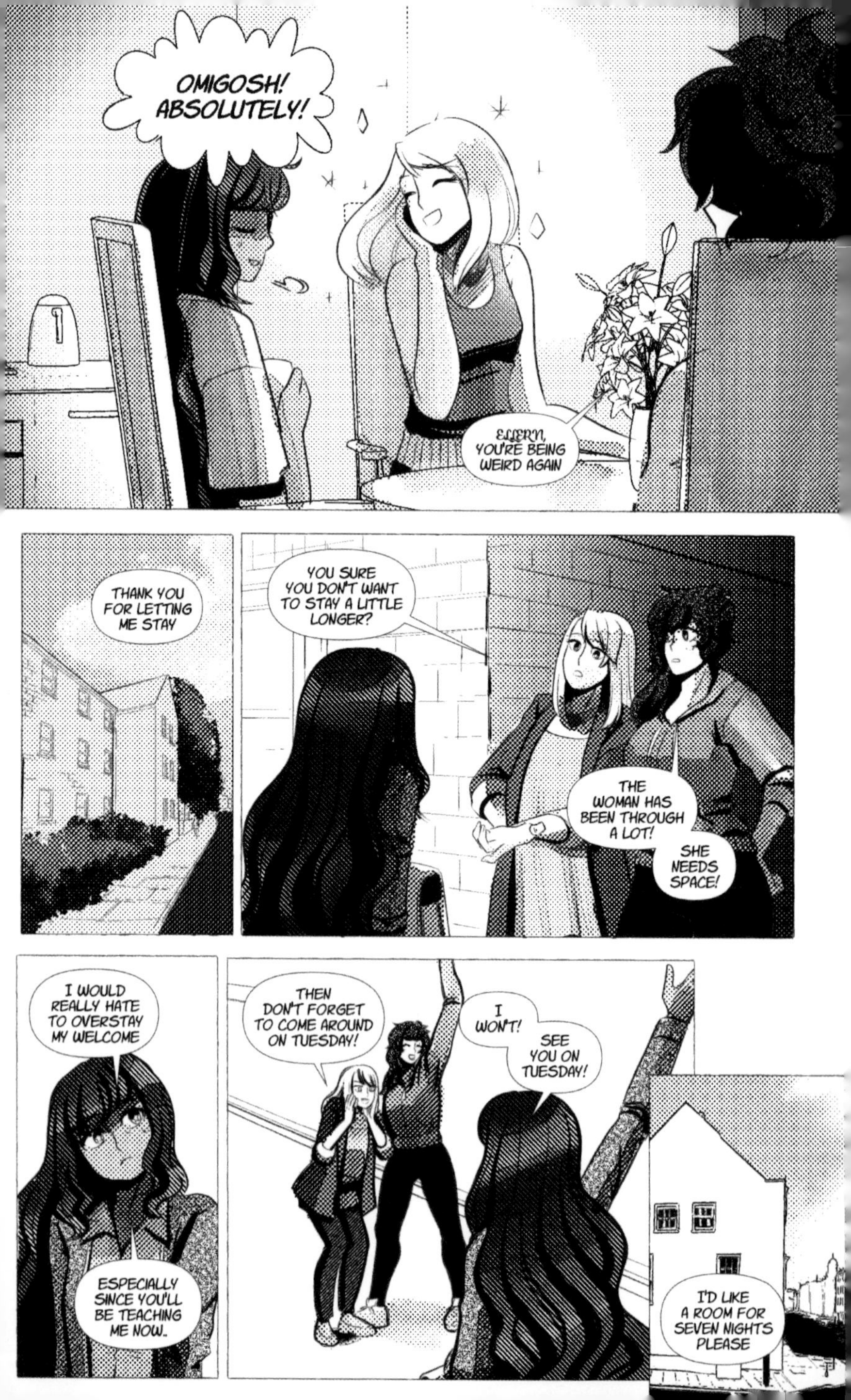
OMIGOSH! ABSOLUTELY!
ELLERN, YOU'RE BEING WEIRD AGAIN
THANK YOU FOR LETTING ME STAY
YOU SURE YOU DON'T WANT TO STAY A LITTLE LONGER?
THE WOMAN HAS BEEN THROUGH A LOT!
SHE NEEDS SPACE!
I WOULD REALLY HATE TO OVERSTAY MY WELCOME
ESPECIALLY SINCE YOU'LL BE TEACHING ME NOW..
THEN DON'T FORGET TO COME AROUND ON TUESDAY!
I WON'T!
SEE YOU ON TUESDAY!
I'D LIKE A ROOM FOR SEVEN NIGHTS PLEASE

SEVEN NIGHTS?

I HAVE A BANK CARD

AH, IT'S OKAY MADAM

H-HERE'S YOUR KEY CARDS

YIKES. EXPLAINS THAT WEIRD LOOK...

PROBABLY OUGHT TO BUY SOME NEW CLOTHES...

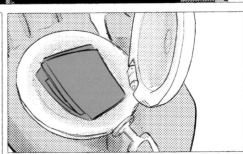

BUT FIRST

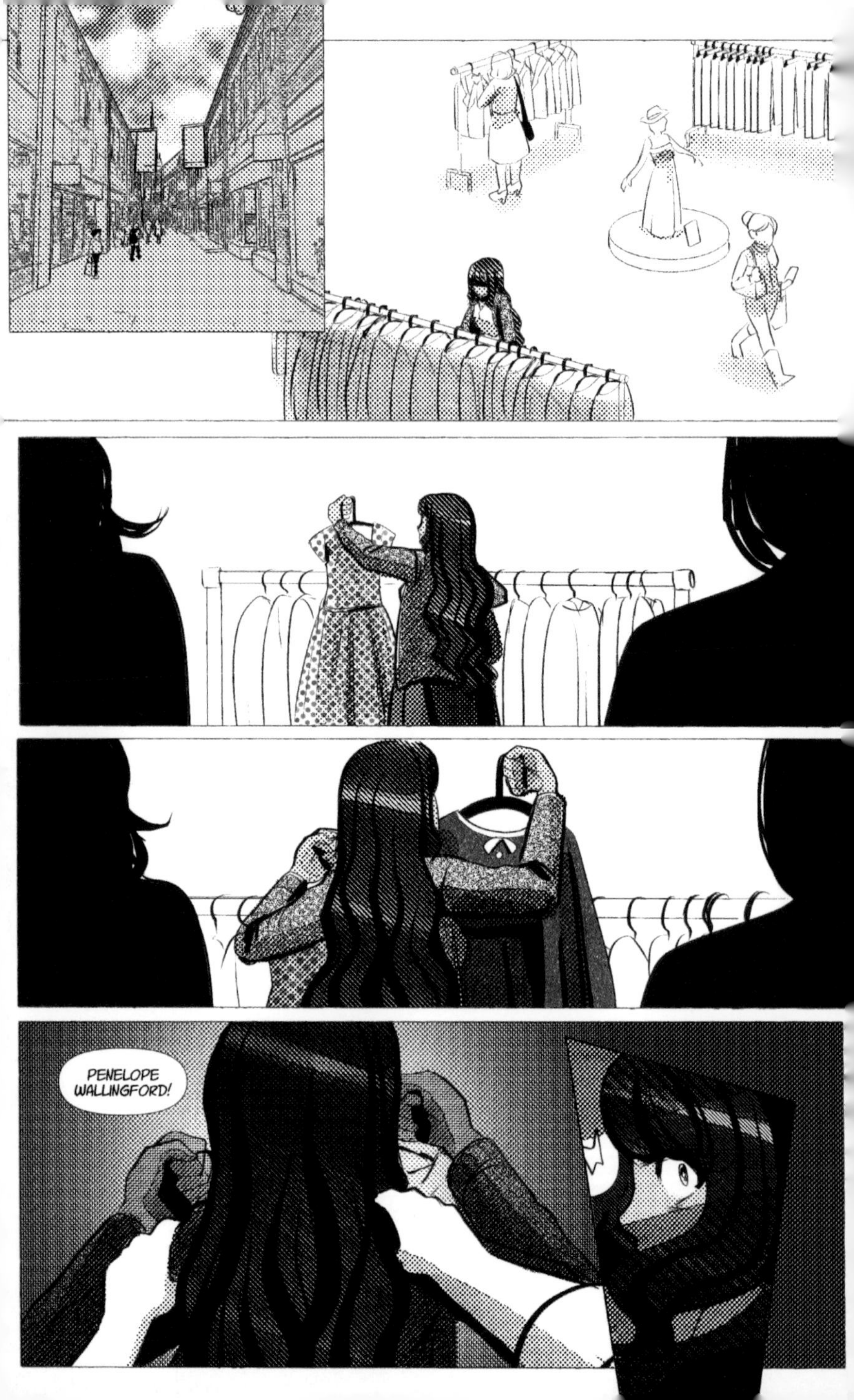
PENELOPE WALLINGFORD!

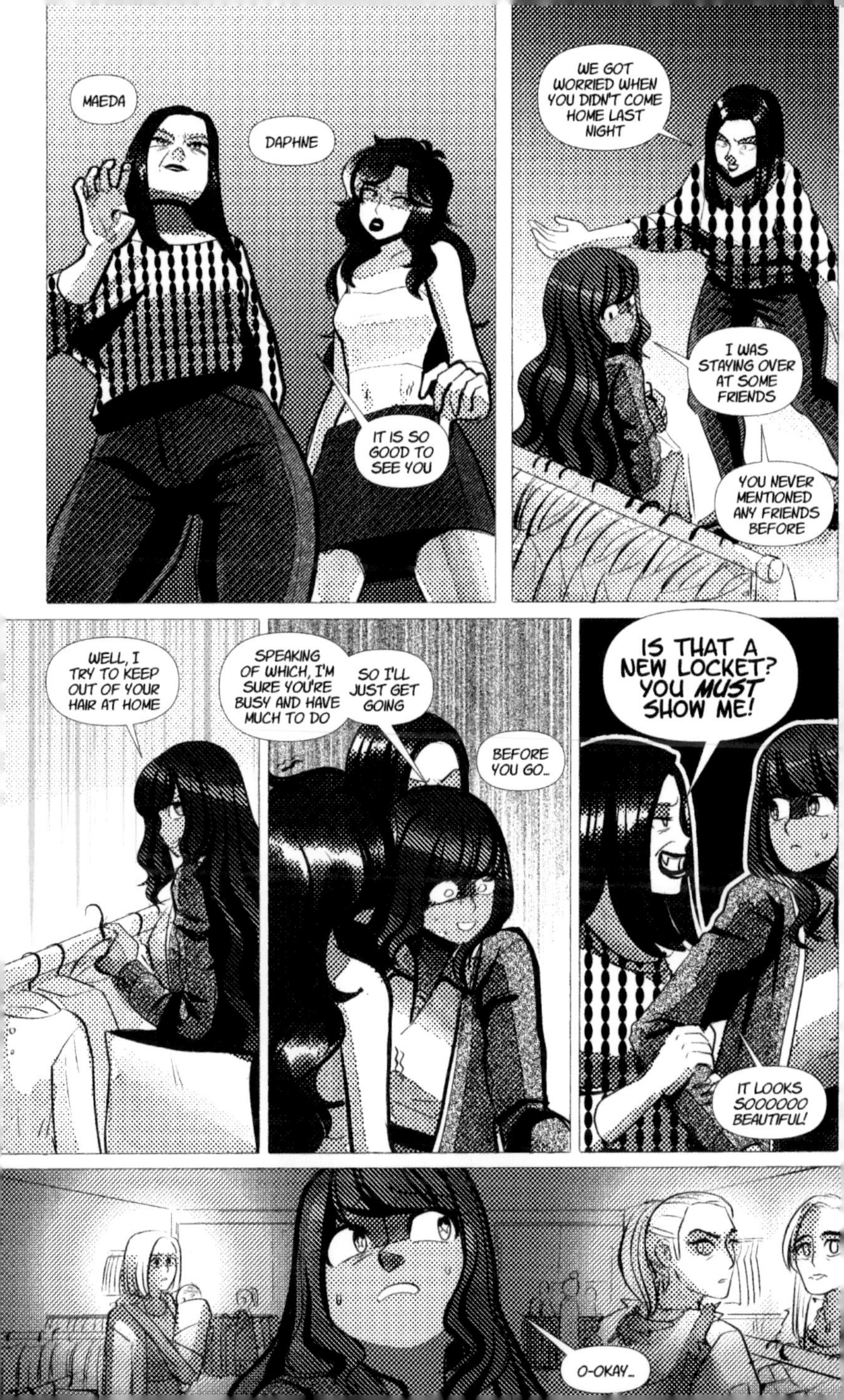
MAEDA
DAPHNE
IT IS SO GOOD TO SEE YOU
WE GOT WORRIED WHEN YOU DIDN'T COME HOME LAST NIGHT
I WAS STAYING OVER AT SOME FRIENDS
YOU NEVER MENTIONED ANY FRIENDS BEFORE
WELL, I TRY TO KEEP OUT OF YOUR HAIR AT HOME
SPEAKING OF WHICH, I'M SURE YOU'RE BUSY AND HAVE MUCH TO DO
SO I'LL JUST GET GOING
BEFORE YOU GO...
IS THAT A NEW LOCKET? YOU MUST SHOW ME!
IT LOOKS SOOOOOO BEAUTIFUL!
O-OKAY...

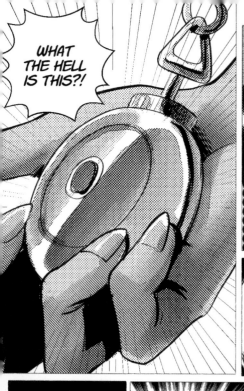

WHAT THE HELL IS THIS?!

IS IT OUT OF MAGIC?!

I GUESS IT IS...

CRACK

O-OUT O-OF M-M-M.....

AAAAAAAAAAAAAAAAAAA
AAAAAAAAAAAAAAAAAA

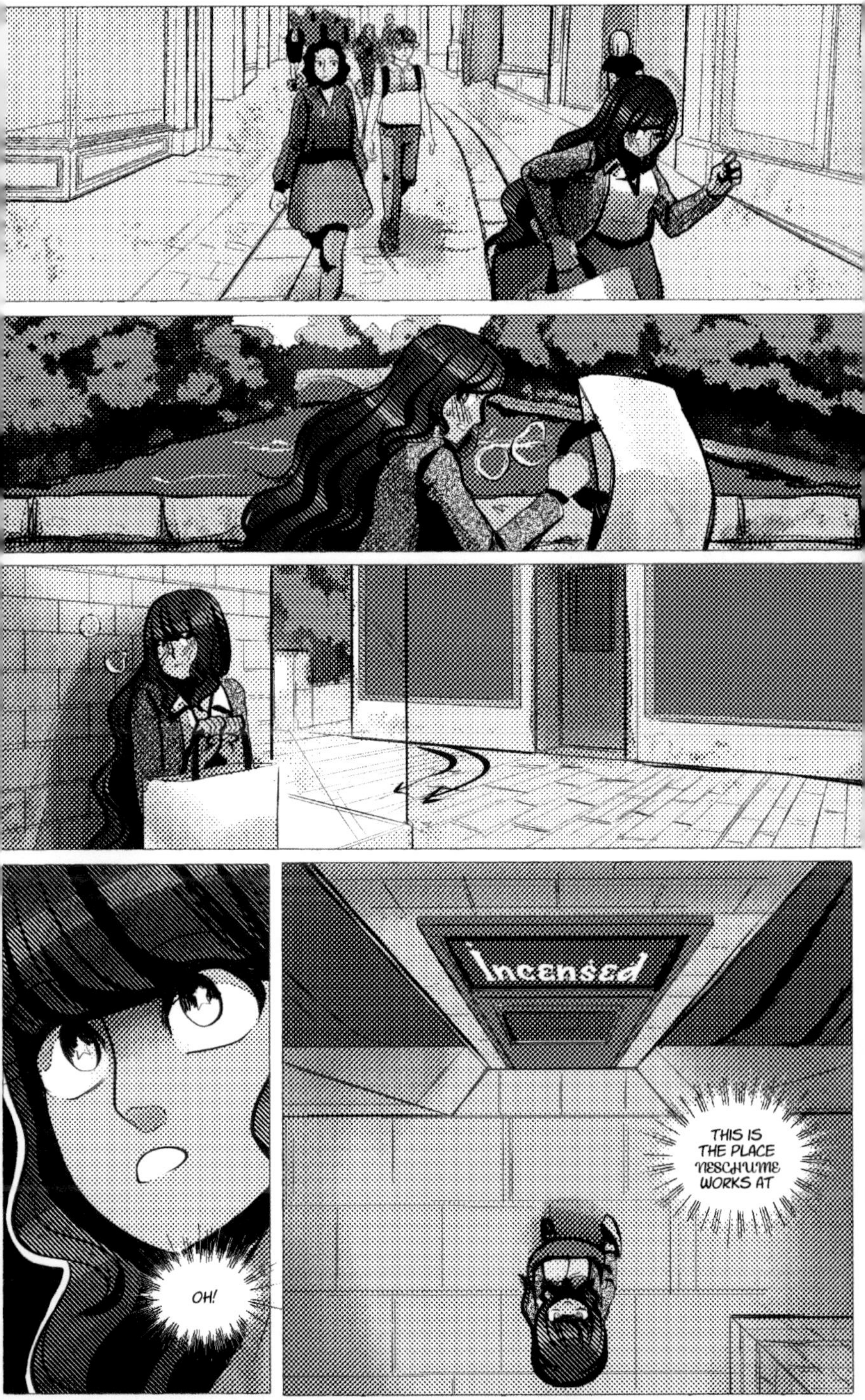
OH!
Incensed
THIS IS THE PLACE NESCHUME WORKS AT

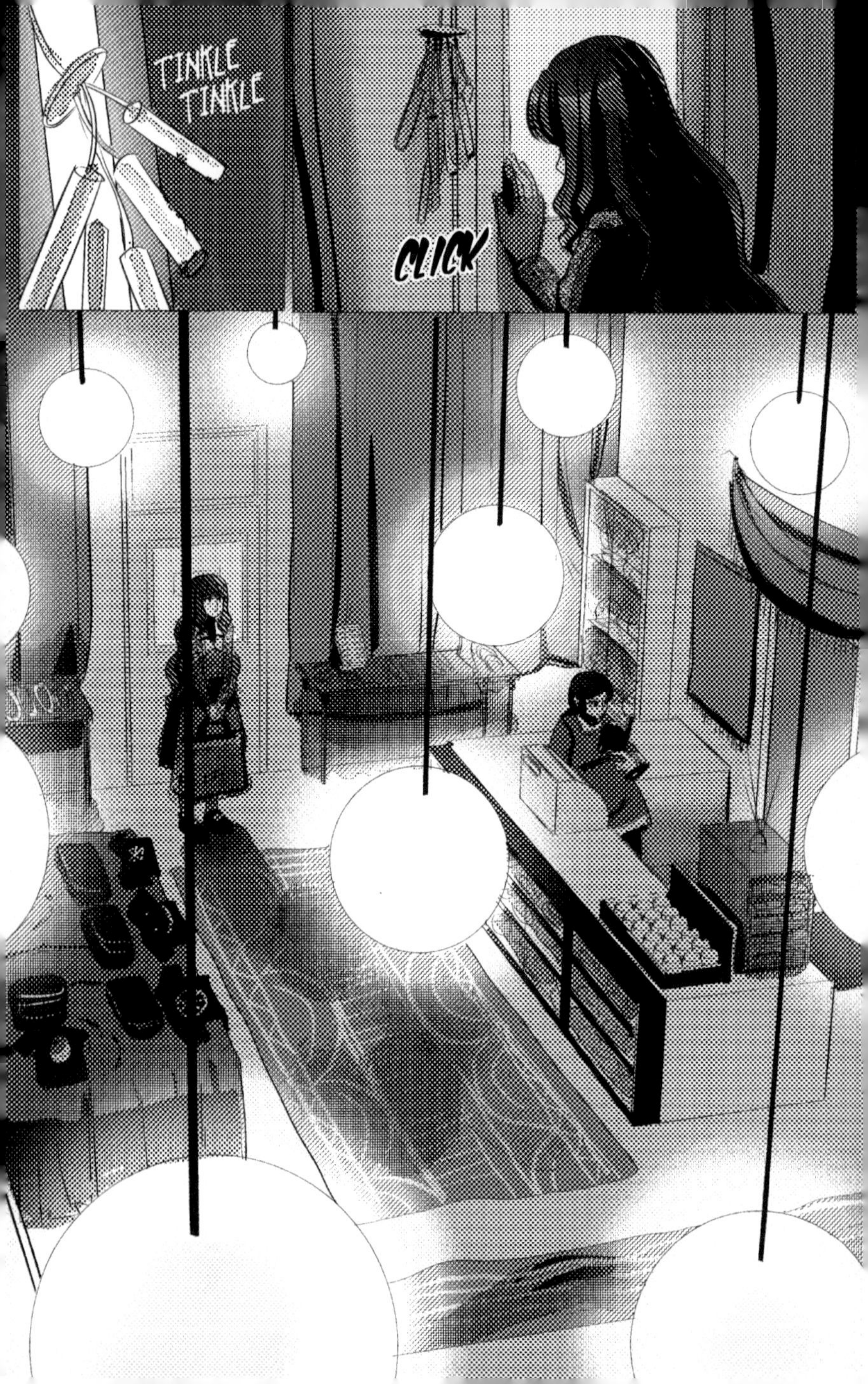
TINKLE
TINKLE
CLICK

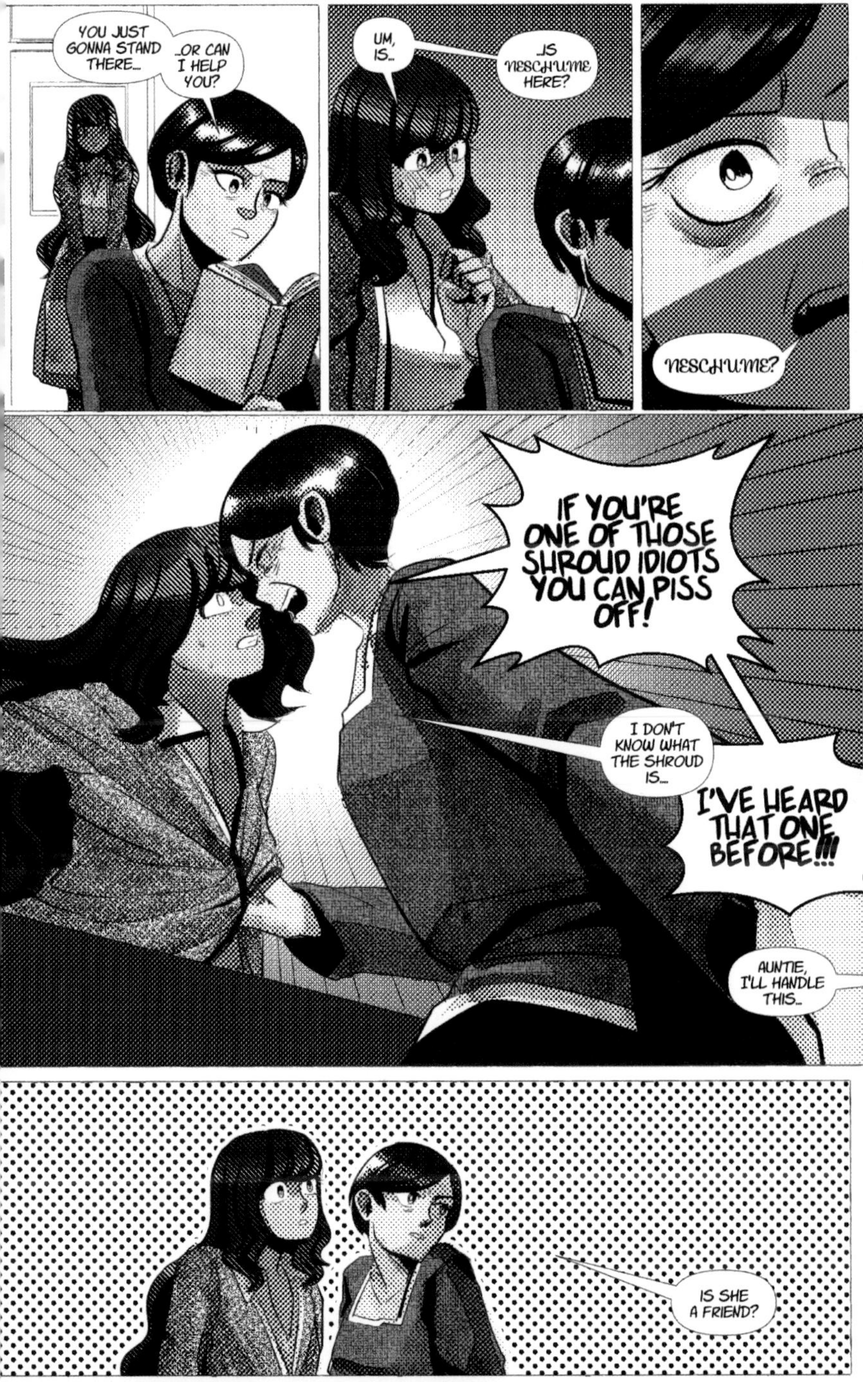
YOU JUST GONNA STAND THERE...
...OR CAN I HELP YOU?
UM, IS...
...IS NESCHUME HERE?
NESCHUME?
IF YOU'RE ONE OF THOSE SHROUD IDIOTS YOU CAN PISS OFF!
I DON'T KNOW WHAT THE SHROUD IS...
I'VE HEARD THAT ONE BEFORE!!!
AUNTIE, I'LL HANDLE THIS...
IS SHE A FRIEND?

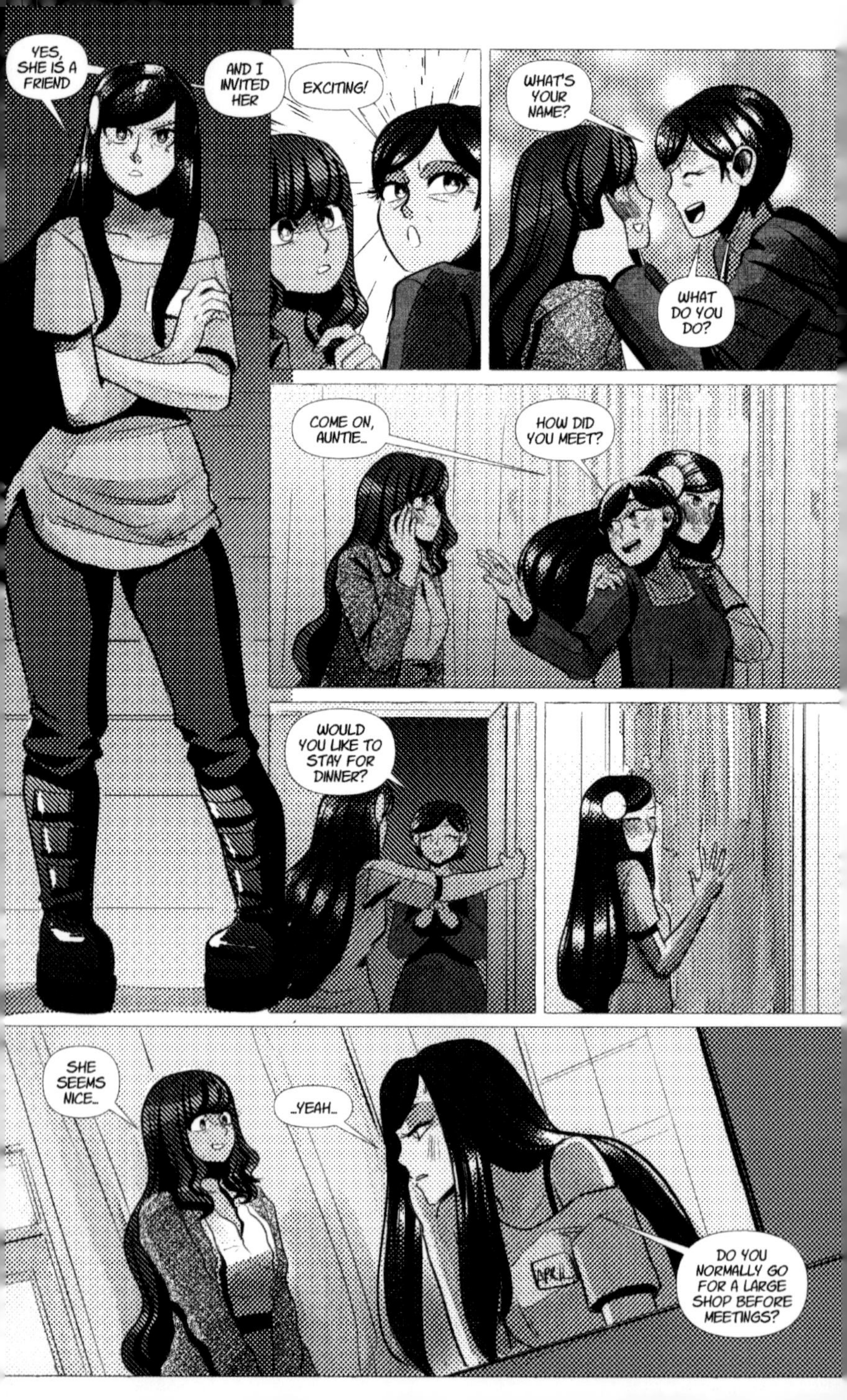
YES, SHE IS A FRIEND
AND I INVITED HER
EXCITING!
WHAT'S YOUR NAME?
WHAT DO YOU DO?
COME ON, AUNTIE..
HOW DID YOU MEET?
WOULD YOU LIKE TO STAY FOR DINNER?
SHE SEEMS NICE..
..YEAH..
DO YOU NORMALLY GO FOR A LARGE SHOP BEFORE MEETINGS?

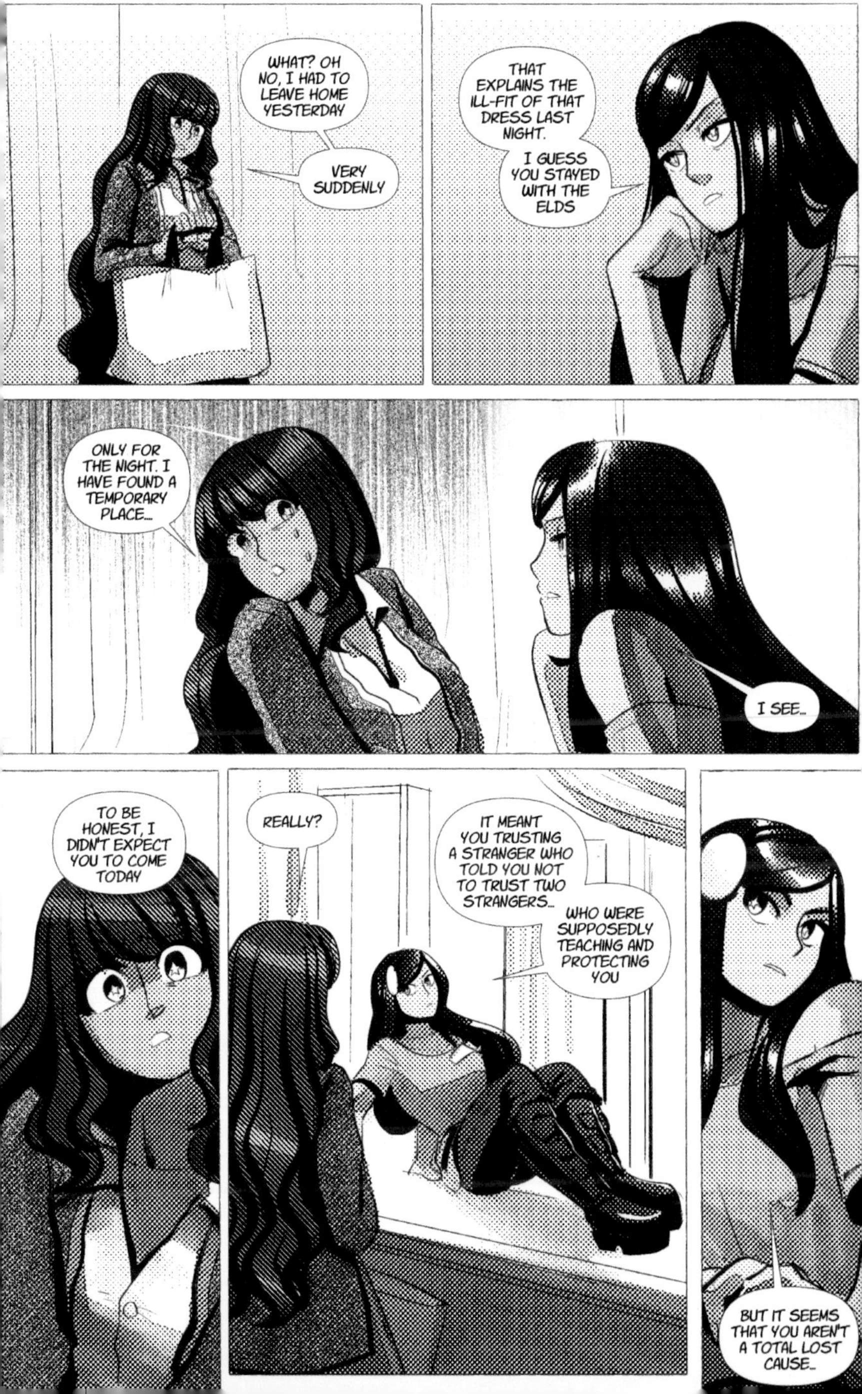
WHAT? OH NO, I HAD TO LEAVE HOME YESTERDAY
VERY SUDDENLY
THAT EXPLAINS THE ILL-FIT OF THAT DRESS LAST NIGHT.
I GUESS YOU STAYED WITH THE ELDS
ONLY FOR THE NIGHT. I HAVE FOUND A TEMPORARY PLACE...
I SEE...
TO BE HONEST, I DIDN'T EXPECT YOU TO COME TODAY
REALLY?
IT MEANT YOU TRUSTING A STRANGER WHO TOLD YOU NOT TO TRUST TWO STRANGERS...
WHO WERE SUPPOSEDLY TEACHING AND PROTECTING YOU
BUT IT SEEMS THAT YOU AREN'T A TOTAL LOST CAUSE...

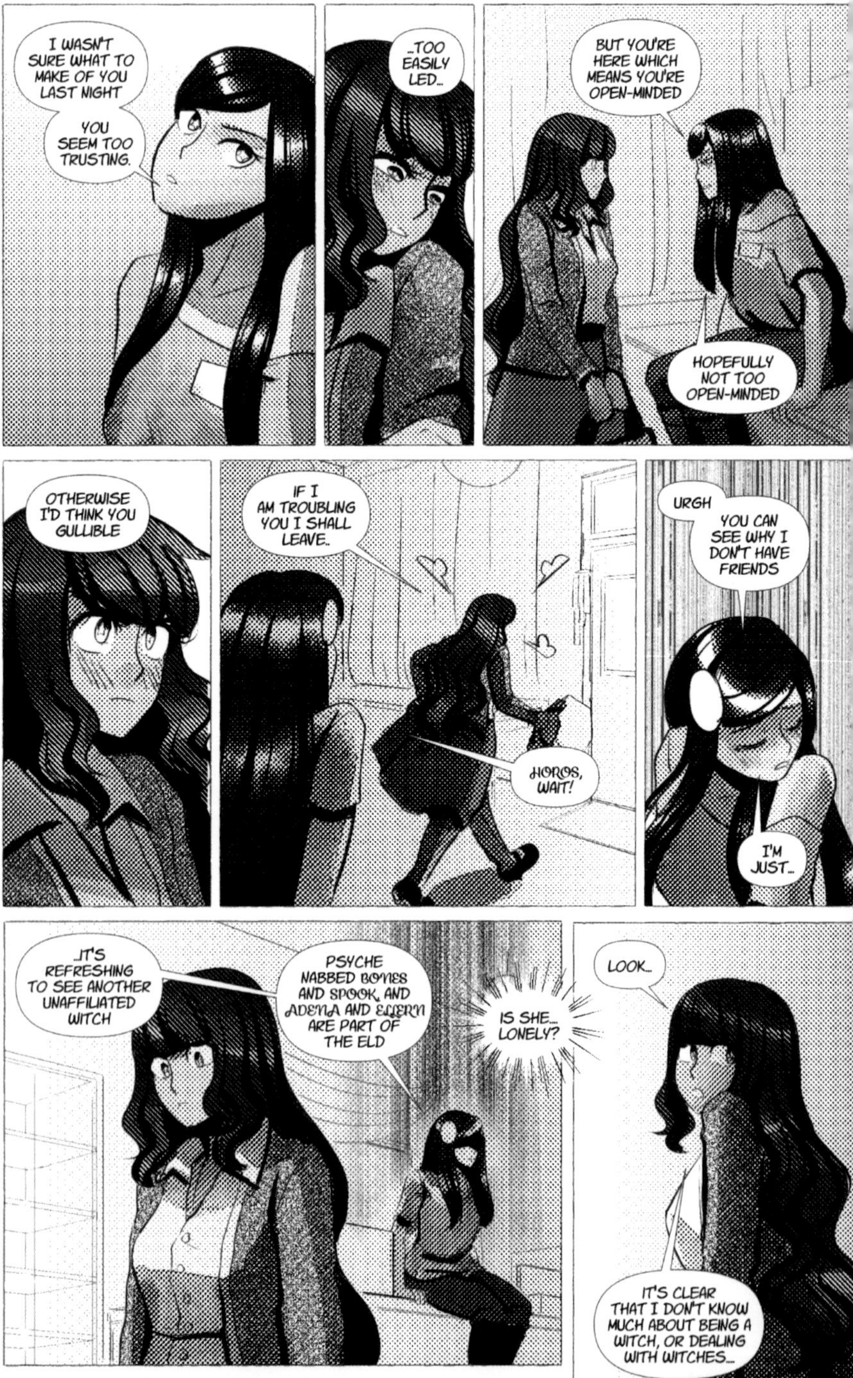
I WASN'T SURE WHAT TO MAKE OF YOU LAST NIGHT
YOU SEEM TOO TRUSTING.
..TOO EASILY LED...
BUT YOU'RE HERE WHICH MEANS YOU'RE OPEN-MINDED
HOPEFULLY NOT TOO OPEN-MINDED
OTHERWISE I'D THINK YOU GULLIBLE
IF I AM TROUBLING YOU I SHALL LEAVE..
HOROS, WAIT!
URGH
YOU CAN SEE WHY I DON'T HAVE FRIENDS
I'M JUST...
..IT'S REFRESHING TO SEE ANOTHER UNAFFILIATED WITCH
PSYCHE NABBED BONES AND SPOOK, AND ADENA AND ELLERN ARE PART OF THE ELD
IS SHE... LONELY?
LOOK..
IT'S CLEAR THAT I DON'T KNOW MUCH ABOUT BEING A WITCH, OR DEALING WITH WITCHES...

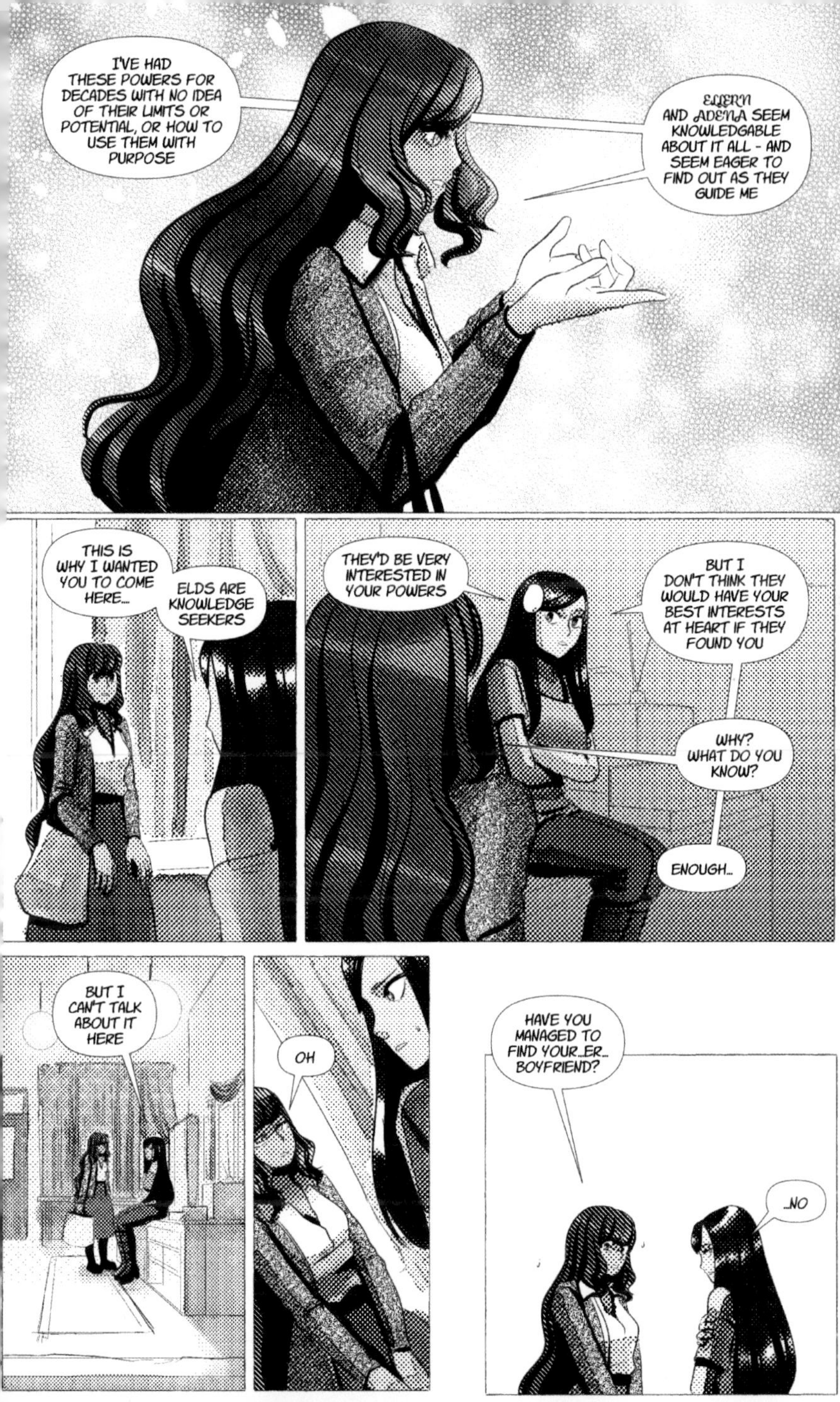
I'VE HAD THESE POWERS FOR DECADES WITH NO IDEA OF THEIR LIMITS OR POTENTIAL, OR HOW TO USE THEM WITH PURPOSE
ELLERN AND ADENA SEEM KNOWLEDGABLE ABOUT IT ALL - AND SEEM EAGER TO FIND OUT AS THEY GUIDE ME
THIS IS WHY I WANTED YOU TO COME HERE...
ELDS ARE KNOWLEDGE SEEKERS
THEY'D BE VERY INTERESTED IN YOUR POWERS
BUT I DON'T THINK THEY WOULD HAVE YOUR BEST INTERESTS AT HEART IF THEY FOUND YOU
WHY? WHAT DO YOU KNOW?
ENOUGH...
BUT I CAN'T TALK ABOUT IT HERE
OH
HAVE YOU MANAGED TO FIND YOUR...ER... BOYFRIEND?
...NO

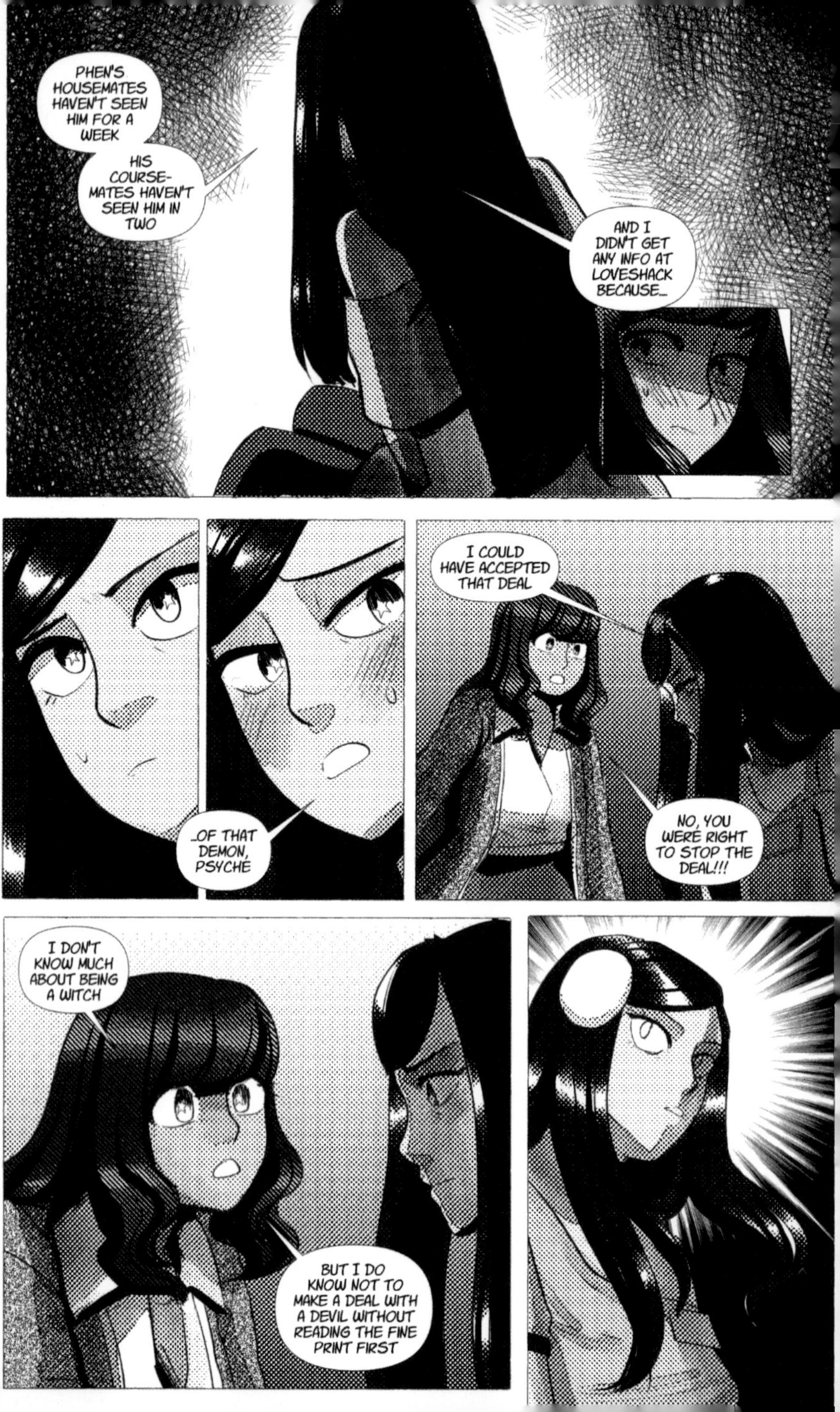
PHEN'S HOUSEMATES HAVEN'T SEEN HIM FOR A WEEK
HIS COURSE-MATES HAVEN'T SEEN HIM IN TWO
AND I DIDN'T GET ANY INFO AT LOVESHACK BECAUSE...
...OF THAT DEMON, PSYCHE
I COULD HAVE ACCEPTED THAT DEAL
NO, YOU WERE RIGHT TO STOP THE DEAL!!!
I DON'T KNOW MUCH ABOUT BEING A WITCH
BUT I DO KNOW NOT TO MAKE A DEAL WITH A DEVIL WITHOUT READING THE FINE PRINT FIRST

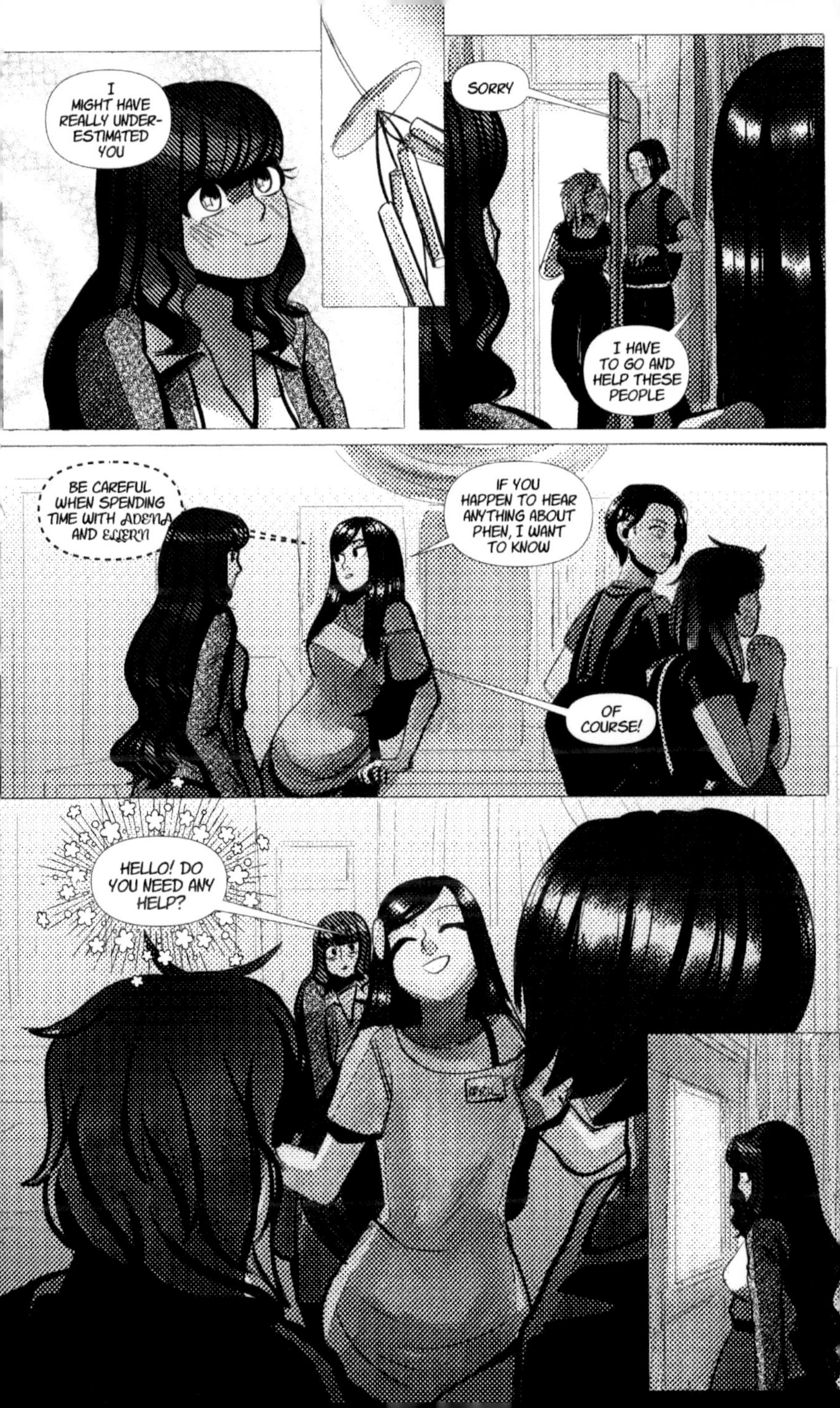
I MIGHT HAVE REALLY UNDER-ESTIMATED YOU
SORRY
I HAVE TO GO AND HELP THESE PEOPLE
BE CAREFUL WHEN SPENDING TIME WITH ADENA AND ELERN
IF YOU HAPPEN TO HEAR ANYTHING ABOUT PHEN, I WANT TO KNOW
OF COURSE!
HELLO! DO YOU NEED ANY HELP?

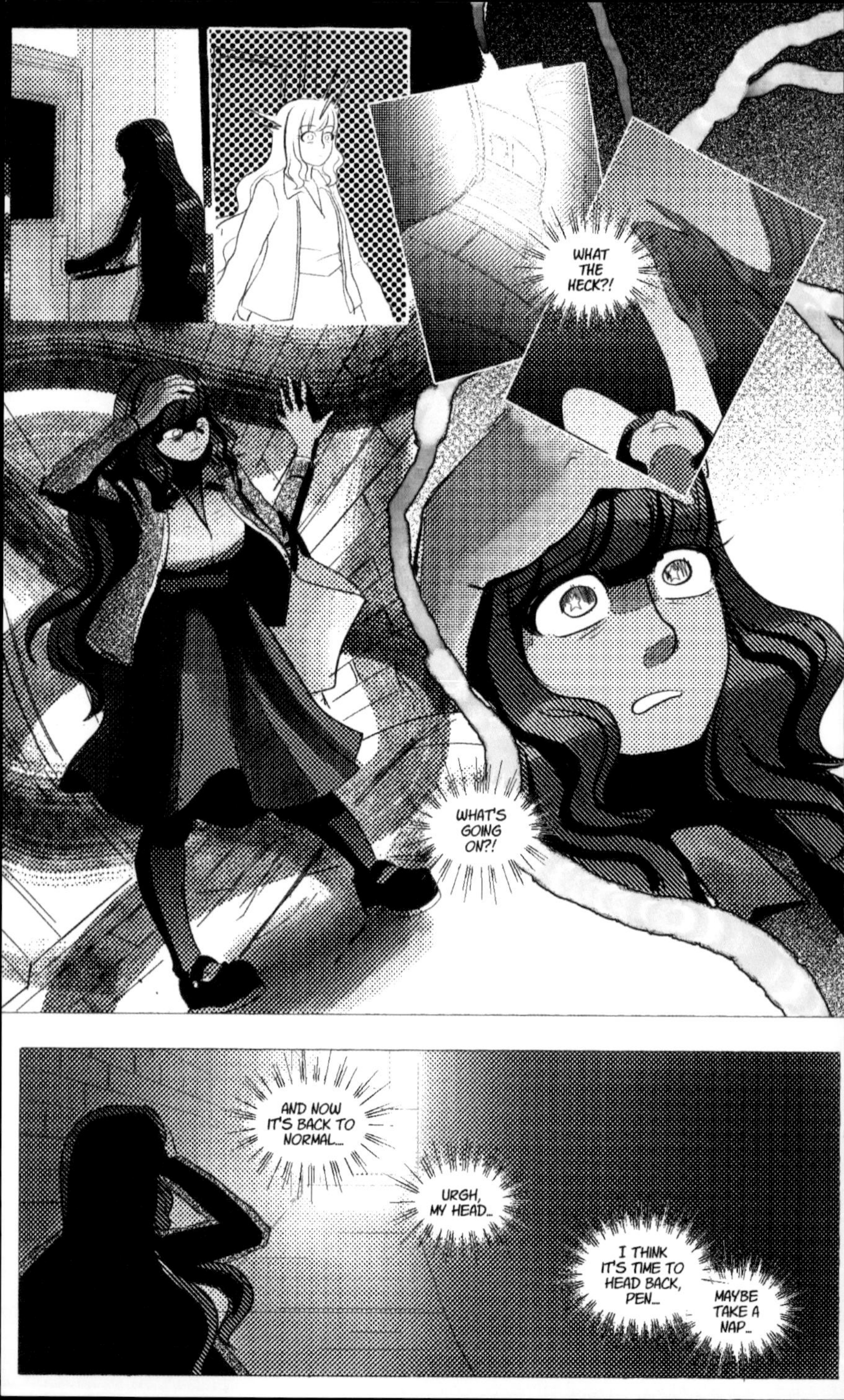
WHAT THE HECK?!
WHAT'S GOING ON?!
AND NOW IT'S BACK TO NORMAL...
URGH, MY HEAD...
I THINK IT'S TIME TO HEAD BACK, PEN...
MAYBE TAKE A NAP...

Chapter 8
A New Home

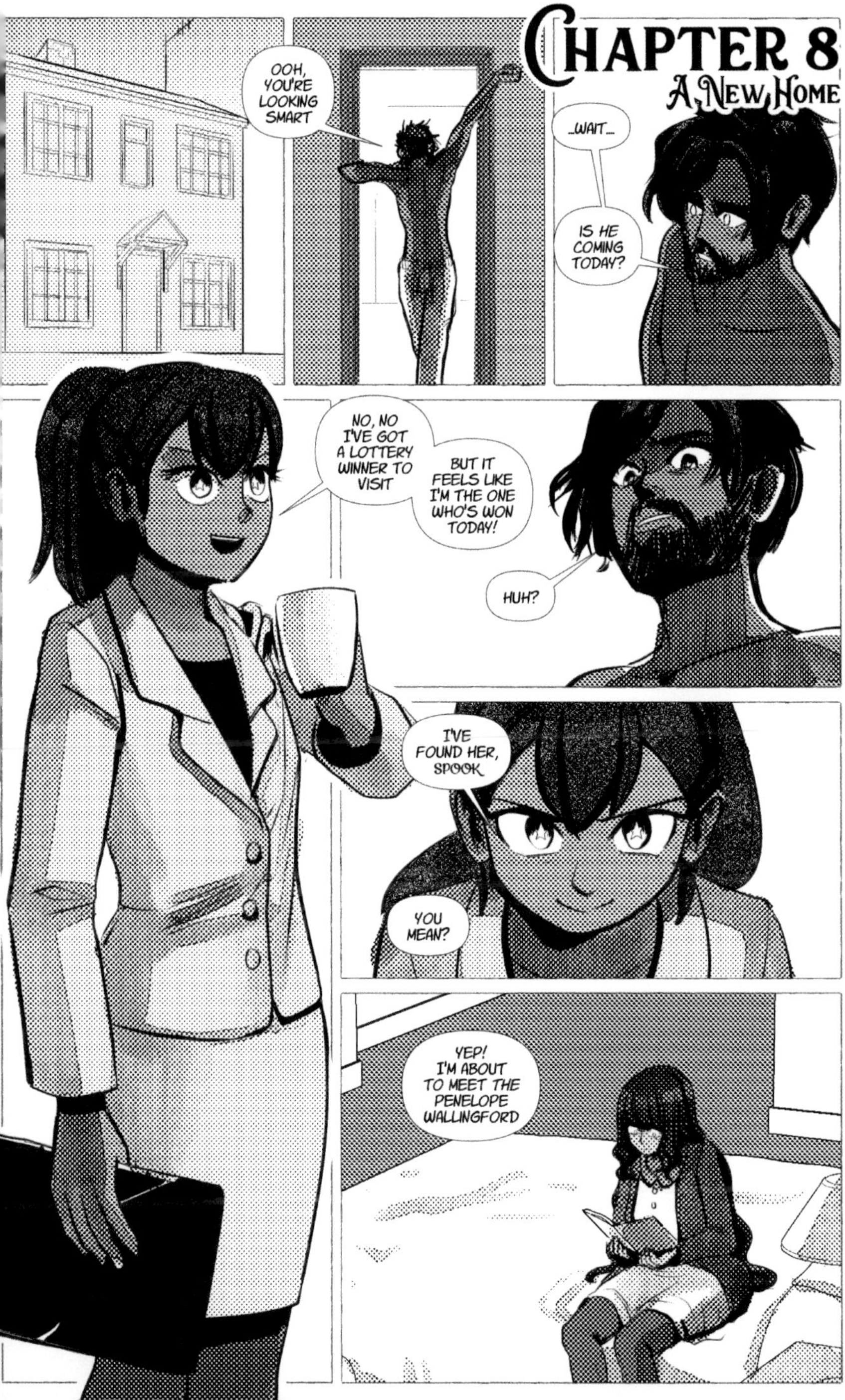

OOH, YOU'RE LOOKING SMART
...WAIT...
IS HE COMING TODAY?
NO, NO I'VE GOT A LOTTERY WINNER TO VISIT
BUT IT FEELS LIKE I'M THE ONE WHO'S WON TODAY!
HUH?
I'VE FOUND HER, SPOOK
YOU MEAN?
YEP! I'M ABOUT TO MEET THE PENELOPE WALLINGFORD

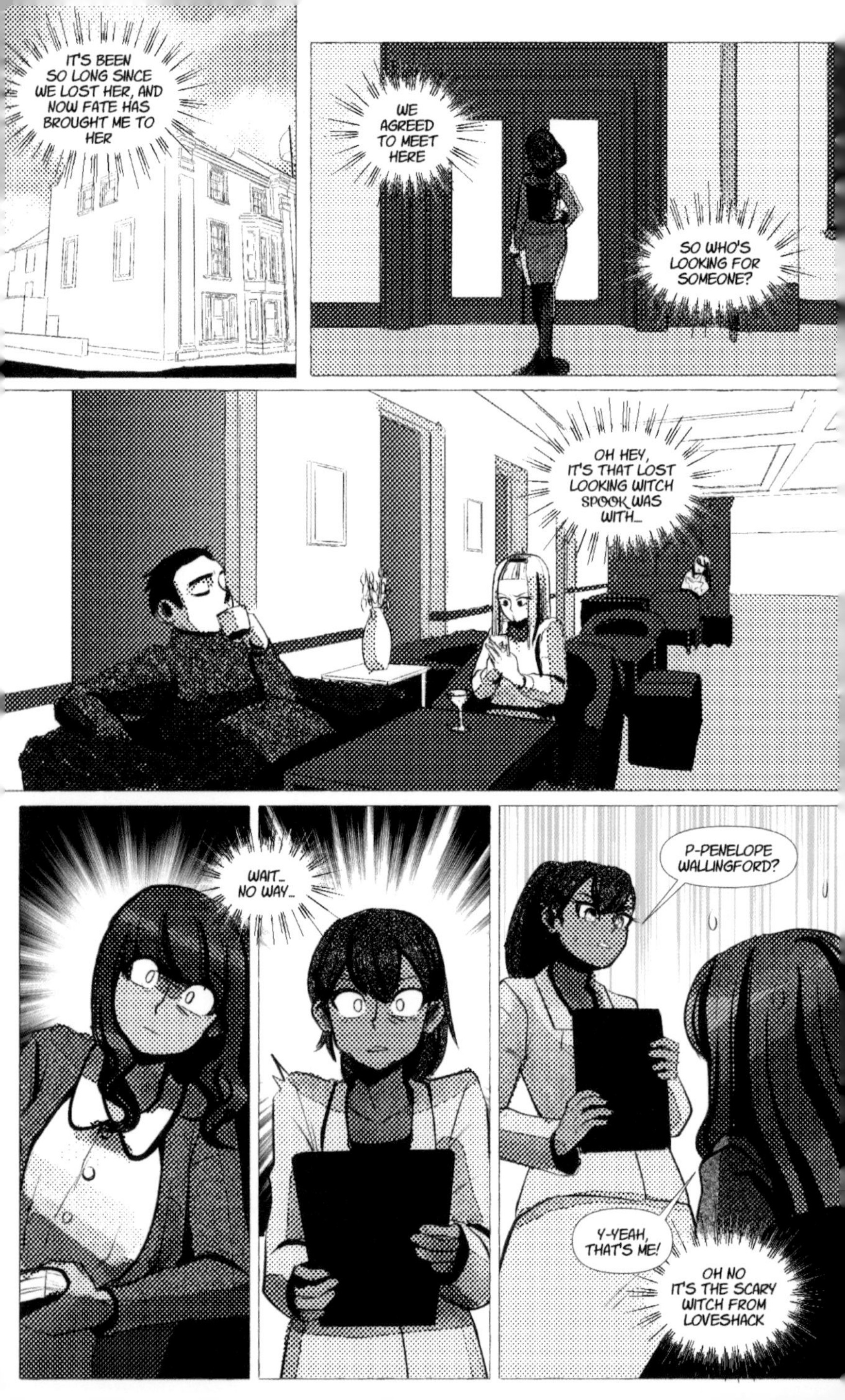
IT'S BEEN SO LONG SINCE WE LOST HER, AND NOW FATE HAS BROUGHT ME TO HER
WE AGREED TO MEET HERE
SO WHO'S LOOKING FOR SOMEONE?
OH HEY, IT'S THAT LOST LOOKING WITCH SPOOK WAS WITH...
WAIT... NO WAY...
P-PENELOPE WALLINGFORD?
Y-YEAH, THAT'S ME!
OH NO IT'S THE SCARY WITCH FROM LOVESHACK

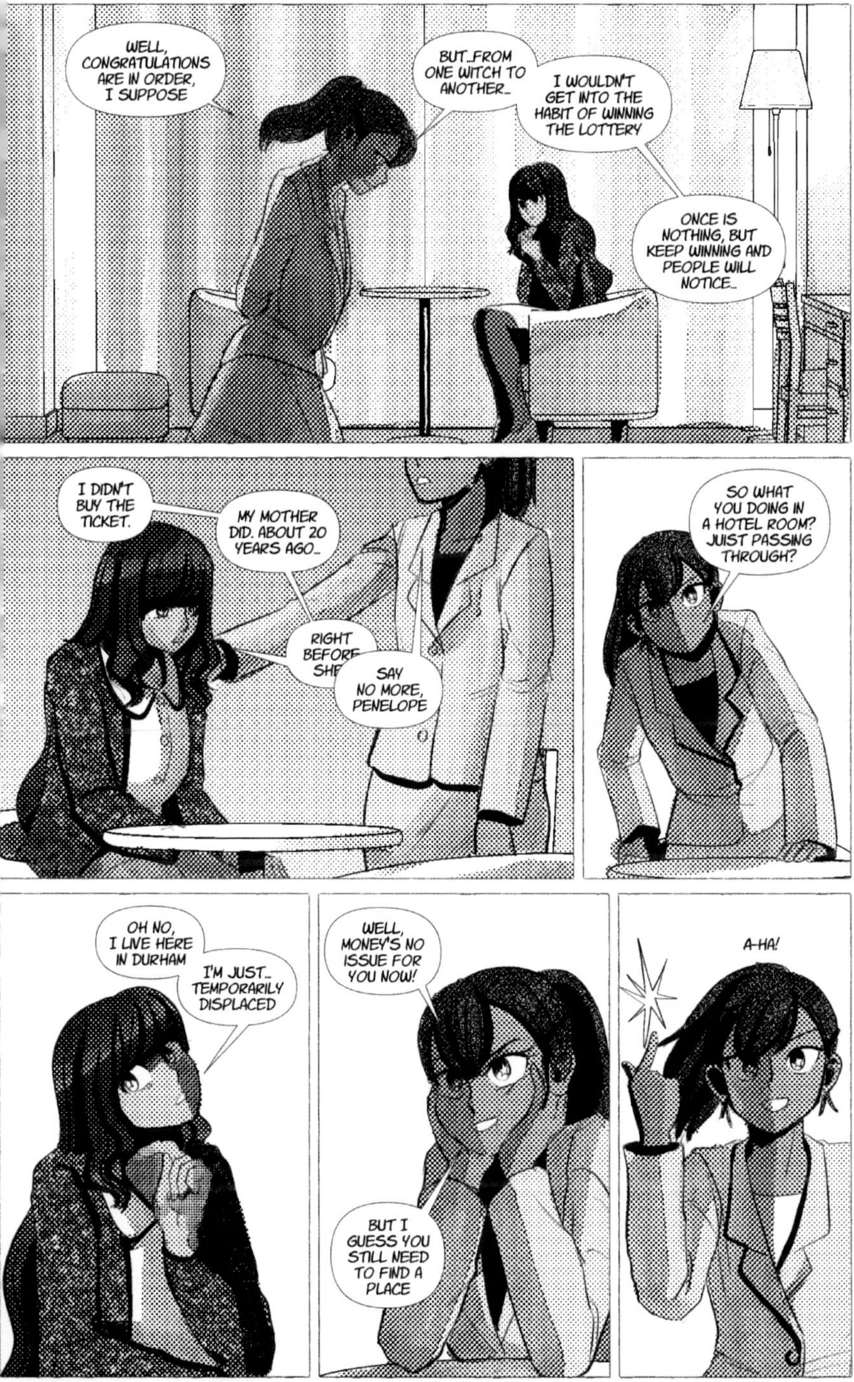
WELL, CONGRATULATIONS ARE IN ORDER, I SUPPOSE
BUT...FROM ONE WITCH TO ANOTHER...
I WOULDN'T GET INTO THE HABIT OF WINNING THE LOTTERY
ONCE IS NOTHING, BUT KEEP WINNING AND PEOPLE WILL NOTICE...
I DIDN'T BUY THE TICKET.
MY MOTHER DID. ABOUT 20 YEARS AGO...
RIGHT BEFORE SHE
SAY NO MORE, PENELOPE
SO WHAT YOU DOING IN A HOTEL ROOM? JUIST PASSING THROUGH?
OH NO, I LIVE HERE IN DURHAM
I'M JUST... TEMPORARILY DISPLACED
WELL, MONEY'S NO ISSUE FOR YOU NOW!
BUT I GUESS YOU STILL NEED TO FIND A PLACE
A-HA!

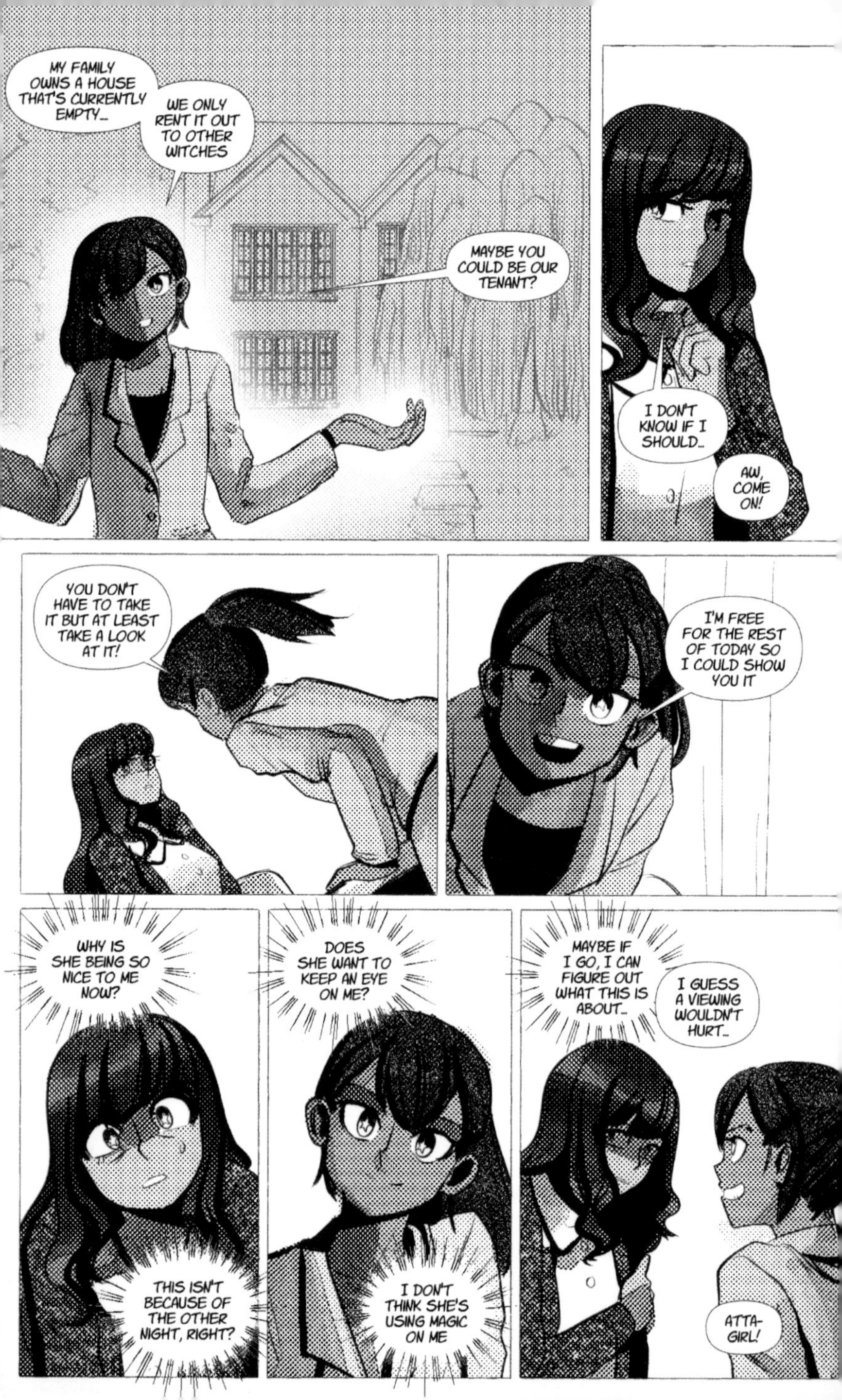
MY FAMILY OWNS A HOUSE THAT'S CURRENTLY EMPTY...
WE ONLY RENT IT OUT TO OTHER WITCHES
MAYBE YOU COULD BE OUR TENANT?
I DON'T KNOW IF I SHOULD...
AW, COME ON!
YOU DON'T HAVE TO TAKE IT BUT AT LEAST TAKE A LOOK AT IT!
I'M FREE FOR THE REST OF TODAY SO I COULD SHOW YOU IT
WHY IS SHE BEING SO NICE TO ME NOW?
THIS ISN'T BECAUSE OF THE OTHER NIGHT, RIGHT?
DOES SHE WANT TO KEEP AN EYE ON ME?
I DON'T THINK SHE'S USING MAGIC ON ME
MAYBE IF I GO, I CAN FIGURE OUT WHAT THIS IS ABOUT...
I GUESS A VIEWING WOULDN'T HURT...
ATTA-GIRL!

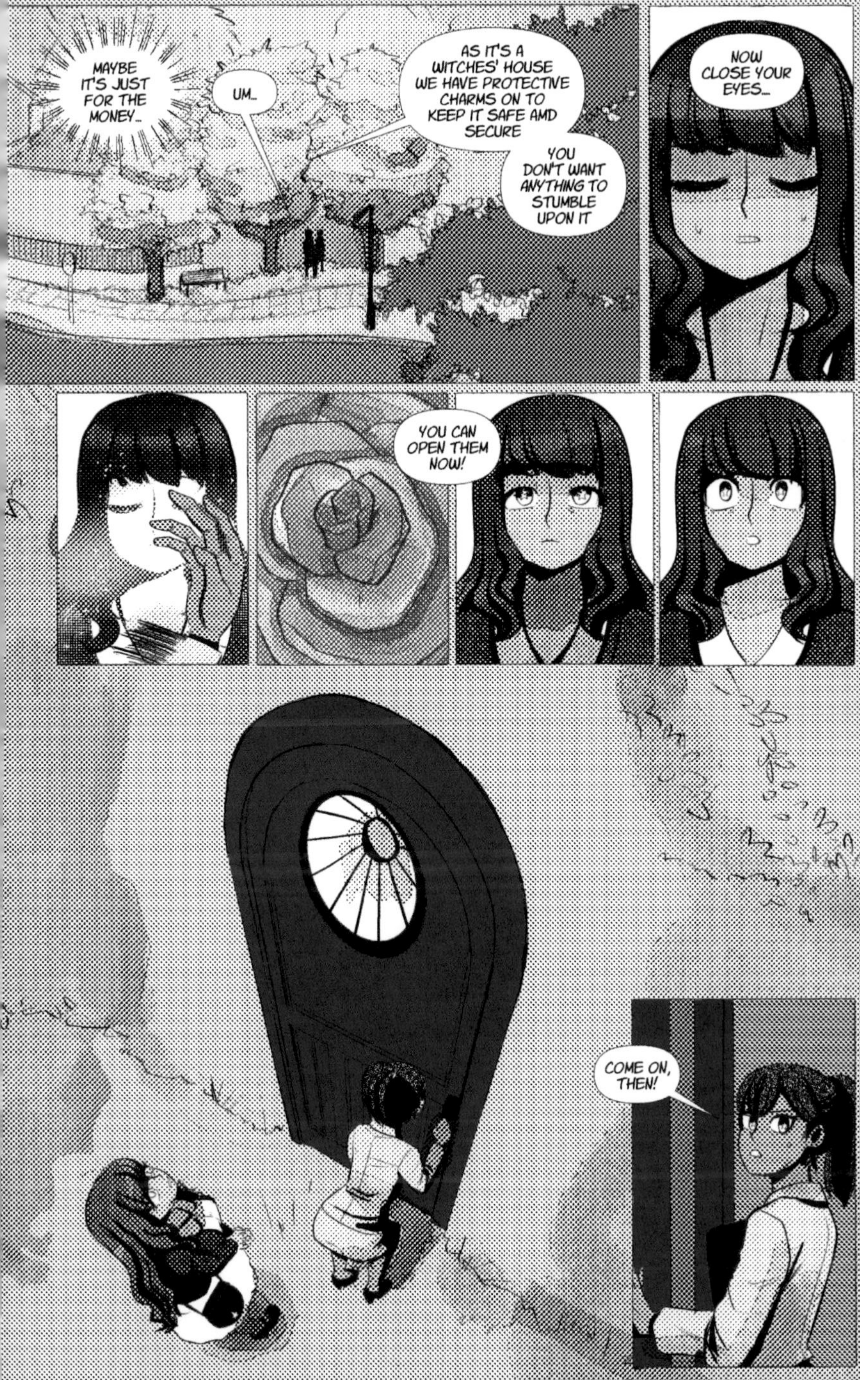
MAYBE IT'S JUST FOR THE MONEY...
UM...
AS IT'S A WITCHES' HOUSE WE HAVE PROTECTIVE CHARMS ON TO KEEP IT SAFE AMD SECURE
YOU DON'T WANT ANYTHING TO STUMBLE UPON IT
NOW CLOSE YOUR EYES...
YOU CAN OPEN THEM NOW!
COME ON, THEN!

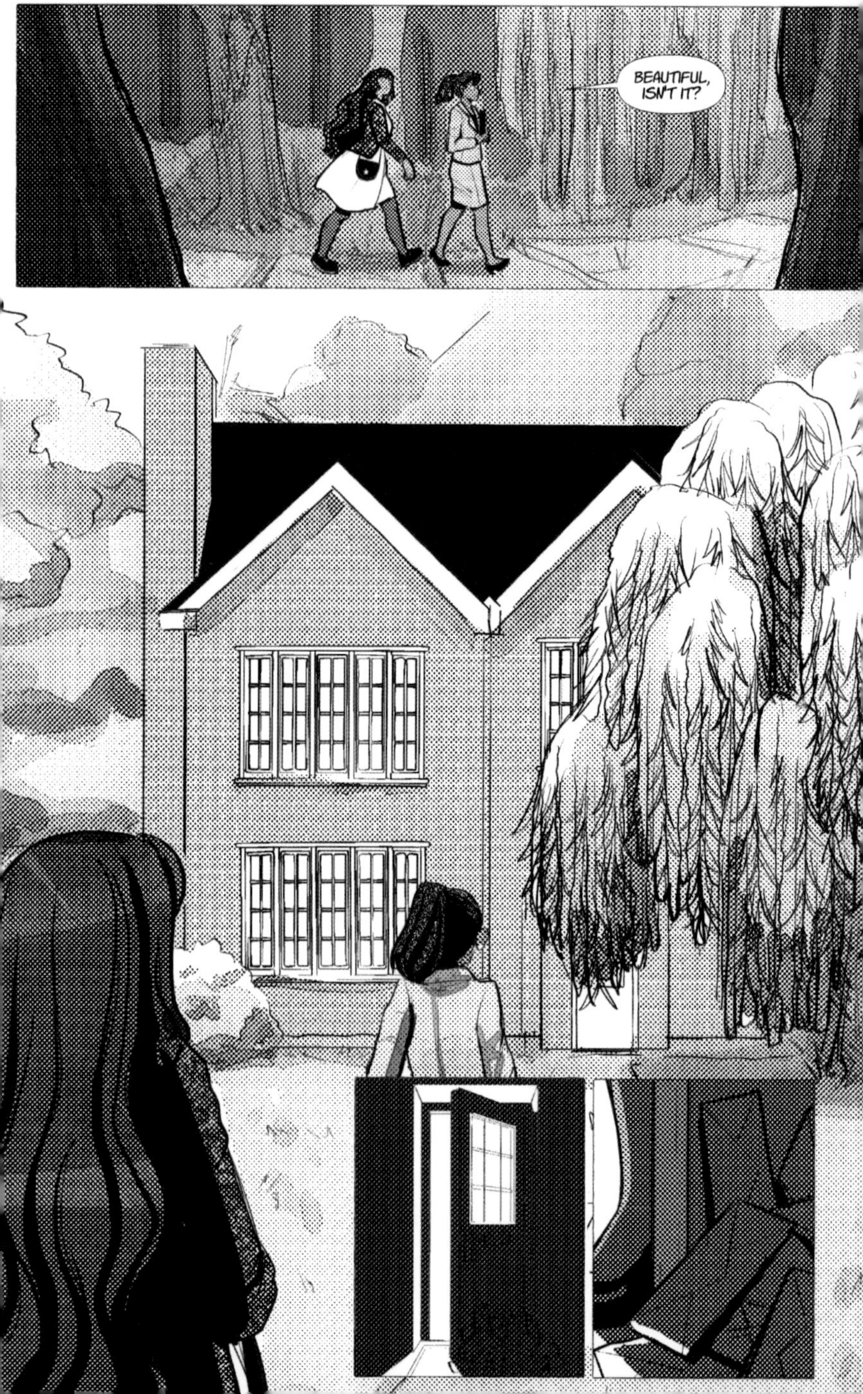
BEAUTIFUL, ISN'T IT?

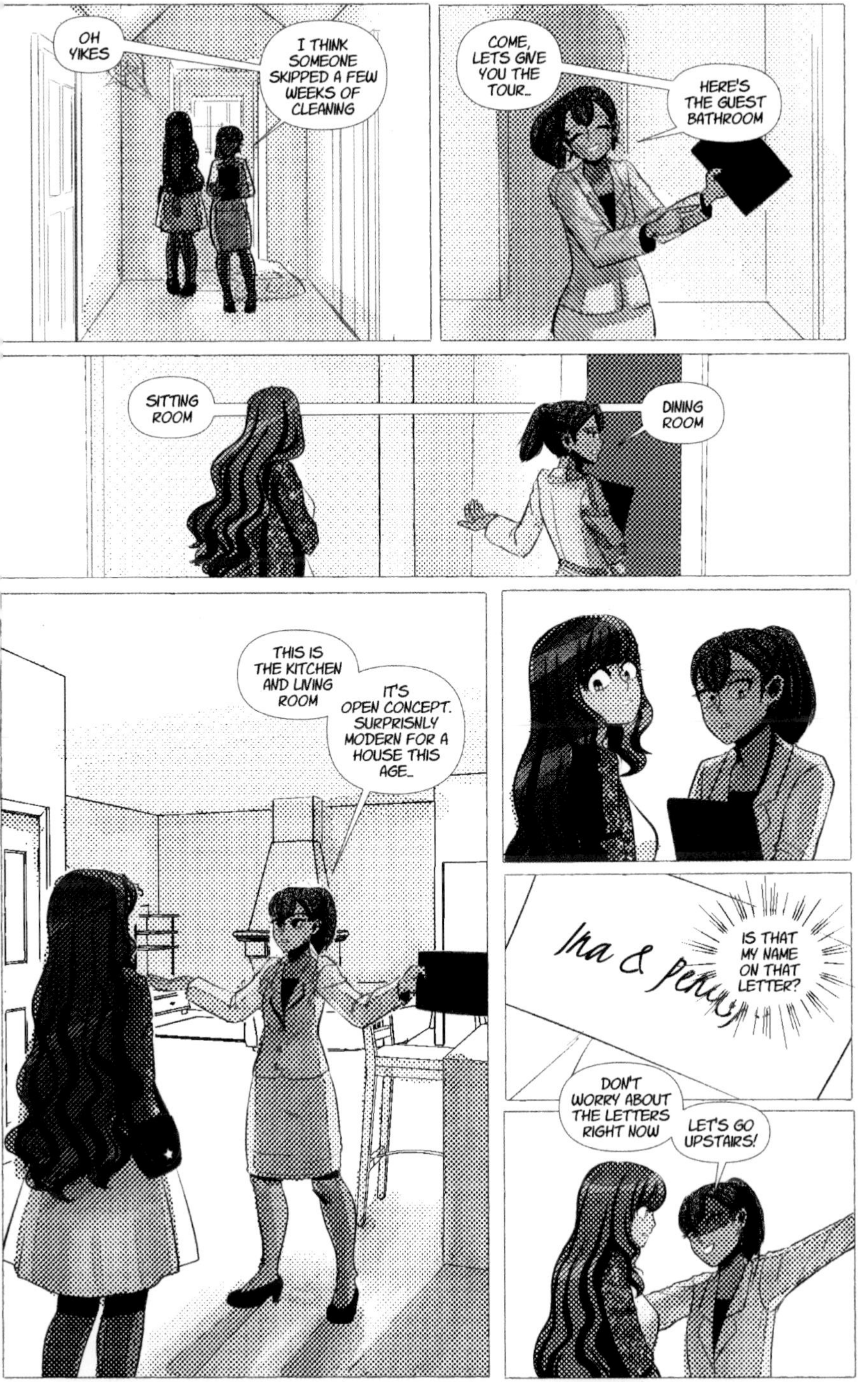
OH YIKES
I THINK SOMEONE SKIPPED A FEW WEEKS OF CLEANING
COME, LETS GIVE YOU THE TOUR...
HERE'S THE GUEST BATHROOM
SITTING ROOM
DINING ROOM
THIS IS THE KITCHEN AND LIVING ROOM
IT'S OPEN CONCEPT. SURPRISNLY MODERN FOR A HOUSE THIS AGE...
IS THAT MY NAME ON THAT LETTER?
DON'T WORRY ABOUT THE LETTERS RIGHT NOW
LET'S GO UPSTAIRS!

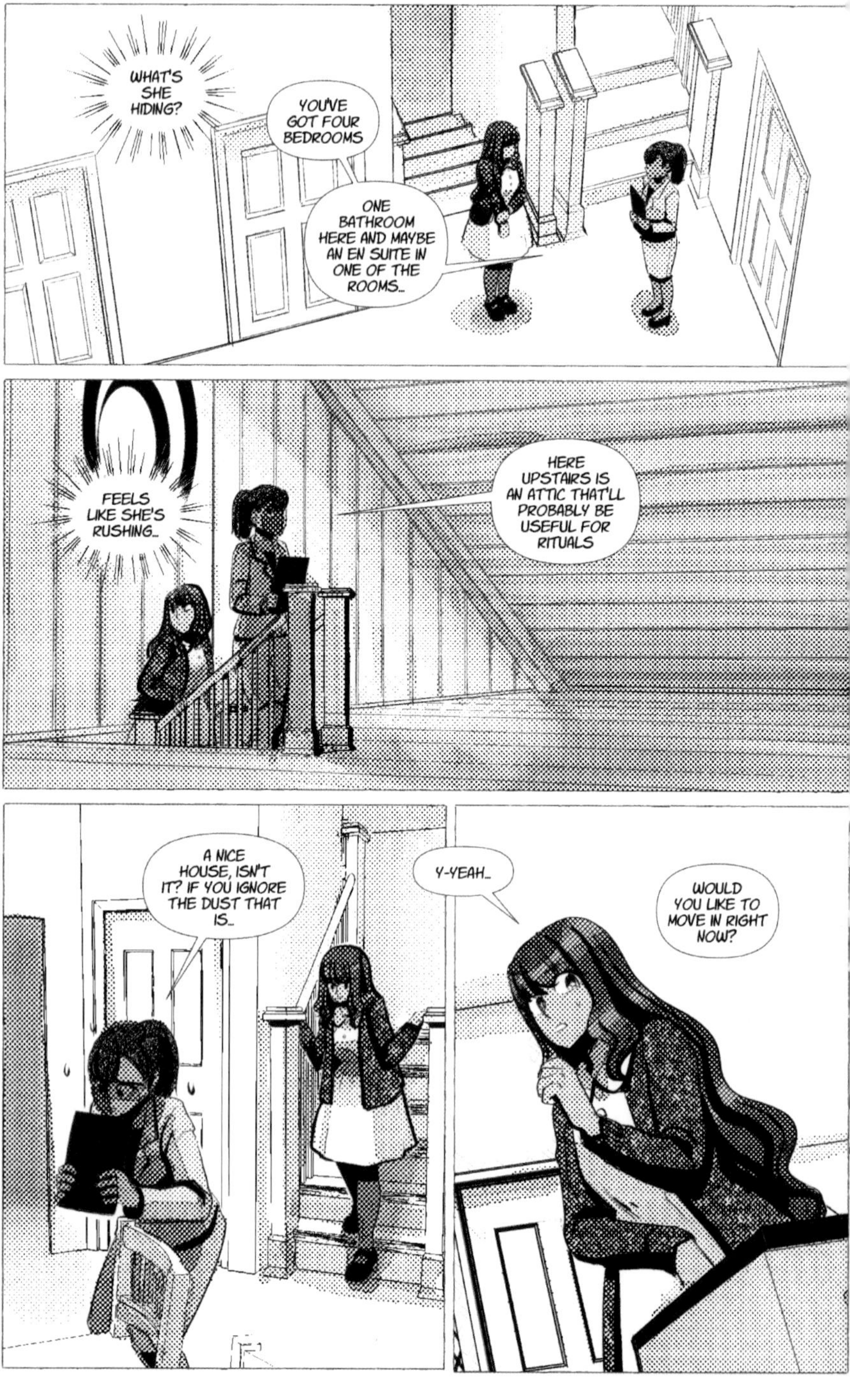
WHAT'S SHE HIDING?
YOU'VE GOT FOUR BEDROOMS
ONE BATHROOM HERE AND MAYBE AN EN SUITE IN ONE OF THE ROOMS...
FEELS LIKE SHE'S RUSHING...
HERE UPSTAIRS IS AN ATTIC THAT'LL PROBABLY BE USEFUL FOR RITUALS
A NICE HOUSE, ISN'T IT? IF YOU IGNORE THE DUST THAT IS...
Y-YEAH...
WOULD YOU LIKE TO MOVE IN RIGHT NOW?

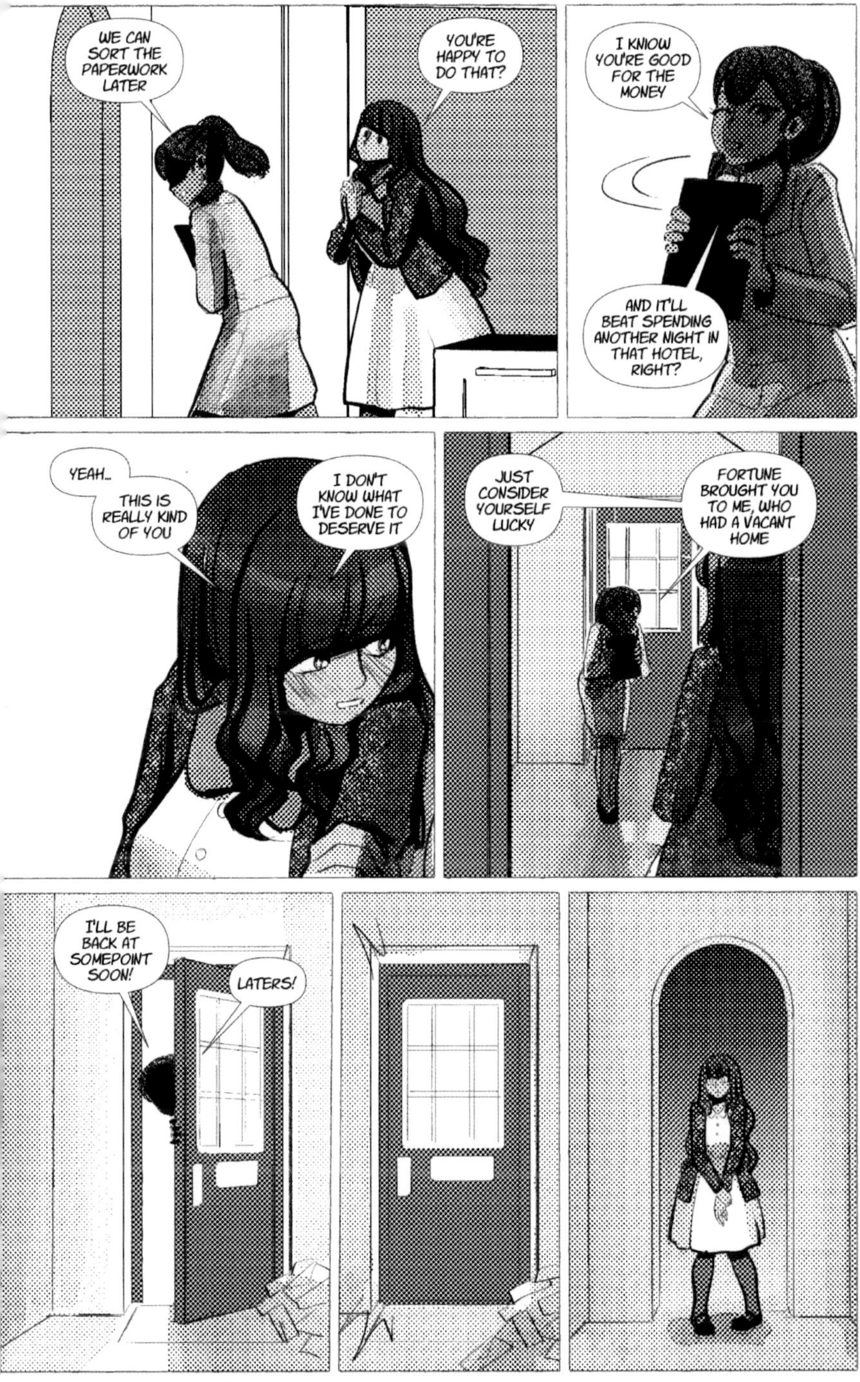
WE CAN SORT THE PAPERWORK LATER
YOU'RE HAPPY TO DO THAT?
I KNOW YOU'RE GOOD FOR THE MONEY
AND IT'LL BEAT SPENDING ANOTHER NIGHT IN THAT HOTEL, RIGHT?
YEAH...
THIS IS REALLY KIND OF YOU
I DON'T KNOW WHAT I'VE DONE TO DESERVE IT
JUST CONSIDER YOURSELF LUCKY
FORTUNE BROUGHT YOU TO ME, WHO HAD A VACANT HOME
I'LL BE BACK AT SOMEPOINT SOON!
LATERS!

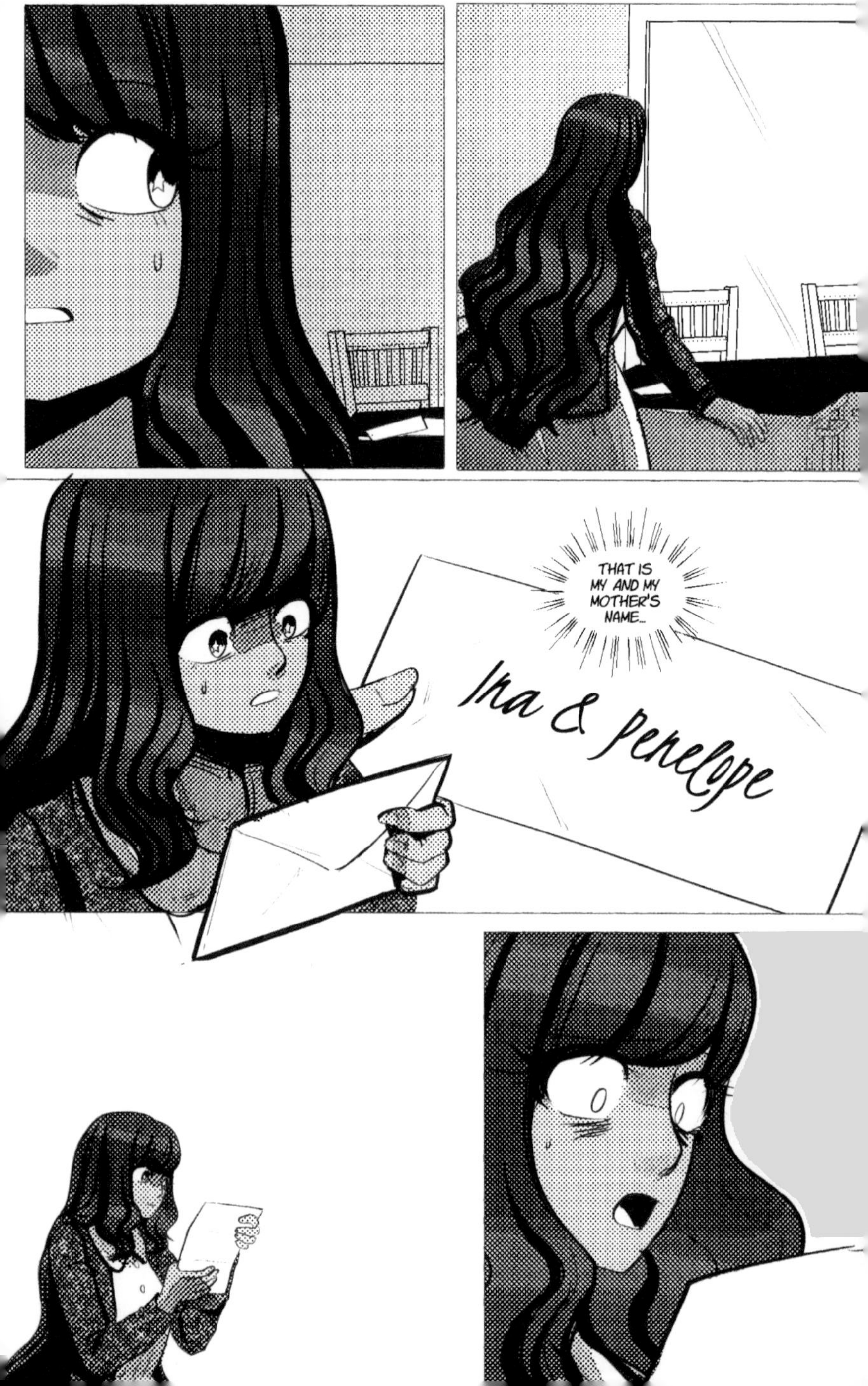
THAT IS MY AND MY MOTHER'S NAME...
Ina & Penelope

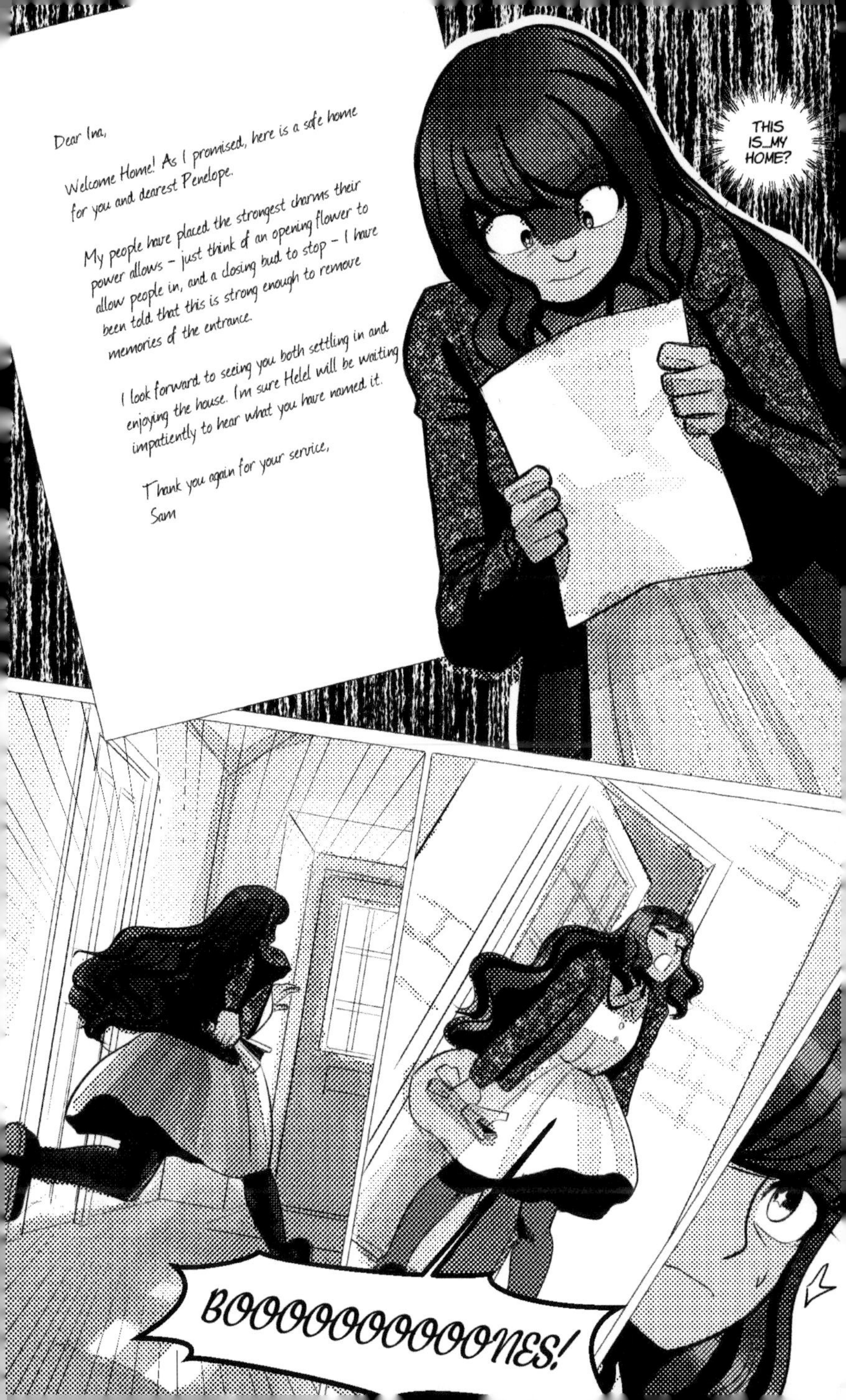

Dear Ina,
Welcome Home! As I promised, here is a safe home for you and dearest Penelope.
My people have placed the strongest charms their power allows - just think of an opening flower to allow people in, and a closing bud to stop - I have been told that this is strong enough to remove memories of the entrance.
I look forward to seeing you both settling in and enjoying the house. I'm sure Helel will be waiting impatiently to hear what you have named it.
Thank you again for your service,
Sam
THIS IS...MY HOME?
BOOOOOOOOOONES!

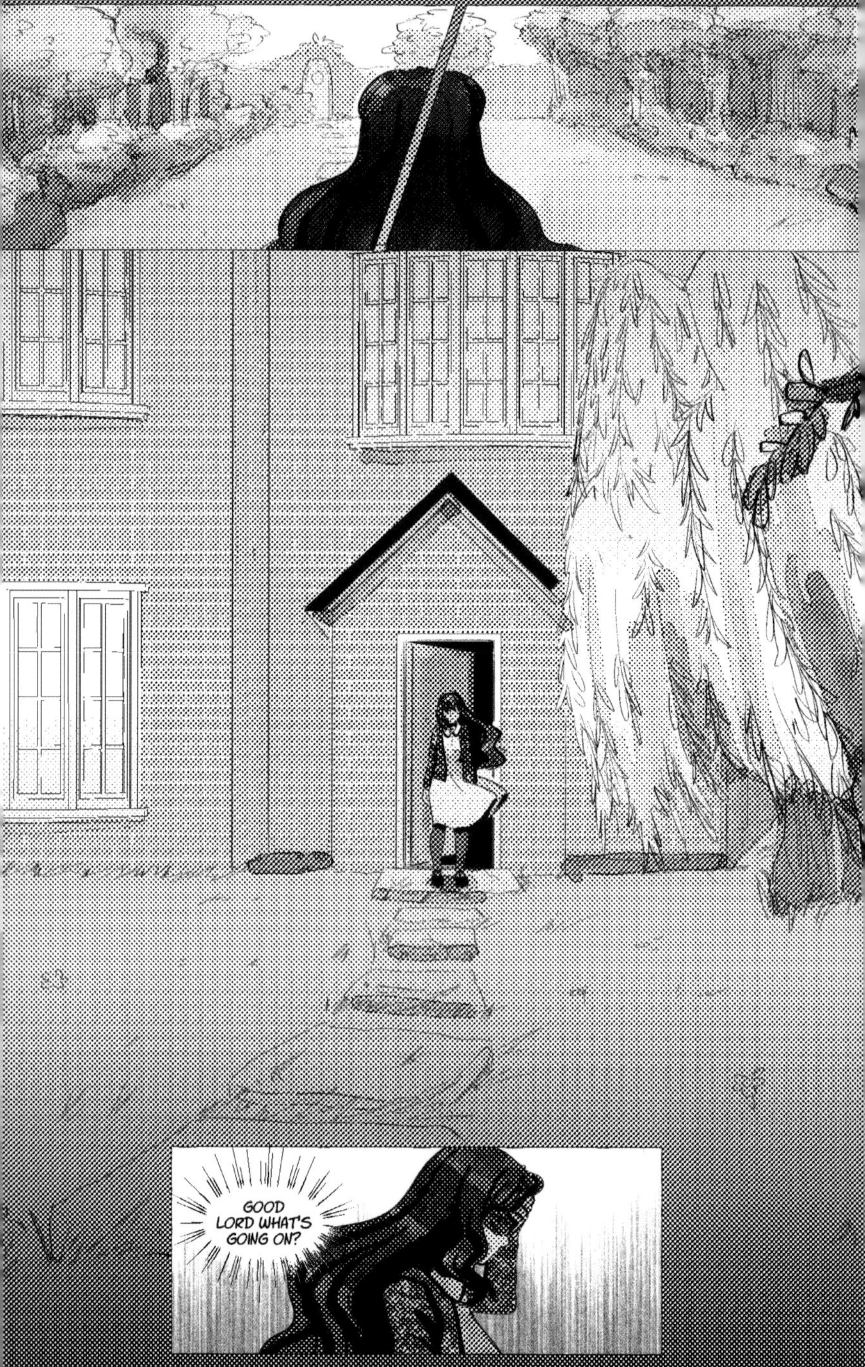
GOOD LORD WHAT'S GOING ON?

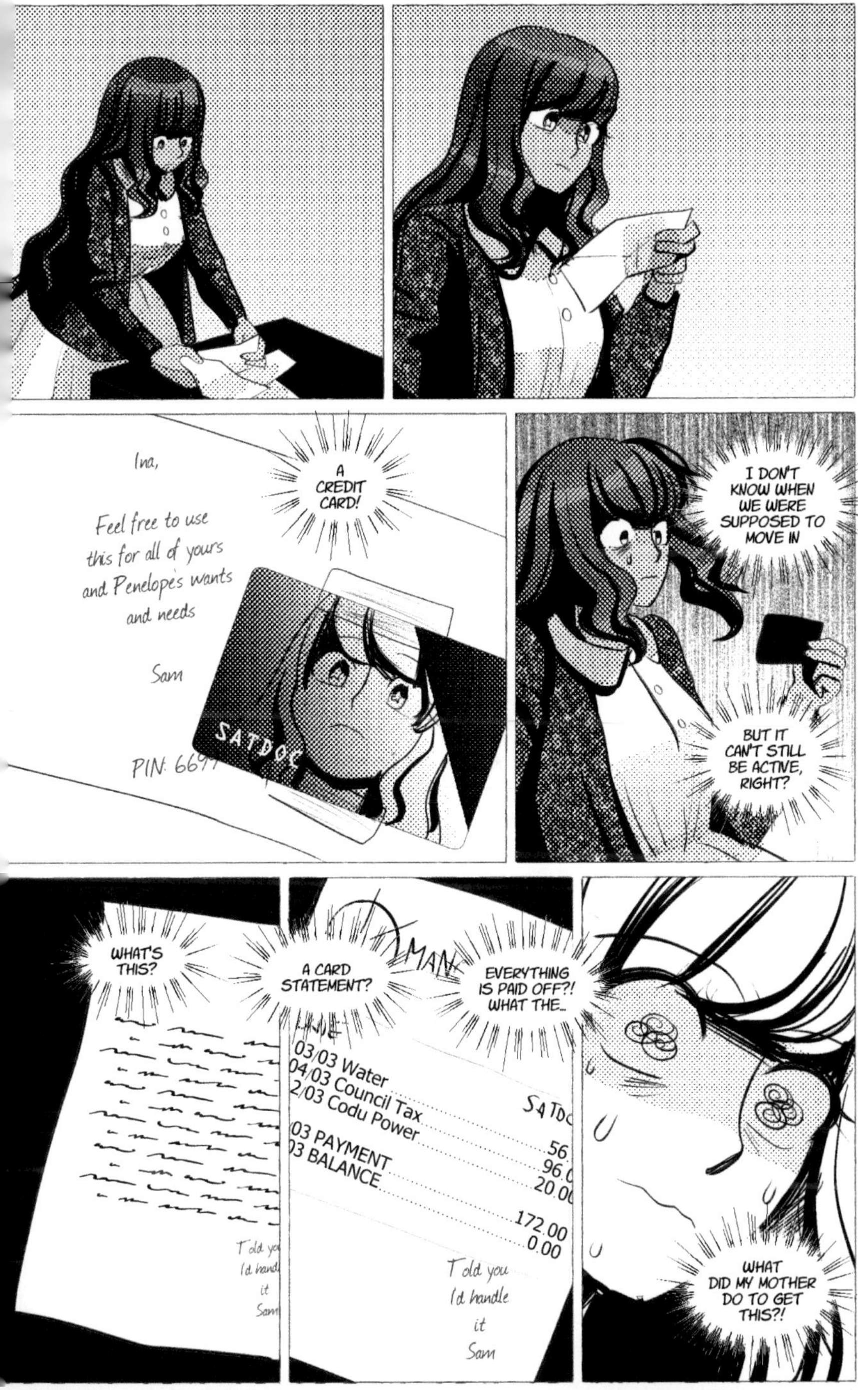
Ina,
Feel free to use this for all of yours and Penelope's wants and needs
Sam
PIN: 669
A CREDIT CARD!
SATDOC
I DON'T KNOW WHEN WE WERE SUPPOSED TO MOVE IN
BUT IT CAN'T STILL BE ACTIVE, RIGHT?
WHAT'S THIS?
Told you I'd handle it Sam
A CARD STATEMENT?
03/03 Water
04/03 Council Tax
2/03 Codu Power
03 PAYMENT
03 BALANCE
SATDO
56.
96.0
20.00
172.00
0.00
Told you I'd handle it Sam
EVERYTHING IS PAID OFF?! WHAT THE..
WHAT DID MY MOTHER DO TO GET THIS?!

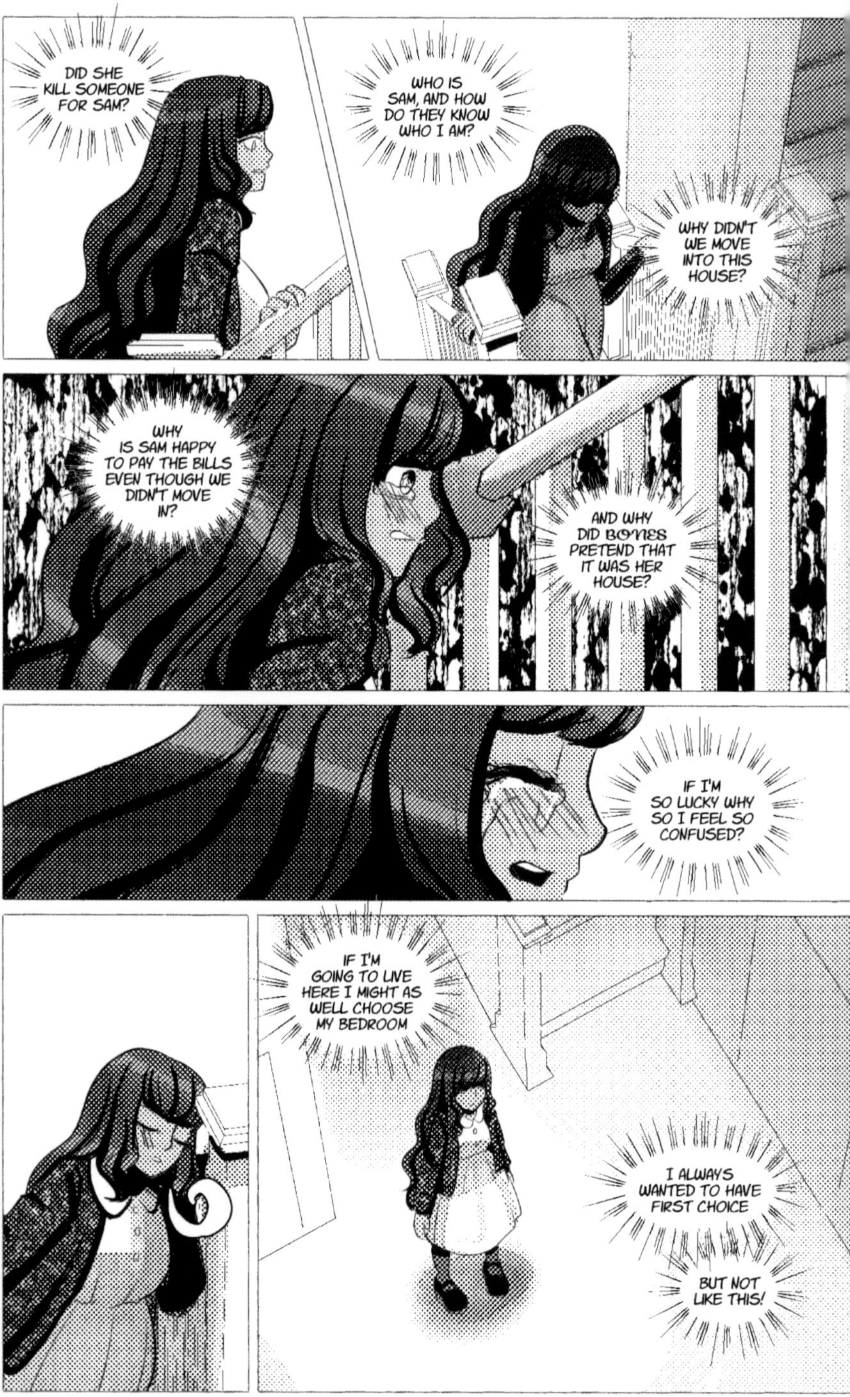
DID SHE KILL SOMEONE FOR SAM?
WHO IS SAM, AND HOW DO THEY KNOW WHO I AM?
WHY DIDN'T WE MOVE INTO THIS HOUSE?
WHY IS SAM HAPPY TO PAY THE BILLS EVEN THOUGH WE DIDN'T MOVE IN?
AND WHY DID BONES PRETEND THAT IT WAS HER HOUSE?
IF I'M SO LUCKY WHY SO I FEEL SO CONFUSED?
IF I'M GOING TO LIVE HERE I MIGHT AS WELL CHOOSE MY BEDROOM
I ALWAYS WANTED TO HAVE FIRST CHOICE
BUT NOT LIKE THIS!

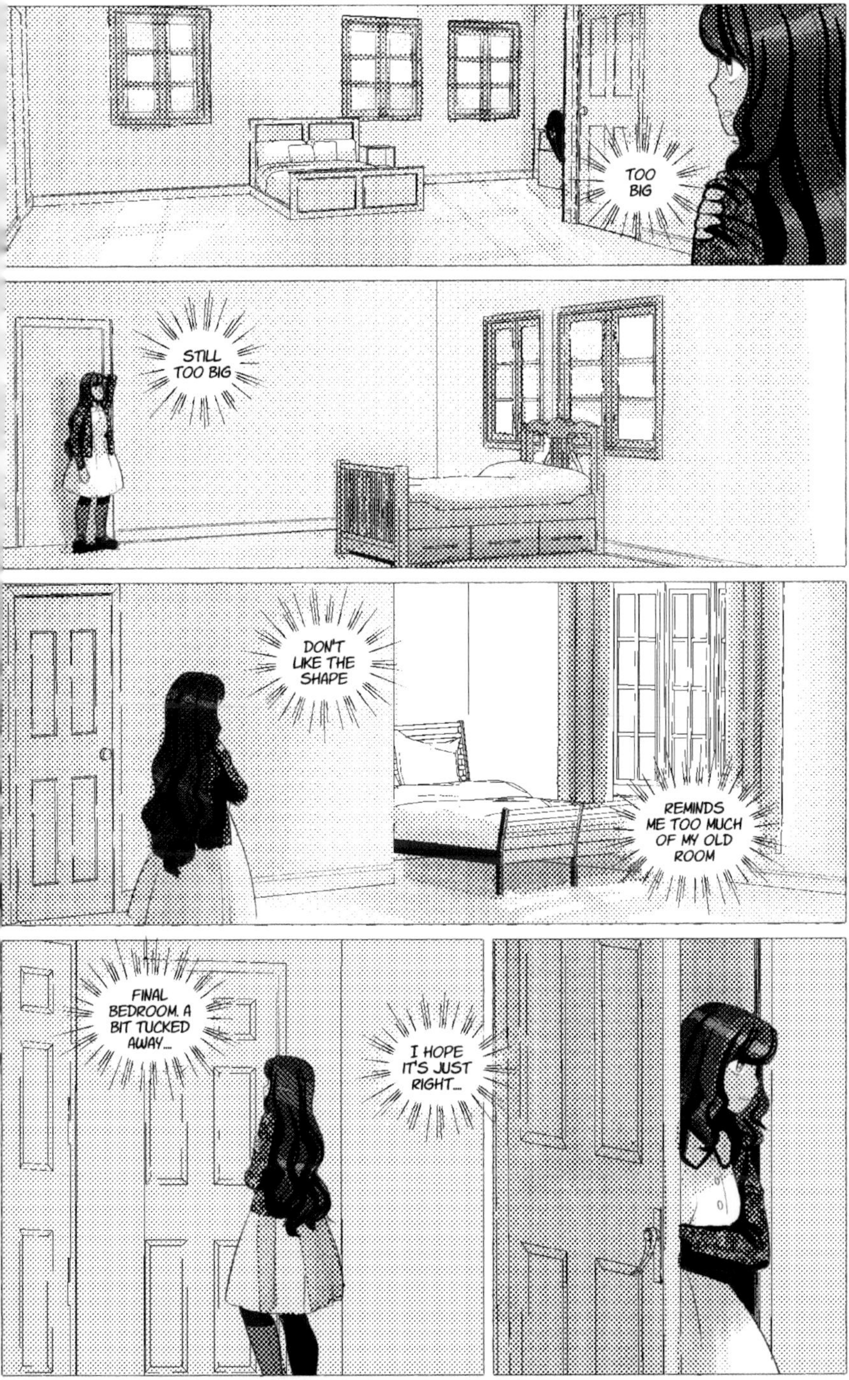
TOO BIG
STILL TOO BIG
DON'T LIKE THE SHAPE
REMINDS ME TOO MUCH OF MY OLD ROOM
FINAL BEDROOM. A BIT TUCKED AWAY...
I HOPE IT'S JUST RIGHT...

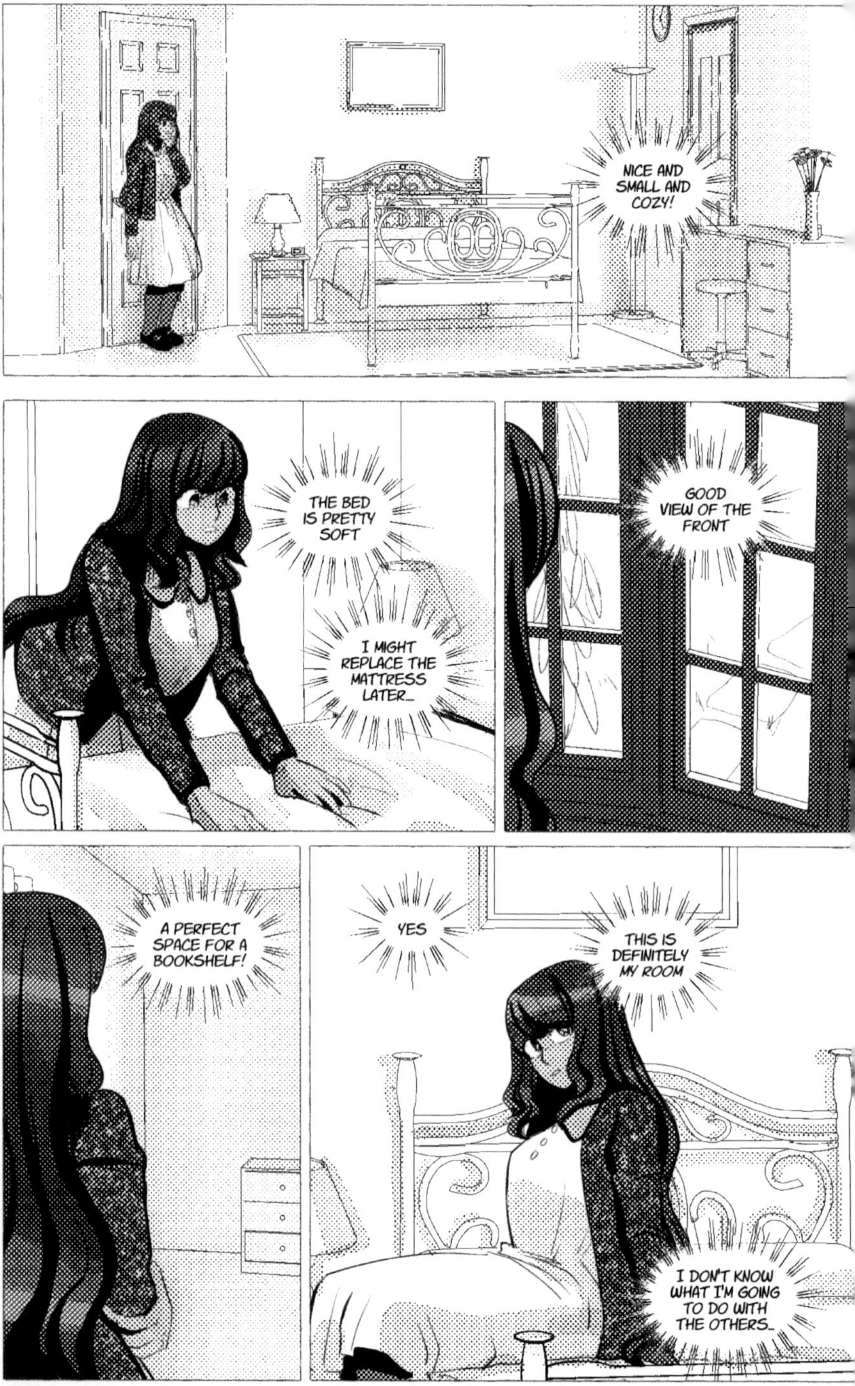
NICE AND SMALL AND COZY!
THE BED IS PRETTY SOFT
I MIGHT REPLACE THE MATTRESS LATER...
GOOD VIEW OF THE FRONT
A PERFECT SPACE FOR A BOOKSHELF!
YES
THIS IS DEFINITELY MY ROOM
I DON'T KNOW WHAT I'M GOING TO DO WITH THE OTHERS...

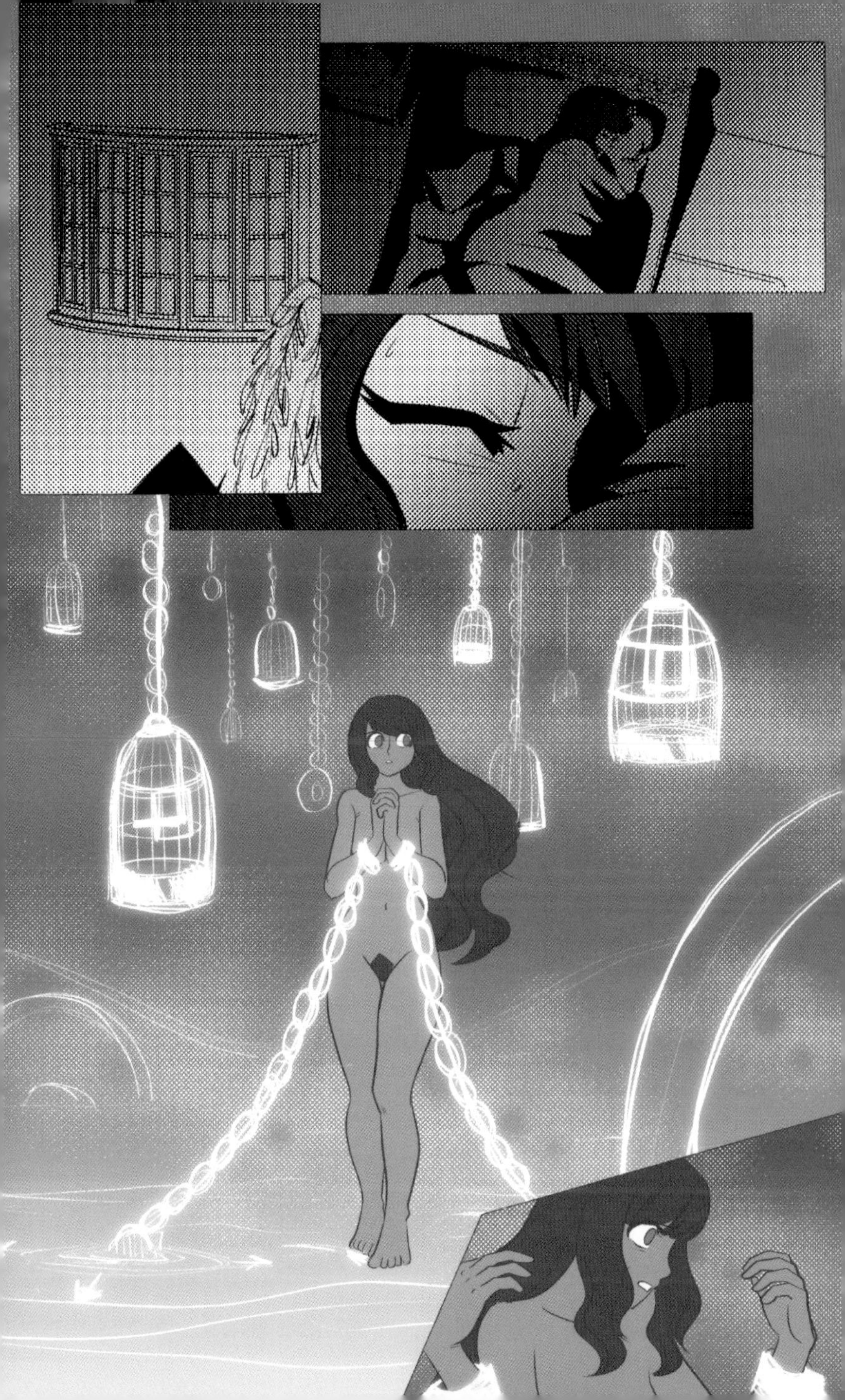

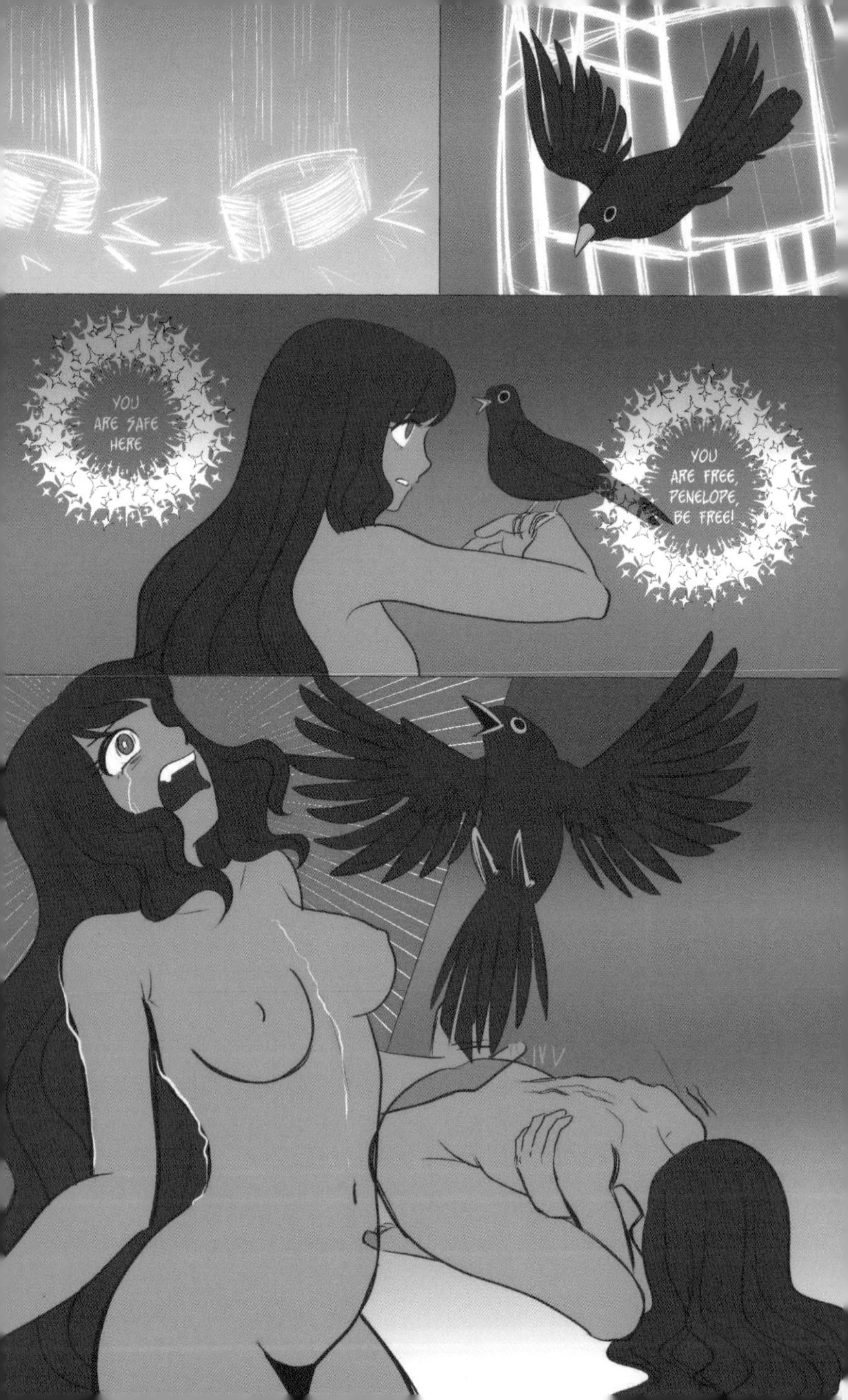
YOU ARE SAFE HERE
YOU ARE FREE, PENELOPE, BE FREE!

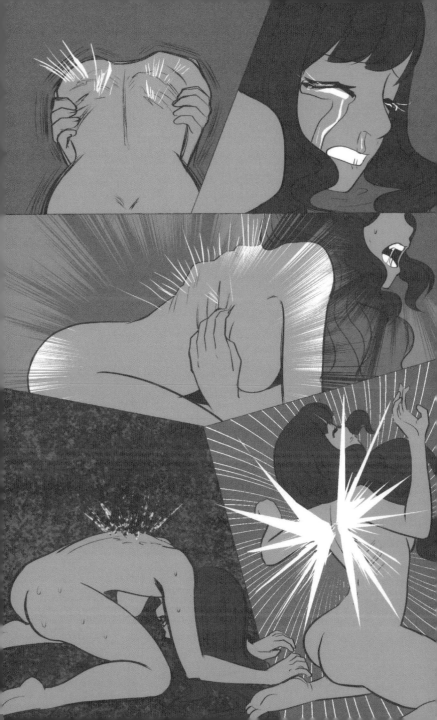

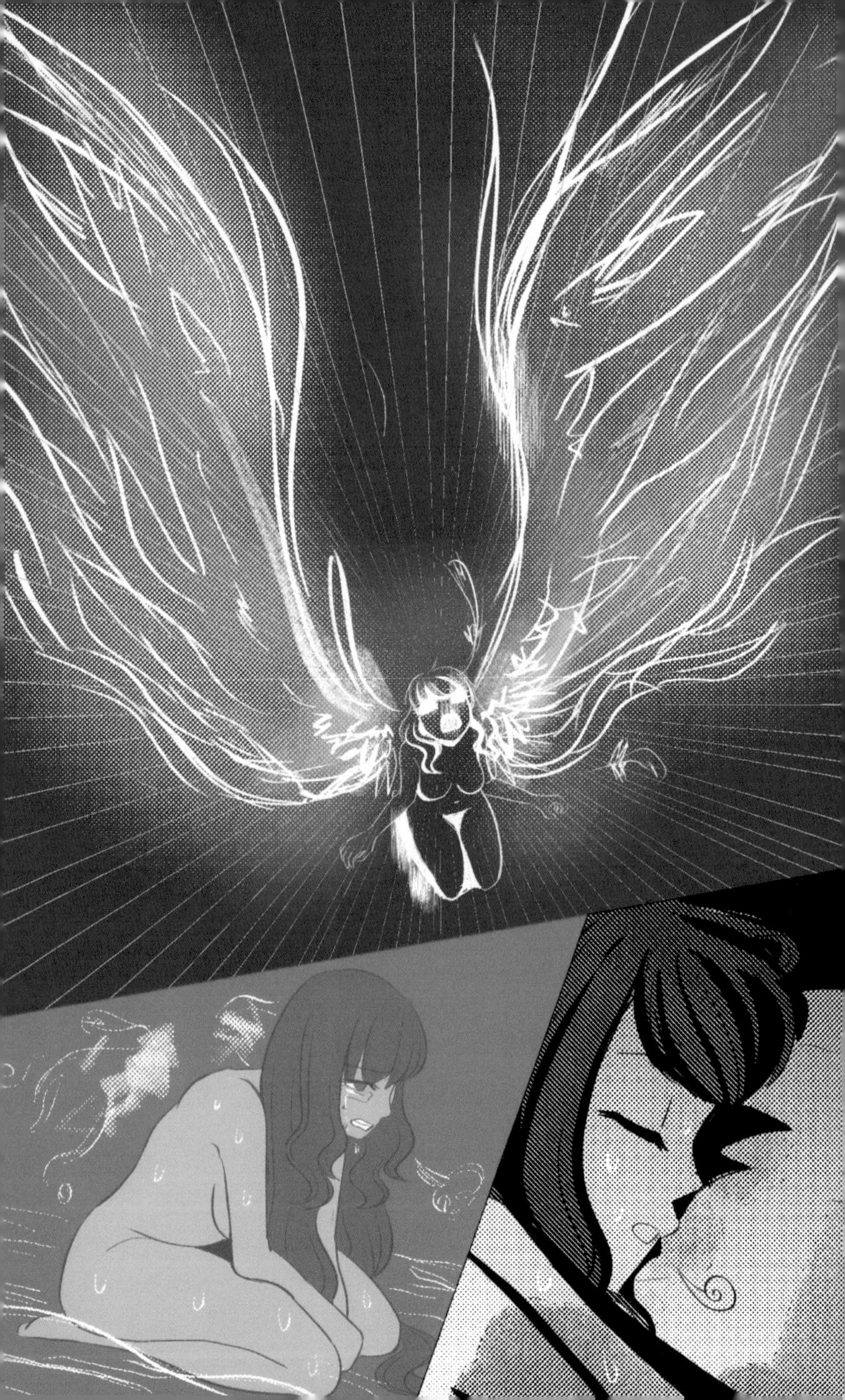

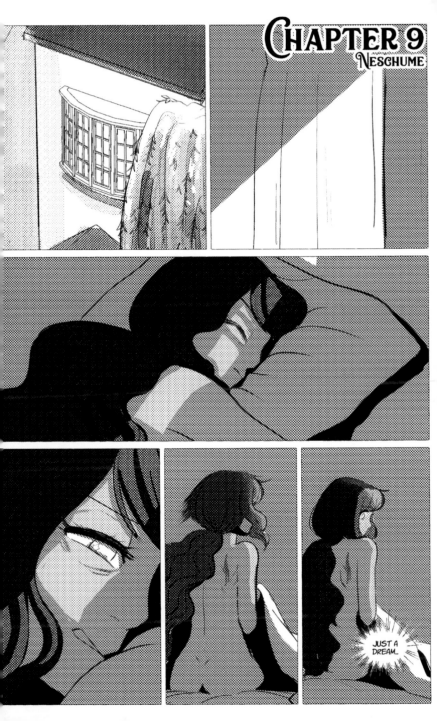

CHAPTER 9
NESCHUME

JUST A DREAM...

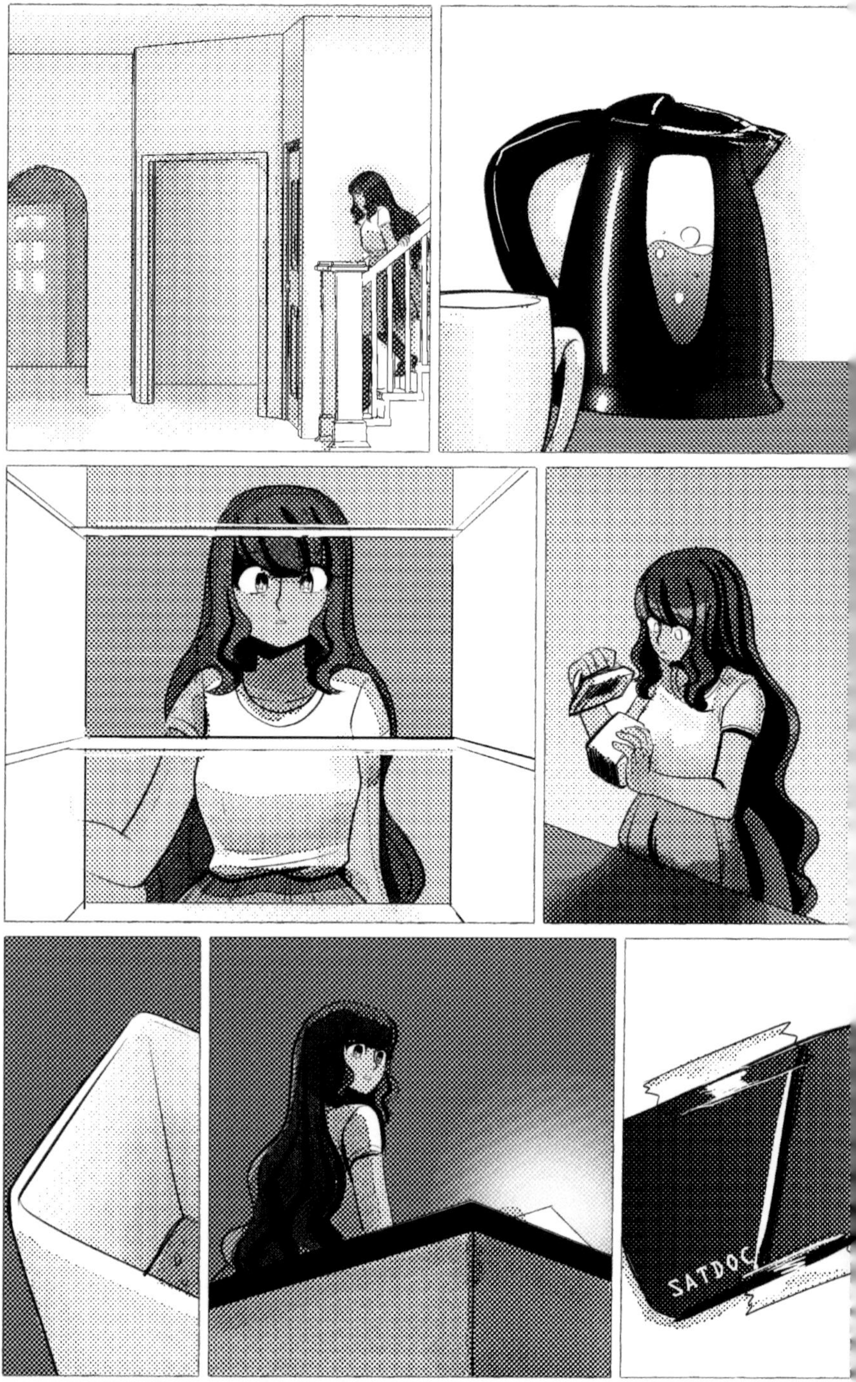
SATDOC

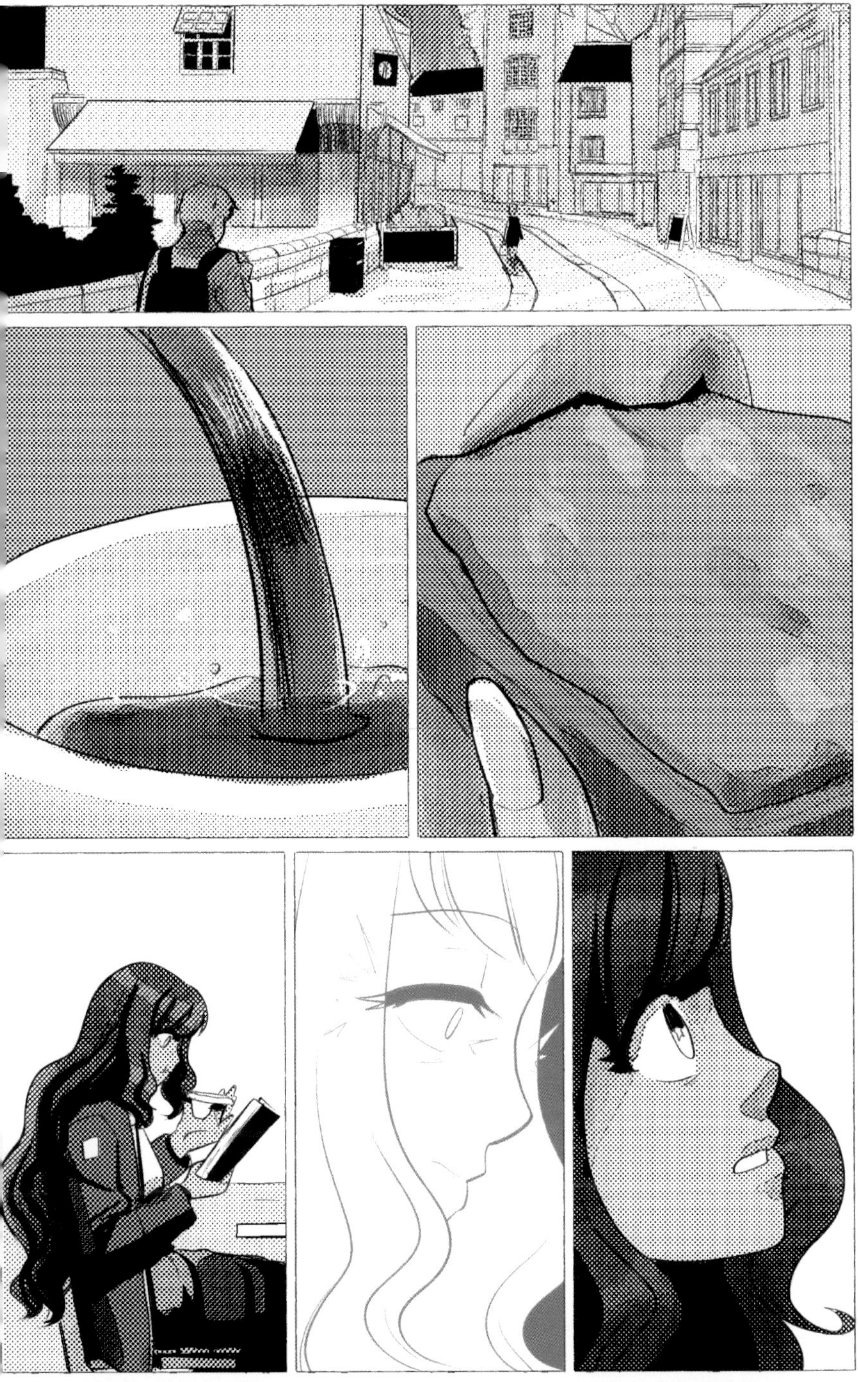

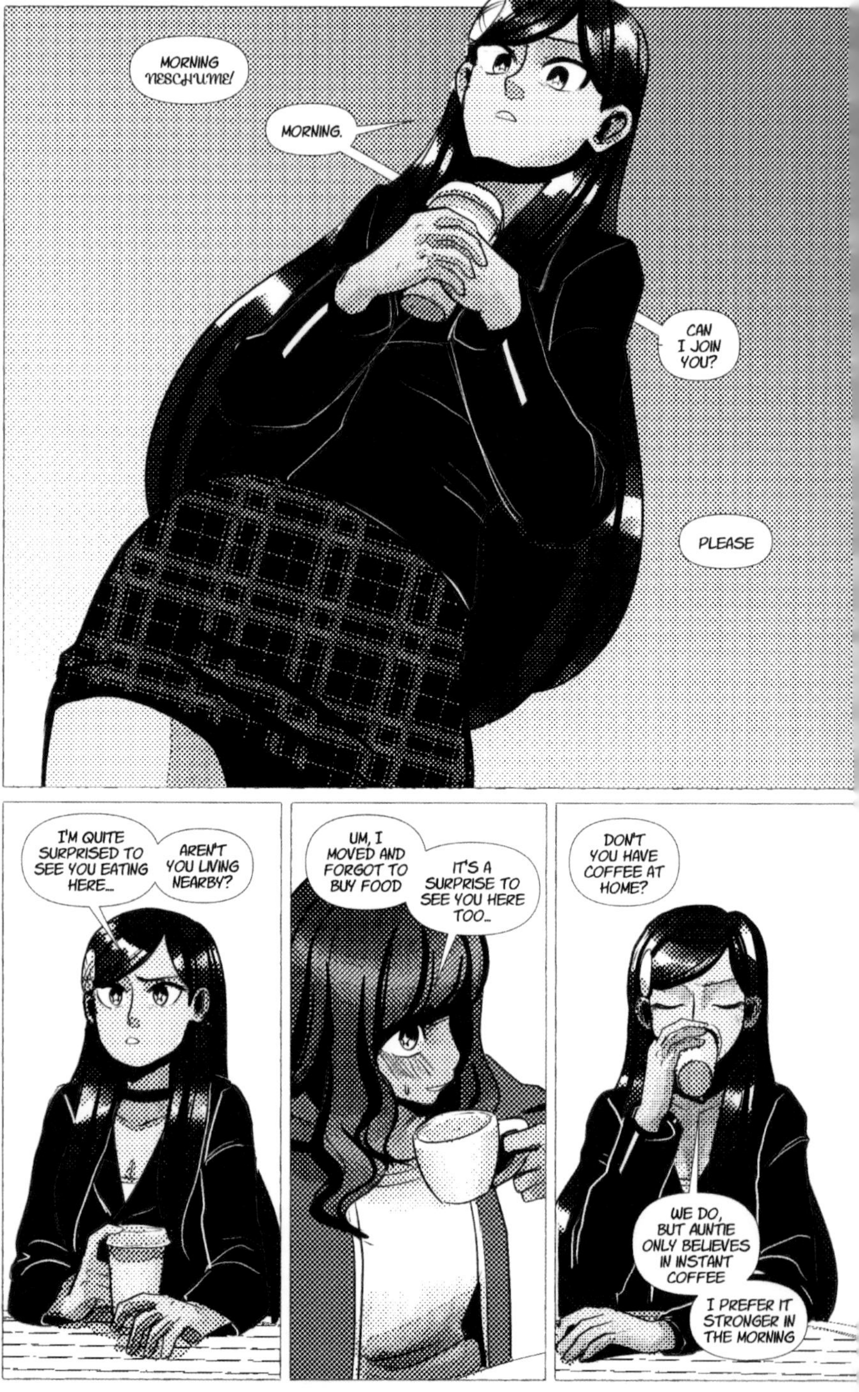
MORNING NESCHUME!
MORNING.
CAN I JOIN YOU?
PLEASE
I'M QUITE SURPRISED TO SEE YOU EATING HERE...
AREN'T YOU LIVING NEARBY?
UM, I MOVED AND FORGOT TO BUY FOOD
IT'S A SURPRISE TO SEE YOU HERE TOO...
DON'T YOU HAVE COFFEE AT HOME?
WE DO, BUT AUNTIE ONLY BELIEVES IN INSTANT COFFEE
I PREFER IT STRONGER IN THE MORNING

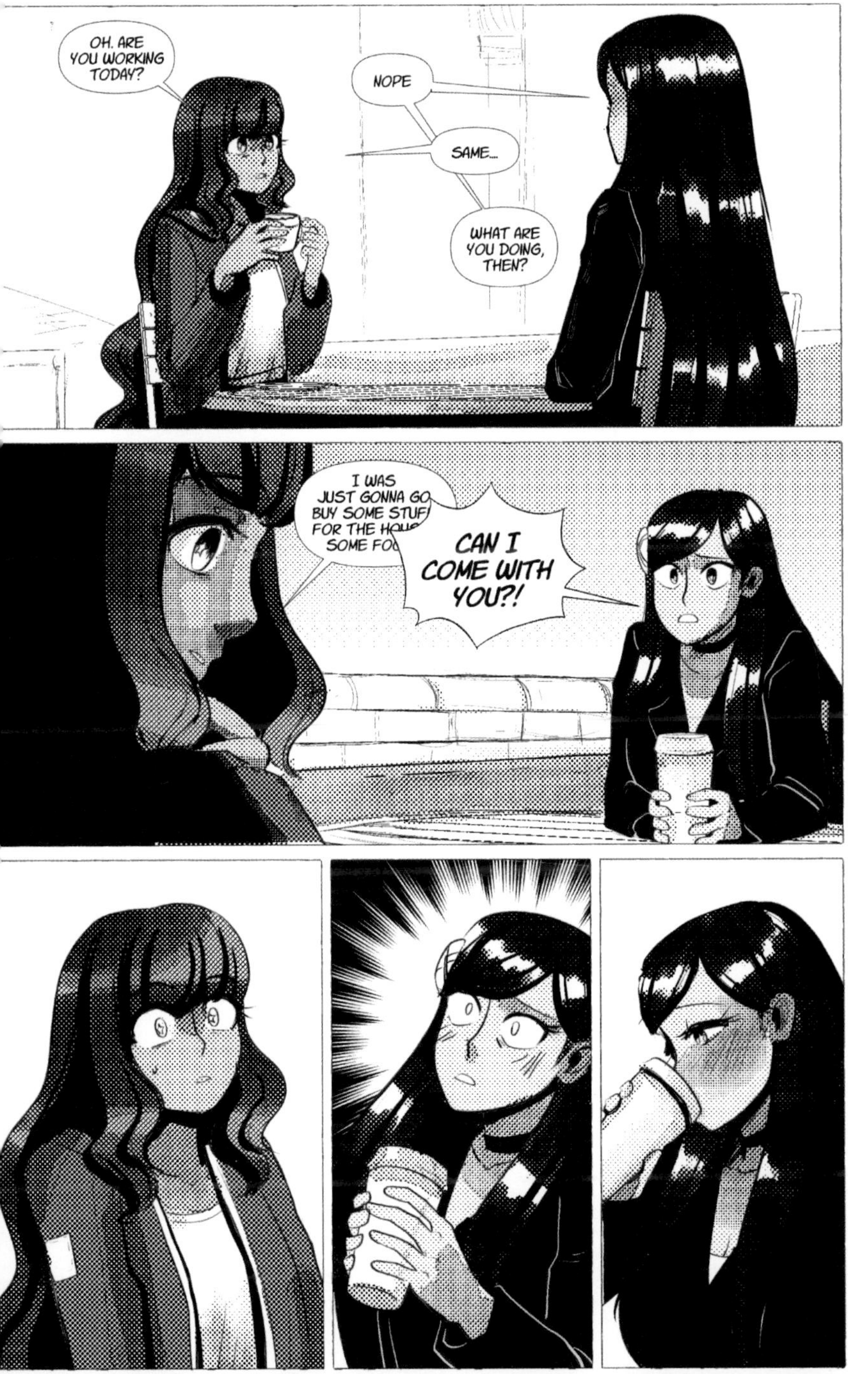
OH. ARE YOU WORKING TODAY?
NOPE
SAME...
WHAT ARE YOU DOING, THEN?
I WAS JUST GONNA GO BUY SOME STUF FOR THE HOU SOME FO
CAN I COME WITH YOU?!

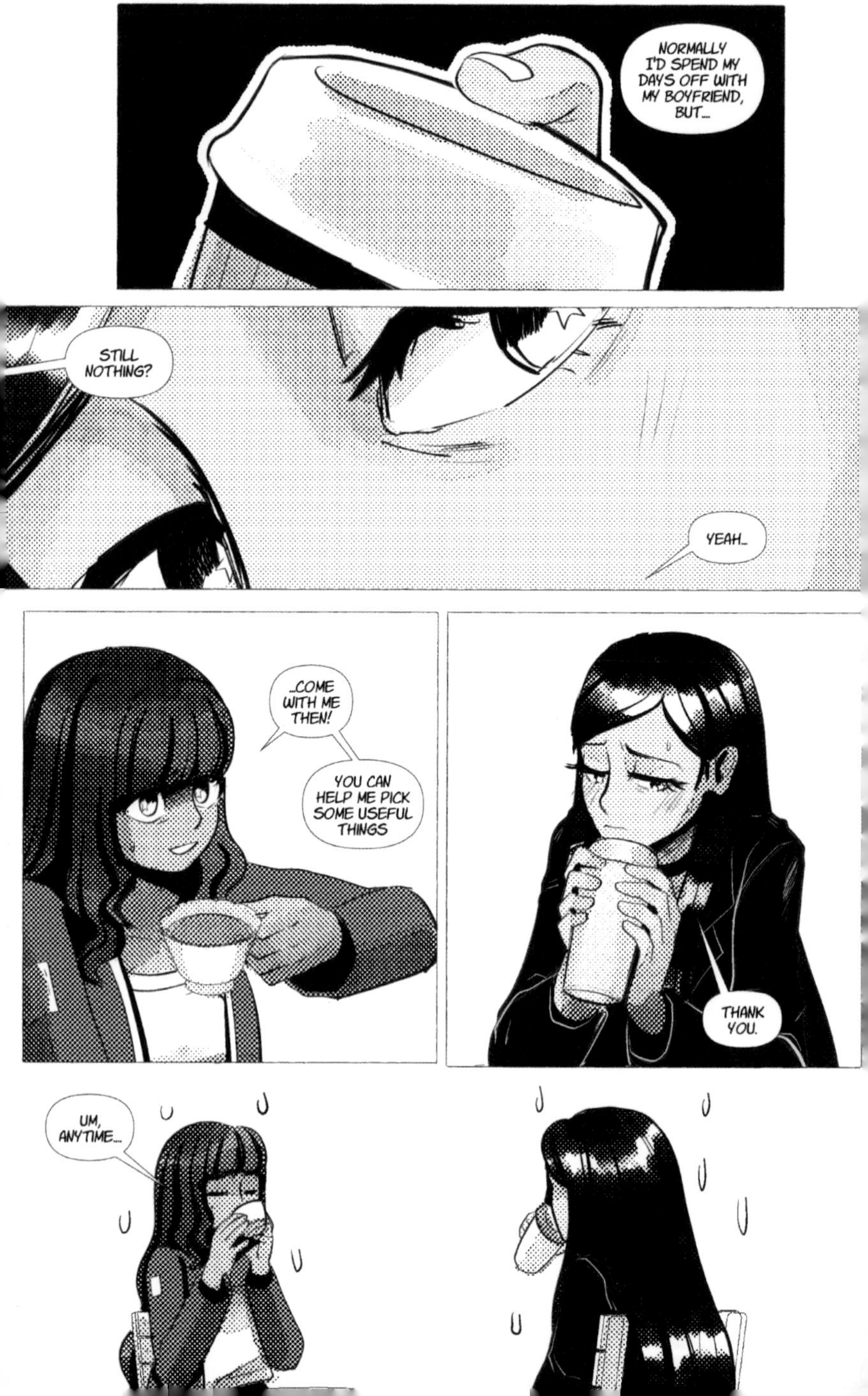
NORMALLY I'D SPEND MY DAYS OFF WITH MY BOYFRIEND, BUT....
STILL NOTHING?
YEAH..
..COME WITH ME THEN!
YOU CAN HELP ME PICK SOME USEFUL THINGS
THANK YOU.
UM, ANYTIME....

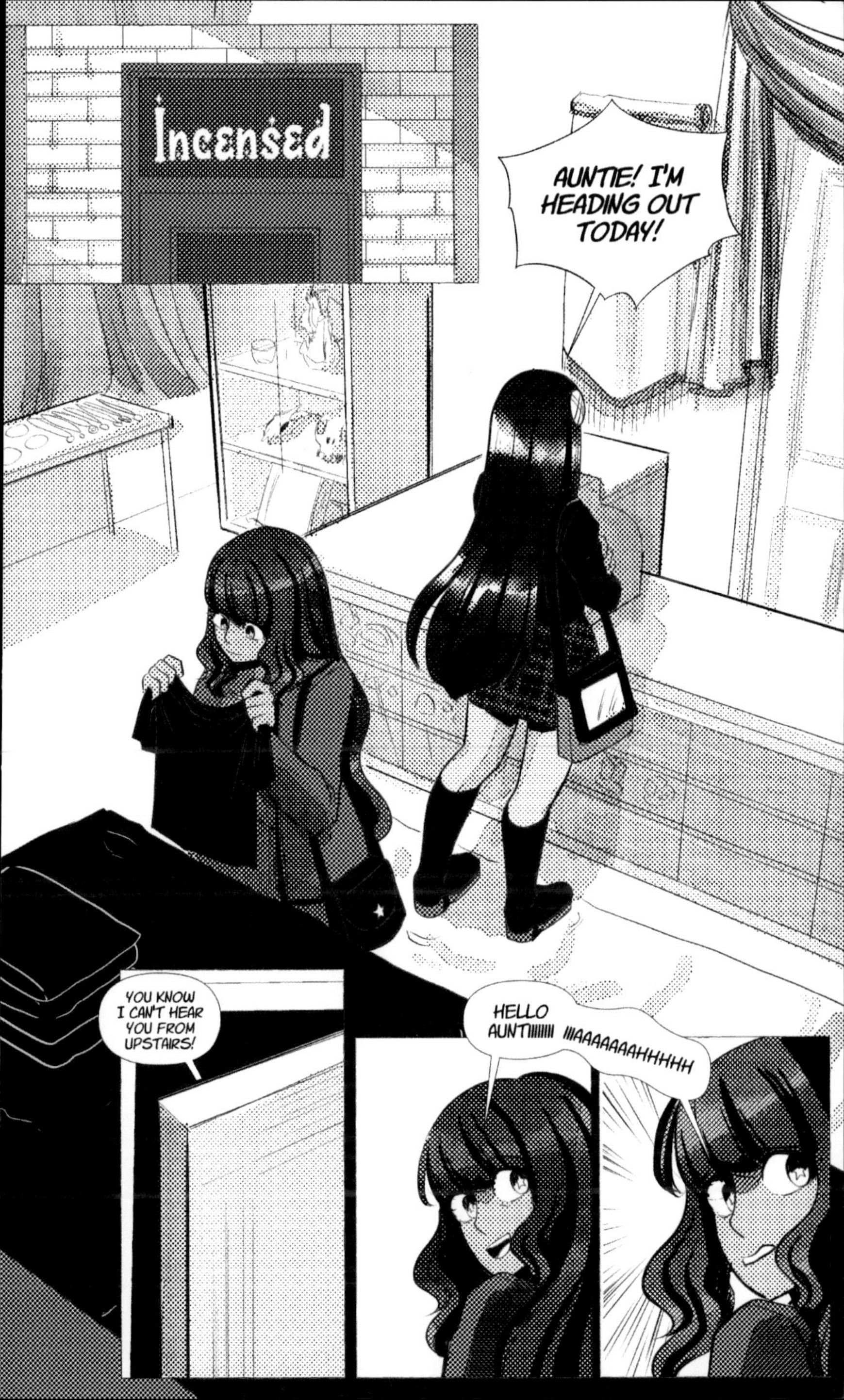
Incensed
AUNTIE! I'M HEADING OUT TODAY!
YOU KNOW I CAN'T HEAR YOU FROM UPSTAIRS!
HELLO AUNTIIIIIIII IIIIAAAAAAAHHHHH

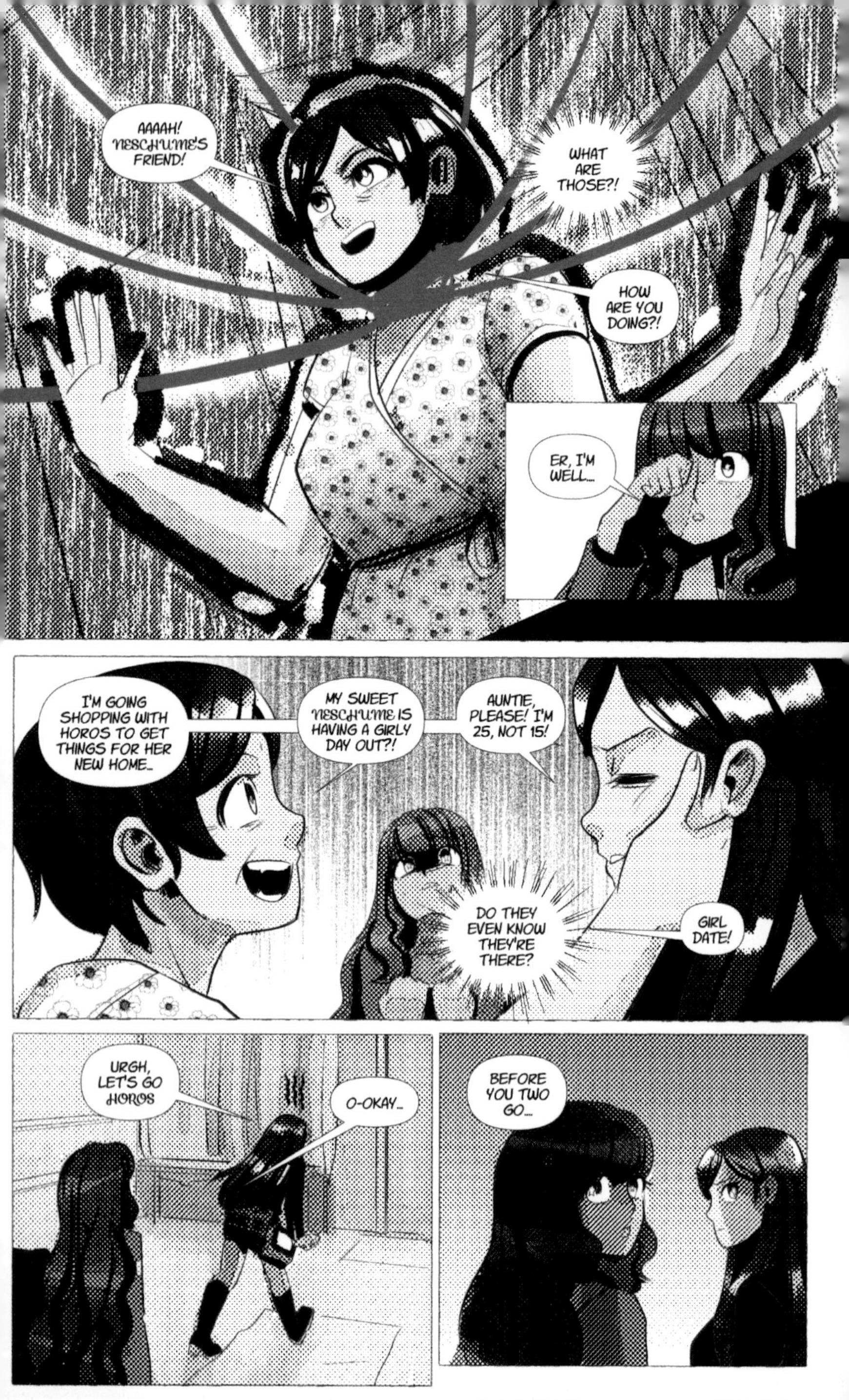
AAAAH! NESCHUME'S FRIEND!
WHAT ARE THOSE?!
HOW ARE YOU DOING?!
ER, I'M WELL...
I'M GOING SHOPPING WITH HOROS TO GET THINGS FOR HER NEW HOME..
MY SWEET NESCHUME IS HAVING A GIRLY DAY OUT?!
AUNTIE, PLEASE! I'M 25, NOT 15!
DO THEY EVEN KNOW THEY'RE THERE?
GIRL DATE!
URGH, LET'S GO HOROS
O-OKAY..
BEFORE YOU TWO GO...

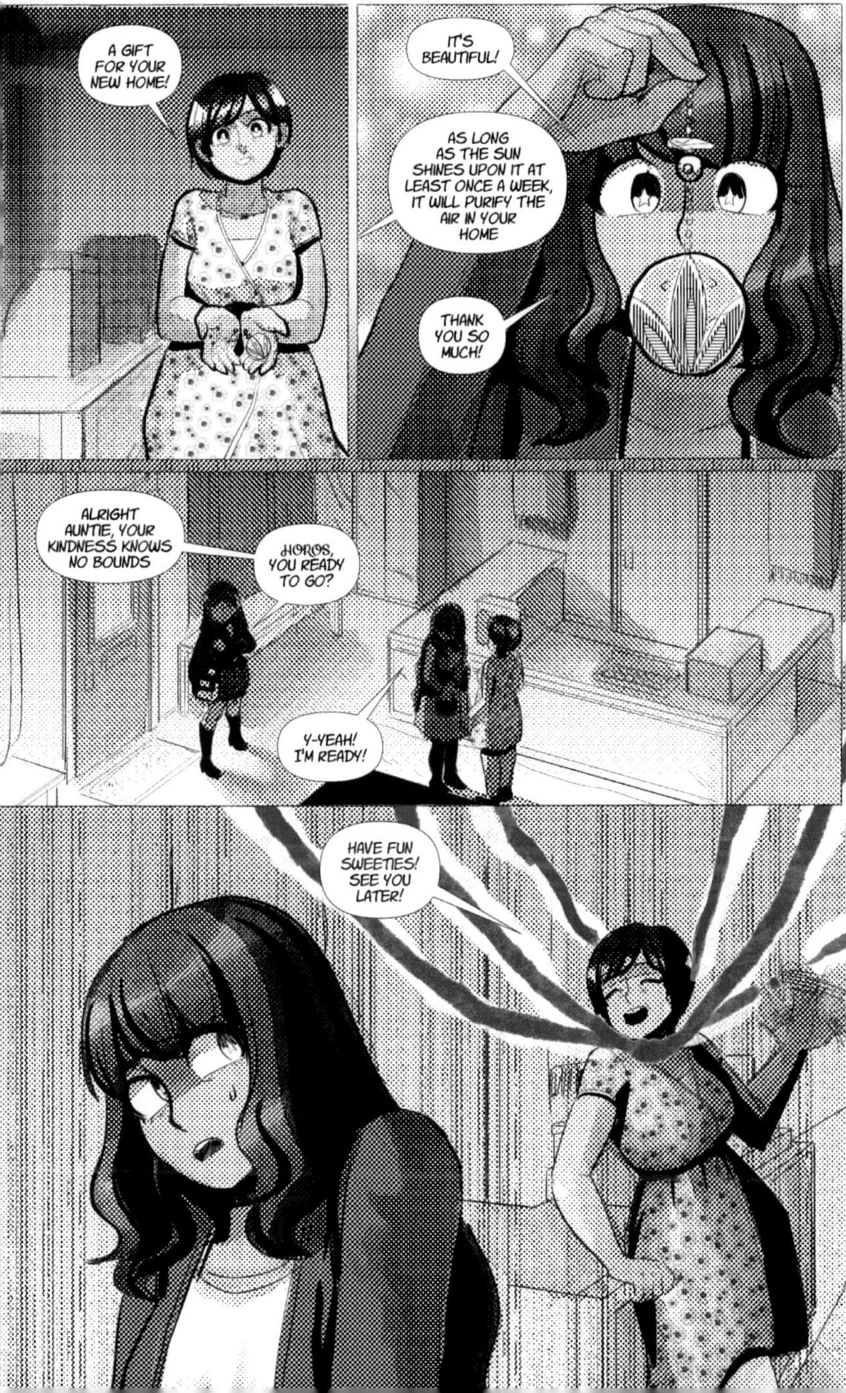
A GIFT FOR YOUR NEW HOME!
IT'S BEAUTIFUL!
AS LONG AS THE SUN SHINES UPON IT AT LEAST ONCE A WEEK, IT WILL PURIFY THE AIR IN YOUR HOME
THANK YOU SO MUCH!
ALRIGHT AUNTIE, YOUR KINDNESS KNOWS NO BOUNDS
HOROS, YOU READY TO GO?
Y-YEAH! I'M READY!
HAVE FUN SWEETIES! SEE YOU LATER!

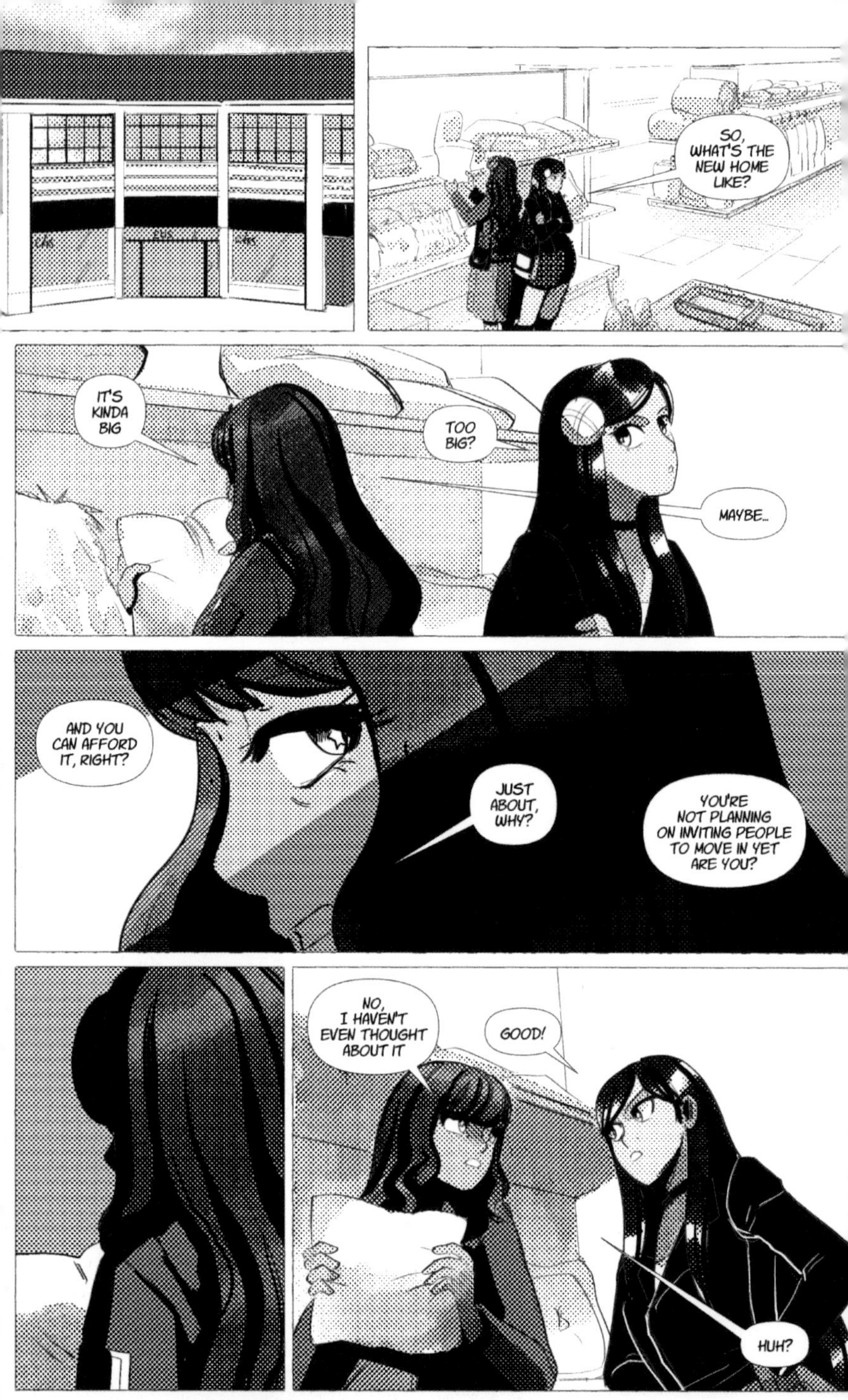
SO, WHAT'S THE NEW HOME LIKE?
IT'S KINDA BIG
TOO BIG?
MAYBE...
AND YOU CAN AFFORD IT, RIGHT?
JUST ABOUT, WHY?
YOU'RE NOT PLANNING ON INVITING PEOPLE TO MOVE IN YET ARE YOU?
NO, I HAVEN'T EVEN THOUGHT ABOUT IT
GOOD!
HUH?

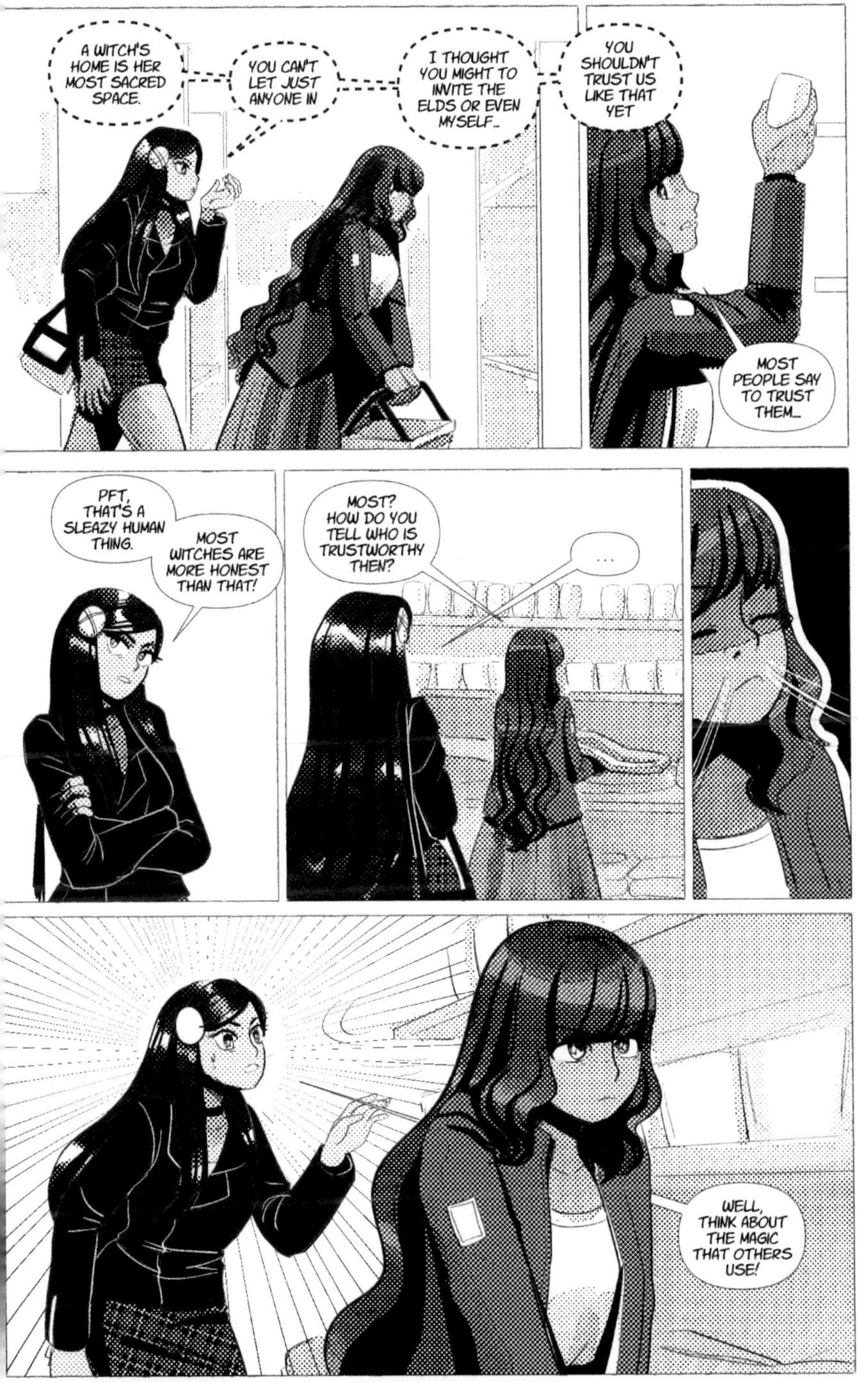
A WITCH'S HOME IS HER MOST SACRED SPACE.
YOU CAN'T LET JUST ANYONE IN
I THOUGHT YOU MIGHT TO INVITE THE ELDS OR EVEN MYSELF...
YOU SHOULDN'T TRUST US LIKE THAT YET
MOST PEOPLE SAY TO TRUST THEM...
PFT, THAT'S A SLEAZY HUMAN THING.
MOST WITCHES ARE MORE HONEST THAN THAT!
MOST? HOW DO YOU TELL WHO IS TRUSTWORTHY THEN?
...
WELL, THINK ABOUT THE MAGIC THAT OTHERS USE!

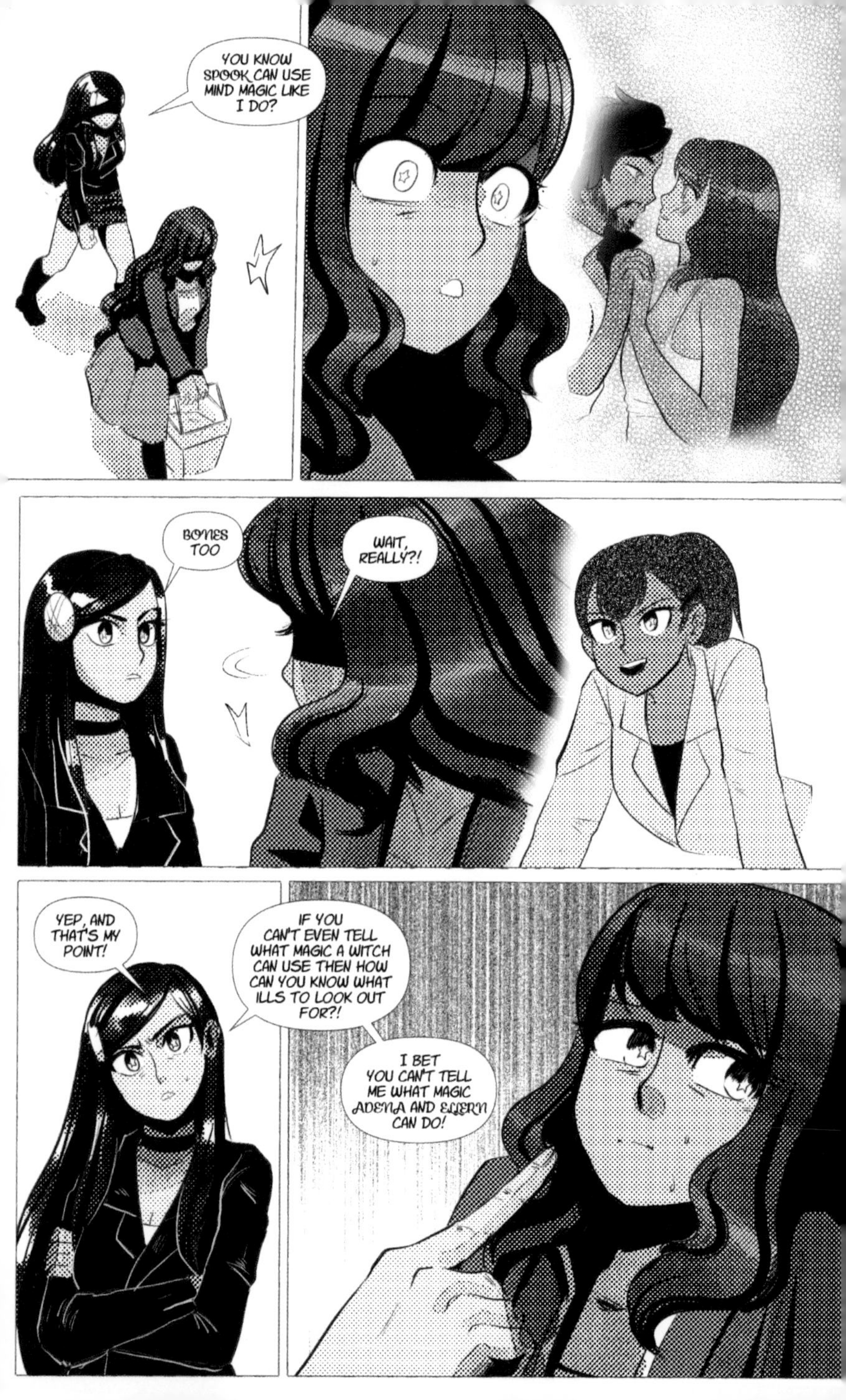
YOU KNOW SPOOK CAN USE MIND MAGIC LIKE I DO?
BONES TOO
WAIT, REALLY?!
YEP, AND THAT'S MY POINT!
IF YOU CAN'T EVEN TELL WHAT MAGIC A WITCH CAN USE THEN HOW CAN YOU KNOW WHAT ILLS TO LOOK OUT FOR?!
I BET YOU CAN'T TELL ME WHAT MAGIC ADENA AND ELLERN CAN DO!

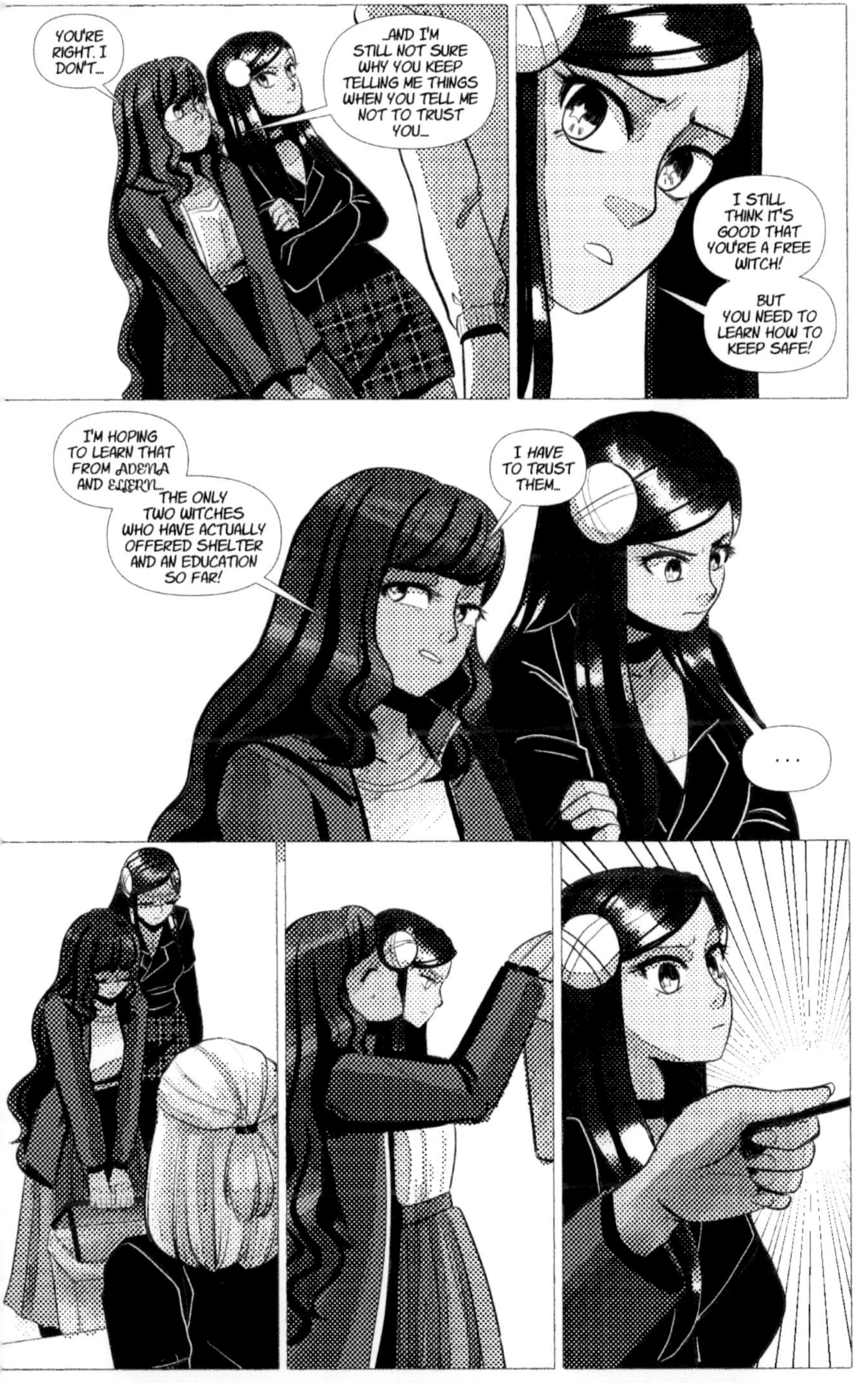
YOU'RE RIGHT. I DON'T...
...AND I'M STILL NOT SURE WHY YOU KEEP TELLING ME THINGS WHEN YOU TELL ME NOT TO TRUST YOU...
I STILL THINK IT'S GOOD THAT YOU'RE A FREE WITCH!
BUT YOU NEED TO LEARN HOW TO KEEP SAFE!
I'M HOPING TO LEARN THAT FROM ADENA AND ELLERN...
THE ONLY TWO WITCHES WHO HAVE ACTUALLY OFFERED SHELTER AND AN EDUCATION SO FAR!
I HAVE TO TRUST THEM...
...

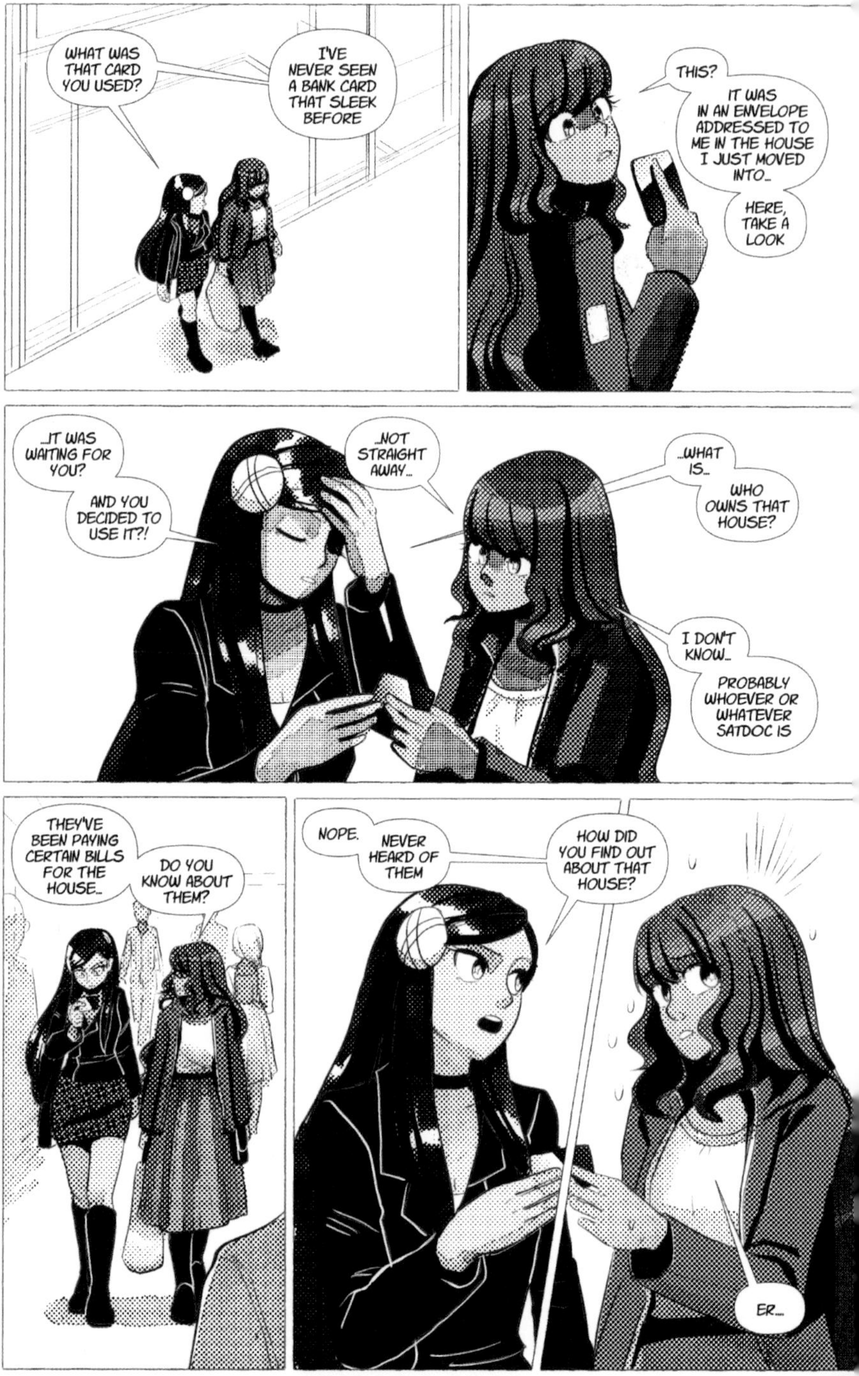
WHAT WAS THAT CARD YOU USED?
I'VE NEVER SEEN A BANK CARD THAT SLEEK BEFORE
THIS?
IT WAS IN AN ENVELOPE ADDRESSED TO ME IN THE HOUSE I JUST MOVED INTO...
HERE, TAKE A LOOK
...IT WAS WAITING FOR YOU?
AND YOU DECIDED TO USE IT?!
...NOT STRAIGHT AWAY...
...WHAT IS...
WHO OWNS THAT HOUSE?
I DON'T KNOW...
PROBABLY WHOEVER OR WHATEVER SATDOC IS
THEY'VE BEEN PAYING CERTAIN BILLS FOR THE HOUSE...
DO YOU KNOW ABOUT THEM?
NOPE.
NEVER HEARD OF THEM
HOW DID YOU FIND OUT ABOUT THAT HOUSE?
ER...

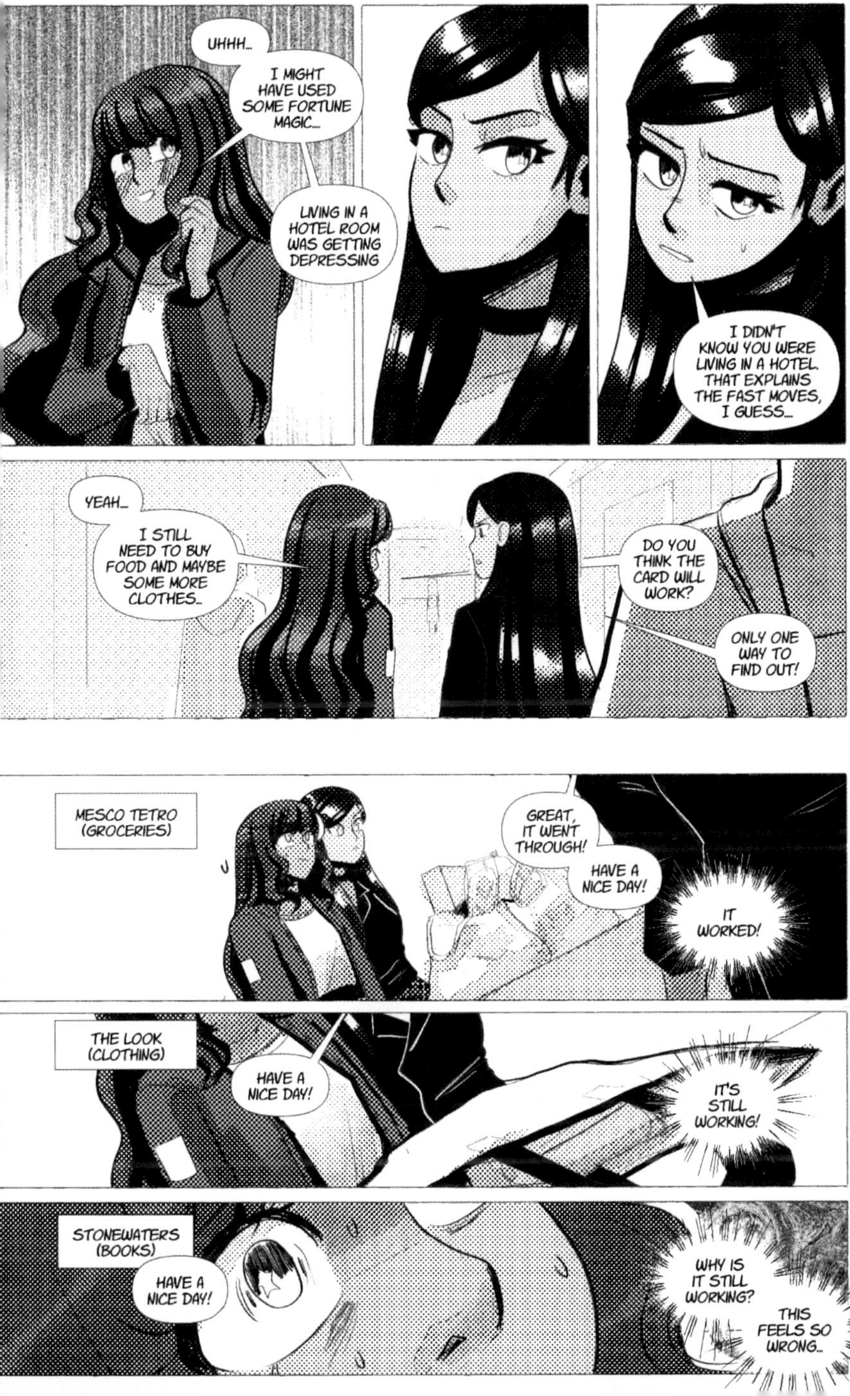
UHHH...
I MIGHT HAVE USED SOME FORTUNE MAGIC...
LIVING IN A HOTEL ROOM WAS GETTING DEPRESSING
I DIDN'T KNOW YOU WERE LIVING IN A HOTEL. THAT EXPLAINS THE FAST MOVES, I GUESS...
YEAH...
I STILL NEED TO BUY FOOD AND MAYBE SOME MORE CLOTHES...
DO YOU THINK THE CARD WILL WORK?
ONLY ONE WAY TO FIND OUT!
MESCO TETRO (GROCERIES)
GREAT, IT WENT THROUGH!
HAVE A NICE DAY!
IT WORKED!
THE LOOK (CLOTHING)
HAVE A NICE DAY!
IT'S STILL WORKING!
STONEWATERS (BOOKS)
HAVE A NICE DAY!
WHY IS IT STILL WORKING?
THIS FEELS SO WRONG...

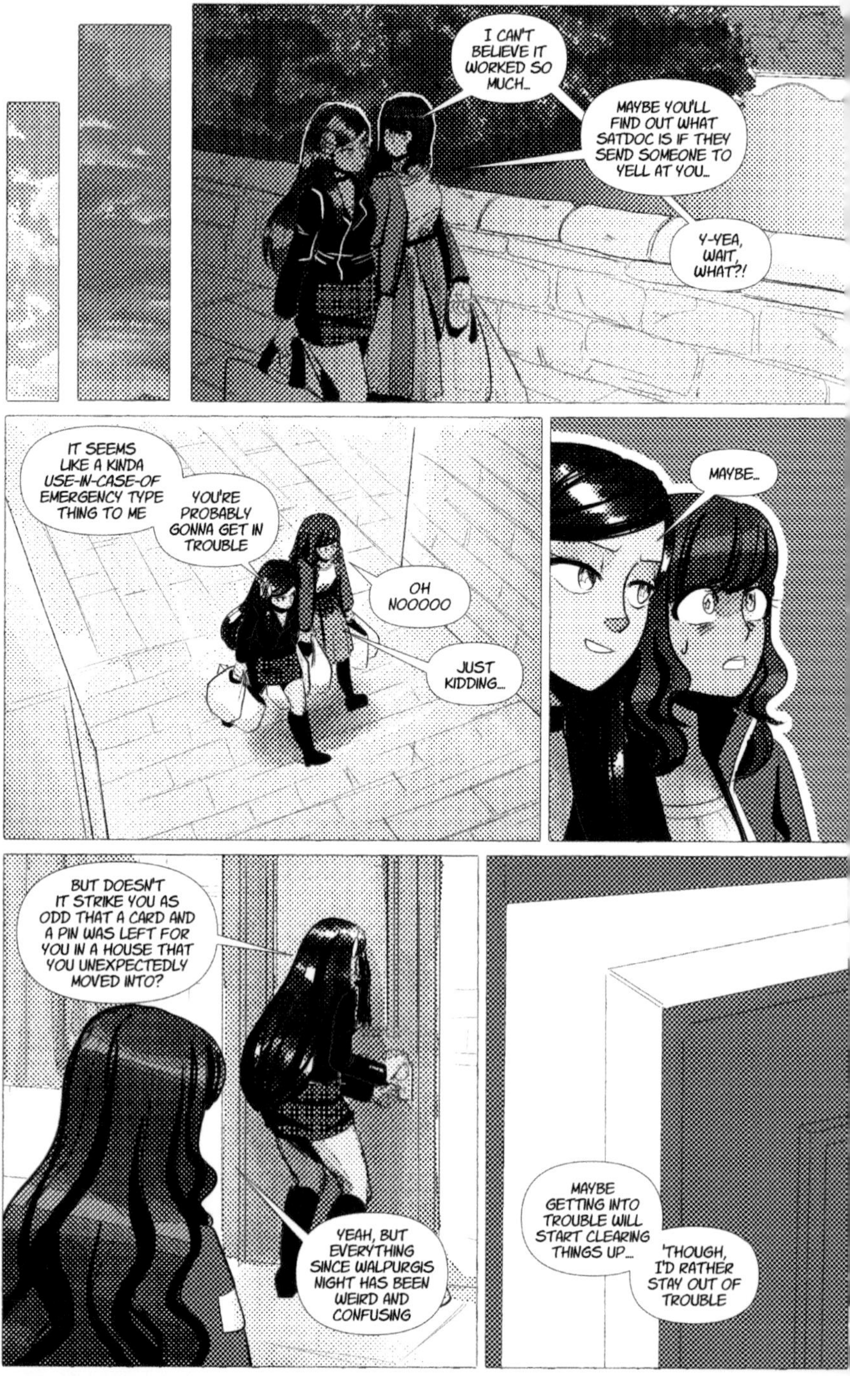
I CAN'T BELIEVE IT WORKED SO MUCH...
MAYBE YOU'LL FIND OUT WHAT SATDOC IS IF THEY SEND SOMEONE TO YELL AT YOU...
Y-YEA, WAIT, WHAT?!
IT SEEMS LIKE A KINDA USE-IN-CASE-OF EMERGENCY TYPE THING TO ME
YOU'RE PROBABLY GONNA GET IN TROUBLE
OH NOOOOO
JUST KIDDING...
MAYBE...
BUT DOESN'T IT STRIKE YOU AS ODD THAT A CARD AND A PIN WAS LEFT FOR YOU IN A HOUSE THAT YOU UNEXPECTEDLY MOVED INTO?
YEAH, BUT EVERYTHING SINCE WALPURGIS NIGHT HAS BEEN WEIRD AND CONFUSING
MAYBE GETTING INTO TROUBLE WILL START CLEARING THINGS UP...
'THOUGH, I'D RATHER STAY OUT OF TROUBLE

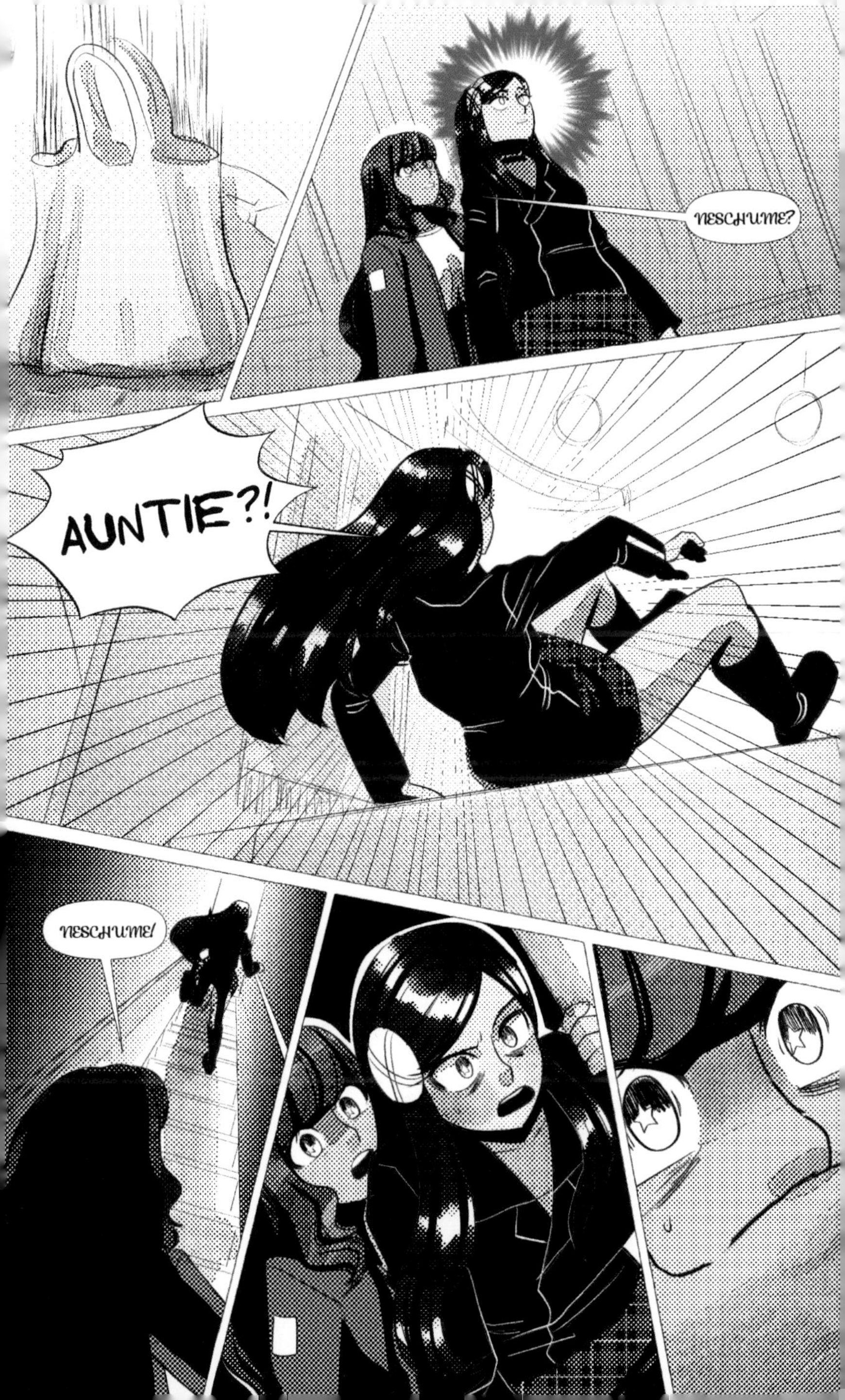
NESCHUME?
AUNTIE?!
NESCHUME!

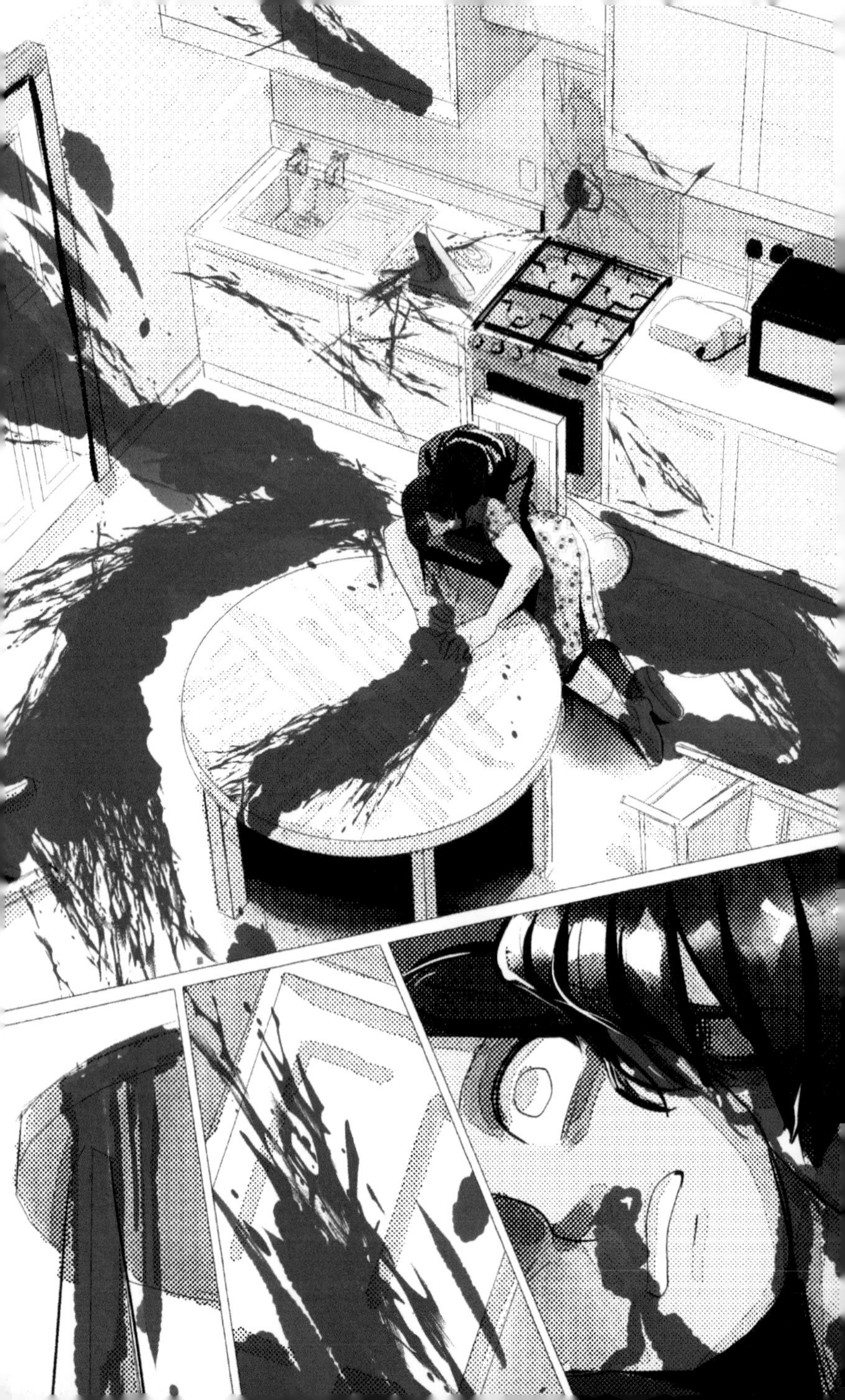

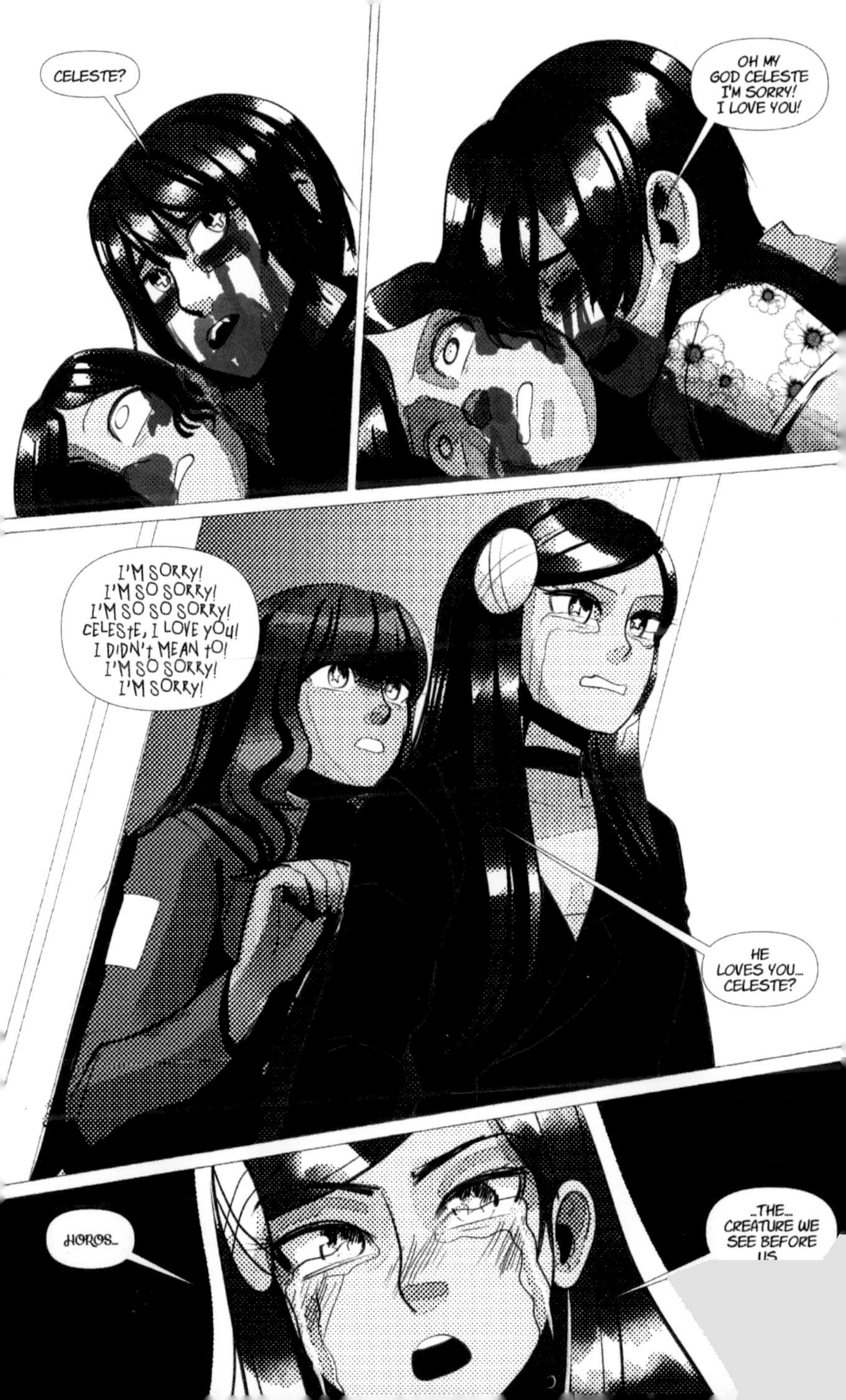
CELESTE?
OH MY GOD CELESTE I'M SORRY! I LOVE YOU!
I'M SORRY! I'M SO SORRY! I'M SO SO SORRY! CELESTE, I LOVE YOU! I DIDN'T MEAN TO! I'M SO SORRY! I'M SORRY!
HE LOVES YOU... CELESTE?
HOROS...
...THE... CREATURE WE SEE BEFORE US

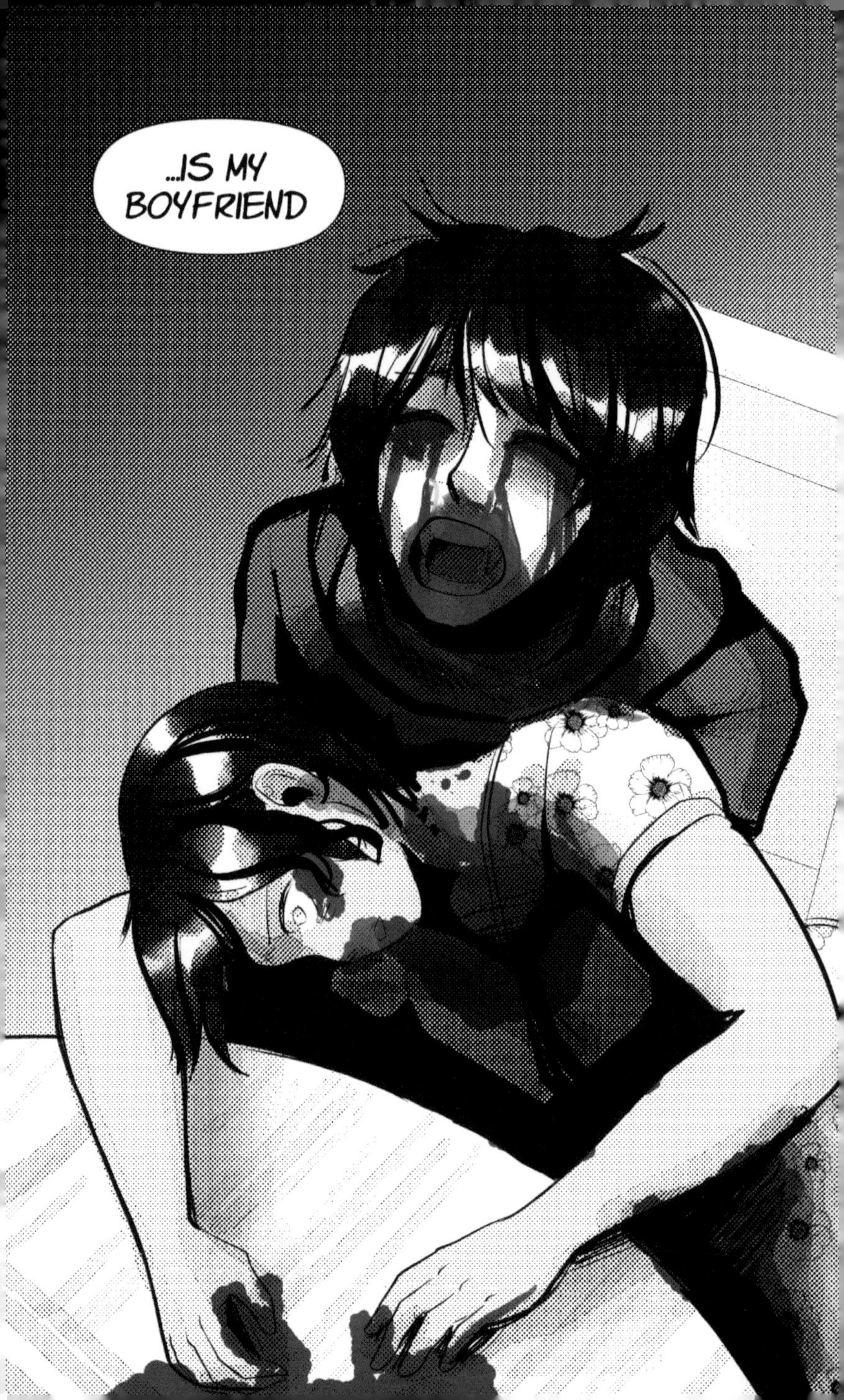
...IS MY BOYFRIEND

About Feff

Feff Silvers (pronouns: she/they) is a British self-taught Creator
hailing from the best county in England; West Yorkshire. She has a
Physics degree but rarely uses it. As well as creating digital art, Feff
often paints traditionally using watercolours. She's trying to work
collage and stamps into her work but it's a little slow-going.

Feff likes phantasmagoria, Malbec, black coffee, creepy Sci-Fi/Cosmic
Horror series, weird Japanese video games, stars, sparkly things,
pretty dresses, comfortable but stylish shoes, bright colours, basking
in the sun and playing with software.

You can catch Feff online at;

- Blog: https://feff.works
- Twitter: @FeffSilvers
- Instagram: @FeffSilvers
- Twitch: FeffSilvers

If you want to tell Feff how much you enjoyed this comic and you
prefer to use email, you can email her at feff@feff.works